TRIGGER WARNING

Possible Triggers: This is your trigger warning. The characters in this book went through many traumas. Some possible triggers include violence, blood, and abuse.

This story is about a FMC who does not have to choose between her love interests. A few of her love interests do not mind crossing swords. So if males touching males is not your thing, then you may not want to go any further. But if you do, please enjoy!

Inspiration Board for Meddling with Madness: https://pin.it/1nLS6th

Dedications:

To my husband, don't worry. They are just book boyfriends. Thank you for your constant support. Love you forever and always.

To the teachers who said I was stupid and couldn't write worth shit. Haha, bitches look at me now!

To my Beta Reader, this book wouldn't have made it this far without you. You gave me the courage and advice to be the author I knew I could be. Thank you!

To those who never felt like they belonged. To those wishing for a happy ending. To those who wanted a place of their own. This is for you. Find your Wonderland.

Meddling
With
Madness
Ivy Cole

Book Cover by D' Arte Oriel

Map done with InkArnate Pro

Editing by Kyla Lee

Photos by Pexels

2nd Edition

This is a fairy tale retelling of Alice In Wonderland. Things will be twisted from the author's view and this will not be the exact retelling of Wonderland. Characters may have the same names and a few of the same quirks but are unique characters from the author's mind. This retelling is a bit darker than the original, so if you do not like violence or blood, you may want to turn around before it's too late.

PLAYLIST

Mad Hatter by Melanie Martinez
Madness by Ruelle
Someone To You by BANNERS
Born for This – Lionel Fabert Remix by CRMNL
Kingdom Dance – From "Tangled"/Score by Alan Menken
Keep Holding On by Avril Lavigne
Sound of Madness by Shinedown
Alice by Avril Lavigne
Game of Survival by Ruelle
Taking a Stand by Henry Jackman
Victory by Two Steps from Hell and Thomas Bergensen
Lovely by Lauren Babic and Seraphim
Panic Room by Au/Ra
Don't Give Up On Me – (From "Five Feet Apart") by Andy Grammer and
Naive
Human by Christina Perri
Live Your Story by Auli'i Cravalho
A Million Dreams (The Greatest Showman) by Ziv Zaifman and Hugh
Jackman
Unsteady by Kurt Hugo Schneider and Madilyn Bailey
Madness by Ruelle
Stay Alive by Hidden Citizens and REMMI

A bit about Wonderland:

Females rule in Wonderland. If a male marries into royalty, he will share the equivalent rank but rule beside the female. The female looks to her male or males for guidance while ruling. Rulers of each Suit are then ruled by the Queen of Wonderland.

How things used to be before the war:

Heartz - Ruled by a Countess and Count, this Suit is known to produce the most painters, singers, and those who work with animals due to this Suit being ruled from the heart. This Suit believes in love and peace.

Dymondz - Ruled by an Empress and Emperor, this Suit is known to produce the knowledgeable Wonderlanders. Healers and Engineers come from this Suit due to the rulers believing in the wealth of knowledge. Mind over heart is the motto of this Suit.

Clubbz - Ruled by a Lady and a Lord, this Suit rules with honesty and believes in hard work. This Suit is filled with the most agriculture due to the high numbers of farmers and fishermen.

Spaydz - Ruled by a Commander and her male counterpart the Commandant, they rule this Suit with honor and often brutality. Most warriors, assassins, mercenaries, and guards are from this Suit. They are taught from a young age to fight and protect.

Heartz
Clubbz
Queen of Wonderland
Spaydz
Dymondz

CONTENTS

CHAPTER ONE
Alyce

May 4th

I startle awake, a cry stuck in my throat. That was the craziest dream I've had in a while. Grumbling, I shove a pillow over my face. Holy whistling tea kettles, that was scary. My phone goes off, the familiar ringtone loud in my otherwise quiet apartment. Ugh. Feeling around for my phone, I finally find it before the song ends. "What? It's too early for phone calls, Edi."

He scoffs. "I'm just checking on my favorite little sister."

Sitting up in bed, I grin and tease, "I'm your only sister. Not much competition."

"And that's why you're my favorite."

Sliding out of bed, I head to my closet to get ready for the day. "I'm fine as usual. The madness hasn't consumed me yet." I feel like I may have put a little too much sarcasm into that retort, but I was tired of the daily phone calls. I knew my brothers loved me, but I wanted them to stop worrying so much.

"How were the dreams?" he whispers.

I sigh. At least he didn't call them delusions like the rest of the family. "They were different last night," I say.

"How so?"

I pick out my outfit for the day and head back to the bedroom. Distracted with trying to get dressed, I answer, "They seemed darker, I guess. Like there's something wrong in Wonderland, and it's calling out to me to fix it."

"That's... concerning."

"I'll be fine. I've got to go, okay? Love you."

"Love you too, Alyce. Be careful," he says before hanging up.

I look down at the phone, brows furrowed. My brothers hardly ever call me Alyce. It's usually Little Sis or Aly. Shaking off that thought, I look up at myself in the mirror. With my long platinum blonde hair, bright blue eyes, blue blouse, and white skinny jeans, I look like a modern-day Alice. To me, that was the point. My family is said to be cursed due to something the original Alice Liddell did. According to tradition, the firstborn female of the firstborn female of the family line must be named Alice and carry the Liddell name.

Dreams of Wonderland pass from mother to daughter when she turns five. Sometimes the dreams are too much, and the mothers fall into madness, not believing that Wonderland is a real place but plagued with dreams of it night after night. My mother was one of those who fell into madness. She thought she had beaten the curse when she had only had sons. When she got pregnant the third time, they didn't realize they were having twins. I was the surprise female. As soon as Alix and I were born, my mom fell into madness and had to be put in a mental institution. When my oldest brother turned eighteen, my dad left. He wasn't much of a father to me, but he loved his sons.

My brothers have been taking care of me ever since I was born. They raised me after our father left, and I love them for it. They've never treated me like a burden. They've been more overprotective than anything else, constantly checking in on me to make sure I don't fall into madness like our mom. But I don't think they realize that I'm different. They hate that

I dress in the colors of Alice, but I think that's the solution. I've accepted that Wonderland is a real place. I believe in magic, and I think that's the difference. I've only visited my mother once. I'd been struggling in school and with friends because I felt like I didn't belong, and I wanted some time with my mother. I hadn't expected that the only words she ever said to me would stick with me for so long.

"You are a terribly real thing in a terribly false world, and that is why you're in so much pain."

Looking at myself in the mirror that has been handed down since the first Alice descendant, I touch my reflection and smile. Sometimes, I can see things when I look hard enough and believe even harder. Things that I see in my dreams. I pull away and finger the tiny sword necklace between my breasts, another heirloom passed down from mother to daughter. I haven't told my brothers what I believe because it would only worry them. But I know one day I'll make it to the other side of the mirror.

Huffing out a sigh, I move back to my closet to pick out a pair of shoes for the day. I have to admit, I absolutely love shoes. There are so many to pick from. I grab my solid black wedges. Classic is always a good look. I groan when I hear my phone ringing again. Seriously?! Do these males think I'm utterly incapable of taking care of myself?

"What?!" Well... shiitake mushrooms. I said that a little more aggressively than I meant to. But if Laurel keeps treating me like a baby... Ugh. I know I'm the little sister, but seriously!

"Well damn, Sis. Way to greet your brother," he teases.

I roll my eyes. "What do you want, Alix?"

He sighs and says, "Am I not allowed to call my sister and wish her a Happy Birthday?"

I gasp and look across the room at my clock. "I didn't even realize. Happy birthday, Alix."

"How do you forget about our birthday?" He laughs.

I giggle. "Well, Edi called first thing this morning. So…"

"Ahh, he give you the third degree about your dreams?"

"I'm sure you can imagine."

Sighing, he says, "Yeah. He called me too to make sure I called you. I was already planning on calling you anyways to wish you a Happy Birthday. I'm sure he called Laurel too. You know how he is being the second oldest and all."

I laugh softly. "Yeah. Laurel stands off a bit, which I like. I appreciate all the things you guys do for me, but sometimes it's a little smothering."

"Which is why I try not to call you too much. Laurel only texts to make sure the apartment is still to your liking. So you only have to deal with Edi's constant badgering."

Smiling, I look around my studio apartment. I love it. "I would hope the apartment was to my liking since he got the fanciest one he could find. I remember him telling me he wouldn't let his little sister live in a run-down, rat-infested room."

"Yeah. Ever since he took over Dad's company, he feels the need to make sure we are all provided for. Especially you."

I huff at the thought. "He has always acted like my dad instead of my brother. Sometimes I wish…"

"He would just be your brother?" Alix finishes.

"Yeah," I whisper.

"Hey, he just needs time to figure out that he doesn't need to be our dad anymore."

I feel a tug in my chest telling me to look back at the mirror. Looking over my shoulder, I see blurry images of people, but I can't make anyone out. Blinking a few times, I watch the images disappear, but I still feel the tug to touch the mirror. I shake myself and tell Alix, "I don't think I have that sort of time." I turn back to my closet in search of a bag.

"What do you mean?" he asks.

"Nothing. I'm fine."

"Aly. You can tell me. I promise."

I nibble my lip, debating whether to tell him my thoughts or not. Then, heaving out a sigh, I throw my bag onto the bed and turn to pack some clothes. "I feel different today," I say.

"Well, we turned twenty-one today." I hear his strained laugh on the other end of the phone.

Folding up my clothes and shoving shoes into the bottom of my bag, I look back over to the mirror. "No, Alix. Today is different. I feel... I feel the tug of Wonderland. In the last few weeks, I've been seeing more visions than usual of Wonderland in the mirror. And my dreams have been more vivid. I'm telling you something is going to happen today."

Only silence greets me after I spill my thoughts. Ugh. Whistling tea kettles! I should have kept my thoughts to myself. "Do you think I'm crazy now?"

"No!" he yells, startling a squeak out of me. He sighs. "No, I don't think you're crazy, Aly. I've been with you since the day of conception. You have been my ride-or-die forever. I've always believed you. We may be fraternal twins, but we have ALWAYS had a connection."

My eyes water at his words. "Yeah?"

"You are my little sister. I will always love you, no matter what. Whether you are here with us or in Wonderland saving the day. I've always felt like you haven't quite belonged here. You have a bigger purpose than staying here being coddled and protected by your brothers. But... " His voice sounds rough, and I hear a soft sniffle in the background.

"But what?" I whisper as I sit down and cuddle the two kitten stuffies on my bed.

"I wish you didn't have to go without me," he whispers.

I feel tears streaming down my cheeks. "Why do you sound like you're saying goodbye?" I ask quietly.

I hear his watery laugh. "I'm your twin. I can tell when you are trying to hold back. You don't want to tell us that you feel the magic of Wonderland calling you to touch the Looking Glass and fall through. Don't forget, I've been watching you forever, Sis."

"Alix..." My throat feels thick, and it's hard to talk.

"I'll keep the guys off your ass, okay Sis? But can you do me one favor?"

I don't hesitate before I agree, "Anything."

"I'm five minutes away. Don't touch the glass till I get there, okay?"

I look at the glass and nod. "I can wait."

"Promise?" I can hear the desperation in his voice.

"I promise."

"Text the others and tell them what's going on, okay?" Before I can form a response, I hear a click. I look down at my phone and laugh. He hung up on me. I wipe the moisture off my face and sigh. Who knew my twenty-first birthday would be so crazy?

CHAPTER TWO
Alyce

Cramming the last of my stuff into my bag, I place my two cat stuffies in the side pockets. My dad never allowed me to get an animal, so my brothers got me my black and white cat stuffies. "Alright, Snowdrop and Kitty, we are going to go on a little adventure. I'm not really sure what's going to happen, so…" Before I can finish that thought, the doorbell rings, and I hustle over to the door and open it. I smile up at my twin standing on the other side. "Hey, Alix." His eyes are a bit red, but I'm sure that's from our heart-to-heart moment. As far as twins go, we look nothing alike. Whereas I look like our mother due to the Alice curse, my brother looks like our dad with dark mussy, light brown hair, and light green eyes.

"Hey, Aly." He smiles as I step away from the door to let him in. "Did you text the others?"

I sigh. "I did, but I don't think they believed me."

Alix takes my hand as I move over to my bed. "They never do."

We sit on my bed as he takes a look around the apartment. "I could stay here to keep the mirror safe if you want?" he offers.

I tug on his hand until he looks at me. "Don't you have a place?"

He shrugs. "Yes, but It doesn't seem right to move the mirror. This is your place, and it's where the mirror belongs whether you're here or not."

My eyes start to water again, and I release my grip on his hand. I shuffle closer to him and wrap my arms around his middle giving him a side hug and hiding my face at his back. I hear his chuckle, but it seems a bit strained. He tugs at my arms. "Hey, come here," he says gently.

I loosen my grip, and he tugs me into his lap. My hands fall into my lap as I try to hold in the sob stuck in my throat. He wraps his arms around me, pulling me close. His grip is a little tighter than our usual hugs, but I don't mind. I shove my face into his neck, inhaling his familiar cinnamon scent. It always seems to calm me, but today it only seems to make the tears fall faster. He's always been my safety blanket, the one person I can always count on. I feel his cheek resting against the top of my head, dampening my hair as he cries too.

"I don't care what anyone says. You are my favorite sister," he mumbles into my hair.

A laugh stutters out of me. "I'm your only sister."

His arms tighten even more around me and he whispers, "And that's why you're my favorite."

I bite my lip, trying to stop the tears from falling. "I'm going to miss you. I promise I'll come back. Even if it's only to visit."

"You have no idea how much I'm going to miss you, Little Sister. I'll hold you to that promise."

I feel the tug of Wonderland again and whine. No! I'm not ready yet!

Alix pulls away slightly. "What's wrong?" I shove my face into his shirt, wiping the moisture and snot away. Yes, snot. There is no such thing as crying pretty. "Ew, gross, Aly!" he cries.

I laugh. Pulling away, I see that he has a smile on his face. He wipes at his face with his sleeve and clears his throat before stating, "So that was a great bonding moment."

I snort. "What? Crying with your little sister isn't normal?" I tease.

He lightly punches my shoulder. "I don't feel like anything with you is normal."

I feel the tug again, and this time it feels as if someone is trying to tug my heart right out of my chest. I gasp, putting a hand over my heart and rubbing it.

"What's wrong, Aly?" he asks, and I look up to find worry in his gaze.

I look at the mirror as it gets blurry again. "The tug is getting stronger."

I hear Alix gasp and look at him only to find that he is not looking at me but at the mirror. "Wow," he utters in shock.

I smile. "So you can see it too?"

He looks down at me, eyes wide. "It's blurry, but I can make out shapes and colors. Is that what you see?"

I nod. "It's been more active lately, though. I think something is wrong in Wonderland," I tell him.

Alix jumps up from the bed and grabs my bag. "I suppose, as your brother, it's my job to escort you as far as I can go."

We walk over to the mirror, and he hands the bag to me. I look down at it, then up at the mirror. I look back up at my brother and say, "Thank you."

His brows knit together. "For what?"

I grin as I rise to my tiptoes and kiss him on the cheek. "For believing me when no one else did."

He rustles my hair and kisses me on the forehead. "You're my twin. I have no reason to doubt you. And after seeing that..." he points to the mirror. "If you're crazy then so am I."

I reach up and touch the mirror. It takes a few seconds, but then the surface shimmers, and my fingers go straight through the glass. I hear a knock at the door behind me, and my eyes widen when I hear my other two brothers. The knock sounds frantic. I look up at Alix to find him smiling. "It's fine. I'll take care of everything," he assures me.

I nod as I continue reaching through the mirror. Half my body is through the glass when I hear the front door slam open. I look back to see

Laurel and Edi staring at me, eyes wide with shock as they see half my body already in the mirror.

"Alix, what the fuck are you doing!? Grab her!" Edi yells as he tries to run through the door at the same time Laurel does, causing them both to get stuck.

I look back at Alix, and he nods. "Go be the savior of Wonderland," he says proudly before pushing me the rest of the way through. I look back to find Laurel reaching for me, but it's too late. I'm falling. Falling down, down, down. As if through a rabbit hole. I smile, remembering the words from the book. *The only way to achieve the impossible is to believe it is possible.* I think I have finally achieved what was impossible for every Alice before me; I believed it was possible.

It feels like I've been falling forever before I hit something soft, then fly into the air and land on the damp ground. I lay there for a moment, grumbling. Groaning, I force myself up from the ground. Wiping my hands on my pants, I sit back on my heels. Looking around, I laugh. I'm definitely not in my world anymore. There are a variety of colored mushrooms all around me, which range in size. I realize now that I had initially landed on a purple mushroom about the size of a horse, I would guess.

I look up at the sky to find large... fish? There are fish swimming across the sky, but they look to be made of a weird substance.

"They are called Jellyfish," a masculine voice says behind me.

I squeal and whip around to find... nothing—hum... curiouser and curiouser. I slowly look back over to the mushrooms and see a smile. Would it be considered a smile if it's quite large and attached to nothing? I furrow my brows, thinking about all the Alice and Wonderland books I've read. My favorite has to be the reverse harem books, though. My favorite is a series by C. M. Stunich. She really had a way with the world, and I loved every moment of it, although many would say it was a little bloody. Well, shattering teacups, I hope I'm not in a Wonderland similar to that.

Thinking about the characters in Wonderland, I remember who the smile belongs to. "Cheshire?" The smile seems to grow, and the canines look a bit sharp. A head, then a body, then a tail shimmer into view. I gasp at the sight. He's like a combination of the old Chesh from the stories and the Chesh from the Tim Burton movie. He has silky grayish-black hair with ombre stripes that start off blue and then fade into pink. His eyes, though, are breathtaking. They are a deep purple with slitted pupils. He disappears again, then reappears on top of my bag.

"You know my name. How does a Surface being know my name?" he asks suspiciously.

"Surface being?" I question, tilting my head to mirror his.

"You are not from Wonderland. A Wonderland being is a Wonderland being, and a Surface being is a Surface being."

I huff out a laugh trying to make sense of his gibberish. "So I'm a Surface being because I'm not a Wonderland being?" I ask.

"I suppose you could be a Wonderland being since you were able to get into Wonderland. But the real question is why are you here?"

Shifting into a more comfortable position, I say, "Well, it's a long story, actually."

Cheshire tilts his head and then erupts in a puff of purple glitter. I squeal when the glitter clears, and I find a male in his place. His ears, which are on the top of his head, flatten at my squeal.

"I'm sorry. I didn't mean to be so loud. I didn't know you could change into a..."

"Male? Yes, most shifters here can shift into a more human form."

"So... you're a shifter?" I ask. I run my gaze over him and realize he's quite muscular. His stripes in cat form seem to be his hair color in human form, and his eyes are still purple and slitted. He must not care about modesty because he's only wearing loose-fitting pants. My eyes meet his, and I feel my cheeks flush with heat.

His eyes seem to glitter at my question, and that he caught me checking him out, but he nods and says, "You were going to tell me a story?"

"Right, um… So my name is Alyce. I'm from the Surface as you pointed out. The females in my family have this sort of curse. I guess you could say that we have a connection to Wonderland. Usually, the females go mad due to the overwhelming dreams of Wonderland and not believing it's a real place."

He points at me. "You believed?"

I nod. "I always thought this was a real place. Two of my brothers thought I would fall into madness like my mother, but my twin brother was the one who believed me when I told him everything. He was actually the one who pushed me the rest of the way through the mirror before my other brothers could stop me," I explain. I feel my eyes sting at the thought of Alix. I hope he's okay and that my other brothers didn't do anything to him. A pair of purple eyes are suddenly in front of me, but instead of the man I had just seen, he's back in cat form. He rubs against my face, and I laugh.

"You looked sad thinking about your brother. I'm sorry," Cheshire says as he purrs against my face.

I rub under his chin. "Thanks, Cheshire."

He jumps out of my lap and turns into a man once more then turns to me with a smile. "You can call me Chesh." He holds out a hand. "It seems you have places to be."

I grab his hand and he easily lifts me to my feet. I grab my bag and ask, "Would you tell me which way to go? You seem to know where you are."

He turns to me with a grin. "Well… that depends on where you want to go?"

I laugh, remembering this conversation in the original Alice in Wonderland story. "I don't care much where."

He starts walking away from me backward. "It doesn't matter which way as long as we get where we are going." He turns back around and begins heading into the dense forest of trees I hadn't noticed yet.

I feel like my brothers would frown upon me following a strange male into a dark forest. I look around, taking in my surroundings; I seem to be between a forest and farmlands. Odd. Turning back to find Chesh now at the edge of the woods, I jog to catch up. I'm unsure who I should and shouldn't trust in this place, so here goes nothing. Hopefully, Chesh doesn't end up being a serial killer or something worse in this version of Wonderland.

CHAPTER THREE
Alyce

So I've learned three things since my fall into Wonderland. One, my brothers made sure that I have no idea how to act around guys, normally due to them scaring off every guy who seemed interested in me. Two, Chesh was still holding my hand as we walked, and I loved the feel of his hand in mine. And three, I should not be this comfortable with a complete stranger, in a strange place, where I have no idea who anyone is. But for some reason, I feel entirely comfortable here in Wonderland. It's like something inside me settled the second I crossed over. Also, being with Chesh feels like catching up with an old friend. Like I've known him forever. Although, now that I think about it, I remember that I've had dreams about certain people from here. I rummage through old memories of dreams and realize he was one of them.

I look up to find him staring at me with curious eyes.

"Is something wrong?" I ask.

"No. I could see the thoughts buzzing around in your head."

Humming, I say, "Yes... well, I was thinking it odd how comfortable I am here." I give a shy smile and add, "With you as well."

He gives me a toothy grin as if that thought pleases him as we continue to walk. "I see the thoughts stopped buzzing so loudly."

I nod. "Yes. I realized that I've dreamed about this place and certain people here my whole life. It's as if I already know you."

"I do hope I was a proper gentleman in your dreams." I watch as his ears swivel in my direction as if to gauge my reaction. It's odd that he has human-like ears in his male form but his cat ears as well. Does that mean he can hear twice as much?

I laugh as I respond, "I didn't realize the Cheshire Cat could be a gentleman. I thought you were supposed to be playful and cause trouble."

"Is this a reference to what this Alice person said?" he asks, turning to give me a wink.

I grin. "Maybe."

His ears flatten slightly against his head. "I'm not saying I'm not playful or that I don't cause trouble, but Wonderland has changed since my more chaotic days."

I squeeze his hand. "My last few dreams have given me the impression that Wonderland isn't as wondrous as it used to be."

He gives a soft growl. "No, it is not."

"Well, I'm here now. I'm not sure what the reason is yet, but I feel like there's a reason I am here, and I'll help in any way I can."

Giving me a quick toothy grin he says, "I believe the fun is the journey of not knowing where you're going but knowing where you've been so that you can continue the fun till you stop where you end up."

I think about his words for a moment. A bit jumbled, but I think I at least understand what he means. It's not about where you're going but the journey to get there. "So may I ask where we are going?"

His ears twitch then settle, facing forward. "Well, if the Surface being must know..." he starts to say, but I interrupt.

"My name is Alyce, but you can call me Aly."

"Ah, Aly then. Since you must know where we are headed..." Before he can finish talking, there is a loud screech, and then Chesh's hand is ripped out of mine as he's flung into the air.

I officially forget my normal curse words and scream, "Fuck!" I hear Chesh's meowing and mewling as he hisses at whatever creature currently has him in the air. I search the area. Tree. Tree. How am I supposed to hide from whatever that creature is with only trees surrounding me? I run further in the direction we were headed and find mushrooms large enough that I can hide under. I hunch under the spongy material and close my eyes as I feel myself beginning to shake.

This brings back horrible memories of school when I would hide from my tormentors. I used to huddle under desks or playground equipment so they couldn't find me. Of course, being known as the freak before you could even understand what made you a freak didn't help. Although, I suppose that explained why my brothers were so protective. Though I had a twin brother who was often with me as much as he could be, there were times when he couldn't be there.

When I hear the flap of wings and Chesh's hisses stop, I sigh. I can't bring myself to look up yet. What if whatever that thing is killed him? Fuck! What am I going to do? I'm in a strange place with large things that want to kill me. I can feel tears stinging my eyes. Chesh. Did I do this? Did my arrival end up causing his death? I didn't even realize I was whispering, "Chesh," over and over until a hand touches my shoulder. I scream, jumping away from the hand.

I look up to find purple eyes watching me, touched with concern. "It's just me, Alyce."

I jump toward him, wrapping my arms around his neck. "Whistling tea kettles! I was so afraid that, that thing killed you. I'm sorry. I'm sorry," I apologize. I bury my face in the crook of his neck and inhale his scent. Strawberries and cream. Interesting smell for a cat. Although, he is a male from Wonderland so maybe that's normal.

Sitting down next to me, he wraps his arms around me and gently tugs me into a comfortable position on his lap. "What do you have to be sorry for? You didn't do anything," he says.

Sniffling, I explain, "If I hadn't shown up, that thing wouldn't have had the opportunity to attack you."

His warm breath tickles my neck, sending a shiver down my spine as he chuckles. "That thing would have attacked me no matter what. It's a Jabberwock. The Queen controls them, and they have been ordered to attack anything that isn't within the confines of the Heartz borders."

I pull away. "The Heartz borders?"

He gently wipes the moisture from my cheeks and licks my nose. Then he smiles wide enough that I can see the tips of his canines. "Yes, we are outside the borders. You actually fell on the edge between Clubbz and Heartz. We're further into the woods of Clubbz now. We are on our way to the Rebellion camp to meet my friends," he explains.

Surprised by the lick, I touch the tip of my nose with my fingers. I suppose the lick did shock me enough that I stopped crying. "How did you get free from the... Jabberwock?" I ask.

He nods, letting me know I got the name right. "Well, my species has been cursed by the Queen, which allows me to change forms, so I was able to free myself." He gently maneuvers me so he can hold me as he stands from the ground. A surprised squeak escapes me, and he raises an eyebrow in question.

"'Uhh... no one has ever been able to lift me like that before."

He shrugs as he says, "You're not that heavy, and you'll find that the males here are much more... muchier."

"Muchier, you say?"

"Well, the males who I confide with have much muchiness. They fight against the Red Queen and are the most loyal males I have ever met. Many are... damaged, but they are brave. I am honored to call them friends and family."

I smile. "Well, I cannot wait to meet these males who have so much muchiness." He continues carrying me through the forest, and thankfully we don't run into any more animals or things that want to kill us. I try to tamper the nervous buzz in my veins by thinking about meeting these other males. I feel this tug in my chest the closer we get. Like meeting these males is what I was always meant to do.

Trying to distract myself, I ask the question I've wanted to ask since the beginning of this adventure. "Why do you have two pairs of ears? You have your human-like ears as well as your cat ears."

His signature grin is back in place. "I would look quite odd in male form with only cat ears, would I not?"

"I suppose so," I agree. "Does that mean you can hear out of both pairs of ears?"

He shakes his head. "No. I could shift my ears and tail away if I wanted. But it requires a lot of concentration due to the Queen's curse on me. So it's easier to let them be as they are."

"Your cat ears seem to twitch in your male form, so does that mean you can't hear out of your human-like ears?"

"If I shifted completely into my male form without the cat ears, I would be able to hear from them. But since I'm in my male form with my cat ears, the formation of ear drums is difficult, and I cannot grow additional ear drums to hear out of four ears."

I sigh. This explanation is more in-depth than I originally thought. "Which ears do you hear out of?" I ask, confused.

He laughs and says, "Sorry. It has been a while since I've had to explain this. I can only hear in my animal form unless I completely shift into my male form. My human-like ears are more for show. It is quite difficult to explain where my eardrums are located and the magic behind them. I'm not sure I understand it myself."

That makes two of us. "I assume there are other shifters here? Is it the same for them?"

He nods. "Unless they have a lot of magic as a shifter, they will most likely have their animal ears in their human-like form as well."

Curiouser and Curiouser. If I'm honest, the magic doesn't really make sense with the ears, but this is Wonderland. Does anything really make sense?

CHAPTER FOUR
Alyce

It feels like we have been walking for hours. Maybe we have. I'm not sure I've figured out how to tell the time in Wonderland yet. I feel myself nodding off to sleep in Chesh's arms when I hear male laughter and yelling. I jolt awake as Chesh smiles down at me.

"Did you have a good cat nap?" he teases.

Grinning up at him, I nod.

He maneuvers me so I can stand as we continue to walk into what looks like a large campsite. "That's good. You'll need all of your energy to deal with our type of company." He slides his hand into mine as we enter the campground.

There's a flutter in my stomach. Is this what getting butterflies feels like? I've never had someone hold my hand like this before or even want to hold my hand. Trying to push the feeling away, I smile up at Chesh. "You guys can't be any worse than my brothers."

He shrugs. "We'll see." Then he clears his throat and calls out. "Hey, everyone, I picked up a wanderer."

Oh, shattering tea cups. Did he have to introduce me like that? Six males turn in my direction, and I feel my cheeks heat. Wow, I've never had this many males staring at me all at once before. This is intense. I wave shyly. "Um... Hey, I'm Alyce."

Their eyes shift over to Chesh and then back to me. As if he can sense how nervous I am, Chesh squeezes my hand. "I suppose I'll introduce you since no one has manners around here."

I hear a gruff laugh and look in that direction to find a male wearing a black top hat with hat pins in it. His eyes are what I think are dark brown but could be mistaken for black in the shadow of his hat. I can see tufts of messy black hair peeking out from under his hat with the sides of his head trimmed short.

Chesh points in the male's direction. "That's..." he starts, but before he can finish speaking I tug on his arm. He looks down at me in question.

"Can I guess who everyone is?" I ask.

Chesh's smile widens, and his canines show as he chuckles. "Sure. Is this another Surface being thing?"

I grin and reply, "Can we say it's an Alyce thing?"

He hums. "I suppose as long as you explain the Alyce thing after. I'm very curious."

"You know curiosity killed the cat," I can't help but tease.

Shrugging, he releases my hand and settles down on a stump a few steps away from me. "I'm a cat. I'm naturally curious, and it hasn't killed me yet."

Rolling my eyes, I say, "I'll explain after, Chesh." He waves for me to do my thing, so I move into the center of their setup. A small pile of wood sits in the center for what I assume is a fire when it's dark. I take a deep breath and look around. All the males are seated on tree stumps or large mushroom caps. Okay, Alyce, this is what you were meant for! I turn and point at the male Chesh was going to start with. "You're the Mad Hatter. Although, the color scheme is way off from what I thought it would be. You are heavy on the black and brown colors instead of bright and vibrant ones. Though this could be similar to Stunich's Wonderland, where it's a bit dark. Though, I hope it's not."

"Alyce!"

I jump at the sound of my name being called, realizing I'm waving my hands around in the air, gesturing wildly. I look toward who said my name and find Chesh laughing. "You seem to be going mad in thought."

Rubbing the back of my head, embarrassed with my mumbling I say, "I suppose I did start rambling."

He gives me a wink. "It was adorable. But I would like to have you continue telling us who you think everyone is."

Taking a deep breath, I refocus. "Right... Okay!" Ugh, that was a little too enthusiastic there, Alyce! I look around and find a pair of males sitting next to each other. They look like twins. I feel a pang of longing for my own twin. Shaking the thought off, I point at both of them. "You two are the Tweedles. But, I'm not sure who is who." Looking at them more closely, I think back over all the Wonderland books I have ever read. I remember in one of the books that Dee was the one who was happy and fun, whereas Dum was more serious and broody.

Humming, I walk a little closer to them. "You know I'm a twin too, so I know I'll be able to figure this out." The twin on the right tries to hide his smile, but I see it. Dee. That's Dee. I'll be able to easily differentiate between them now because he has light purple hair that's short and spiky. He also has unique eyes. His right eye is a light purple and the other is a light teal. I point at him and state, "You're Dee." I point to the male beside him. "That would make you..."

"Rook," he interrupts. His voice is deep and a bit rough, like he doesn't use it very often. His hair is the same except for it being a light teal instead of purple, and his eyes are the mirror opposite of his brother's.

I quirk a brow in question but nod. "Rook. Nice to meet you both." I can't blame him for not wanting to be called Dum. Who would like to have that name? Turning slightly, my gaze stops on a male with blue butterfly wings. They remind me of the Blue Morphos back home. Wow. Beautiful.

I try not to check him out, but well, I fail completely. He's smaller in stature but muscular like a runner. Lean and fit. His tan skin makes his wispy blue hair and bright blue eyes pop.

I point at him. "You." My voice squeaks a bit, and my face grows hot. He gives me a soft smile. Clearing my throat, I manage to say, "Um... you're the Caterpillar."

His voice is soft and melodic as he responds, "I was once a Caterpillar. Now, I go by Mor." He flutters his wings as if to emphasize the reason he goes by Mor.

I nod. "We have Blue Morpho butterflies on the Surface. Your wings remind me of them." He gives me another soft smile. I feel my face flush again, and I turn quickly to hide my blush. My eyes meet a pair of dark mocha eyes and shift to the brown rabbit ears on top of his head. They twitch at my scrutiny. I take in the male himself. He's broad and muscular with light chocolate skin. Interesting. My eyes drift back up to his ears as they twitch again. I wonder if he has a fluffy tail? I hear a squeak, and that's when I notice a mouse on his shoulder.

"If I had to guess... The March Hare and the Dormouse?"

A voice whispers in my ear. "He goes by Arch, and the mouse is Dor." Startled, I shriek and hold a hand to my chest as I see a floating cat hovering beside me.

I take a shuddering breath. "Whistling tea kettles! I don't remember the Cheshire in the books sneaking up on Alice this much. I think I may need to put a bell on you," I admonish.

He gives me a toothy grin, his eyes sparkling with amusement. "I wouldn't be much of a spy if I didn't stay silent, now would I?"

"I'll make you wear it when you're around me," I mumble. He gives me a quick lick on my nose before exploding into a puff of purple glitter. He settles onto the stump once more in his male form with a smile.

A sensual male voice interrupts, "I'll buy the bell if you can put it on him. I think we all would appreciate the cat not sneaking up on us."

I turn to look at who said that and find the last male of the group taking off a top hat that has gears and a clock on it. Once it's off, I gasp. He has piercing red eyes, not like blood red but softer, like the red eyes of an Albino. They're not harsh, just surprising. His white rabbit ears stand tall before one flops in half. I smile. It must be exhausting to keep your ears upright all the time. However, his were hidden under the hat at first. They would have been at an awkward angle while he wore the hat, isn't that uncomfortable? His hair is white as well. It's short but looks soft and fluffy from here. Oh, I wonder if he would let me pet his head? Wait... what? Did I actually think that?!

"Um." Wait, what were we talking about again? Chesh... bells... oh! He said he would buy a bell for Chesh. "Yeah. I could figure out a way to make him wear it." The male smiles at me. That's when I notice the clock tattoos on his arms. I'm assuming he has them all over his body. The clocks are all different, some are ticking, and others are broken. He must notice me looking.

"I can control time for anyone who I have touched," he says as he wiggles his hands, which are covered by white gloves. I now notice he's wearing a red button-up shirt with his sleeves rolled up, which is how I was able to see the tattoos.

"I see. So, you're the White Rabbit?"

He nods. "I go by Rab."

I nod, looking around and finding an open spot to sit. Sitting down, I look at Chesh beside me. "So that's everyone."

He nods. "In our group, yes, but there are other warriors around the camp. So now you have to tell me what the Alyce thing is."

I laugh and try to explain, "It's not really an Alyce thing. There are books on the Surface about Wonderland and all the characters here, so I wanted to see if I could guess who everyone was. Everyone here is a bit different than in the books, though."

"How so?" Mor asks curiously. I watch as he takes out what looks like a cigarette. Interesting. I guess the way he smokes here is different, but he still smokes.

"Um, in the original Alice in Wonderland book, the Caterpillar, Cheshire, White Rabbit, and the March Hare are all animals. They can't shift forms."

"You said in the original Alice. Does that mean there are different versions?" Dee asks.

I smile. "Yes. There are many different versions. Other authors have written various adaptations of the book. My favorite is a version by C.M. Stunich. It's pretty epic."

"Why is that one your favorite, Aly?" Chesh asks as he grins.

If I blush anymore, I'm going to be permanently red. I groan. "It's my favorite because it's an RH book."

"What's an RH book?" Chesh asks poking at my reddening face with a laugh.

Covering my face with my hands, I mutter, "Reverse harem."

"Now, now, Aly. You know we need more information than that. We aren't from the Surface. These are new terms. Please explain." Chesh tries to pull my hands away from my face, but I refuse to move them.

Fine, I think, taking a deep breath. "A reverse harem is when a female character doesn't have to choose between her love interests. They are often all male." I can't believe I said that all in one breath. I don't hear anything for a few minutes, so I peek between my fingers to see what's happening.

The first thing I see is a grinning Chesh. I haven't seen his grin that wide before. Hatter is beside him, and he looks a little confused if I'm being honest. Does he not know what I meant? I am NOT explaining this further if he doesn't understand. Moving on, I look at Arch next. He has a slight tilt to his lips and is looking at Hatter. I can see him holding back a full smile and shaking a bit as if holding back laughter. Dee grins about as wide as Chesh and pokes his brother beside him. Rook, because he didn't want to be called Dum, is rolling his eyes at his brother, but I can see the slight tilt of his lip. Mor's wings are slowly flapping back and forth, and he has a thoughtful look on his face. Ugh... what is that look supposed to mean? I look at Rab next. He seems to have a slight flush to his cheeks as he looks anywhere but at me.

I let out a groan as I squeeze my fingers tighter against my eyes, so I can't see anything. Chesh tries to pry my hands away from my face, and I reluctantly let him. I refuse to look at him, though. He places a finger under my chin, lifting my face and forcing my eyes to meet his. He caresses my bottom lip with his thumb and orders softly, "Aly, look at me."

Ugh. I can't deny him when his voice is all purry and soft like that. I blame my brothers. I was not ready for the male encounters of Wonderland! They did not prepare me for situations like this! I lift my eyes to meet his, and I can see his smile has softened. "Females in Wonderland often have multiple lovers. That isn't taboo here. I think it's more taboo not to have multiple partners."

"So you're not weirded out that I read that sort of stuff?"

Chesh's grin widens again. "On the contrary. I'm sure you've picked up a lot of ideas from those books," he purrs seductively against my ear, and I shiver. Holy whistling tea kettles. That's hot. I can feel myself becoming slick and wet with need. Well, maybe real men can make me hot like the ones in my books. Chesh takes a deep inhale as he runs his nose up my neck causing goosebumps to erupt all over my skin.

He growls. "I can smell you. And you smell purrfectly delicious, my Little Kitten."

Oh, shattering tea cups. I moan. He licks up my neck, and I shiver in pleasure. A throat clearing breaks me out of my haze. I pull away from a grinning Chesh as I try to drag myself out of my needy haze. Ugh, this is what happens when your boyfriends are fictional, and the only pleasure you get is from a machine with batteries.

"Sorry," I squeak out.

"Oh, no need to be sorry. We were thoroughly enjoying the show. We just figured, coming from the Surface, that you wouldn't want six other guys watching you. At least not at first," Dee teases, winking at me.

"Also, we were discussing the differences between us and the original Alice book before we got off topic. Although, I didn't mind the detour," Mor adds.

"Right." Clapping my hands and trying to shake off the last of my lust, I ask, "Right, where was I?" Thinking for a moment, I finally remember. "Animals. Right, um, the Tweedles." I gesture toward them. "They are usually made out to be cowards and often talk in riddles." I see a fire blazing in Rook's eyes, and I can tell he's about to say something, so I wave my hand in the air to cut him off. "I can see you aren't cowards. You look like warriors. Although, in the books, the Tweedles always speak in riddles. They also interrupt each other a lot, finishing each other's sentences." I shrug.

Dee laughs. "We don't talk in riddles, but we used to finish each other's sentences quite frequently."

I grin at him. "My twin and I would do that all the time. It would annoy my other brothers a lot."

"All the more reason to do it," Dee adds.

I agree, laughing. "Exactly!" Twins bonding over doing twin stuff. Who would have thought? "And lastly, the Mad Hatter." I nod toward the huddled figure, getting us back to our original conversation.

He raises his face enough so I can see his dark gaze. And he's... glaring at me? Well, that's not intimidating at all. I snuggle a little closer to Chesh and turn to whisper, "Why does he look so mad?"

I can feel Chesh shrug as he says, "He's not mad." He looks in Hatter's direction to see the glare he's sending our way. "Well, maybe he's a little mad. But he hasn't had much to be happy about in a long time. Once you make a face long enough, it gets stuck that way, right?" He gives me a toothy grin.

I remember him mentioning that they have been fighting against the Red Queen. "I suppose if you have been fighting against a Queen for so long, there wouldn't be much to be happy about."

"It's not that," he whispers. "We all find something to smile or laugh about. It helps to not give into the madness."

A snort escapes me as I say, "I thought this was Wonderland. Aren't you all mad here?"

He laughs throatily. "I never said we weren't mad here."

I sigh and ask, "So why can't he find the laughter?" I look back to see Hatter still glaring at us. I suppose having a secret conversation right after nodding at him would be considered rude.

He huffs against my ear. "His story is his own to tell. But there's a reason he's standoffish and broody."

I nod. Shifting away from Chesh, I take a deep breath and say, "In the original Alice, he's mad. As in crazy, and his hair color is different."

"What color is his hair?" Arch asks. I look around the group and find everyone looking as if they are holding their breath. Curious.

"It's Red. Why?" It's as if the once sweet-smelling air surrounding us has suddenly become sour. I flinch at the sound of a deep growl and a thump. I look over to see that Hatter has thrown the hat pin he was twirling to the ground, staring straight at me.

I scream when he suddenly charges at me, but Chesh throws himself in front of me and hisses at Hatter. Hatter peers down at me. I've never seen someone consumed by madness; his eyes look crazy and angry at the same time.

His voice sounds gravelly as he sneers at me, "I would kill myself before I ever let my hair turn red!" He grunts as he turns and stomps off toward what I assume is his tent. Ripping open the flaps, he stumps inside, the flaps fluttering closed behind him.

I can hear everyone huff out a breath as Chesh snuggles in beside me. "Seems you hit a nerve, Kitten."

Looking around the group, I find Arch's eyes. They look sympathetic. "I'm sorry, I didn't mean to make him upset," I apologize.

Arch sighs. "It's not your fault. The hair color thing is just a sore spot for him."

I look back at Hatter's tent and sigh. I can feel a tug to go to him. I'll admit I've always felt the need to help others, but I never got the chance. It's hard to help when everyone thinks you're crazy or that they will catch the crazy. But this is Wonderland. I may have only been here for half a day, but I already feel like I've been here forever. I feel like I belong here. Like I'm meant to be here, getting to know these men. That there's a connection between us.

Sighing, I stand. "I'll go talk to him."

"Not sure that's a wise idea, Kitten," Chesh warns.

I turn and scratch between Chesh's ears and laugh when he starts to purr. "No fair. That's cheating, Kitten."

I grin. "I'll be fine. If I need help, I'll yell for you, okay?" I promise.

He nods. I give him one last stroke before heading toward Hatter's tent. Gripping the flap, I take one last deep breath before shoving my way through.

CHAPTER FIVE

Alyce

I gasp as I enter the tent. Well, what I thought was a tent. It's nothing like the tents we have back home. It looks small on the outside, like the tents I'm familiar with, but the inside... wow... it's the size of my studio apartment. Two large beds sit in the corner as well as a tub. In the opposite corner, there's what I assume is a workout area. That is where I find Hatter, throwing sharp hat pins at what I think is a dart board. It looks like the cap of a large mushroom to me. He hits the bullseye every time. Maybe this wasn't such a good idea.

His deep, gravelly voice greets me, "You shouldn't be in here."

I jump slightly but stand my ground. "I wanted to say I'm sorry. I didn't mean to upset you."

He throws another hat pin. Another bullseye. "Alright. You can go now."

Ugh... he's one of those. Walking toward the workout area, I sit against the wall so I can see his profile. Wow. I expected to fall into the wall due to the floppy material, but it's solid. Curious. I look around the room again before sitting quietly and watching him throw his hat pins.

He huffs and says, "You don't have to sit with me. You should go out there and have fun with the others. They are better company than I am. I don't like new people."

"Well, it's good that I'm not new then. I'm quite old, actually. I'm twenty-one, in fact. Just turned twenty-one today," I retort. I hear him huff out what I think is a laugh. I'll take it.

"I suppose you're right. But I still think Chesh is better company. Even Dee and Arch are better company than I am."

"Who said I wanted better company? Maybe I want the company of the brooding man." That thought suddenly makes me feel homesick. This man reminds me so much of Laurel. The oldest, and the one who took on the most responsibility. He hardly ever laughed or smiled anymore. And I left without saying anything, only a text. I can feel my eyes stinging with unshed tears. Ugh... I feel like the original Alice from the book. I've cried so much today. I could probably flood Wonderland with how much I've cried today. I huddle down into myself to hide my tears. I don't want Hatter to know I'm crying. I cover my mouth to hide the sobs that wish to escape.

"Shit! Please tell me you're not crying. Damnit, I knew I was bad company!" he exclaims.

I shake my head and suck in a deep breath. "I'm fine," I manage to say before gulping down another sob. I hear him sigh, then suddenly, he's sitting next to me. He brushes his shoulder up against me, and I lean into it.

"I have no idea what to do when a female cries. I haven't seen a female cry in a very long time," he admits, then lets out an exasperated sigh. "I suck at this."

That makes me laugh. He sounds so lost. My brothers are the same way. "You're not doing too bad. It's not your fault. My emotions are really high right now. It's my birthday today, and I fell through the Looking Glass, leaving behind my brothers. They're all older than me. You remind me of the oldest one. He's very serious, never laughing or smiling. The only time we could ever get him to laugh was when my twin brother and I pulled a prank." I heave out a sigh before saying, "I suddenly got homesick because when I was falling through the mirror, I looked back and saw his face. He looked so scared. I wish I could tell him that I'm fine."

"Do you want to go back?" he asks curiously.

Humming, I think about it. "Someday. Just to visit. I never felt like I belonged there. That world never made sense. But here, as crazy as it sounds, it makes sense. I feel like I belong here."

He grunts. "You are under no obligation to make sense to anyone."

Grinning, I wipe my face with my sleeves. "Ugh. I hate crying."

He bumps his shoulder against mine and says, "I have siblings as well. We would fight too. I am the youngest," he tells me.

"Ah, I can relate to being the youngest." Looking over at him, I notice his brows knitted together as he looks down at a hat pin. He's twirling it around, hilt over tip.

Sighing, he throws his head back against the wall, tapping it a few times before he closes his eyes and says, "My family and I aren't on the best of terms right now."

I bump my shoulder into his this time. "You don't have to tell me anything."

I can see the tilt in his lips. "You trusted a complete stranger. I can at least give you this little bit of information so you know why I was so angry about the hair color." He tilts his head slightly and opens one eye. "It doesn't mean I trust you completely, though," he says gruffly.

I smirk at him. "Oh, of course."

He turns back and looks up at the ceiling before explaining, "The Hatter's are a group of mercenaries and assassins. Depending on what you want done depends on the group you talk to. Although, with either group, as long as the money is good they will do just about anything. It's only family who can become a Hatter. When we are born, we have blond hair, the essence of purity. If you see an older Hatter with blond hair, they chose not to become an official Hatter but a hatmaker. The hat-making business is a front for the group. Any family not born into the family is also part of the hat-making business."

I lean my head against his shoulder, and I feel him stiffen for a moment before relaxing. "Anyways, if you become a Merc, you're a soldier. You have the training and often are hired to take out groups that need to be killed. They are often paid large sums of money and will only go after targets they choose. If you become an Assassin, you are trained for stealth and quick kills. They do it for the pay, but also for the thrill of killing. They often don't care who the target is."

I notice him pause so I mumble, "I'm still listening."

He grunts but continues, "The hair color doesn't discriminate between which path you choose. It's more of a marker of who you are as a person, and it allows those who wish to hire you to know how far you are willing to go. As you can see, my hair is black. It means I will only kill the guilty."

"What do you mean by guilty?"

He sighs and says quietly, "Guilty is based on personal morals. I won't kill if it conflicts with my morals."

I snuggle a little closer to him. Mmh, he's so warm and smells like a combination of black licorice and mint. Who knew those would smell so good together? Humming, I ask, "And what are those morals?"

I can feel his eyes on me, but I don't move. I'm extremely comfortable. "Are you snuggling me?" I can hear the apprehension in his voice. Has no one ever snuggled this male before?

"Am I making you uncomfortable?" I ask as I shimmy away. "Sorry, you're warm and smell so good." Oh, whistling tea kettles! Did I say that out loud!? I can feel my face growing red. Before I can shimmy too far away, he grabs my arm. I look up to find his cheeks are also slightly pink.

"I smell good, do I?"

I shrug and reply, "You smell like black licorice and mint. It's an odd combination, but it smells familiar and nice."

He pulls me back into his side. "Familiar?"

"I'm not sure how to explain it, but all of you seem familiar to me. Like I've known you all my whole life. You and Chesh are the only ones who I've been close enough to, to know what you smell like, though. Do you guys wear cologne or something?" I'll take that as a no by the confusion on his face. "Natural scent. Got it."

"Does it matter if it's my natural scent or not?" He sounds slightly offended by the idea.

My eyes widen. "No!" I yell. His eyes widen a bit at my loud protest. "Sorry. No, it doesn't matter. Males on the Surface usually use cologne over their natural scent. Your natural scent is amazing, though."

There's a slight tilt to his lips. "So you like my natural scent?"

Burying my face into his shoulder, I groan. "Yes, can we move on now? Back to the original conversation. You were telling me about your morals."

He snorts but does as I say. "I don't kill women or children. No matter what."

"So what would cause a Hatter's hair to turn red?" I ask gently.

His face darkens. "A Hatter with red hair has chosen to kill no matter who the target is. The darker the red the hair is means they have killed more guilty than innocent, but they still kill the innocent. The brighter the red hair, the more they fall into madness. They kill marks as well as those around them."

I gasp. "I'm sorry! I didn't know."

He squeezes my thigh. "I know. That's why I'm explaining this to you." We sit there in silence, and finally, after a few minutes, he softly says, "We can go back to the camp, I'm sure everyone is worried about you."

I laugh. "Chesh was a bit worried, but I told him I would yell if I needed help."

He hums. "I wouldn't blame him for being worried. That's the first time I've ever seen him hiss at someone. I'm convinced that cat would go to war for you."

I smile. "He is a protective cat. I like that about him." Then, sighing, I snuggle closer into his shoulder. "Do you mind if we sit here for a little while longer? I like the silence."

"Sure."

I nod my thanks and settle in next to Hatter. My body seems to relax from the warmth radiating off of him. With each breath I take, I fall deeper and deeper into relaxation, surrounded by his delicious licorice and mint smell.

"You falling asleep, Alyce?"

I mumble what I think is a no, but I'm not sure. Finally, I hear a soft chuckle, then he says, "You're safe here." With those words, I let myself fall. For the first time in sixteen years, I don't dream of Wonderland. Instead, I dream of monsters I thought were lost and forgotten.

CHAPTER SIX
Chesh

"Shouldn't one of us go in there and check on her?" I ask, my tail twitching with irritation and worry.

Rab clears his throat and replies, "You seem quite attached to this female already, Chesh."

"She not only has the name Alyce, but she also carries the Liddell name. That means something, does it not?" I growl out. It's none of his business who I get attached to.

"That's not what I asked."

My ears twitch in irritation. "You did not ask anything. You made a statement, so I replied with a statement as well."

Dee snickers. "He does have a point, Rab. If you want to know the answer to the question running around in that skull of yours, ask."

I ignore everyone and look over at Arch only to find his eyes on the flaps of Hatter's tent as well. His brows knit together as he feeds his pet mouse. "Arch, do you think we should go in there and check on her?"

He shifts his gaze to mine. "She said she would yell if she needed help. Have you heard a peep?"

Growling, I admit, "No. I suppose not."

"Why are you getting so attached to this woman?" Rab asks.

"I am under no obligation to make sense to you," I say, growling. What is up with me? I don't normally growl at anyone. Maybe my little kitten is getting under my skin more than I thought.

I look over to Rab and watch as he raises a brow. I sigh then answer his silent question, "I don't know. There's something about her that feels familiar. Like she belongs here. With Wonderland and with us. Plus the way she smells…" I purr when I remember her smell.

"What does she smell like?" Mor asks.

"Like roses." I watch as everyone cringes at the thought. "No, not like the roses here. Like what they used to smell like but softer and with a touch of sweetness." The guys around me still look unconvinced, and I let out a frustrated mewl. Trying to think of a way to get them to understand, I look around the group of males. Then I remember I rubbed myself all over Alyce earlier. Smiling widely, I jump up and run over to Dee. "Smell me!"

Dee's brows knit together briefly before he shrugs. I grin. This male never questions my crazy, odd behavior. He shifts to smell the crook of my neck and lets out a groan. I laugh when he grabs onto me and pulls me closer. His nose is against my neck now as he takes a deep inhale. "Spaydz above…" Dee groans again.

"Does she not smell delicious?" I pull away and give Dee a toothy grin.

"You're right. She does smell familiar in a way. Not from this time, but maybe from a time before?" Dee questions.

"A time before?" Rab asks.

"Didn't Alice from times past have many lovers?" Rook questions.

"The original Queen of Wonderland?" Arch asks quietly. There are eyes and ears everywhere, so we need to keep this to ourselves. We don't want the Red Queen to know what we think to be true.

"So you think our Alyce is a descendant of the original Alice?" I ask.

"I thought she was killed by her sisters. The Red and White Princesses," Mor adds.

I look at Mor. "I have heard the ramblings of Wonderlanders who believe that she escaped through the Looking Glass."

Rook runs a hand down his face. "What additional ramblings have you heard?"

I move back to my original spot, thinking over the ramblings I've heard. "They say that her lovers forced her to escape Wonderland so her sisters couldn't kill her. That her lovers were part of the original rebellion in Wonderland against the rule of the Red and White Queens. It's said that the Red and White Queens were not Wonderland's original rulers but Alice. And when the Red and White Princesses fought against the Queen's lovers, they won the fight, which is why they now rule over Wonderland. Well, used to rule over Wonderland until the Red Queen decided she wanted all the power for herself."

The circle is quiet for a moment before Rook speaks up. "So what does that have to do with us feeling connected to this Alyce?" he asks.

Wow, the grumpy male admits to feeling connected to someone other than his twin brother. Curious. I'm about to say something before I'm interrupted by Rab who says, "Maybe the connection is that the original Alice had lovers from all four Suits. Perhaps the Queen of Wonderland took lovers from all four Suits, so there were ties to each Suit for peace and representation."

We all look at each other. Our group has at least one person born from each Suit even if we don't align with the Suits anymore. Standing, I stretch before saying, "I'm going to go check on Aly. It's been too quiet for my liking."

"As opposed to loud?" Arch raises a brow.

"If it were loud, I would have checked on them sooner." Making my way over to the tent, I listen from the outside for any sign that I need to jump in quickly. The only thing that greets me though is silence. Hum. Curious. Opening the flap quietly, I make my way through and look around the room. My eyes snag on two figures sitting on the ground. I shift into cat form and disappear, so I can quietly float over them and not be seen. The sight that greets me makes me grin.

Alyce has her head resting against Hatter's shoulder. Her eyes are closed, and her mouth is slightly agape. I can hear the soft whispers of her breathing, which leads me to believe she's asleep. I look over to see Hatter staring down at a hat pin with a small smile on his face. Seems our sweet Alyce has thawed our dark, mad Hatter.

"I know you're there, Chesh," Hatter whispers.

I shift back into my male form before becoming visible. I make my way over to them and sit beside the large male. "Seems you bored our sweet Alyce to sleep."

His gaze shifts over to her briefly before meeting mine. "I told her I was horrible company, but she wouldn't leave."

"Is that why you have a smile on your face?" I ask, grinning. His glare meets me, but I can tell it's lighthearted.

He rolls his eyes and sighs. "She opened up to me. Started talking about her family on the Surface." He looks back at her briefly, then drops his head back against the wall with a quiet thump. He closes his eyes. "I'm a stranger. I trust no one."

"For good reason," I interrupt.

He groans. "Maybe. I know how I portray myself. I have those I trust and no one else."

I can feel the 'but' he wants to say but can't. So I help. "But?"

Heaving out a breath, he replies, "But she feels familiar. Like I know her from a time before."

I nod and say, "The others and I were also talking about this. We think it's connected to the original Alice. We believe the ramblings of the past could have some truth to them."

"The original Alice," he states.

I lay my head against his shoulder, mirroring Alyce. A cat always loves a good cuddle.

He snorts. "Everyone seems to be a cuddler today."

I purr. "You often don't let others touch you, so I'm only taking advantage of your good mood," I tease.

"For good reason," he grunts.

I cuddle closer, purring louder. "For good reason," I agree. I feel the tightness in my chest growing. He has a good reason. I wouldn't want others to touch me either if the reminder of the only physical touch I'd had was branded into my skin. I shiver at the thought.

Hatter

I had forgotten how nice companionship could be. With Chesh on one side and Alyce on the other, I felt surprisingly comfortable. It was odd seeing them asleep. I was the last person people went to, to seek comfort and definitely not one they felt comfortable sleeping next to. The only being in Wonderland I thought I felt that comfortable with was Arch. He and I were similar in many ways. We knew what each other wouldn't tell others. We were the monsters of Wonderland. Worse than the Jabberwocky and Bandersnatch because we looked human. We could blend into society, and no one was the wiser.

I stiffen when I hear the flaps of my tent rustle once more and look up to find Arch in the doorway. I groan when I see a smile playing on his lips; I'm never going to live this down.

"I was a little worried when the cat didn't come back out," Arch says as he raises an amused brow, "I see he's taking a cat nap."

I roll my eyes. "It seems my broody image is failing me now. I can't seem myself when I look as I do now."

Arch moves closer. Sitting on the floor across from me he asks, "As you look now?"

I look at Chesh beside me. He has a soft smile on his face as he purrs in delight. He seems to be having great cat dreams. What do cats dream of anyways?

"It isn't often I see Chesh able to cuddle next to you. He usually seeks out Dee or me to get cuddles."

I grumble, "I didn't have much choice. He cuddled without asking."

Arch snorts. "I know Chesh. He doesn't seek affection where it's not wanted. He doesn't force himself on anyone."

"I guess you're right." I look up at Arch before switching my gaze to the sleeping Alyce on my opposite shoulder. "It didn't seem right to refuse him when she fell asleep on me as well."

"Are you alright?" he asks.

I look up to find my long-time companion's worried eyes. I think about the question. Am I alright? The affection from these two does feel a bit odd, but not in a bad way. "I believe I'm alright, Arch."

"Would you like me to help you move them?"

I'm about to say yes when I notice Alyce mumbling. I look up at Arch, then back at the woman beside me. Her brows are knit together, and her breathing hitches. I move the shoulder Chesh is lying on and say, "Chesh, wake up."

The cat yawns and complains, "But I was so comfortable."

I smirk. "Yes, I'm sure, but something seems to be wrong with Alyce."

Chesh seems to wake up faster at the mention of her name. "What's wrong?"

"I'm not sure." Both males move closer as she whimpers.

"Should we wake her?" Arch asks.

I have no idea what to do, but she seems distressed at whatever she's dreaming about. Suddenly, she jerks awake with a startled scream. Chesh covers his ears with a whine as Arch and I back away to give her some space.

She looks around the room, breathing heavily. Her eyes have a wild look to them as she takes in the room. I watch as realization lights her eyes. She looks at Chesh and winces. "I'm sorry, Chesh." I watch as she crawls over my lap and into his. She rubs at his ears.

Chesh purrs and says, "No reason to be sorry. You must have had quite the fright to scream so loudly."

Suddenly, the flaps to my tent are ripped open as Dee and Rook rush in with swords drawn. They lower them once they see everything is fine. Rab and Mor enter behind them as well.

Alyce turns in Chesh's lap and gives them a sheepish smile before apologizing. "Sorry! Everything is fine."

Arch moves in closer to her. "What were you dreaming about to cause such a fright?"

Her cheeks are slightly tinted pink from what I'm assuming is embarrassment. "Well, I used to only dream about Wonderland. Now that I'm here though, I guess that means I am dreaming of other things."

Chesh pulls her closer as she shivers. "It's okay, Little Kitten, I've got you." She seems to relax and snuggles in closer to Chesh.

"What were the dreams about?" I ask. Everyone's gaze shifts to me, and I raise a brow in question. What? I do talk. Just not often. I turn my gaze back to hers, and I'm familiar with that look. Those eyes are haunted by the monsters of her own world.

"In my world, I was considered cursed. Some people did mean and horrible things to me when I was a kid because of that. I'd forgotten about it. I never dreamed about it, so I thought I'd forgotten the trauma." She looks up at me, and I can feel my cold dead heart breaking a little for her.

Without thinking, my hand brushes against her cheek. Her eyes close as she sighs and leans into my touch, seeking comfort. My inner monologue is yelling at me. My thoughts start to spiral, and I get stuck in my head. Don't trust her! She's just like the others. She'll betray you just like your family. I can feel the pulse of every brand on my body as if new. The brands my family gave me when I refused to side with the Red Queen. When I refused to spill innocent blood. Sighing, I pull away and stand. I need to distance myself.

As I turn away, my eyes meet Arch's. I see the mournful look he gives me before he nods. He's the only one who understands. This is all too much. I'm feeling too much. I head toward the flaps of my tent when I hear her soft voice.

"Did I do something?"

I don't hear anything else as I rush out of the tent. The ache in my chest doubles, and I grunt. This woman. She's making me feel again, and I don't know what to do with that. I need to get some air. I need to regroup and harden my heart again because the emotion I'm feeling right now is something I haven't felt in years.

Fear.

Change is bad. Change means something new. And in my experience, new things often mean something bad.

CHAPTER SEVEN
Alyce

"Did I do something wrong?" I ask worriedly as I look toward the flaps Hatter hustled out of. I knew the moment his eyes darkened that he had closed himself off to me.

Chesh cuddles closer to me. "You didn't do anything wrong. Hatter is fighting his own monsters right now. He'll come around."

I suppose Chesh would know. These men have known Hatter a lot longer than I have. Huffing, I say, "Alright, well that was a nice nap, but I'm still exhausted. Is there somewhere I can stay the night?"

Chesh purrs against my neck. "You can use my tent."

"I don't want to be a bother," I say.

Chesh shuffles me off his lap, then stands up and holds out a hand. "No bother. I don't use my tent very often. I'm usually in cat form sleeping in a tree, or roaming. So if you would like to be alone, that's fine."

I grasp his hand, and he pulls me up. Did I want to be alone? I'm in a new world with strange things and even stranger men. Looking around the tent at the other males, I debate what I want to do as I gnaw on my lip.

Chesh tugs my hand and assures me, "None of these men will enter the tent without your consent, Aly."

Eyes widening, I squeak out, "No! That wasn't what I was thinking at all."

Chesh tilts his head in silent question.

Groaning, I explain, "I don't want to be alone in a strange place where something can sneak up on me and kill me. But it may be awfully awkward to ask the males I just met if one of them could at least stay in the tent with me so..."

Chesh nods. "It's not awkward. Do you have a male in mind who you wish to accompany you tonight?"

I stare at him mouth agape. "Um...I didn't realize I could choose?"

Chesh shrugs and nonchalantly asks, "Is there a male you wish to get to know better, a male you feel safer with, or a male you want to cuddle with? It is entirely up to you."

They weren't kidding when they said multiple partners weren't taboo here. "Would all of you feel comfortable staying in the tent with me?"

The males look at each other and then back at me with a shrug. Arch raises a hand. "If you wouldn't object, would you mind if I stay and check on Hatter?"

My brows knit together in confusion. "Of course not, why would I object?"

Arch shrugs and explains, "If Wonderland women wish to lie or stay with the male of their choosing and the male wishes otherwise..." He rubs at his neck, looking uncomfortable. "They can be beheaded by the Queen for displeasing the female."

I gasp in horror and quickly reassure them, "I would never do that." I look around the room. "To any of you!" I see all of the males relax a little. "If you do not wish to stay in the room with me, that's fine. I won't make you do something you don't want to do."

"It's not that I wouldn't want to enjoy your company in whatever way you would give it. But Hatter is like my... well he's my closest friend, and my loyalty is to him first, you see," Arch replies.

I move toward him and grab his hand. Gripping it in mine, I look into his eyes, so he can see the truth behind my words. "I wouldn't expect you to pick a stranger over your friend."

He squeezes my hand gently. "Thank you. You don't know how much that means." He gives me a quick peck on the cheek before heading toward the tent flaps.

"Arch!" I call after him. He turns and I smile. "Can you tell me how he is in the morning? I feel like I may need to stay away from him a bit."

Arch grins. "I'll inform you about him in the morning. But if I may be so bold as to say..." He pauses, and I nod for him to continue. "I wouldn't recommend you stay away from him. I know his greatest fear, and I can say with the utmost confidence that if you stick by him, he will open up to you."

I nod as he exits the tent. Message received. I turn to the others and ask, "Anyone else?"

Chesh raises his hand. "I wish to stay in the room with you!"

I laugh at his excitement. "Alright."

Dee and Rook raise their hands as well. "We can guard the outside of the tent if that would make you feel better," they say together, which is hilarious.

Nodding, I tell them, "That would be amazing, thank you." Looking toward Rab and Mor, I raise a brow. "You haven't said your wishes yet."

Rab shrugs. "There will be a person in the room with you as well as guarding the outside. I'm not sure what else we can provide."

"That's not what it's about. It's about you voicing what you want to do in this situation," I say.

"If you wouldn't mind, I wish to join you in the room," Mor states. I nod, looking toward Rab again.

"I'll stand guard inside the room. Since I have Mor's clock, I can stop time if any intruders get through the twins, then Mor can disarm them before they can get to you."

Chesh purrs with excitement. "Now that we have sleeping arrangements settled. Let us be off."

Lying in Chesh's bed, I have to admit this is the most luxurious bed I have ever been in. The blankets feel like silk, the pillow is made of down feathers, and the bed is cloud-like. I moan in pleasure as I shimmy down into the blankets.

"Comfortable, Aly?" Chesh asks, laughing beside me. I look over to find him in cat form. He circles a few times before lying down beside me.

"This bed is amazing," I gush.

He purrs. "A cat loves its comforts."

I look over to find Mor standing next to a chair. I watch as he flutters his wings before they disappear in a blast of blue glitter. I guess Chesh isn't the only one who has bursts of glitter. Mor settles gracefully onto the chair beside Chesh. I look to my other side to find Rab, ears still twitching on the top of his head, sitting in the chair by my side. My eyes bounce between the two of them and I ask, "Are you guys not going to sleep?"

Rab pulls out a book, which seems to have poofed into existence. "I am the extra guard, so I will not be sleeping."

I shift to look at him better. "What book are you reading?" He turns the cover so I can see. "Tea?"

He shrugs. "I like tea. I've been looking at broadening my palette of flavors."

"Can I try some?" I yawn and watch as his ears twitch before he nods.

"I'll pour you a cup in the morning."

Humming, I say, "Sounds good. What about you, Mor?" I shift on the bed to look in his direction.

He smiles. "I'm your second guard in here. I'm also here to soothe you if you have another nightmare."

"How are you going to soothe the nightmare away?" I ask curiously.

"I sing."

Grinning as I burrow under the blankets, I ask, "Will you sing for me?" Accepting my request, he begins to hum. His soft, melodic voice engulfs me in warmth, and my body relaxes as the sound calms me. Humming contently, I fall asleep.

When I wake, there is something warm wrapped around me, and I am extremely hot. Grunting, I try to push at whatever has me in its death grip, but it seems to cling to me harder. Whistling tea kettles! I'm burning up! I push against it again with no luck. Giving up, I whine, "It's too early to wake up, but I'm being baked alive!"

I hear soft laughter before someone says, "I believe Chesh has claimed you as his cuddle partner."

Fearing the room will be bright, I slowly open my eyes. Squinting, I look around to realize that the tent is softly lit with lanterns. I sigh and open my eyes wider. I find Chesh next to me, no longer in cat form. No, he's in his male form with his face squished into my boobs, purring. The blankets are wrapped around me in a cocoon, so my arms are stuck at my sides while he cuddles me like a body pillow.

I hear snickering and turn toward the noise as best I can in my position to find Rab grinning as he stands next to the bed. He sips from his teacup, then raises it in greeting. "Morning, Alyce."

I groan as I look back toward Mor. Jutting out my bottom lip, I pout. He just raises a brow while smirking. Damn, I thought that would have worked. Sighing, I beg, "halp!"

He seems to ponder my request then nods. Moving over to the bed, he grasps Chesh's tail and gives it a tug, causing Chesh to jolt awake.

Turning toward Mor with a hiss, he howls. "Hey! What's with the brilliant idea to pull on my tail?!

I try to free myself from my blanket prison, but damn, he wrapped me up good. When I realize I'm stuck, I whine, "You wrapped me up in a cocoon of death! I'm baking to death and you wouldn't move."

Chesh turns back to me and winces. "I suppose I did get a little carried away with making sure you stayed warm."

Raising an indignant brow, I ask, "A little?"

He shrugs, pulling at the blankets to free me. "You shivered, and I don't know how cold is too cold for Surface beings, so I wrapped you up tight and thought what better way to keep you warm than with body heat?"

I rip my arms out of the blankets and wave them around. Airing out my sweaty self, I wriggle farther out of the blankets. "So you shifted?"

He nods, smiling. "I'm bigger in my male form, so I can cover more body surface that way."

Humming, I nod. That makes sense. Although, his male form wasn't the only big thing that greeted me this morning. I guess morning wood affects all males, no matter the species. Is it species? Would shifters be considered a different species? Shaking the newest conundrum from my mind, I turn and point at Rab. "You promised me tea."

"That I did." He moves from the bed over to the small kitchenette, but I can't see what he's doing since his back is to me. My eyes roam over him. The button-up he's wearing shows off his strong shoulders. The material ripples as he moves. My gaze lowers, and I bite my lip as I grin. That right there, ladies, is a fine ass. His black slacks seem to cup his cheeks perfectly. I must have made a sound because when my eyes finally venture back up, Rab is looking over his shoulder with a knowing grin.

His ears flop in half as he turns with a teacup in hand. "Do you approve of what you see, Alyce?" His voice is deep and sensual, causing me to shiver as goosebumps spread across my skin.

"Uh... maybe." My voice squeaks at the end. Smooth, Aly. Real smooth. Clearing my throat, I change the subject, "So what kind of tea did you make?" Our fingers brush as he hands me the teacup and saucer. A tingle of Wonderland magic seems to pass between us, and a shiver runs down my spine. It's not unpleasant. It's actually really... nice.

"Lemon tea. It's sweetened with honey."

"You guys have bumblebees here?"

He looks confused. "We have Bubble-bees."

Looking up at him, I ask, "Bubble-bees?"

He nods. "Bubble-bees. They are bubbles with stripes and they float around. If you're not careful you'll pop them."

I look over my shoulder at Chesh and Mor to make sure they aren't laughing. This seems like a joke, except no one's laughing, so I guess this is a real thing. Wonderland did have weird things in the original book. I don't remember Bubble-bees, though. Shrugging, I ask curiously, "Alright, how do they make the honey if they can pop?"

"Honey doesn't come from Bubble-bees. It comes from honey ants," Mor says from behind me.

I set the tea on the side table. "Please tell me I am not drinking ants."

Chesh laughs. "No, silly. Honey ants are... hum... well, it's quite hard to describe to someone who isn't from here."

Mor speaks up, "Their body is wooden, so you're not eating the ant. The ant is covered in honey. That's what we use as a sweetener."

"So I'm drinking the body fluid of the ants?"

"I'm not sure if body fluid is the right word. I suppose all I can say is that it's a Wonderland thing." Mor shrugs.

Picking up the tea cup, I try not to think about how weird this is and accept that this is Wonderland. I was planning on staying here anyways. Buck up, Alyce, this is your new normal.

CHAPTER EIGHT
Alyce

Sipping the last of my tea, I had to admit it was delicious. Handing the teacup back to Rab, I look down and realize I'm still in my clothes from yesterday. They are rumpled and extremely dirty from my fall into Wonderland. Looking at Chesh, I ask, "Is there a way I could shower?"

He nods toward the opposite corner of the tent. "There's a tub behind those curtains. I'll have to go to the creek to get some water for you."

Mor stands from his chair and says, "I can get the water." He nods toward Rab and asks, "Could you get the firewood to heat the tub?" Rab nods and makes his way out of the tent.

I raise a brow. "Heat the tub?"

Chesh makes his way over to the curtains in the corner as he explains, "Most of us usually just take a quick rinse with water from the creek, but for you, we are going to heat up the water so it's not cold."

He pulls the curtains toward a hook on the wall. I see a copper-looking tub raised a few inches off the ground with some ash underneath. "So you heat the water by setting a fire underneath?" I ask.

He kneels and shovels the ash from underneath the tub into a bucket. "It's a small fire. We heat up the water, and then put out the fire so it doesn't continue heating the tub."

Humming, I respond, "That makes sense. Wouldn't want a cooked cat."

"I assure you, I would not be delicious." Chesh laughs. I hear the flaps of the tent rustle, and I look over my shoulder to find Mor, Dee, Rook, and even Arch carrying buckets of water.

"I see you grabbed some extra hands," I say with a laugh.

Mor smiles. "Fewer trips to the creek this way."

I wander over to watch as they each empty a bucket of water into the tub. The buckets are huge by my standards, and the tub is full before Arch can empty his second bucket. He sets the bucket beside the tub and nods in my direction. "In case the tub gets too warm, you can add this in."

"Thank you." I look at each male. "All of you." They each give me a nod. Dee gives me a wink as he leaves, and Rook, who's still a bit broody, gives me a nod as he follows his brother.

Mor smiles and says, "I'll leave you to your bathing." He nods and exits the tent.

Arch is about to leave, but I stop him. "Is Hatter alright?"

He smiles but it seems sad. "He is doing as well as usual."

I nod. "Thank you."

His brow furrows. "For what?" he asks.

Also confused, I reply, "For checking on him and making sure he's doing okay. For giving me an update. You didn't have to let me know how he's doing."

Arch shrugs. "You asked me last night to give you an update."

Reaching out, I grip his arm. Giving it a gentle squeeze, I say, "I know, but you didn't have to. I want you to know that I'm not like the females here in Wonderland. If you don't want to tell me something, I won't force you."

He looks into my eyes for a moment, and I see something click in his gaze. He nods, his smile becoming genuine. "Thank you."

I arch a brow, now it's my turn to be confused. "For what?"

"For caring." He bends and places a quick kiss on my cheek before turning to leave.

Reaching up, I touch my cheek. Smiling, I look up to find Chesh with a wide grin. "What?" I ask, wondering what that grin is for.

He's about to talk when Rab walks back in with an armful of wood. He looks between the two of us and asks, "Did I miss something?"

"No! Nothing at all," I squeal.

Rab smirks. "Nothing sure looks like something to me," he teases as he kneels on the ground and places the wood under the tub. Pulling out a box of matches from his pocket, he lights the wood pile.

"Even if it was something, I'm not telling you." I stick out my tongue.

He laughs and wiggles his brows. "I'm sure I could persuade you."

Before I can blink, he is standing in front of me causing me to let out an indignant squeak. He caresses my cheek with his gloved forefinger as his voice turns sensual. "Also, be careful with that tongue of yours, or I may wish for it to be put to better use."

Shattering tea kettles. My underwear dampens instantly. I can feel the pulse between my legs signaling that my needy cunt is ready for action. Calm down, Alyce! You just met these guys! Do not add sex into the already complicated situation. Taking a shuddering breath, I focus. "I see. Well, I'll make sure to keep my tongue to myself then."

He turns with a deep chuckle. "You do that, Alyce," he says as he walks out, leaving only Chesh and me together.

Huffing, I point toward the bath. "Is the water warm?"

Chesh's smile has grown tenfold. "Three males under your control and two who are smitten with you. Two more to go, and you'll have the most sought-after males in Wonderland all to yourself."

I growl out, "I don't have anyone under my control, nor do I want to control them. They are their own men, and they are going to stay like that."

Then I whisper under my breath, "Even if I find each of you appealing in your own way."

"Oh, so you find me appealing?"

Groaning, I reply, "Obviously. Now, can I take my bath so that I may suffer in my embarrassment alone?"

He has an amused grin on his face as he douses the flames. Turning, he gestures to the tub. "All warmed up and ready." Chesh brushes his tail softly against my fingertips, making my breath catch before he casually says, "We find you appealing as well, Alyce."

I wait until he walks out of the tent before I whip the curtain around myself. Feeling safe now that I'm hidden from view, I cover my face and let out the girliest squeal of my life. Am I proud of it? No. Will I deny I did it if I'm ever asked? Yes. But what am I supposed to do when I'm surrounded by seven of the sexiest males I have ever seen in my life!? I'm sorry book boyfriends, but these males are most likely, okay definitely, taking your place in my spank bank. And don't you dare deny having a spank bank. Every woman does.

Confirming that I am in fact alone, I slip out of my dirty clothes, folding them up and placing them in the corner. Yes, I folded my dirty underwear. Every woman does that when they go anywhere other than their own house. It's an unwritten rule.

I'm about to slide into the tub when I notice that the water is pink. Is that normal? I take a closer look at the water and notice little flower buds. Curious.

"The creek has natural healing properties, that's why it's that color."

The scream that I screamed was a scream that I have never screamed before. Covering my lady bits with my arms and hands, I turn and find... nothing. Shattering tea cups! "Cheshire!" I hear his laughter behind the curtain.

"Sorry. I came back to explain the odd color of the water since you're not from Wonderland."

"Sure. You just wanted to have a peek at the goods, didn't you?"

"By goods, do you mean your naked body parts?"

"Yes, Chesh," I squeal. I can't see him on the other side due to the curtain being solid, but I feel the change in air pressure that goes with his shift.

"I am a gentle cat and would never peek unless I was welcome to. My only wish was to ensure you knew about the water." I must be silent for too long because he whispers, "Alyce?"

I nibble my lip then sigh. "Promise?"

"I promise. If I am lying, may my ability to shift be taken away forever."

Well, how can I argue with a promise like that? "Alright, Chesh. I believe you."

"You do?" He sounds shocked by my words.

Turning away from the curtain, I slip into the tub so he can't see me anyways. Moaning from the warmth seeping into my body, I answer. "Of course. You promised on your ability to shift. I assume that's important, is it not?"

I can hear him shifting nervously from foot to foot. "Yes. It's very important."

"Then why would I not believe you?"

He's quiet for a moment, and I can see the outline of his finger as he caresses the curtain from his side. "The females here wouldn't have." He sighs. "But you are not a female from Wonderland, so I suppose I should not expect the same reaction."

My chest aches for these males. It seems like the females here treat males like possessions instead of males with feelings and emotions. "I'm sorry, Chesh."

He snorts. "There is nothing for you to be sorry about."

Swirling my fingers around as I play with the flower buds, I sigh and say, "I know, but I'm still sorry that the females here seem to be bitches."

"I'm not sure what the word bitch means, but considering how our conversation is going I'm inclined to agree." We are both silent for a moment before he speaks again, "I'll let you enjoy your bath, Aly. If you need anything just yell. One of us will be able to hear you and help."

His steps whisper away. I wait until I can't hear his footsteps anymore before plunging myself under the water. I hold my breath for as long as I can, thinking of as many impossible things as I can. Although, my prior impossible things are now my reality, so maybe I should re-evaluate the meaning of impossible.

The burn in my lungs becomes too much, and I surface with a gasp. Wiping the water from my eyes, I look around and find a fluffy purple towel on the ground waiting for me. Now, I would love to say I'm a graceful person. To say that I stood and reached over the tub, grabbed the towel, and stepped out of the tub with no problem. That's what I want to say happened. Unfortunately for me, that's not what happened.

Standing, I reached over and down to get the towel. Wrapping the towel around myself, I stepped one foot out of the tub and onto the textured ground. Now, apparently, my balance was off, and to compensate I put more weight on the leg that was still in the tub. Do. Not. Do. For future reference. Due to the slippery nature of the copper, my foot slid out from underneath me, making me lose my balance, and sending my ass crashing down onto the side of the tub and then onto the ground. Hard.

"Shattering Tea Cups!" I yell. My ass! Ouch. That is going to bruise so badly! Refusing to move, I continue lying on the floor, gasping in pain. The guys must have heard my screaming though because the ruckus of feet rattles the floor. Oh. No. Please, no. Whoever is in charge of my life needs to lay off. This is too much embarrassment for one person to handle! "Please don't open the curtain!" I cry out.

"Alyce? You okay?" Mor's soft melodic voice greets me.

"Doing great," I grunt.

"You don't sound great." Dee's normal happy tone sounds more serious now.

Ugh! For the love of hearts! "Yep, doing great. Just wanted to get more acquainted with Chesh's bathroom floor."

"Why are you on the floor, Aly?" Arch asks.

"Please tell me everyone is not on the other side of this curtain. I'm going to die of embarrassment if you tell me every single one of you is out there." I hear whispering on the other side and catch bits and pieces.

I laugh when I hear a whispered, "Get out. She'll die if we are all in here." I would bet the voice belonged to Chesh.

"I'm not going to actually die, Chesh. It's just an expression." I giggle as I lie on the floor because what else can I do? I'm wrapped in a bath towel, laughing on the floor because I slipped, and now there are seven extremely hot guys on the other side of the curtain thinking I will actually die of embarrassment.

"Not to sound redundant, but why are you on the floor, Alyce?" Hatter's deep, gravelly voice seems to echo through the tent.

Sighing, I mutter, "I slipped when I was getting out of the tub."

"Do you need help?" Chesh asks.

Did I need help? I try to pull myself up by grabbing onto the side of the tub when a twinge of pain radiates up my back and through my asscheeks. Grumbling to myself, I lie back down. Sighing, I say, "Yes. But can everyone leave except..." I try to think about who I have had the least interaction with. Maybe if I pick someone I haven't spoken to a lot, someone who hasn't flirted with me, it will make this less embarrassing. Rook. "Rook. Please. It will make it less embarrassing with fewer of you watching."

I hear the shifting of feet until it's quiet again, then Rook's husky voice comes from the other side of the curtain. "Are you covered, Alyce?"

"As best as I can be."

He grunts and pulls the curtain to the side. I watch his face come into view as he makes his way around the tub. He looks down at me and raises a brow. "How bad is it?" he asks.

I can feel my face heat. "My back hurts if I try to sit up by myself."

He nods. Crouching down, he slides one arm under my knees and the other behind my upper back. He looks into my eyes and says, "I'm going to lift you. If it hurts too much let me know."

I nod, lifting my right arm around the back of his neck. I bite my lip as he lifts, and a sharp pain shoots up my back. Without thinking, I shift my fingers into his hair and squeeze. I hear him grunt as he shifts me a bit to get a better hold on me.

We stand there for a moment until I open my eyes and find him watching me. I realize my fingers have a death grip on the short hairs at the back of his head. Releasing my grip immediately. "I'm sorry!" I exclaim.

His eyes seem to search mine. "Are you alright for me to move?"

I nod, ducking my head. I was close to ripping the hairs out of his head. I hadn't realized I'd been doing it.

He sets me down on the edge of the bed before looking around the room. "Is there anything else I can get you?"

I look around and find my bag on the chair Mor was sitting in. I point toward it. "Would you mind getting me my bag?"

He nods, reaching over and placing it beside me.

Opening the bag, I reach in and grab a pair of undergarments and my black yoga pants. As I search through my shirts, I realize I did not pack for the rugged woods of Wonderland. I managed to remember to pack decent jogging shoes and socks but no reasonable shirts. Huffing out a sigh, I flop back onto the bed, looking up at the ceiling. What should I do?

"Is there something wrong?"

From my vantage point, I peer over to see Rook giving me a questioning look. I squint at him for a moment, thinking. I suppose I could ask to borrow one of the guy's shirts. I take a moment to debate who to ask. Rab and Chesh are the smallest as far as muscles go, so their shirts wouldn't be too huge. But, Chesh never seems to wear a shirt. Which leaves Rab. "Would you mind asking Rab a favor for me?"

He shrugs. "I suppose, as long as it's not too large of a favor."

Sitting up, my back twinges, and I cringe. That was a stupid idea. "Could you ask him if he would mind letting me borrow a shirt from him? It seems I didn't pack appropriately for this adventure."

He seems to think about it for a moment before turning and leaving the tent. It's only a few minutes before he's returning with a red button-up in hand. He holds it out to me, and I smile up at him. "Thank you, Rook."

He gives me a puzzled look. "I didn't give you my shirt. I only retrieved what you requested."

These males have obviously never had a well-mannered female in their life. Sighing, I say, "I understand, but I still want to thank you for asking for me. Could you also thank Rab for letting me borrow his shirt?"

Still seeming confused he replies, "I suppose, but I'm not sure how thanks from me will matter." He points toward the flaps of the tent. "He is standing right outside the tent."

Laughing, because what else can I do? I raise my voice enough for Rab to hear. "Thank you, Rab, for letting me borrow your shirt."

He laughs from the other side of the flaps. "You are welcome, Alyce."

I point toward the flaps. "See? He accepted my thanks."

Rook shakes his head. "You are a curious female, Alyce."

Arching a brow, I ask, "Is that a good thing?"

I see the hint of a smirk on his face as he turns to leave. "Not sure yet. Get dressed so we can have a meeting."

CHAPTER NINE
Alyce

Walking out of the tent, I wince with each step. Man, I hit that tub hard. I make my way over next to Chesh, and he holds out a bottle for me. It looks similar to the beer bottles back home. I nod toward the drink and ask, "What's that?"

"It's called a Drink Me. The medical officers in the rebellion came up with it. It relaxes your muscles and helps with pain. It also has some healing herbs."

I shrug, sitting down next to him. Taking the bottle, I take a swig. My body instantly relaxes, and the pain in my back lessens. "That's amazing." I feel a tingle in my body. Curious. Then suddenly, I feel my body compress. The feeling makes me dizzy, and I close my eyes. It takes a second for the dizziness to wear off, but when it does, I open my eyes. Except when I do, I realize that everything around me is huge. Uh oh.

I look around. Wow, this is crazy! Looking in the direction I last saw Chesh, I see him looking down at me, a look of horror on his handsome face. He's massive. I look down at myself and blush. Note to self, clothes do not shrink with you. Reaching down, I pull Rab's shirt up to cover my near-naked body. Looking back up at Chesh, I try not to panic as I ask, "Do you have any Eat Me's?"

He's still standing there, a shocked look on his face, so I look around the group, only to find all the males looking at me in a similar manner. Seems the Drink Me's and Eat Me's are the same in this world as they are in the books. Waving one arm in the air as the other holds up Rab's shirt, I yell, "Do we have any Eat Me's?"

Chesh snaps out of his shock. "Eat Me's? Yes! We have Eat Me's. I'll go get one!" Chesh yells as he races off in the direction I assume he got the Drink Me from.

Huffing out a sigh, I sit and wait. I watch as Arch makes his way over to me and settles himself on the ground in front of me. "What type of magic is this?" he whispers so as to not hurt my small, delicate ears.

I have to yell to be heard. "It has to do with the Alice books."

He cocks a brow. "The Alice books?" he asks.

"In the books, if she has a Drink Me it makes her small. If she eats an Eat Me, it makes her tall."

"As big as a house, as small as a mouse." He nods.

"I expected to be smaller, so this is nice."

He grins. "Would me calling you mouse offend you?"

I laugh. "It seems rather appropriate at the moment."

He looks over at Hatter for a moment, and I see the smirk Hatter tries to hide. "Yes, Arch. A very appropriate nickname," Hatter agrees.

I watch Arch's ears perk up at the praise. Curious. Looking between the two of them, I can see that there's a connection there. I wonder if they are more than friends. If not they have a serious bromance going on. Arch looks back at me with a slight pink tinge to his cheeks. I'll bet they are more than friends. I look around to see if anyone else noticed the exchange, but no one seems to pay them any mind.

Chesh rushes back with a large square pastry in hand. "I found an Eat Me!" he calls as he settles next to Arch and holds the pastry out to me. "I'm not sure how you want to eat this."

He still seems panicked, so I stand while still trying to keep the shirt covering me. I walk towards his outstretched hand. "Everything is fine,

Chesh. Thank you for getting the pastry for me." I'm about to repeat myself because I didn't yell when Chesh's ears twitch.

"It's my fault. I gave you the drink," he mumbles.

"Chesh, can you hear me when I talk regularly?"

He nods, pointing at his ears. "I'm a cat."

"Can you put the pastry down, please?" He sets the pastry down beside me, and I grip his large finger with my tiny hand. "Can you shift into your cat so you are at my level?"

His brows furrow, but he does as I ask. In a puff of purple glitter, he is in front of me as a house cat. Still large by my standards, but it's better than looking up at his tall male form. He shuffles a little closer to me and lays his head on his forepaws.

I reach up and pet him between the eyes, and he closes them as he purrs. "Now, Chesh, I want you to know that I don't blame you at all for what happened. You didn't know what was going to happen. I should have told you that in the books the Drink Me's shrink Alice, but I assumed that what I was drinking was a normal drink for Wonderland. I now know that there is something in there I can't drink. The same with the Eat Me's."

His large eyes blink at me. "Are you sure?" he asks quietly.

My heart breaks a little at the caution in his voice. Was it the females in Wonderland who caused these males to second-guess their actions? Or did something else happen? I kiss his wet nose and say, "I'm very sure."

He enjoys my pets for a moment before scooting back. "You should probably change back."

I look down at myself and realize that the clothes I borrowed will not magically appear back on my body when I get big again. Looking back at Chesh I ask, "Would you mind telling the guys to turn around? My clothes won't be on when I change back."

He boops his nose against my face and says, "Of course, Kitten." I love that his voice is back to his playful nature. In a puff of glitter, he's back in his male form. "Alyce would like us to turn around. She will be naked when she changes back and would like some privacy."

The males look at each other and nod. Arch shifts from his position on the ground to stand and turns, facing the opposite direction. The others come closer, forming a circle around me. Once they are in place, they each turn so that their backs are to me. I smile, my chest filling with gratitude. They are blocking me so none of the soldiers who happen to walk by will see me changing.

Dropping the shirt, I move quickly, grabbing my undergarments and clothes. Taking as large of a bite as I can of the Eat Me, I feel the familiar tingle race through my body as I seem to grow at a rapid pace. I'm quickly back to my normal size, and I race to put my clothes back on. Buttoning up the shirt, I say, "Thanks, guys. I'm good now."

They each briefly look over their shoulder to check before moving back to their original seats. "So we were going to have a meeting, right?" I ask as I pull on my socks and tie my shoes.

"Yes, we were going to talk to you about the ramblings we've heard around Wonderland about the original Alice," Rab mentions across the circle.

I nod. "Sounds good. I can compare what I've read to the information you have." My stomach chooses that moment to growl. Looking at the males with a blush, I ask, "So... what's for breakfast. I don't think the tea was enough."

Dee shrugs. "We can't cook, so we usually go into the settlement closest to us. We are currently deep in the woods of Clubbz. I would say we should be safe from the Queen's grasp if only a few of us walk into the settlement at a time. Otherwise, we normally snack on plants and wildlife that we catch."

I can see that the males didn't think about having to cook for me. I laugh and say, "It's fine; I can cook. Do any of you have a skillet I can use? If someone could start a small fire, I can cook over that."

The males all look at me with surprise. "You know how to cook?" Mor asks.

"Is it not normal for a female to cook in Wonderland?"

Arch shakes his head and explains, "The males often do the housework and cooking. We are considered possessions and are treated as such. It's rare to find females who allow their husbands to work outside of the house while doing the housework themselves."

Hatter nods beside him. "The closer we get to the Clubbz and Dymondz border you'll find more females who treat their males as equals."

I hum. "Curious." Pointing to Chesh I say, "Since you are my mighty hunter, would you catch us some animals that we can cook up?"

"As you wish." Chesh grins as he shifts into a cat the size of a tiger then races off into the woods.

Wow. He's huge! Shaking myself, I look between Rab and Mor. "Who knows the plants best in the group?"

Mor raises his hand and says, "I know the plants the best."

"Would you mind gathering some plants and herbs for me?" He nods and takes off flying in the same direction Chesh went. Looking toward the twins, I ask, "Would you two mind gathering some firewood?" They nod as well.

Clapping my hands together, I think for a moment. Arch comes up beside me holding out a cast iron skillet. I smile up at him. "Thank you." He nods, moving back over to his seat next to Hatter. "Do we have a small table or somewhere I can prepare everything?" I ask them.

Rab nods as he heads off into his tent. Snapping my fingers, I run back into Chesh's tent. Opening my bag, I reach in and pull out my phone. Turning it on, I see that I still have ninety-eight percent battery. I'm glad I remembered to turn it off before throwing it into my bag. I brought my backup battery too, unsure if Wonderland would have plugs, but I wanted to save it for when my phone was almost dead. So turning it off when not in use was the best idea.

Walking back out to the group, I find Rab has brought out his small end table. I shrug. I can work with that. Chesh and Mor come back into the clearing at the same time, and Chesh is holding several animals in hand. I have no idea what the animals are, but I suppose they look similar to foxes. Although, their pelts are every color of the rainbow.

They set the animals and plants next to the table and sit. The twins come back and start the fire for me. Scrolling through my phone, I find my Spotify app. I'm so glad I downloaded my playlists because I have absolutely no signal in Wonderland. Clicking on my 'keep smiling' playlist, music blares from my phone. I set it down on the large mushroom next to the table. Seeing a knife already on the table, I pick up the animals Chesh caught and begin preparing our morning meal. Singing softly to myself, I bop to the beat.

"What is that device?" Lost in the music, I jump at Dee's voice.

Grinning, I nod down at the device. "It's a cell phone or mobile device. You can take pictures and videos and talk to people. I currently have it playing music from an app."

"Curious. May I touch it?"

"Go ahead. Click the small button on the right and the screen will light up. Swipe your finger across the screen and it will unlock the phone."

Dee picks up the phone and sits next to me. His eyes widen as he clicks through random apps. He lifts the phone up so I can see. "What is this image?"

I look down to see he has my folder open with my camera app and gallery app. "The one on the left is the camera app where you can take pictures. The one on the right is my gallery. It's where all the pictures I've taken are."

He nods, clicking on the gallery. He laughs as he scrolls through my pictures. "Who are these males you keep making faces with? And what is this writing at the bottom?"

I turn to see what picture he is looking at. The picture is of me cross-eyed with my tongue sticking out. Alix is to my right, blowing a raspberry on my cheek. Edi is on my left throwing up bunny ears behind my head, and Laurel is taking the picture. His face is on the far left side. He's laughing as he takes the picture. It's one of my favorites because it's the only one I have that shows he used to laugh all the time.

Smiling, I reply, "The one on the right is my twin brother, Alix. On the left is the second oldest, Edi, and the one taking the picture is the oldest, Laurel. The note on the bottom says to our favorite sister."

"Are you not the only sister?" he asks in confusion.

I laugh. "Yes. When I was around six, I think, Laurel had made a comment that he was glad he only had one sister, but Edi had said that he wouldn't mind having another sister. The comment made my six-year-old brain freak out thinking that Edi wanted to replace me. Alix had said that it didn't matter if we had another sister because I would always be his favorite. It stuck from that point on."

I watch Dee's eyes skip over to his brother before looking back at the photo. "I would have felt the same way. A twin bond is strong, though. But having an older brother would be nice too." He looks back up at me. "Did you like having brothers?" he asks.

I snort. "Don't get me wrong, I love my brothers. I wouldn't change having older brothers for anything, but sometimes they could be too much. Often too overprotective for my liking but..." I shrug, not sure what else to say.

Dee nods. "It's nice knowing someone will always have your back."

I hum in agreement. "It is."

Moving over to the skillet, I throw the meat in to cook. Moving back over to the table, I look around to find something to wipe it off with. As if reading my mind, Rab hands me a wet rag. I murmur my thanks as I wipe down the tabletop and grab the rest of the ingredients. The smell of the meat is making my mouth water as I chop the herbs and mushrooms. I'm not a fan of mushrooms, but I chop them up finely so I won't be able to feel the texture.

Throwing in the rest of the ingredients, I let them cook. I already made sure the skillet was on embers instead of the raging fire it was before so it's simmering. Sitting next to the skillet, I look up at Rab expectantly. "So you were going to tell me about the original Alice?"

CHAPTER TEN
Alyce

I stir the food as I listen to Rab. He seems to be the leader of this group of males. He does have a calm yet authoritative voice. I wonder if he's assertive in the bedroom with that voice. Mhm. I bet he is. All sexy and dominant. I squeak when Chesh's face suddenly appears in front of mine. His eyes narrow for a moment then dance with amusement.

"Are you paying attention, Kitten?" he purrs.

Whistling tea kettles! I feel my cheeks heat. "Yes! Until I got slightly distracted."

His knowing grin widens. "And what would distract you? Did the rabbit's voice make you daydream?"

Unable to look Chesh in the eyes, I turn my gaze back to Rab. There's a smirk playing on his lips as he asks, "Do I need to repeat myself, Alyce?"

Groaning, I reply, "Yes."

He arches a brow. "Yes, what?"

I bite my lip as a rush of heat shoots right down to my core, and I whisper, "Yes, please?"

He smiles darkly. "Such a good Little Alyce."

Oh, sweet tea! Who knew I had a praise kink?! I shift my eyes to meet Arch's and I find him grinning, but his cheeks are tinted pink. Guess we both like it when broody, strong men praise us. I clear my throat, trying to get us back on track. "So... anyways."

Rab chuckles. "Right. As I was saying, the original Alice was the Queen of Wonderland. Each Suit had a monarch as well. The Queen of Wonderland ruled over the people who chose to live within her borders. She made rules for all of Wonderland, and then the monarchs of each Suit had the option of adding onto them. The monarchs of each Suit were under the rule of the Queen of Wonderland. The Queen then had advisors who were often her sisters. The original Alice had two sisters, the Red and White Princesses."

"Wait, so I understand correctly, there is the Queen. So where I'm from there's a President who rules over the United States." He nods for me to continue. "Then each state has a representative who is in charge of that state's wellbeing. So that's what the rulers of each Suit do?"

He nods. "It sounds like it. Any other questions?" I shake my head for him to continue.

Then I hold up a hand. "Wait, sorry, do we have bowls or something for me to put the food in to eat?"

Mor stands. "Keep going. I'll get the bowls."

Rab nods and continues, "The rumors are that the Red and White Princesses didn't like their sister being in charge and wanted more power for themselves. So the sisters tried to kill the Queen to gain her power."

"By power, you mean control over Wonderland?" I ask.

"Not just that, the Queen of Wonderland had magical powers herself. No one knows exactly what they are anymore. But the Red and White Princesses only had a small amount of magic themselves. Thinking that killing their sister would then transfer the power to them, they started a war over Wonderland. They tried to kill her, but she escaped through the Looking Glass in her personal chamber, which was guarded by her husband and lovers."

"So she fled with an additional Looking Glass in the hope of returning?"

Rab nods and says, "That's the thought."

Mor comes back with bowls, and I spoon a heaping of food into each bowl figuring these males probably eat a lot. Mor hands a bowl to each of them. "Why didn't she come back through the Looking Glass?" I wonder aloud.

Chesh speaks up, "My thought is that maybe she found herself trapped on the other side. She would have had to put a spell on the Looking Glass so no one could follow her. Maybe she used up the last of her magic doing that. I assume there's no magic on the Surface?"

I shake my head. "No." Does that mean by being a descendant of the original Alice that I have powers? Will they appear the longer I'm here in Wonderland? Huffing out a sigh, I ask, "So there was a mention of a war happening not too long ago. What happened?"

Surprisingly, it's Rook who speaks up, "The White Queen disagreed with the way things had been done. She didn't agree that the descendants of the Red and White Princesses should have control over Wonderland."

"Okay, so what caused the war? Because that sounds like a good thing."

Rook nods. "It would have been great. The Red Queen on the other hand disagreed. She thought they needed more power to be able to rule more forcefully in case the people of Wonderland disagreed with their rule."

I sigh. "So the Red Queen started a war to take over Wonderland."

"She took over Heartz first and is still trying to take over more land."

"Why Heartz?"

Dee smiles sadly and answers, "They are not born fighters. Heartz is filled with those who wish to be peaceful. Spaydz is filled with warriors and is surrounded by mountains, so it's harder for her to take control of that Suit. Clubbz is split. The closer you get to Heartz, the more you will find that people will report anything and everything to the Queen in order to make sure they don't lose their heads. The area closer to Dymondz has more rebels due to the White Queen providing guards and soldiers to the area. Clubbz is filled with farmers and fishermen. It's not in their nature to fight, but they will if they have to."

"Okay then, so we need to make our way closer to Dymondz to help in the war." Temporarily shocked silent, the males look at each other and then back at me.

"You would join the war?" Rook asks in amazement.

Apparently, I'm not done surprising these males. I shrug. "If I can at least visit my brothers one last time before joining the ranks, I will." The males still look shocked. Groaning, I say, "I don't know why I'm here, but apparently, I'm where I'm supposed to be. I supposedly have some power running through my veins from the original Alice. I'm not sure what it is or how to control it, but I guess we will find out when it happens."

Still stunned, Rook nods. "There's still a Looking Glass in the Queen of Wonderland's castle. We will have to go to the White Queen first, though. She somehow sealed it up so her sister couldn't get into it," he tells me.

Shoving a spoon full of mish-mash ingredients into my mouth, I groan at the explosion of flavor. This is amazing. It's quiet for a moment, and I look up to find all the males shoveling food into their mouths. I'm not even sure they are breathing between bites. I laugh. "You guys can eat slowly, it won't disappear." At least I don't think it will, this is Wonderland.

The males look chastised. "Sorry," they all whisper in unison.

I wave a hand at them. "No need to be sorry. I just don't want you to choke because you are eating so fast."

Chesh wipes at his mouth and says, "We don't normally get cooked meals like this."

"I can cook anytime," I offer, smiling softly at each of them.

Arch raises his bowl in my direction. "It's delicious." The others hum their agreement.

I grin. "I wasn't sure how it would turn out considering I'm not familiar with the ingredients here." Rab licks his bowl clean which makes me laugh, and I watch as each male does the same.

Mor stands, collecting everyone's bowl. He goes to grab mine, but I hold my hand out for the bowls he's already collected. "I can clean the dishes."

His eyes widen only briefly before he smiles brightly. "It's alright, Alyce. I don't mind. You cooked, I can clean."

He has a stubborn air about him so I concede, handing my bowl to him. "Thank you." He bows as he heads toward his tent. "So when would you guys like to head out toward Dymondz?" I ask.

"It will take between a week to two weeks to get there. We will have to walk through the woods so we aren't spotted." Rook looks at his brother for confirmation.

Dee nods his agreement before saying, "We should pack up this afternoon to at least start getting some distance. The other warriors can stay here at camp while we make our way to Dymondz."

Everyone stands, making their way to their designated tents. I notice Dee and Rook share a tent as well as Hatter and Arch. I expected Dee and Rook to share, but I thought Hatter and Arch would have their own tents. I figured they just often hung out with each other in one tent. Curiouser and Curiouser. I jump up from my spot. "What can I do?"

Chesh turns and says, "You can help me, Kitten."

I nod, heading back to Chesh's tent. Once inside, he points to my bag. "If you want access to your bag as we walk, you'll want to put it outside of the tent."

A little confused, I simply do as he says and grab my bag and place it outside the tent. I wasn't sure how they were going to pack and carry everything inside these tents. As I watch, Chesh moves a few breakable items into drawers then looks around the room and nods. "That should do it."

He grabs my hand as we make our way back out of the tent. "How are you packing everything in here for travel?"

Chesh throws a grin over his shoulder. "You'll just have to watch and see."

We walk back out to our meeting area, and Arch looks around and asks, "Everyone good to go?" Everyone nods. He pulls out a small remote and pushes a button. Suddenly, all of the tents implode on themselves, each one leaving behind only a large backpack.

"That. Was. Awesome!" I squeal excitedly.

Arch laughs. "Not really. It's just a bit of magic and technology put together."

I launch myself at him, wrapping my arms around his neck. He grunts but lifts me, so I can wrap my legs around him. "You are amazing! Did you make your pistol too?!"

I watch as color seeps into his cheeks. "I did."

I grin up at him and say, "That's impressive!"

His cheeks grow even pinker with my praise. "Um... thank you, Aly." I give him a peck on the cheek before wiggling for him to let me down. I look over my shoulder to find Hatter smirking as he looks at Arch. His eyes meet mine and his smirk falls. I give him a smile and blow him a kiss. His eyes widen, and then his brows furrow and he sends me a very unconvincing glare as he turns to get his pack.

I laugh, turning to Chesh as he makes his way over to me with his backpack. He grins as he looks between Hatter and Arch and comments, "I see you noticed."

"Noticed what?"

He bumps my shoulder. "I know you noticed."

Sighing, I admit, "Okay, yes I noticed."

"You don't seem to mind," he replies as he takes my hand in his while we wait for the others.

I shrug. "Why would I mind?" I watch as Arch comes up next to Hatter and places a gentle hand on his back. Hatter turns, giving him a quick smile. Arch points to the pack and Hatter rolls his eyes but hands it over to him. I smile. "They look happy when they aren't pretending around me."

Chesh hums and explains, "A relationship between two males in Wonderland is taboo. If the males are pleasuring each other for the female's enjoyment that's different. But to have feelings for another male…"

I squeeze his hand. "Again, I feel like the females here are bitches. I think they are amazing together."

"Alright, let's go!" Rab yells as he turns and starts walking, heading in what I assume is the direction of Dymondz. Mor walks next to him, closely followed by Hatter and Arch. Chesh tugs me and we start walking behind them with Dee and Rook bringing up the rear.

I tug on Chesh's arm to bring him closer and whisper, "To find someone you can trust no matter what is amazing. It's amazing Hatter trusts Arch, and to have feelings for that person and know that they wouldn't hurt you." I sigh and admit, "I've wished for that my whole life."

Chesh whispers back, "You didn't find that on the Surface?"

I shake my head sadly. "The only people I trusted were my brothers. I made the mistake of trusting people when I was younger." I shutter at the passing memories.

Chesh squeezes my hand and says, "You can trust me."

I look into his eyes and find the truth of his words, making me smile. "You can trust me, too."

He gives me a peck on the cheek. "Are you ready for some adventuring?" he asks excitedly.

I look at the males in front of me and then look over my shoulder at the others. Looking back at Chesh, I grin. "As long as I'm with you guys, I can't think of a better adventure."

CHAPTER ELEVEN
Alyce

It's starting to get dark, and we still haven't found a spot to camp for the night yet. I'm distracted as I watch small orbs of light flicker into view and then disappear. They seem to be everywhere, and they remind me of the fireflies back home.

Rab turns to the group. "This looks like a good spot to spend the night. We'll pack up early tomorrow morning to make some more headway." The others spread out, placing their tents in a circle around a clear spot where we can make a campfire.

I continue looking around and find more flickering lights. Arch notices my wandering eyes, so I point toward one of the flashing lights and ask, "What are those?"

He looks toward where I'm pointing and says, "Fireflies."

"Fireflies?" I think about that. This is Wonderland, they wouldn't have normal bugs here. As I watch, Chesh snatches an orb out of the air, quickly blows on it, then pops it into his mouth with a satisfied chirp. "What do fireflies taste like, Chesh?" I ask curiously.

Pondering the question, his brows knit together. Then looking at the others, he asks them, "How would you describe the taste of a firefly?" They all shrug. He looks around for another orb and snatches it before blowing on it. He holds it out to me. "For you, Aly."

I look into his palm and find a dark red orb about the size of a grape. Picking it up, I sniff it; it smells like rum and cherries. Shrugging, I pop the orb into my mouth and chew. The flavors of dark rum and sweet cherries explode in my mouth. Humming, I say, "It tastes like cherries and rum."

Arch nods. "That would make sense. They have cherry bodies that are on fire due to the rum. They just sorta float through the air."

I look around at the tents and ask, "Won't they set the tents on fire?"

Shaking his head, Arch pulls out the remote and presses a button that makes all the tents release and inflate. "I made sure the tents were made out of a non-flammable material in case we ever got attacked at camp," he explains.

Wow. He's thought of everything it seems. I shift my bag on my shoulder and head toward Chesh's tent. It's the tent I was invited to stay in indefinitely so... but before I take another step Mor calls my name.

"Alyce?" I watch his wings flutter in quick succession before closing. Is he nervous?

I give him a soft smile. "Yes?"

"Would you do me the honor of staying in my tent with me tonight?"

My eyes widen in surprise. "Really?"

His brows knit together. "If you don't want to that's fine. You didn't seem to mind the thought of spending time with us, so I..." Before he can continue rambling, I run over and place my finger against his lips. That seems to do the trick because his eyes widen at my touch, and he stops mid-sentence.

"I would like very much to spend time with you, Mor."

He seems frozen in shock for a moment before his eyes soften. He removes my hand from his lips, placing a quick kiss on the tip of my finger before threading his fingers through mine. "Very well, Alyce. Thank you for your company."

We continue into his tent as the others file into theirs. Looking over my shoulder quickly, I see if I can spot Chesh and find him looking right at me with a soft smile on his face. I nip at my lip, trying to figure out if he's upset that I agreed to stay with Mor tonight instead of him, but his grin just seems to grow, and he winks at me. He gives me a flirty wave before disappearing into his tent. Okay. I'll take that as he doesn't mind me staying with Mor. I feel a flutter in my chest at the thought.

Mor points to a chair in the corner. "You can set your bag over there if you wish."

Making my way over, I place my bag on the chair and look around. So far, the tents look similar in size as well as layout. I look toward the bed to find Mor's blankets are blue, but they look just as soft as Chesh's.

Mor is on the other side of the tent, and I watch him as he pulls his shirt over his head causing me to gasp. "Wow."

He looks over his shoulder at me and asks, "What?"

I walk over to him. I'm about to touch his back but stop myself before asking "May I touch you?"

"If you wish," he replies.

I look up at him. "It has nothing to do with what I wish. I want to make sure it's okay with you. I won't ever touch you if you don't want me to," I tell him seriously.

His brows knit together. "I've never been asked before," he whispers, looking unsure of himself.

I wet my lips before saying, "Well, I'm asking."

He looks away from me for a moment, and his wings seem to shiver as he sighs. His gaze meets mine over his shoulder, and I gasp at the emotion in them. "I wish for you to touch me."

I feel his muscles tense for a moment as my fingers graze the tattoos of Morpho Butterflies on his lower back. Underneath the tattoos, my fingers brush over several scars. "If you don't mind me asking, what are these scars from?"

His voice is still melodic but deepens a bit as he answers, "While I was in my butterfly form, several of my butterflies did not make it in the war against the Red Queen. They are a part of me through magic, though, a piece of me in each butterfly, so when a butterfly falls, a new scar appears on my skin."

I rest my hand against the scars. "I'm sorry."

"You have nothing to be sorry for."

"I suppose," I whisper. My fingers continue moving up his back to where his wings meet his back. They are so beautiful. Thinking of the butterflies back home, I ask, "If I touched your wings would it hurt you?"

"What do you mean?" he asks curiously.

"Back on the Surface, when you touch a butterfly's wings you can rub off the protective scales. Also, their wings are extremely delicate, so you can easily break them."

He shakes his head. "You won't hurt my wings by touching them. They are made from magic and are very sturdy."

Nodding my head, I reach out slowly and brush my fingers across the blue patterns. He shivers at my touch, so I ask, "Are you okay?" I don't want to hurt him.

"Yes, but they are sensitive," he rasps, but his voice seems strained. With the next swipe of my fingers, he moans. Ah. That kind of sensitive, got it. "If you keep doing that..." he groans.

"Do you wish for me to stop?"

"No," he grunts. He leans his hands against the wall while spreading his legs slightly.

"So you wish for me to keep stroking you?" I ask. Wow! Was that me? I didn't even realize I could sound all seductive like that.

"I wish for it! Please, Alyce," he whines at the end.

I move my other hand up to the opposite wing and stroke both at the same time. As I watch, sweat beads against his skin, and his breathing increases. I run a finger down the center of his back, and he arches into my touch as his hands on the wall turn into fists.

"This seems to be more sexual than I originally thought."

"I agree," he pants. "If this is too much for you..."

I run my finger up his back again, circling the area where his wing meets his shoulder. "I've never done this before," I whisper.

He lets out a breathy laugh. "You are doing amazing if I do say so myself."

I grin. "Is that so?" I wrap my hand around the base of his wing, wondering if the sensations feel the same as holding his cock? As I lightly run my fingertips up one wing, I squeeze the base of his wing.

He lets out a deep, keening sound. "Alyce!" I switch hands and do it again. "I'm so close, Alyce. Please. I wish for it so much," he begs. I guess that answers that question. Putting a hand around the base of each wing, I switch up my grip so my thumb can press into his spine; I figure that is probably where most of his nerves are. I stroke both thumbs over his spine before pressing and squeezing at the same time.

A guttural shout echoes throughout the tent. I release my hold on his wings and they sag, touching the floor. Mor is now resting his head against the wall, breathing hard.

I smile to myself. That's the first time I've ever made a guy come, let alone come in his pants. He turns to face me, looking briefly down at the large wet stain on the front of his pants. Thankfully, they are black. He looks back up at me, his cheeks a dark pink. I don't think it's all from the pleasure. "I've... I've never had that happen before," he says breathlessly.

A laugh bubbles out of me. "That makes two of us."

He reaches for me and says, "I will return the gesture."

I stop him with a smile. "You don't have to do that."

He shakes his head, stating, "But I must."

I take his hand in mine and look him in the eye, so he knows I'm serious. "You don't. That was for you and only you. I don't want you to feel like you need or have to return the gesture to make me happy or to want to be in your company."

His brows knit together in confusion. "You don't want me?"

Damn the females of this world; they have really messed up the males around here. Reaching up, I caress the side of his face and explain, "It would be an honor to be with you, Mor. But I want it to be because we both want it, not because you feel obligated to return pleasure simply because you received pleasure. If I'm honest, it was very pleasurable to watch you fall apart like that."

His eyes widen. "Do you speak the truth?"

I nod. "Of course. If you really want to return the gesture..." I hesitate for a moment before asking, "Could we possibly just lie in bed and cuddle?" I feel so juvenile asking that question.

His eyes seem to brighten at my response. "You wish to be held? By me?"

Confused, I answer, "Um... yes?"

He nods enthusiastically then grimaces looking down at his pants. "Can I change my pants first?"

I jump. "Of course!" Turning to give him some privacy, I head toward the bed. Before jumping in, and without turning around, I ask, "Can I borrow a shirt to sleep in? These clothes are a little dirty, and I don't want to mess up your bed."

I hear Mor come up behind me. "Will this work?" he asks.

Turning, I see he's holding out a light blue tunic. I nod appreciatively. "That should do it." Shimmying out of my yoga pants, I turn and sit on the bed. Taking my shoes off next, I pull my pants off the rest of the way. I look over my shoulder to find Mor sitting on the opposite side of the bed, facing away. Quickly unbuttoning Rab's shirt, I pull it off and throw Mor's shirt over my head. Pulling the shirt down, I shift so I'm under the blankets.

Mor takes notice and turns before burrowing under the blankets as well. He lifts the blankets a little to beckon me closer. I shift closer to him until my ass hits his front. I'm surprised to find he's not hard at all. History has shown me that when a female touches a male's cock in any way, he instantly gets turned on. He tugs me a little closer and wraps his arms around my middle.

"I've never..." he pauses, "I've never cuddled someone before."

"Why's that?" I yawn. Being surrounded by his warmth and fresh rain scent makes me tired instantly.

He sighs against my neck and answers quietly, "Most females who want my company only want one thing."

"Sex?"

"More for their pleasure than mine. My race was cursed by the Queen, so to find a male of my species is rare alone. But to find one of my race not under the influence of the Queen is very uncommon."

He's quiet so I speak up, "If I may say. The pleasure of your company is pleasure enough. I would be more honored to call you a friend than a random lover. You are an amazing male, Mor."

He tightens his hold on me. "Thank you for saying that, Alyce." I hum, letting him know I heard him. I feel myself relaxing, but before the darkness takes me I hear, "Being in your company is a pleasure as well, Alyce."

CHAPTER TWELVE
Alyce

Waking to the feel of arms around me would normally send me into a panic, but the smell of rain keeps me calm. I snuggle deeper into the warmth, and I'm greeted with a soft male chuckle.

"We need to get up, Little Butterfly."

I groan. "Five more minutes. It's too warm and comfy in here to leave."

"I have let you sleep for as long as possible, but the others are ready to leave."

Mor does have a point. Sighing, I twist around to look up at him. He is somehow already dressed, and his hair is wispy as if windblown. Does he wake up like that? No bedhead, just wispy blue hair? He bends and kisses me on the nose. "Did you sleep well?" he asks.

I yawn as I stretch. Surprisingly, I haven't had another flashback. Here's to hoping that was a one-time deal. I smile up at him. "I slept amazingly. You?"

I see the flash of surprise in his eyes before he smiles. "Very well, thank you for asking." He motions to the table behind me. "Dee has provided you with one of his cloth undershirts."

I flip over to find a dark purple long-sleeved shirt. It will most likely hit me around my knees. "Thank you."

Mor rolls out of bed and heads toward the door. "We thought you could wear those tight pants you wore yesterday, so you wouldn't go through too many of your clothes. We will be able to get you more clothes once we get into Dymondz territory."

I nod as I laugh. "The tight pants? You mean the yoga pants?"

He grins. "They are tight are they not? Dee mentioned how wonderful your butt looked when he caught a glimpse of it as you were walking yesterday."

Dee. That cheeky bastard. "Is that a good thing?" I ask.

Mor laughs. "He seemed quite happy mentioning it, so I would say yes."

I make a shooing motion and say, "Alright well, out you go. I'll be out shortly." He gives me a wink before leaving the tent. These males. Shaking my head in amusement, I pull Mor's shirt off, fold it, and put it on the table, then shimmy into Dee's large shirt. I was right; it hits me at my knees. It could be a dress. I grab my pants from the floor and slide into them. Putting my shoes on quickly, I keep having to shove the sleeves up my arms because they are so long.

Walking out of the tent I call, "Hey guys?" I have my arms raised in the air, letting the long material flap back and forth. I start to giggle because the flapping of the material as I move reminds me of those wacky waving inflatables they have outside car dealerships. I start full belly laughing as an image pops into my head of me waving and flapping about.

"Is she alright?" Rook asks worriedly.

I hold up a hand. "Give me a sec," I say, tears in my eyes from laughing so hard. I hold my belly, trying to get my giggles under control. "Sorry, it's a Surface thing. There are these things there that flap and wave in crazy directions, and the way I was waving and flapping my arms all over reminded me of it."

Chesh grins. "You did look quite silly. But also adorable, Kitten."

I wave my arms again, trying to find my hand under all the fabric. "The sleeves on this shirt are too long. I can't get them to stay when I roll them up."

Dee inspects the sleeves. "We could cut them."

I pull my arms away and exclaim, "This is your shirt! I don't want you to ruin it."

Dee grins. "It's only a shirt." He turns toward Arch and asks, "Could I borrow your knife?" Arch pulls a knife out from behind him and flips it, holding the hilt out to Dee. Dee holds out his other hand. "Let me see where I need to cut."

I hold out my arm, and he makes a small cut where the sleeve lands right below my wrist. He tugs a little on the fabric. "Alright, pull your arm up inside your shirt," he instructs.

I do as he says, and in one quick movement, he slices through the fabric. I squeak, surprised by how quickly and easily the knife cut it. He looks up at me in concern and asks, "Are you alright?"

I nod. "I'm fine. I was just surprised by how well that knife cut through the fabric."

"If it didn't cut through fabric, I would be worried that I haven't been doing my upkeep correctly," Arch murmurs from behind Dee.

Dee repeats the process on the other sleeve. I wiggle my now free fingers and say, "Thanks, Dee. If I ever figure out how to get you another shirt to replace this one I will."

Dee ruffles my hair affectionately. "Don't worry about it, I have plenty of shirts. This one can be yours to wear until we can get you more clothing."

I feel myself blush. "Thank you." I look around to find the other males smiling at me.

Chesh slides up next to me, grinning. "Like I said. Not like other females."

"Still wondering if that's a good thing," I mutter.

He slides his fingers through mine, tangling our hands together. "It's like breathing fresh air for the first time."

I think on his words for a moment. Thinking back to our conversation about Hatter and Arch, I remember him saying that not many females would approve of their relationship. Looking into his playful purple eyes I say, "That sounds lovely. I feel like there's a lot of trust being put into the thought of me being different than other females, but I feel like just an ordinary female."

He rests his forehead against mine. "I don't think I'm placing my trust in anything ordinary." He pulls away with a smile. "Sometimes the ordinary to one can look extraordinary to others." He tugs me to follow the others.

"You think I'm extraordinary?" I ask in surprise.

"You are Alyce. My Kitten. A female who literally fell into this world and met seven broken males. Who, without thinking twice, has taken on helping not only those males but Wonderland itself. This world isn't yours to fix, but you are willing to try anyways. Does that not sound extraordinary to you?"

I shrug, slightly embarrassed. "It sounds like someone who didn't feel like she belonged in her own world, so she came to another to find out who she is."

"Have you found her?" he whispers.

Thinking about his question, I glance at the males in front of me. First, there's Rab. A male who takes on the leadership position seemingly without question. He seems to shoulder a lot of weight, and I want to help him with that. I want to be someone he can rely on to help shoulder the heavy burden he carries. Then there's Mor. He carries deep wounds underneath his beauty. He's the most beautiful and ethereal male I have ever seen. In the past, females have taken advantage of that, forgetting his beauty within. I want to show him that not all females are the same. And Hatter. Cloaked in darkness and anger, it sounds like he lost his family because they chose to side with the Red Queen. I know he doesn't trust easily because of that, but I want to be able to stand next to him alongside Arch. To help and support him always. Then there's Arch. A loyal male who stands next to his best friend no matter what. He seems to feel the need to support Hatter by himself, but I want him to know he can lean on me, and that he no longer has to do it alone.

Switching my gaze to look behind me, Dee gives me a smile and a wave. I wave back with a smile of my own. Dee. He stands next to or behind his brother. A male often lost in the shadow of his older brother, but he doesn't mind. I want him to realize that he shines by himself. That he has skills and qualities that are just as important as his brother's. I look over to Rook. He's a shadow of his past that haunts him. He double-checks himself constantly and will always protect others before himself. I want him to realize that the past is just that, and we should live in the present. The past will always be there, and we should learn from the things we can't change.

Looking up at Chesh, I smile. Last but not least is Chesh. My crazy and fun male. He hides behind smiles and laughter, afraid to show who he truly is as a male. The first male I met in Wonderland. He's stuck by my side every step of the way through this new adventure, never once making me feel small. Always willing to explain. I tug him down for a kiss. I think I've found out who I want to be, which will slowly change to who I am. That female starts with these males. It may be fast, but I've never felt more like myself than when I'm with them.

I pull away with a grin and say, "I think so."

Chesh grins back. "Then I'm excited to get to know this extraordinary female."

Facing forward once more, I realize that we've fallen behind, but Dee and Rook have stayed back to make sure we are guarded. Tugging on Chesh's hand, I cheer, "Here's to adventuring!"

He laughs as I tug him to run with me. "To adventuring, Kitten."

I look over my shoulder laughing and call out, "Let's go, Dee! Rook! Let's catch up so we don't get left behind!"

Dee laughs as he begins to jog. Rook shakes his head, but I can see the smile he tries to hide. He begins jogging to keep up. "We only fell behind due to you walking so slow."

"I don't walk slow!"

Chesh laughs, the sound a beautiful melody. "You do have small legs, but that's okay, you have me." Poofing into a cloud of glitter, he's now the size of a tiger. "Hop on!"

I grab onto the hair at his nape and jump up as we continue to run. I squeal, squeezing my legs behind his front legs, so I don't fall as he takes off. When I feel like I have a good grip with my legs and I won't fall off, I lift my arms in the air, laughing as we pass Hatter and Arch.

I wave as I giggle and call out, "Hey guys!" I can feel Chesh laughing under me. We are about to pass Rab and Mor as well when Mor explodes in a cloud of blue glitter. I laugh as I'm suddenly surrounded by thousands of Blue Morpho Butterflies. They flutter and swirl around me as Chesh continues to run. Chesh circles around so we stay with the others but continues to bob and weave through them. A few of the butterflies land on my outstretched arms. One lands directly on my nose, opening and closing its wings, blinding me each time the wings open.

"Mor, I'm trusting you to make sure I don't fall off because I can't see anything," I say with a laugh. In response to my words, the butterfly on my nose flaps its wings open and stays that way. Alright. Trust exercise it is. "Alright, I'm trusting you and Chesh to keep me safe." I close my eyes and enjoy the world around me.

I can feel bursts of warmth as we hit random beams of sunlight streaming through the trees. The smells of the woods seem more intense now that I'm not able to see anything. Keeping my arms outstretched, I feel like I'm flying as the wind whips through my hair.

"If flying feels like this it's amazing, Mor." A butterfly lands on my ear, and I giggle as it tickles me with its soft movements.

I hear his soft voice whisper into my ear. "What does it feel like?"

"Like... I'm lighter than air. I'm free from the confines of gravity, and I can enjoy the freedom of floating through the clouds. The sun beams stroking my wings, filling me with warmth."

"You make flight sound like a dream."

"It is a dream. I've never flown through the air like you. It's what I imagine flying would be like."

"Open your eyes and we will show you what flying is like," his voice whispers as the butterfly at my ear flutters away. I feel wings brush against my eyes then the butterfly on my nose is gone. I open my eyes to see that Chesh is running toward a raised rock. "Trust us, Kitten?" he asks.

Without hesitation I say, "Yes!" I watch as the butterflies around us combine and in another puff of blue glitter, Mor is there flying next to us in his male form.

He smiles at me and instructs, "Stretch out your arms."

I nod, not realizing I had lowered my arms to sit in my lap. I lift my arms out wide as if I have wings. My heart beats rapidly as Chesh quickens his pace. He runs up the rock and with a powerful push of his rear legs, he jumps into the air.

I squeal as I feel myself become weightless but gasp when I see the world around me. The sun beams down through the forest and hits tiny objects, making the world around us seem to shimmer. It's beautiful in its simplicity. I feel myself sliding forward as Chesh nears the ground and lower my arms to thread my fingers into his scruff as he lands roughly. I shift forward slightly but catch myself before I fall face-first over the front of Chesh. He trots to a stop and looks over his shoulder at me. "Are you alright?" he asks.

Huffing out a laugh I exclaim, "That was amazing!" Mor lands beside us as I ask, "Can we do that again sometime!?" They both laugh as the others catch up to us.

Mor nods in answer. "We can do that whenever you like." Feeling the rush of adrenaline draining from my body, I fall back against Chesh's back.

"Is she alright?" I hear Rab ask.

I throw two thumbs up. "I'm recovering from my adrenaline high."

Rab's red eyes are suddenly in front of my face. "Are you sure?" he asks worriedly.

I grin. "I'm better than ever. I should probably walk, though. My butt is starting to go numb." I go to lift myself off of Chesh when I suddenly lose purchase on his back and slide off, falling to the ground. Squealing as I fall, I land on my belly. Shattering tea cups! Defeated, I shove my face into the grass as I hear the pop of Chesh shifting.

"Are you alright, Aly?"

I give him an unenthusiastic thumbs up from my position.

"I feel like that's a sarcastic thumbs up," Dee mutters from somewhere beside me.

He's not wrong, but damn it for him realizing that. Huffing out a breath, I push myself up off the ground and onto my knees. I look up expecting to find their faces filled with amusement, but instead, I'm greeted with varying degrees of concern.

Dee holds out a hand to help me up. "Are you alright?"

I nod. "I think my leg fell asleep. The only thing damaged is my pride."

"Why would your pride be damaged?" Rook asks from beside Dee, holding his hand out as well.

Grabbing both of their hands, I let out a very un-lady-like grunt as I stand. "It's embarrassing to keep falling on my ass in front of a bunch of attractive males," I whisper.

The twins look at each other, and Dee arches a brow. "What does our attractiveness have to do with your pride?"

Running a hand down my face, I explain, "On the Surface, it's embarrassing to fall in front of men you find attractive. They often laugh and snicker at you, which then damages your pride."

Arch comes up and kneels in front of me, brushing grass and dirt off my yoga pants. "That seems ungentlemanlike and rude. Why would watching a female fall make a male laugh?"

Surprised by his reaction, I stutter out, "Um... they find it funny, I suppose."

I look up at Rab's voice asking, "How would watching a female fall be funny?" His arms are crossed over his chest, and he seems a bit peeved at the thought of a male laughing at a female like that.

Looking at all the other males, I'm a bit lost for words. I didn't really understand it either. Shrugging, I say, "I guess some males find weak females funny."

"How is a weak female funny?" Rab growls, and a chorus of growls follows behind his.

I can only shrug. "I'm not a male, so I don't know."

"A male is supposed to cherish and protect his chosen female. Especially if they are weak. It's our job to make them feel safe and make them stronger, if they wish," Hatter barks out. I jump at his sudden aggression. He sees my reaction and deflates. "I'm sorry, Alyce."

I shake my head. "You're fine." He must hear the truth in my words because he nods. I look at the others. "So I think you repaired my pride." I laugh.

Rab laughs too. "Alright. If everyone is good to go, we should get some more distance in before settling down for the night."

Arch stands from his kneeling position, and I reach out for his hand. I pull him down and kiss his cheek. Pulling away, I thank him. He arches a brow. These males have never had a single female thank them for anything in their lives. Learning curve I suppose. I point down to my now clean leggings. "For brushing off my yoga pants. You didn't have to."

His eyes brighten as he smiles and says, "I wanted to."

"And that's why I'm thanking you." He nods, brushing his lips against my cheek before heading back to his walking position in our group. Hatter gives me a nod before following Arch, and Rab and Mor have already started walking at the front of the group, leaving me with Chesh and the twins.

I'm still holding the twin's hands, so I go to release them, but they both tighten their grip on me. I look up at them. They look at each other and then back down at me. "Would you mind walking with us?" they ask, echoing each other's words.

I look toward Chesh. He sends me a grin and a wink before shifting into his Bandersnatch form. My eyes widen at his size. Compared to his largest cat form he's now the height of a large horse. "Wow! I can see now how you fought off the Jabberwock."

He boops my face with his large nose and says, "I'll take the rear." He waits for us to start walking before following behind. We continue walking till dusk, and I enjoy being able to walk with the twins. I like being able to spend time with each of the guys.

The hand Dee is holding swings slightly, and he grins down at me when I shift my hold. I'm now holding his thumb while my wrist is in his grip. His hand is so large, my normal hand-holding tactic felt weird. Adjusting my grip on Rook's hand, I hold onto his pointer finger as he holds my wrist lightly. I look between the two males and grin when I realize they've positioned themselves so that they still have access to their swords if needed while still holding my hand.

CHAPTER THIRTEEN
Alyce

We have officially been on our adventure for a week now, and I've learned so much about these males on the journey. I've learned their tics, tells, and quirks. Well at least a few of them. Rab seems to have control issues. As if he feels the need to be in control of our surroundings and what's happening at all times. If he feels like he doesn't have control, his tail twitches. He often takes his top hat off, holding it under his arm as his ears twitch in several directions. It's an odd tell, but I've only noticed him take his hat off a few times.

With Mor, his quirk is with his wings. He can often hide his emotions and how he's feeling on his face, but his wings give him away every time. Chesh, like most cats, gives himself away with his tail and ears. If he feels overwhelmed I notice he disappears, but I can usually still feel his body heat beside me. Hatter plays with his hat pins, usually twirling them, although if we are camped out he will throw them at the ground as if there is an invisible target that only he can see. If he wants to hide while everyone is around, he will pull his top hat down to shield his eyes. I think his eyes give him away the most, which is why he tries to hide them.

Arch seems to feed off of Hatter's mood. If Hatter seems upset or frustrated, I'll find Arch sitting as close to him as he can get. If Hatter seems to be in a better mood, Arch will play around and joke with Chesh. Dee is similar in that he feeds off his brother. If Rook seems upset or frustrated, Dee will bump him and try to make him laugh. The happier Rook seems, the more Dee plays and jokes with Arch and Chesh. Dee often walks behind Rook, letting him take the lead. Rook. I sigh. Rook has been harder to pin down. He always seems to be in control. Ever watching and waiting for an ambush. But I've noticed the more stressed or unsure he feels, the more rigid he holds himself. He talks and interacts with the others less as he watches his surroundings. The more confident he feels, the more relaxed he seems, and the more he smiles with Dee.

Rab interrupts my thoughts. "Does this spot look good to settle in for the night?"

Rook nods. "Seems secure enough. I haven't seen much activity in this area, and there aren't any signs of anyone passing by."

Dropping my bag beside a large mushroom, I stretch. The others set up their tents in a circle like usual. Settling down on the mushroom, I wait for the others. They have made it clear that they want me to rest while they set up the camp. I tried helping out once but ended up tripping and falling on my face. What I tripped over, I have no idea, but from that point on, they said I wasn't allowed to help set up.

Thinking over what I've learned the last few days, I realize that the feelings of friendship I wanted with them have grown into something more. I wouldn't mind dating them all. Chesh made it clear that females around here often have multiple lovers, but I want a relationship, not a fling. Do they date in Wonderland? Is it even called dating?

I bend over to open my bag, trying to find my phone so I can play some soft music as we relax for the night. I'm rummaging through my bag when I find an envelope. Hum. It must have been buried under everything; I hadn't noticed it before. I pull out the envelope to find my name scribbled across the front. I immediately know who wrote it. Alix. I know his writing better than anyones. We purposefully learned each other's handwriting, so we could pose as each other on assignments. I open the letter to find his familiar whimsical writing.

Hey Little Sis,

I'm sure you're having the time of your life in this new world of yours. I know you're also probably freaking out because we did not prepare you whatsoever to have relationships with people who aren't your brothers. We know who you are and love you no matter what. You're my twin, so you know I will always have your back. I know that there are probably boys in this new world as well. We also probably didn't help in that department considering we scared off every single guy who even looked your way. But they were totally not good enough for you, and I'm sure the guys there aren't either. That's probably just the words of a big brother, though. You will know if a guy is worthy of your time and your love. I'm sure you feel like you belong there more than you ever did here, which is why I'm sure the guys there will be better, too. I want you to know that I read all the Alice in Wonderland books too. I wanted to know what you were going through. I wanted to be there if you ever needed anyone. Whenever you talked about Wonderland, you always had a smile on your face. That's when you were the happiest I've ever seen you. So my parting words till I see you again are these: the secret, my dear sister, is to surround yourself with people who make your heart smile, only then will you find your Wonderland.

Love you so much,

Your big brother

I look up to find each of the males surrounding me. They are all kneeling in front of me with varying degrees of concern and sympathy on their faces. I realize that everything is blurry, and I touch my face to find that I'm crying. I let out a sob as I hug the letter to my chest. I miss my brothers desperately, but I understand what Alix was saying. Who knew that in order to find my Wonderland I had to fall? And not only did I fall through the Looking Glass, but I'm falling for the males surrounding me too.

"Kitten?" Chesh whines anxiously as he slides onto the mushroom beside me. He wraps his arms around me and pulls me into a hug.

What if I'm not able to get to the Looking Glass in Wonderland? What if I'm never able to see my brothers again? A soft keening sound escapes me as the ache in my chest deepens. I didn't realize I would miss my brothers this much.

Chesh lifts me onto his lap, wrapping his arms around me tightly. I shove my face into the crook of his neck as my sobs intensify. He makes a distressed whimpering sound and cries, "What do I do?!" He rocks me as he shifts a hand into my hair and holds my head against his neck.

"Little Butterfly," Mor whispers as I feel his hand settle on my thigh. He squeezes softly. "It's okay. We are here. Let it all out." I feel the others surround me, each placing their hands on me where they can. It's not sexual, just a male of Wonderland trying to comfort a female in pain.

I release everything. All the pain of my past, and the fear of coming to a new world. The fear of never seeing my brothers again. The pain of leaving them behind. The guilt of seeing their faces filled with fear as I fell through the Looking Glass.

After what feels like forever, I find myself finally calming down. I feel my face vibrating and realize Chesh is purring as he rocks me in his arms. I can't help but smile. He's trying to soothe me.

I pull away enough to wipe my face. I let out a watery laugh when I notice the amount of snot covering Chesh's shoulder. He never wears a shirt, and I now feel bad because of how soaked he is. "I'm sorry! I snotted all over you and got you all wet. I know cats hate being wet."

Chesh gives me a small smile and reaches up to wipe under my eyes. "I will live, no need to be sorry. Are you okay now, Kitten?"

I huff out a shaky breath. "I feel like I purged everything I've been holding back since I got here."

Dee's unsure voice comes from beside me. "Does that mean you feel better?"

Realizing my abrupt purge of tears may have made them uncomfortable, I apologize, "I'm sorry if my random outburst of sobbing made you all uncomfortable."

Dee shakes his head, but it's Hatter who speaks up. "We may not know what to do when a female erupts in tears, but we would never make you feel like it's wrong to show emotion. If you feel like crying, then cry."

I give a shaky laugh. "Alright." I look toward Dee and say, "There is something all of you guys could do that would make me feel better."

I almost laugh when all of them nod eagerly. I bite my lip, not sure if everyone will be okay with this request. "Could I have a group hug?"

Dee smirks. "You want all of us to hug you at the same time?"

I nod shyly. "Please?" They all shuffle in close, wrapping their arms around each other and squishing me in the middle.

I laugh as Chesh purrs louder while rubbing his cheek against mine. "Are you feeling better?" he asks.

Feeling the warmth of the males surrounding me seep into my soul, I sigh. "Yes. So much better." I get squished even more as they tighten their hold on each other. I erupt into a fit of giggles. "Don't smash me!"

Dee laughs. "We want to make sure you can feel how much we want you to feel better."

I squeal, "I feel it! I feel it!"

Arch chuckles. "Are you sure?"

"Yes!"

"We just want you to know we care," Chesh says as he kisses my cheek.

I grin, my tears forgotten, and tell them, "I can feel it."

CHAPTER FOURTEEN

Alyce

"Alright everyone, look alive. We are entering a part of the woods that happens to have some dangerous plants. Follow our lead, and we should be fine," Rab announces from the front of the group.

I have no idea what these dangerous plants could be. But between Rab, Mor, Hatter, and Arch being between me and the possible dangerous plants, I should be fine.

Chesh bumps my shoulder. "I have a riddle for you."

I arch a brow. "Alright, hit me."

Chesh gasps. "Why would I hit you?!"

Face palming, I forget that these males have no idea about the expressions we use on the Surface. "Sorry, Chesh. It's an expression. It means tell me."

His ears twitch. "What an odd expression. Anyways, the riddle. Why is a raven like a writing desk?"

"Hey! That's the riddle I told you," Hatter yells from up ahead of us.

"Well, I'm asking it now."

I giggle. "Alright. I'm assuming there isn't a true answer."

Chesh grins wider. "You would be correct."

"But to answer the riddle. It can produce a few notes, though they are very flat, and it is nevar put with the wrong end in front," I say.

Mouth agape, Chesh yells to Hatter, "She has an answer for your riddle, Hatter."

I can hear the amusement in Hatter's voice as he replies, "I heard, Chesh. Very clever."

I'm laughing at Chesh's awed face when suddenly, I'm looking up at the sky. What in the name of Heartz just happened? My hands and legs feel restrained, so I lift my head to look at what's going on. My wrists and biceps are being held down by what looks like vines, and my ankles and thighs are not faring much better. Wiggling only causes the vines to tighten. Shit! Looking around for the guys, I find them chopping away at the vines trying to take hold of them.

I can feel panic rising within me. Don't freak out, Alyce. That is all in the past now. The guys will finish chopping these rude plants and have you out in no time. Taking a deep breath, I let it out slowly, trying to keep my fears and nightmares away. It's in the past, Alyce. They can't hurt you here. I feel like I have everything in control until a vine slides across my abdomen, then I'm lost in the visions of the past.

"Alyce, come play with us!"

I had just turned thirteen, and a group of popular girls from school invited me to play with them after school. Alix had gone off to hang out with some of his friends, so I figured it would be fine. Making my way over to the girls, I sit next to them at the park behind the school.

"So is it true?" one of the girls asks.

"Yeah, is it true?" the brunette asks.

"Is what true?"

"That your mom went crazy and is now in a mental institute," the first girl says.

I shrug. "I suppose it's true. Why?" Suddenly, a group of girls come up from behind me and slam me down onto the ground. "What's going on?" I cry out as my arms and legs are pinned down, and I'm starfished across the ground.

"We figured we would make sure everyone knew who the freak was in this school." The brunette laughs.

One of the random girls lifts up my shirt as another one hands a box cutter to the brunette.

"Stop! What are you doing?" I scream as loud as I can. After a few minutes of no one coming to my rescue, I realize that everyone from school has left. Even my brother. I scream and fight as another girl sits on my chest to keep me still.

I cry as the brunette girl carves into my skin. "Psycho. There, that should keep everyone away."

I scream until my voice is gone.

Hatter

I hear a haunting scream. A scream full of pain and fear. I look around my surroundings, cutting away vines as they try to attack. Looking around, I finally see a still form lying on the ground. Alyce! I run, hacking at the vines as I go. I slide next to her and start cutting the vines holding her down. She's lifeless. There's no movement from her other than her mouth gaping with a scream. I look into her eyes. Glassy and haunted. I know those eyes; I've seen them enough times in the mirror.

I hear the others running up behind me, and I put out a hand. "Stop! Don't come any closer yet."

"What's wrong with her?" Chesh whines, putting his hands over his ears to block out her screaming.

"She's stuck in a nightmare," I answer.

"We need to help her!" Dee exclaims as he begins to walk toward me.

I spin and look at him. "Stay where you are. The more people around the worse it will get. Just let me handle this." He looks at me silently for a moment then nods.

Looking down at Alyce, I try to think. What would help snap her out of this nightmare? I try talking to her first. "Alyce? Sugar? You need to come back to us now, alright?" My voice sounds far gentler than I ever thought it could. She's still not responding though. Placing my fingers against her cheek, she flinches slightly. "It's okay, Sugar. It's just me, Hatter."

She stops screaming finally, but her eyes are still vacant, like there's no one home. Shifting positions, I pull her head in my lap, running my fingers through her blonde hair while caressing her cheek with my other hand. I continue talking to her, "You should really come back soon. You know how Chesh is. He would be so lost without you."

As I talk to her, the light slowly comes back into her eyes, and she starts to blink. I bend my head slightly, so the others can see me as I smile down at her. "Hey, Sugar. You back yet?" No response. "If you come back, I'll tell you a secret that no one else knows. Except Arch. But he doesn't count."

I watch as she licks her lips and rasps, "Hatter, is it a secret worth knowing?"

My heart tightens as she rasps my name. I swallow the lump in my throat and force out a chuckle. "That depends on who you ask."

She gives me a weak smile. "I'll take it to my grave then."

"My given name is Tarrant. I go by Hatter because I hate it," I admit to her.

She giggles. "Tarrant."

Hearing her say my name gives me an unexpected thrill. "You can't tell anyone." I try to give her a stern glare, but I'm not sure it came across the way I wanted.

"Can I call you Tar when we're alone or with Arch?" she asks quietly.

I think on it for a moment and shrug. "I suppose. As long as I can call you Sugar?"

She snorts. "You picked a nickname I hate."

I grin before saying, "Then it's an even trade."

"Can we come check on Aly now?" Chesh whines from further behind me.

Sighing, I help Aly to sit up as the others close in. I watch Chesh shift into his cat form and bury himself in her lap. She laughs as she strokes between his ears while he purrs in contentment. I stand from my spot and back away so the others can get closer.

Arch takes my spot as he sits next to her. Dee mirrors him on the other side, asking if she's okay. Rook lays a hand on the top of her head giving her a smirk when she smiles up at him. Rab and Mor both bend down to place kisses on opposite cheeks, and she laughs as her face gets smashed between them.

I look at how happy she is with all of us around her and can't help but smile. I didn't have a sugar cubes chance at keeping my distance from her. The happiness she radiates draws in the broken parts of each of us. She makes us feel whole.

A little while later, I'm in my tent, lying on my bed, trying to figure out my feelings for the new female who has entered our lives. I told her my name. My real name. A name I haven't used in years. Arch was the only one who knew it, and he hardly ever used it. I pinch the bridge of my nose trying to stave off the headache I feel coming on. I only get headaches when my emotions are all over the place. An unfortunate side effect of the training we had. I hear the rustle of tent flaps and look up to see Arch making his way into the tent.

Apparently, my need is written all over my face because he takes one look at me and strips down, his cock already erect. "Such a good hare aren't you, Archy?" I growl out.

He swallows before kneeling in front of me. "Yes, Hatter."

Threading my fingers through the short hairs on the back of his head, I tug. He whines which makes me smile down at him. "Say my name," I order.

His eyes widen for a moment then glaze over in pleasure as I move my other hand to one of his ears and tug. "Tarrant," he says with a groan.

A shiver races down my spine, and I grunt as my pants feel suddenly tight. Tugging him up to me, I slam my lips to his, biting and nipping his lips until he opens for me. I tangle my tongue with his as he reaches between us and unbuttons my shirt. I'm thankful that I had already removed my holsters and suspenders earlier.

He shoves my shirt off, running his nails down my back. Groaning, I flip him onto the bed so that he's below me. He's panting and looking up at me with hunger shadowing his eyes.

I tear my pants off as fast as possible, quickly throwing them across the room. "How much do you want my cock inside you, Archy?" I ask teasingly.

He keens as he reaches up and pulls on his own ears. "So much, Tarrant," he says breathlessly.

Positioning myself between his legs, I reach down and stroke his cock. He's already panting as he tugs and pulls on his ears. With my thumb, I wipe the precum already leaking from his cock and use it as lube as I circle his tight hole. Squeezing his cock hard, I begin pumping him faster as I thrust my thumb inside him. Tugging on his ears, he comes on a wail, and ribbons of come cover his abdomen.

"I came too fast," Arch whines.

I laugh. "You were a bit worked up, weren't you? It's okay, I wanted you to come anyway."

I run a hand across his abdomen, collecting his come with my fingers, and then run it up and down my own stiff shaft. Lifting myself, I place one hand right above his shoulder to keep him in place. With my other hand, I tease my cock around his entrance.

I watch as his eyes shift to the entrance of the tent. I turn to look, but he catches my face with his hands and turns my face back to his. "Look at me," he says.

Looking into his eyes, I slowly push myself inside him and groan. It's been too long since I've felt the tight walls of his ass squeezing my cock. He keens as I fully seat myself. He's panting below me, and I watch as his cock stiffens again. I smirk. Got to love the recovery time of shifters.

"Fuck me, Tarrant!" he snarls. Seems I'm not the only one that needed this. I fuck him the way he likes. Reaching up, I grip one of his ears and shift my other arm to hold most of my weight. Making sure he won't move in this position, I tug roughly on his ear as I slide out and thrust back in, hard. He keens, "Yes!"

I continue fucking him hard and fast. I feel sweat beading between my shoulders, and I'm panting. I can feel myself getting close. "You need to come, Archy," I demand.

He shakes his head, and whines, "I can't."

"You will!" I demand, trying to put as much dominance in my voice as I can.

He wails, "I can't, it's too much!" He opens his eyes, and I can see the need in them. They are glassy and pleading with me.

Nodding, I shift my upper body, so I can grab his cock. I look at him before I help. "You are in charge of your ears. Understood?"

He reaches up, instantly grabbing his ears.

"When I say pull, you tug your ears, and I'll help you come, okay?"

He nods, whimpering. "Yes. Please."

Sliding out of him, I command, "Pull!" Arch pulls his ears as I slam into him hard. I grip his cock tightly as I pump. He keens and he explodes.

Ribbons of come spray his chest as I continue to pump him through his release.

I come soon after from how tightly he squeezes my cock. Fuck. I groan, slowly pulling out, then collapse on the bed beside Arch.

"Do you feel better now?" Arch asks teasingly.

A booming laugh escapes me. "You seem to be sassier after having met Alyce."

"Is that a bad thing?" he whispers.

I turn to him with a wide smile. "Not at all, Archy. I'm glad you are gaining more confidence in yourself."

He grins at me. "I think she's helping you as well."

Humming, I ask, "You think?"

He turns and snuggles into my chest. "Yeah. I like it."

I couldn't even argue. I liked it too.

CHAPTER FIFTEEN
Alyce

Holy Shattering Tea Cups! I'm still reeling over what I saw last night. I was planning on thanking Hatter for helping me with the vines, so I went to his tent to find him, but I wasn't expecting what I found. I want to squeal so badly. They are together! I was so afraid that Arch would say something when he saw me, and then Hatter almost turned around. That was so close!

A hand waves in front of my face, startling me, causing me to squeak in surprise. Chesh's ears flick back at the high-pitched sound. "Are you alright, Aly?" he asks.

I look around to find the others have all stopped what they were doing. Rab and Mor are looking back at us, confused by the sound I made while Hatter just looks at me quizzically. My eyes meet Arch's, and I feel my face flush instantly. He just gives me a smirk and a wink. Oh, Whistling Tea Kettles!

I wave at the others frantically. "I'm fine. I'm fine. Just having a..." What could I say? Ugh! "I was daydreaming okay!" I screech out in embarrassment.

Chesh is snickering beside me as he looks between me and Arch. I look back over to Arch to find his cheeks coloring too. Hatter is looking between Arch and me, completely confused. I let out an exasperated sigh and try to change the subject. "Can we keep moving, please!?"

Rab and Mor shrug as they turn to keep walking. Hatter gives me one last arched brow before turning around. Arch is biting his lip, and I can tell he's trying not to laugh. I turn to look at Dee and Rook. Dee is openly laughing while covering his mouth to dampen the noise meanwhile Rook shakes his head in amusement.

I turn and continue our walk for the day. Please tell me everybody doesn't know what is going on!

"Oh they know," Chesh whispers.

"Know what?"

He points to Arch's back and then to me. "Something happened between you two."

"Nothing happened."

He turns toward me and starts walking backward. "It's written all over your face, Kitten."

Sighing, I tug him toward me so that we are walking side by side. I pull him down so I can whisper in his ear, "So you remember that conversation we had about Hatter and Arch?"

"Yeah." He nods and continues our whispered conversation.

"So are they in a relationship?" I didn't want to say too much in case no one else in the group knew exactly what was going on. It's one thing to assume, it's quite another to know.

He pulls away a bit, looking down at me with narrowed eyes. "Why?"

Considering his reaction, I'll go with he knows. "I don't care if they are in a relationship, Chesh."

His eyes stay narrowed for a moment as if assessing the truth in my words. "They may be depending on what you know."

I sigh. "I know, Chesh."

"What exactly do you know?" he asks

I tug him back down and say, "That they are in a sexual relationship. Although, with the way they look at each other, I think it's more."

His eyes widen in surprise. "How did you find out?"

My cheeks flare bright red with embarrassment. "I may have walked into their tent when they were about to... well, do it."

"What!?" he whisper-shouts.

"Shhhhh!" I look back to the front of the group and find Arch looking over his shoulder. He raises a brow at me in silent question, so I give him a shy wave and a fake smile. Turning back to Chesh, I admonish, "You need to be quiet!"

He nods apologetically. "Sorry. How... When... Why were you walking into their tent?"

"I wanted to thank Hatter for saving me from the vines. He's usually brooding or throwing hat pins. Or both so I didn't think anything of it." Sighing, I run a hand down my face. "I didn't mean to walk in on them. Arch saw me in the doorway, and Hatter was about to turn around when Arch stopped him. I ran out quickly after that."

He hums and asks, "So Hatter doesn't know you saw them?"

"No."

"Are you going to tell him?"

I groan. "I have to! But I don't know how I'm going to tell him without it sounding like I invaded their private time."

Chesh shrugs. "Tell him the truth. You were wanting to thank him for the help, and you accidentally walked in on them but left immediately. It would sound like you were invading their private time if you stuck around to watch."

"I would never do that! I mean I would gladly watch, but only if they knew and were okay with it."

Chesh grins. "So my little Kitten likes some male cross-play huh?"

Bumping his shoulder, I say, "You knew I liked the idea when we talked about them the last time."

"It's one thing to say you like it when you suspect they cross manly swords. It's another entirely when you know they cross manly swords and accept them for who they are."

Nodding, I agree, "I suppose you're right."

After walking for a few more hours, Rab announces that it's time to settle down for the night. Everyone goes about setting everything up while I sit in my designated spot on a mushroom. Biting my lip, I look around. Maybe once Hatter sets up their tent I should go talk to him. That way it's out of the way, and there's no way for a repeat of last night to happen.

Hatter's tent inflates with all the others, and he walks in followed by Arch. Taking a deep breath, I try to prepare myself for this completely awkward talk. I screech when a hand lands on my shoulder. Looking up, I see Chesh peering down at me, his gaze full of concern.

"Are you alright, Aly?"

Groaning, I wipe a hand down my face. "I don't know why I'm so nervous to talk to them. I feel like butterflies are swirling around in my stomach."

Chesh's eyes roam down to my abdomen and back up. "That sounds like an odd sensation." He sits next to me before asking, "Why are you so nervous? It's just Hatter and Arch."

"That's just it! It's Hatter and Arch. Hatter and I aren't on the best of terms already. It's not like we are best friends or anything. I'm not entirely sure we can even be considered friends. Yeah, he helped me out of the vines but maybe..." I growl in frustration. "Ugh! I don't know. And Arch! Arch is amazing, and he's so nice. I think we are at least friends, but I don't want to upset him because of what I accidentally did."

Chesh twines his fingers with mine. "Aly, look at me."

Sighing, I do as he asks. "What?"

He smiles softly at me. "You are thinking way too much about this. Yeah, Hatter may be a little embarrassed that you saw him, but I see the way he looks at you when you are looking elsewhere. He cares for you, Aly. We all do. Arch won't be upset. I've seen him sending you winks and smiles all day."

"But... what if..."

He pecks me on the cheek and pulls me to stand. "You'll never get to the best part of the adventure if you focus on the what-ifs. You have to move forward to find out if it's an if or an is."

Internally groaning because I know he's right, I nod. Taking a deep breath, I turn and head toward Hatter and Arch's tent. Here we go.

Walking up to the tent, I announce myself this time, "Hey Hatter? Arch? It's Alyce, can I come in?" Who else would it be, Aly?! You are the only female in this group, of course, they know it's you!

"Come on in," Arch yells.

Taking one last deep breath, I push aside the flaps to enter. I instantly hear the thump of a hat pin hitting a target. Great, he's throwing hat pins. Hopefully, I'm not his next target. When I walk in, I find Arch lounging on his bed.

He looks over to me with a smile and asks, "What can we do for you, Aly?"

Anxiously wringing my hands behind my back, I smile tentatively. "I was actually wanting to talk to both of you. Oh! And thank Hatter as well."

"Thank me for what?" Hatter asks as he throws another hat pin.

"I wanted to thank you for saving me from the vines."

"You don't have to thank me for that. I was just able to get to you the fastest, any of the others would have done the same."

I nod. "I'm sure they would have, but you still helped, and I want to thank you for it."

"You are welcome," he says.

Toeing the ground with my shoe, I say, "You also helped me snap out of the memories I was stuck in." I shiver. "They weren't the best memories. So thank you."

He turns so he's facing me. "I did what I would have done if it were…" His eyes skip over to Arch briefly before he looks back at me. "If it were a friend."

I caught that brief look. Okay, onto the next part of this conversation. "I also wanted to talk to you and Arch about something else. Would you mind coming over here? I feel like I'll be a ping pong ball, bouncing between you guys."

He shrugs, moving closer and sitting on his bed next to Arch's. "Alright, what do you wish to speak to us about?" he asks.

Should I ease into this or rip off the bandaid? Biting my lip, I debate. I'm about to open my mouth to ease them into what I saw when my panic takes over. "I saw you two yesterday evening when you were having an intimate moment!" I snap my hand over my mouth, wide-eyed. SHATTERING TEA CUPS!! I can't believe I just did that!

Hatter's mouth drops open in shock, and Arch is looking between him and me trying to figure out what to do in this situation. Hatter closes and then opens his mouth, and sputters, "You… you saw…"

I can already feel tears filling my eyes. Waving my hands in front of me, I explain what happened, "I'm sorry! I didn't mean to walk in on you. I left immediately! I know having a relationship with a male in Wonderland is considered taboo, but on the Surface, it's completely normal. I wish I hadn't seen you! This is something I would rather you guys have come to me about when you felt comfortable with me!" I'm not entirely sure they understood most of what I said considering how fast I was talking.

Arch jumps up from the bed. Heading toward me, he holds out his arms. I involuntarily flinch. He stops, eyes wide. "Alyce?"

I cover my face in embarrassment and to hide the tears forming in my eyes. I know Arch would never hurt me. "I'm sorry," I whisper.

"Mouse? Can I hold you? Please?" I nod, and without hesitation he wraps his arms around me, engulfing me in a strong hug. "Hey. It's okay. Take a deep breath for me, Little Mouse."

"I'm sorry, Arch."

"There's nothing to be sorry for." Then in a whisper, he says, "I saw your face. I know you didn't mean to interrupt." He holds me until I calm down, then he pulls away slightly. "Give him a moment to digest the fact that you know, alright?"

Nodding, I pull away. Eyes meeting Hatter's, he still seems a bit shocked, but his eyes are slightly narrowed. "So you're saying you saw us?"

"Yes," I whisper.

"You don't mind that Arch and I have a sexual relationship?"

I look between him and Arch and shake my head. "Not at all. Although, I feel like there is more than a sexual relationship between you two."

He grunts while Arch laughs. "And if it were?" he asks.

I smile at both of them. "That's awesome. I've always wanted a relationship with someone who understands and accepts me the way I am."

Hatter arches a brow. "So if you walked in on us again, what would you do?"

"I've actually been thinking about that. I can't exactly knock on a door, so I can promise to always announce myself if I want to come in. Or I can just avoid your tent in general and only come in when invited. Although, I should probably assume if Arch is also in here then I shouldn't bother you. I wouldn't want to be a bother. Also..."

"Alyce!" Hatter's voice booms.

I jump and squeak, "Yes?"

I see the smirk on his face. "You were rambling."

Tugging on my hair anxiously, I mutter, "Yeah. I tend to do that."

Arch bumps my shoulder. "It's adorable, Mouse."

Hatter tips his hat, so I can no longer see his eyes before he shocks me by saying, "You should join us at a future time."

Arch shivers and looks down at me with a grin. "Oh, the fun we could have."

Flushing, I awkwardly say, "Oh... um... sure. Future time... sounds great. Um... I'm going to go outside now and help with... something. Yeah! Something." Rushing out of their tent, I run across the camp and into Chesh's tent. As I fling the flaps open, I see Chesh in the corner, but in my rush to hide, I ignore him and continue rushing over to his bed. Jumping up onto it, I shove my face into the pillow and squeal.

I hear Chesh laugh behind me. "So it went well I take it?"

I hold a thumbs up in the air.

CHAPTER SIXTEEN

Alyce

Chesh pokes my back and says, "It's time to eat."

With my face still shoved into the pillow, I groan. How am I supposed to go out there after having that conversation with Hatter and Arch?

"You need to eat. Would it help if I gave you something to help with your nerves?"

I turn to squint at him and ask, "It's not like the Drink Me is it?"

He shakes his head. "Mor made sure it doesn't have any of the same ingredients. I made him check several times before I even thought about offering it to you."

I roll over, facing him. "Will it really help?" I ask hesitantly.

He shrugs. "It helps Rab and Rook when they can't sleep."

Humming, I agree, "Alright, I'll try it. What could go wrong?" Those are the famous words of EVERY drunk girl by the way. He hands me a vial filled with a blue swirling liquid. I look back up at him and ask, "So do I drink the whole thing?"

"Yes, the effects should kick in pretty quickly."

Taking the cork out of the bottle, I salute the air. Bottoms up! Chugging the solution, I try not to groan at the explosion of flavor that crosses my tongue. Handing the vile back to him, I grin. "That was delicious."

"How do you feel?"

No random effects yet. "I feel fine." But as the word fine crosses my lips, my body instantly feels warm and fuzzy. I giggle. I can't help it, my brain feels like fireflies and cotton. Hum. I bet this is what being drunk feels like. Giggling again, I boop Chesh on the nose. "I feel amazing!"

He arches a brow. "Are you sure?"

I jump up from the bed and squeal. "Oh, shit! The ground is moving!" I yell.

Chesh stands up beside me. "Should I carry you?"

Holding my hands out to my side, I say, "Maybe if I move slowly I can make it?" I walk forward a few steps and proceed to lose my balance. Chesh catches me, swinging me up into his arms. I grin. "Yay! You saved me! You're like a knight in shining armor. You know I never liked the knight or the prince. A princess can be a badass too!" I boop him on the nose again and say, "But I like you."

Chesh smiles. "I'm not entirely sure what you are talking about. I'm assuming the drink affects you differently than Wonderlanders."

"I think I'm drunk. I've never been drunk, you know? So I could be wrong, but that's okay, I feel amazing!"

Chesh carries me out of the tent and places me on top of the same large mushroom I sat on before. He boops me on the nose, and I giggle. He grins. "Stay right here and don't move," he orders. I nod as he walks away to grab me something to eat. I look around the circle and find that everyone is looking at me. I wave awkwardly as I giggle.

"What's wrong with her?" Mor asks, pointing at me with his fork.

I squeal when Chesh appears next to me. "Wow. You're like a... like a...um. Shit! You're like a magical person!"

Chesh shakes his head in amusement. "It seems our Aly reacted to the drink I gave her to calm her nerves. I believe the Surface word for it is drunk."

Dee laughs. "It also seems like she is using normal curse words now."

I moan as I shovel the food Chesh brought me into my mouth. "This is so good. I love Wonderland food!" Finishing my food quickly, I look around the group. "We should play a game!"

Arch laughs. "What kind of game do you want to play, Mouse?"

I look over to Arch and say, "You're really handsome. I love your fluffy hair. Is your tail fluffy?! Oh! Can I touch your ears?! I bet they are really soft!"

Arch flushes red. "Um... thank you." He turns to look behind him. "I suppose my tail is fluffy." He looks over to Hatter briefly before looking back at me. "I guess you can touch my ears."

"Oh! Can I really? I'll be gentle, I promise!" I reach out as far as I can, but I can't reach him. "I can't touch the pretty ears, Chesh!" I whine.

Chesh laughs. "You're still sitting, Kitten." He looks over at Arch and tells him, "You should probably come over here, she says the ground moves when she tries to walk."

"It does!"

Chesh grins. "I know, Kitten."

Suddenly, Arch is in front of me on his knees. "Wow! You're so fast!" I reach out a hand and gently touch his ear. Sighing, I nuzzle my cheek against it before exclaiming, "It's so soft. I love it." I rub it against my cheek a few more times before letting go. "Thank you!"

Arch is bright red as he nods. "You're welcome."

I turn my gaze to Rab. "Can you take your ears out? I love seeing them. You always have them hidden under your hat. They are so pretty and white."

Rab arches a brow but does as I request and takes off his top hat. Setting it beside him he looks back at me. "Better?" he asks.

I grin widely. "Yes!" I look over at the twins and notice they don't have their armor on. I lick my lips and point at them, stating, "You two are sexy!"

Both of their eyes widen before Dee laughs. "Thank you, Aly."

I drunkenly nod. I'm stating the obvious, am I not? Looking over at Mor, I jump up as I point at him. I wobble for a sec, and Chesh puts his hands on my waist to steady me. "Thanks," I tell him.

Chesh nods. "I've got you."

Looking back at Mor, I say, "You! You are amazing." In my drunken state, I do remember that many females have complimented him on his beauty and nothing else, so I say, "You are amazing and wonderful and kind and generous and awesome!"

His wings flutter at a rapid pace before settling closed. His eyes glisten for a moment as he smiles. "Thank you, Butterfly."

Plopping back down on the mushroom, my gaze meets Hatter's. He raises a brow.

I put my hands together in a pleading motion and ask, "Can you take off your hat, please?"

He seems to weigh my request before slowly taking his hat off. I groan as his messy black hair is revealed. "I love your fucking hair! It's so swooshy and messy." I lay my head against Chesh's shoulder adding, "I just want to run my fingers through it." Sitting quietly for a moment, I remember. "The game!" The males around me all laugh.

"I asked what game you wanted to play, Mouse?"

Tapping my finger to my lip, I think. "I want to play twenty questions, but, like, where I get to ask you questions and you get to ask me questions."

"So we just ask questions?" Chesh wonders.

"Yeah! Like I would ask you and Mor why your curses don't affect you the way they do most of your species?"

Chesh shrugs and explains, "There aren't many of my species left. But as far as the effects of the curse, I can only say that the male or female has to be strong-willed. Also having strong magic helps. I have strong magic, that is how I am able to seamlessly shift into several forms."

Mor answers next, "There were many of my species, but most were killed during the war. To be able to control the Jabberwock, strong magic is required. My specific breed is rare, and with it comes more magic."

I'm not entirely sure I'll remember this info tomorrow, but at least I now I have the answer. I point toward Rab. "I forgot to ask you earlier. Why do you always wear that hat? It seems like it would be uncomfortable for your ears."

Rab sighs. "There are only a few with my abilities. We are either in hiding or dead. Many rabbits with my ability hide their ears, so we aren't easily recognizable. I can't pass for a Hare, so I keep them covered."

My smile dampens. "I'm sorry. If you need to put it back on you can. I just love looking at them."

Rab smiles. "As long as it's dark and no one is around, I should be safe."

"Are you sure?" I ask, narrowing my eyes.

He laughs. "Yes, I'm sure. Continue your game, Little Alyce."

Studying him for a few more minutes, I finally shrug. I gesture toward the guys. "Now it's your turn." The guys look at each other.

"What's your favorite color?" Chesh asks.

Hum. Favorite color. "It's so hard to pick a favorite, but I often gravitate toward light blue."

"So you don't have a favorite?" Chesh laughs.

Shaking my head, I reply, "I like all of them equally." I gesture for the guys to ask another question.

"What's your favorite flower?" Rab asks.

"Blue roses!" The others follow after with their questions.

Mor smiles and asks, "Favorite person?"

I laugh. "How can you have a favorite person?"

He shrugs. "Fine, who's the person you feel closest to?"

"Here or the Surface?"

"Both."

Thinking for a moment, I furrow my brows. "I supposed on the Surface it would be my brother, Alix. Here? I'm not sure, but I want to be close to all of you."

Mor nods. "Seems like a good answer."

I yawn as Dee and Rook ask. "Favorite memory?"

"Here or the Surface?"

Dee smiles. "How about both?"

"Um... on the Surface it would have to be when all my brothers came and stayed the night with me after a hard night at work. They brought over my favorite ice cream, and we binge-watched Supernatural, because who can be upset watching Jensen Ackles while eating ice cream?"

"Who is this Jensen Ackles?" Dee asks seriously.

"Yes, did he do something inappropriate while you watched him?" Rook questions.

I laugh. "He's an actor. He plays different characters on tv."

Dee looks confused. "What's a tv?"

"Um." Stupid hazy brain. I try to explain. "It's like a magical box that shows you images. Sort of how you saw the pictures of me and my brothers on my phone, except they move."

Humming thoughtfully, Dee nods. "Sounds interesting. You didn't answer the other part of the question, though."

I roll my eyes. "You interrupted me." I think about that, trying to get my fuzzy thoughts together. "Um... Here?" I look around at the males in front of me, then say, "I don't think I can choose. I have too many."

Rook smirks. "That's an acceptable answer for now."

Yawning again, I feel my eyes getting heavy. Hatter and Arch are in front of me and ask, "Want to stay the night with us, Mouse?" I nod. Arch scoops me off the mushroom and heads to their tent. I snuggle in close, sighing at his comforting leathery scent.

Before I realize what's happening, I am tucked into a bed. Opening my eyes enough to see around me, I notice I'm in Arch's bed. "Where are you going to sleep?" I mutter.

Arch runs his fingers gently through my hair. "Don't worry, I'll sleep in Hatter's bed."

"Where will Hatter sleep?"

Arch laughs softly. "In his bed too."

Humming, I mumble, "Cuddling is nice. I love cuddling. I wish I could cuddle with you." I snuggle down into the blankets.

"Do you want to cuddle with both of us?" Hatter asks.

I smile and say, "Best cuddle ever." A puff of black glitter erupts beside me, making me sneeze. I look to see what happened. There is now a dark brown hare sitting on the edge of the bed beside me where Arch used to be. I push the blankets down squealing, "Yes! I want to snuggle!"

Arch moves up and under the blankets laying against my side as he places his small head on my arm. I pet his head for a moment and his eyes close. I smile down at him, whispering, "You are so soft."

Hatter sighs and makes his way over. Kicking off his shoes, he pulls back the covers and slides in beside me. I grab Arch, moving him so he's laying on Hatter's chest. I shift so I can lay on my side. "Scootch over."

Hatter shifts over more, so I can lay in the crook of his arm. Placing my arm across his chest, I shift Arch so he can lay in the crook of my arm on top of Hatter's chest. I sigh, snuggling in closer to the two males. I'm engulfed in the comforting, familiar scents of leather, black licorice, and mint.

Humming in contentment, I quickly fall asleep.

CHAPTER SEVENTEEN

Alyce

Needing to refill our supplies and wanting to have a decent night not spent out in the woods, the guys recommend a settlement between Clubbz and Dymondz. I wasn't about to complain about the accommodations we had while camping in the woods, though. They were much better than camping on the Surface. The tents alone are magical. Literally. Magical. You think you are walking into a small one-person tent, and poof! It's the size of a decent studio apartment on the Surface.

You won't hear any complaints from me. Although, the way the guys keep describing the settlement we are heading to makes the tents sound small in comparison. Huffing out a sigh, I walk faster. I am going to enjoy a fantastic soak in the amazing life-size tea cups they were talking about. Rab mentioned different tea bags you can put in the bathwater to help with any ailment you have.

I was bubbling with excitement as we made our way out of the woods. I squeal in delight, looking around. "Are you serious?!"

Dee laughs. "I'm assuming that was an excited squeal, not a squeal of fright."

"This is so adorable!" I exclaim, looking around at the multi-colored houses. Each house has a large mushroom with a cutout on the stem for a door. The walkways look like bricks with small flowers between each one instead of dirt or mortar. There are farmers tilling their fields, and the females seem to be working in the flower beds around the small homes.

I jump up and down in excitement. "Please tell me we are staying in one of these amazing houses!" I hear all of the guys chuckle, but I don't care. This is amazing.

Mor comes up beside me and points. "We are staying in that inn."

I follow his finger to the inn in question. "No. Way." I gape. The inn he pointed to looks like a cottage, but is larger than what a cottage usually would look like. It's the size of a two-story home on the Surface. It also has several mushrooms growing from its roof. I look more closely at the mushrooms and find dormers attached as well as small balconies.

I look back at Mor, smiling. Without warning, I grab his hand and start running toward the inn. "Let's go slow pokes!" I call out.

The others call out to us, but all I hear is Mor laughing beside me. Rab is suddenly in front of us and then gone again in a blink. He reappears several paces closer to the inn than he originally was. "No fair! You can't use time magic! That's cheating!" I yell as I try to run faster.

Rab is grinning. "You never said I couldn't use magic."

I huff when I notice Chesh appear next to Rab. "You hitched a ride too!"

Chesh shrugs. "A cat never passes up an opportunity to get where they are going as fast as possible."

I look back to find Hatter and Arch walking at their normal fast pace, while Dee and Rook are shoving at each other as they try to catch up.

I finally make it to the entrance of the inn and bend over gulping down big breaths. Teacups and crumpets! I'm out of shape! Holding up a hand, I pant, "Give me a sec, guys."

Dee comes up behind me, patting me on the back softly. "You didn't have to run so fast. We were going to end up here whether slow or fast."

"Not the point." I try to say through my panting.

"Then what was the point, Kitten?" Chesh kneels on the ground, bending to look up at me.

"Not sure right now, but there was a point." I take in another deep breath, then straighten. Placing one hand on my hip, I point to the entrance with the other then call out, "Onward!"

They all laugh as we enter and check in with the older lady at the desk. I watch in fascination as two males come up on either side of her and kiss her on opposite cheeks. The older lady's eyes light up. She turns to each male and kisses them quickly. "Can you show these males and female to their room?" Both males both nod and turn to us, gesturing for us to follow them.

We walk up a few flights of stairs before coming to a stop in front of a pastel blue door. One of the males unlocks and opens it, while the other gestures us inside. "Welcome to Bubble-bee Inn."

The other male hands the key to Rab as he bows. "Have a bee-utiful stay," he says before the males leave us to ourselves.

All the males look at me, and I arch a brow in question. "What?"

Hatter smirks. "You were so excited to get here." He gestures toward the open door.

Oh. OH! I nod excitedly as I race into the room. I squeal again and exclaim, "This is too much! How am I going to handle all this cuteness? I could just die!"

Chesh races toward me and grips my arms. "Oh, please don't die from the cuteness! We can make it ugly!" He turns around about to do just that, but I grab his arm.

"It's a figure of speech, Chesh." I pull him toward me and kiss him lightly on the nose.

He begins purring. Standing up to his full height, he looks down at me with narrowed eyes and says, "I wish these speech figures would cease. They will make my glorious fur fall out from all the stress." I watch as his ears flatten on the top of his head, a clear tell of his unease.

I tug his arm so that his face is level with mine. Reaching up with my other hand, I scratch the space between his ears. His eyes close as his purring increases. I give him a quick peck on the lips. "I'm sorry, Chesh. I'll be more mindful of my words from now on."

He brushes his nose against mine before he pulls away. "Thank you, Kitten."

I turn to find the others in various states of relief at my words. I hadn't realized that a figure of speech so normal on the Surface could have such a different meaning here. Returning to my previous perusal of the room, I see a door in the corner. Sliding my hand into the Chesh's, I pull him with me as I investigate.

Opening the door, I find a large bathroom. Wow. The bathtub really is a lifesize teacup. There is even a saucer under it. I'm not well-versed in the world of teacups, but I think I remember this one being a Burford. Above the cup, there are several drawers, and I move closer to find that they're labeled with different types of tea. A few I recognize as herbal teas. Chamomile. Lavender. Ginger. Peppermint. There are so many!

"Would you like to take a soak?"

I look back at Chesh and ask, "Really? Don't we have other things we need to do?"

He shrugs. "We need to get a few more supplies, but Dee and Rook can go get those. Hatter and Arch can go find us a snack to last us till the festival tonight, and that will leave Mor and I to guard you."

I look back toward the tub longingly. A soak does sound wonderful. "Are you sure?"

He laughs as he tugs me toward the tub and sets me on the handle of the cup. Chesh turns a few knobs on the wall and the teacup starts filling from the bottom. Curious. Opening a few drawers, he sniffs the contents.

He opens a few more before nodding. He grabs a few bags which look like drinking tea bags if I'm honest, and drops them into the tub.

The smell of strawberries and vanilla fills the room. Wow. I didn't even know you could make a tea with strawberries and vanilla. I look toward Chesh as he walks over to a cabinet and pulls out a white fluffy towel. He walks back over and places the towel inside the saucer.

I point toward the tub. "Strawberry and vanilla?"

He grins. "It's a strawberry and vanilla green tea. It's the closest to my smell that I could find." He turns back toward the wall and turns the knobs to stop the water.

"To smell like you," I whisper.

Turning back toward me, his grin widens as he slides up next to me. Placing his lips next to my ear, he whispers, "I would love for you to smell like me, Kitten. It means my scent is all over you." He pulls away to look into my eyes. "Although, this is Wonderland. My scent marking you doesn't mean much. Only that I belong to you and no other female can claim me." His teasing tone was gone.

My eyes widen. "What do you mean by your scent marking me doesn't matter?"

He sighs and explains, "In Wonderland, females can have multiple males as partners. You won't find that many males normally approach you, though. But with my scent on you, they may see it as you being open to partners."

I snort. "I think the seven of you are enough for me."

His eyes widen in shock. "You want to claim the seven of us?" He asks, sounding unsure.

I nip at my lip. "Only if you guys want me to claim you. I don't want to claim anyone who doesn't want to be Claimed. And I really hate the word claim. It makes it sound like I own you, and I don't. You are your own males and I..." Chesh's lips are on mine in a second, and I moan. I was rambling anyways. Kissing is so much better. He moves his lips against mine in a soft caress, lightly brushing his fingertips across my cheek as he pulls away.

His grin is soft as he murmurs, "Yes."

I look into his purple eyes and ask, "Yes, what?"

He pulls away even more. "We wouldn't mind being Claimed by you. We know you would treat us as equals and not possessions. That's a rare thing in Wonderland. It's even rarer for those of our ranking in Wonderland society."

I reach up and caress his cheek. "Of course we are equals."

Turning, he kisses my wrist. "And that is the reason we would die before allowing any other female to claim us. You are special, Alyce."

"I'm not that special."

He laughs, booping me on the nose. He scurries out of my reach, heading toward the door but turns before leaving. "Enjoy your soak, Kitten. Mor and I will stand guard. We will have an outfit ready for you when you're done."

Shaking myself out of the haze Chesh put me in, I strip out of the clothes I've been borrowing from the guys. Sliding into the cup, I groan. No offense to the guys and their tent tubs, but this is amazing! I close my eyes, enjoying the warmth and smell of strawberries mixed with vanilla.

Opening the door a crack, I peek out. I don't see anyone, so I look down to see if Chesh left me clothes as promised. Sighing, I look around again, but I don't see anything. "Mor? Chesh?" I call.

I watch as Mor walks in from a door on the opposite side of the room. He looks up and his eyes widen. "Alyce? Is something wrong?"

I look down at myself and then back up at him. "Chesh said there would be clothes waiting for me, but there wasn't any outside the door."

Nodding, he sighs and walks toward the bed that has a box sitting on it. Grabbing the box, along with the small bag beside it, he turns back toward me. He holds them up. "He was supposed to deliver these to you. Seems he got distracted."

I smile. "Seems so." He holds the box out for me to take, but I look down at myself. I don't think the towel will stay on if I grab both the box and bag. I look back up at Mor. "Could you put them on the counter for me?" I open the door wider for him to come inside.

He nods. "Of course." He glides over, placing the box and bag on the counter. Turning back to me he smiles and asks, "Did you enjoy your soak?"

I nod. "Yes, it was very nice."

He walks by me, but I notice him sniffing. "I see Chesh choose a scent similar to his."

I blush, holding my towel tighter against my body. "Yes. Seems he wanted me to smell like him tonight."

Mor dips his head in acknowledgement. "That he did." I watch as a series of emotions play over his face before he sucks in a breath. "If I may ask something?"

"Of course!" I watch his wings flutter in rapid succession before tucking together.

"Would it not offend if I pick the next scent you bathe in?"

My brows knit together in confusion. "Why would it offend me?"

He reaches up and tugs on his winged earrings, looking slightly embarrassed. "There is a tea that smells similar to newly fallen rain."

It takes me a moment before it clicks. Newly fallen rain. That's what he smells like. I reach up and tug lightly on his opposite earring, and his eyes meet mine. "I'd love that. Thank you for offering."

He beams at me. "You are most welcome." He looks around the room and then blushes. "Oh! I'll leave you to dress, Alyce." He shuffles out the door before closing it softly behind him.

I laugh as I turn to the counter to open the box and bag they left for me. Dropping my towel, I open the bag first. Sighing with a smile, I pull out a pair of classic white underwear. I'm thankful that the underwear isn't lingerie, but I'm still wondering who would... Chesh. Chesh would buy me underwear no doubt. Laughing, I slip them on. Continuing my search through the bag, I pull out a floral head wreath next. It's got white blossoms with lace ribbon woven between. Reaching into the bag again, I pull out a silver chain with a blue rose dangling from it. It's beautiful.

I set it on the counter and move onto the box. Opening the box, I gasp. Inside, lying on sheets of white paper, is a light blue dress. I gently pull it out. Letting the bottom of the dress slip through my fingers, I stare. Undoing the ribbons to the corset bodice, I slip it on and cinch myself in. I look at myself in the mirror. The sleeves are a sheer light blue that fall off my shoulders. The dress bodice has white blossoms sewn throughout, and a flowing skirt that hits at my knees with the same blossoms scattered throughout.

Peeking back into the box, I find a pair of white flats that look to be made of lace. I slip them on and finish my look by placing the head wreath on. Snatching the necklace, I leave the bathroom. Opening the door, I'm greeted by all my males.

Holding up the necklace, I say, "I need some help with this."

Rab breaks away from the group and walks over. Taking the necklace from me, I turn, grabbing my hair and pulling it up and away from my body. He slips the necklace around my neck, clasps it into place, and gives my shoulders a light touch before stepping away. The necklace sits perfectly so that the rose rests between my breasts.

Looking up at the guys, I smile. Giving a twirl, I ask, "How do I look?"

I watch as the males glance at each other before speaking in unison, "Like a Queen."

Blushing, I dip my head in thanks. I grin as I face Dee. "So you said Festival. What happens at a Wonderland Festival?"

Dee steps towards me holding out his elbow. "This isn't a typical Wonderland Festival."

I slip my arm into the crook of his elbow when Rook steps up to my other side, also holding out his elbow. "This is a Clubbz Festival. Lots of food and dancing."

My eyes widen. "Dancing?!"

Both twins arch a brow. "Yes," they say in unison.

Hopping up and down with excitement, I say, "Well then, let's go!"

CHAPTER EIGHTEEN

Alyce

I'm not sure what will come first. Collapsing from jumping around with too much excitement or spontaneous combustion from pure happiness. The twins lead me into an area around a large fire pit. There are vendors on the outer sides forming a circle. Looking around, I try to take in all the sights. There is so much to see. The night sky is glittering with stars as bubble-bees flutter past, reflecting the rainbow colors of the fire.

I tug on the twin's arms and exclaim, "I don't know what to do first!"

Chesh circles between my legs before shifting into his male form with a grin. "It doesn't matter what we do first because we are doing it all!" He holds his hand out to me, but I look between the twins. I don't want to leave them out. They both arch a brow at me.

"Is it okay if I go with Chesh?"

Dee seems puzzled. "Why wouldn't it be okay for you to go with Chesh?"

Nibbling my lip, I look between them. "I don't want to leave you out since you brought me here." They both press kisses to my cheeks, squishing my face.

Dee pulls back with a smile. "You can go have fun with Chesh. All of us will follow behind."

Rook pats my hand as he steps back and places it in Chesh's. "We will not be left out."

I tug Dee down for a quick kiss on his lips, then pull my arm from his and place it in Chesh's. Quickly grabbing Rook, I pull him down and place a kiss on his cheek as well. "Thank you."

He looks puzzled by my thanks but nods. Turning to Chesh, I grin wide and ask, "Adventure?"

He tugs on my arm, pointing toward our first merchant of the night. "Adventuring!" I'm dragged behind him as he takes me to each vendor. He feeds me bites of food, not allowing me to feed myself. When we get to a flower crown merchant, I make each male get one, which makes me laugh. Rab and Hatter have to hold their top hats under their arms but agree to my request.

I look at Rab, arching a brow as I gesture toward his exposed ears. He gives me a reassuring smile. "We are in safe territory. It's fine."

I smile back. "Now we're matching!" I squeal. I'm not sure what drink Chesh gave me, but he assured me it wasn't made with what was in the Drink Me's or Eat Me's. It makes me feel all warm and fuzzy.

"Are you enjoying yourself, Sugar?" Hatter asks, smirking at me.

I giggle. "So much so!"

I hear music coming from the center of the festival. Turning around, I see a few Clubbz people playing what looks like instruments. Tugging on Chesh's arm, I say, "Dance with me!"

He chuckles. "I may be graceful like a cat, but I cannot dance. You will have to ask Dee or Rook for that."

I turn my gaze toward the twins. "Dance with me?" I begin swaying to the music.

Dee holds up his hands, looking towards his brother and then back at me. "If it were a formal dance, I would be your guy. But this is more of a 'feel the music' situation." He points to his brother and says, "He's your guy."

I hold my hands out toward him, wiggling my fingers. "Dance with me, Rook." He looks like he's going to decline so I add, "Please?"

He sighs, taking my hand. "One dance."

I smile up at him and nod as the tempo of the music increases. "One dance."

Rook twirls me out and then back into his arms. He wraps one arm behind me, holding the center of my back while he holds my hand with the other. We begin to twirl and skip around the fire. The tempo builds, and when there is a bounce in the tempo of the song he shifts his grip and lifts me into the air. I flair my arms out each time, laughing as I feel the whisper of wind brush across my face.

As the beat builds faster, Rook follows. We spin faster and faster as he lifts me into the air. I can feel that the song is about to end as Rook spins me away from him. I continue to spin as I let go of his hand, remembering all those tutorials I watched as a kid about dancing. I begin to pirouette and my dress flares out as I do. Once the instruments stop, I freeze. I look around me, breathing hard, only to find everyone staring at me.

Looking around, I finally find Rook. His mouth is agape and his eyes are wide. Unsure as to why they are looking at me like that, I walk up to him. I wait until I'm next to him to ask, "Did I ruin the dance?"

Shaking himself, he says, "No! You were... mesmerizing. You looked like a celestial being with the way the fire lit your dress."

Dipping my head, I whisper, "I find that hard to believe."

He places a finger under my chin and forces my eyes up to meet his. "You were beautiful. I would dance with you forever."

"Really? Forever? That seems a bit long," I tease.

He places a gentle kiss to my lips, and I suppress a gasp. "Sometimes forever only lasts a second." He pulls away from me with a smile, then says, "I think my brother wishes for some time with you."

I look behind me to find the others all looking at me with soft smiles, but Dee is bouncing up and down with a wide grin. I laugh. "I see."

Rook waves over his brother. Dee runs over, picks me up, and twirls me in the air. "You were amazing. I've never seen someone look so beautiful as they danced!"

I look over and see Rook walking back to the others. I think back to my conversation with Chesh; I never really figured out if they date in Wonderland. Chesh called it claiming. "Hey, Dee?"

He places me on the ground with a smile. "Yes?"

"Do Wonderlanders date?"

Arching a brow, he asks, "What's dating?"

Well, that answers that question. Back to claiming. "What does it mean for a female to claim a male?"

His eyes widen. "You wish to claim a male?"

I groan. "I don't even know what claiming means. On the Surface a female dates a male she likes, and if they like each other a lot they end up getting married. I don't know what the equivalent of that would be in Wonderland."

"I suppose claiming would be the equivalent of dating on the Surface. It means a bit more here, though. When a female claims a male that means the male is her property. He belongs to only her, and he cannot end the arrangement between them without the female's consent."

"That does not sound like dating to me. Dating is when a man and woman agree to date each other. They are equals in the relationship, and if either party wants to end the relationship they can."

He hums. "That sounds much better than claiming."

"I know," I sigh. I swing my arm that's holding Dee's hand.

"If I may ask, why were you asking about claiming?"

I sit on a large mushroom and tug Dee to sit beside me. Looking up, I have a direct line of sight to the others. "Chesh and I were talking earlier, and he mentioned scents and claiming. He said all of you wouldn't mind being claimed by me. But I hate that word. I don't want to claim you; I want you to want to be with me, too."

Dee squeezes my hand. "We do want to be with you."

I look up at him and ask, "Really?"

He grins. "Of course. Claiming is just a word we use in Wonderland. You can call it whatever you want."

"What if we changed what claiming meant to us? What if I said I wanted to claim all of you, and I wanted you to claim me? What if we belonged to each other? I would only belong to you seven."

Dee's eyes gleam in the light. "You would wish us to claim you?"

"Well, yeah. We're equals." He smashes his lips to mine, and I squeak in surprise, but it slowly morphs into a moan.

He pulls away, reaching up to caress my cheek. "I wish to claim you, Alyce."

SHATTERING TEA CUPS! I don't think he realizes how sexy that sounds. Or what that means on the Surface. Knowing my cheeks are pink, I clear my throat. "I want you to claim me." Seriously! Alyce! "I mean, I want to claim you, too!"

He smiles down at me. "Good."

"What's going on over here?" I hear a voice ask.

I squeal, pulling away from Dee, and looking over at Chesh. He has a wide grin on his face. "Um... Dee and I were talking about the conversation you and I had earlier."

He raises a brow. "Is that so?"

"I have claimed our Alyce." Dee says proudly. I'm stuck on how he said ours. My eyes meet Chesh's wide ones.

"You claimed her?" He asks, sounding confused.

Dee nods. "She has allowed us the opportunity to claim her as well." It sounds so weird when he says it like that. I open my mouth to explain it to Chesh when suddenly, he drops to his knees in front of me.

"Would you allow me the honor as well?"

He looks so scared that I'm going to say no. Grinning down at him, I say, "As long as I can claim you, too."

He mewls happily, wrapping his arms around me. "Of course, Kitten! I would like nothing more."

Seeing the ruckus Chesh is making in his excitement, the other males start making their way in our direction. Once they are close enough, I sigh. "Alright, I want to be completely upfront. I like all of you, and I talked to Dee and Chesh. I want you to know that you have the option to say no. But I would like to claim you all; however, there is a rule that I've put into place upon agreeing to my claim."

The males around me are wide-eyed but nod. "In order for me to claim you, you also have to claim me. I want this to be an equal relationship. I DO NOT own you." I emphasize the 'do not'. I want them to understand.

Arch steps forward, grabbing Hatter's arm as well. He looks at Hatter then back at me. "We wish to be claimed. We would be honored to claim you as well."

I smile up at Arch, then move my gaze to Hatter's. "Are you sure?"

Hatter nods. "Yes."

I nod. "Then I claim both of you as mine, and in return, I am yours."

Hatter's smirk widens. "Thank you." They both step back as Mor steps forward.

"It would be my greatest wish to be claimed by you. I would be honored to claim you in return."

I smile up at Mor and say, "Then I claim you as mine. It's my greatest wish to be claimed in return."

Mor bends and places a kiss on my lips. "It's an honor to grant this wish." He steps away allowing Rab to stand in front of me. Chesh moves to sit on my other side as Rab falls to one knee. He places his top hat in my lap as he lowers his head. "Time has been my only companion for many years. It would be my greatest pleasure to be claimed by you and to claim you in return."

I tug on the tip of his exposed ear and he looks back up at me. "You are an amazing rabbit, Rab. It would be an honor to claim you and be claimed by you."

He gives me a lopsided grin as he stands, taking his top hat with him. Rook slides up and stands rigidly in front of me. I reach my hand out to him, and he takes it. I feel the slight shake of his hand as he grips mine tightly.

"It's okay, Rook." I say as I smile up at him. "You and your brother are not a package deal. If you don't want to do this, it's fine."

He shakes his head "That's not it." He looks around the group and then back at me, and I can see the hesitation in his eyes.

"Would you guys mind if I talked to Rook alone, please?" The males standing nod and walk back over to the spot where they were standing before heading my way. They still have me in sight, but this allows me some privacy.

Chesh presses a kiss to my cheek before looking over to Dee. "Come on, Dee."

Dee looks between me and his brother and asks, "Are you sure?"

I smile and pull him over for a kiss. "We will both be fine, Dee. Could you get me more of those awesome stick things to eat?" He nods, following Chesh to the vendor stands.

I pull Rook down to sit next to me. "What's running rampant through that brain of yours?" I ask gently.

He sighs. "It would be a great honor to be claimed by you. An even greater honor to claim you as well."

"But?"

He brushes his finger across the top of my hand as I hold on to his other one. "I have failed important people in the past. It would be horrible if I failed a female who claimed me." His eyes meet mine, begging me to understand, and I can see the pain behind them. "It would be devastating to fail a female who allowed me to claim her in return."

"I find it hard to believe that you could fail me," I tell him honestly.

"What if I can't protect you? What if something happens to you because I wasn't vigilant enough? What if..."

I pull him in for a kiss, interrupting his words. I brush my other hand across his cheek, and feel his lips tremble under mine. Pulling away, I look into his glassy eyes filled with fear and doubt. "Someone once told me that you'll never get to the best part of the adventure if you focus on the what ifs. You'll have to move forward to find out if it's an if or an is."

"I'm afraid of the 'is,'" he whispers.

"Then it's a good thing there are six other males who will be looking out for me. You aren't doing this alone."

He sighs, pressing his forehead to mine. "I claim you."

I smile. "And I claim you, Rook."

CHAPTER NINETEEN

Alyce

Last night. Sigh. Last night was amazing. Amazing and crazy. I can't believe I claimed seven males as my own. I bet this was not what Alix had in mind when he said he hadn't prepared me for guys. I smile as I look to either side of me. I'm currently smashed between Dee and Rook.

I have to say, they are amazing snugglers. Each twin has an arm across my chest, holding me tight. Their head's moved overnight and now their faces are currently shoved into either crook of my neck. I have an inkling that it has to do with the bath I took last night. They had spent ten minutes looking through all the different tea bags. In the end, they found a few they liked and threw them all in the bath at the same time. I was slightly confused, so I asked, "Why are you putting so many bags in?"

They had looked at me and then back at the tub before stating, "It smells like you now."

I sniffed my shirt in confusion. "I still smell like strawberries."

Dee grinned. "I know, but I like your normal scent better."

I sniffed the water after they left, but I couldn't figure out the smell. It wasn't anything I was familiar with, but it had a sweet floral smell.

Considering that their noses are shoved into my neck, I think the scent stuck. Dee's breathing changes as he snorts and then cuddles closer to me. I giggle quietly. He's so cute! Rook mumbles something then pulls me tighter to him. Dee grumbles and pulls me back.

I laugh. "Guys?"

Dee's voice is deep from sleep as he says, "Not yet. Want to cuddle longer."

"Agreed," Rook rumbles.

They each lift a leg over my thighs snuggling in closer. Well, hello. I know males have morning wood. Apparently, it's normal, but holy whistling tea kettles! These males are packing. Like, 'how is that going to fit' size. My face flames with heat due to my sharp left turn into the gutter. Oh no! Now I'm getting warm for a completely different reason.

I wiggle, in an attempt to get out of this twin sandwich. They both groan into my neck. Bad idea, Alyce! Why would you wiggle?! I feel Dee shift and nibble on my ear, causing a shiver to run down my spine.

"Good morning, Aly," he says, his deep voice filled with sleep not helping my situation.

"Good morning," I squeak. With all these males around I really need to do something! I have some serious blue ovaries going on. "I need... I need to pee," I blurt out, hoping my voice didn't sound as breathy as it did in my head.

Dee rolls away, allowing me to jump out of bed. Rushing to the bathroom, I close the door behind me. Fuck, I'm glad we are at this inn instead of in the tents right now. Rushing over to the toilet, I relieve myself. Washing my hands, I look at my reflection. My cheeks are flushed, and my nipples are peaked under my shirt. Biting my lip, I caress the peaked nipples and bite down even harder when a pulse of heat flares between my legs.

Fuck! I look over my shoulder at the teacup bathtub. Well, a girl's gotta do what a girl's gotta do. I tear my clothes off and quickly make my way over to the tub. There's a knock at the door, but before I can say anything, the door opens.

Dee peeks around the corner. "Aly do you..." his words cut off abruptly as his eyes take in my naked body. I'm too shocked to even consider covering myself, and my nipples harden even more under his penetrating gaze.

"Yes?" My voice comes out breathy. Fuck! I rub my legs together to try and provide some relief from how turned on I am and watch as Dee licks his lips.

His grip on the door tightens, his knuckles turning white with how hard he's gripping it. "Did I interrupt something?"

Fuck it. I already claimed them right? "I was about to relieve myself of my sexual frustration from being surrounded by seven sexy males all the time and not having sex."

"Who said you couldn't have sex?" he asks huskily.

"I didn't want to move too fast. I didn't want you guys to think I was using you."

His grin looks feral as he pushes the door further open to show Rook standing right behind him. "You wouldn't be using us. We belong to you, and you belong to us right?" Rook asks from behind his brother, his deep voice filled with desire.

"Yes," I whisper.

Dee unbuttons his pants and quickly shoves them down, his cock standing proud as he says, "Then let us help you."

Fuck yeah! He prowls towards me while Rook shoves his pants off. Dee lifts me, and sets me on the counter as his lips slam against mine. I wrap my arms around his neck and thread my fingers through his purple hair. His hands roam up my body until he gets to my nipples. He flicks them before squeezing my breasts. I groan into his mouth.

He pulls away panting. "Your breasts are amazing." I moan as he circles my nipple with his thumb.

Rook comes up beside us and asks, "Where do you want me?"

I reach for him and he comes willingly. I grip the back of his neck and crush my lips to his. He threads his fingers into my hair tugging softly, making me moan again.

"How do you want us, darling?" Dee asks.

I pull away from Rook, panting. "I don't... I don't know. I've never had two males at once," I admit. Truth is I've never had sex with a guy before. But I did accidentally pop my own cherry when I was eighteen from fucking a dildo too hard. What!? I was worked up after reading a sex scene. You try reading *Den of Vipers by K.A. Knight* without getting worked up!

He smiles. "Do you have any issues we should know about?"

I shake my head. "No, I'm pretty open to anything."

Dee looks up at his brother. "Together may be too much for her first. Cunt n' suck?"

What in Wonderland?! "What's a cunt n' suck?" Dee moves to whisper in one ear while Rook moves to the other.

Dee nips at my ear and then blows softly. "One of us fucks your cunt."

Rook tugs lightly on my hair while whispering, "While you suck the other."

I moan at the thought. Yes! "Who do I get to suck off?"

Dee caresses my lips with his thumb, murmuring, "My brother will have the pleasure of experiencing your succulent mouth this time."

Rook moves, throwing a towel over the lid of the toilet and sitting on it. He looks right at me with a sensual smirk playing across his lips. "Let's show our darling pleasure."

Dee lifts me off the counter, patting my ass. "Off you go."

I kneel down in front of Rook, and he sucks in a breath. He reaches out and caresses my cheek. "You are breathtaking. Having you kneel in front of me feels wrong."

"I want to do this," I tell him, letting him see the truth in my eyes. I shift so I'm on my hands and knees, and then I spread my legs a bit and lift my ass in the air.

"Fuck, darling. You could make me come just from looking at you," Dee growls from behind me.

I smile up at Rook as I lick the tip of his cock. He sucks in a breath, threading his fingers through my hair. "Dee, I would hurry the fuck up. You may not be able to see her face, but I can."

"Is our little darling secretly a seductress?" Dee teases as he kneels behind me.

Lifting one hand, I grip the base of Rook's cock, cuz let's be honest, even if I deep-throat his cock, there is no way it's all fitting. I squeeze as I suck the head of his cock into my mouth. I hear a thump and looking up, I see Rook resting his head against the wall. His eyes are half-lidded, looking down at me.

I slide my mouth over his cock until he hits the back of my throat. I swallow and he grunts. His grip on my hair tightens. "Fuck!" he yells. I suck as his cock slides back out of my mouth.

Rook pants as the vibrations of my moan run down his cock, and Dee circles my clit with his cock.

"Dee, hurry the fuck up!" Rook roars.

Dee laughs. "Alright, alright. Aly, it seems you got my brother worked up there."

I grin around Rook's cock. Dee slowly thrusts into me, and I whine around Rook. "She wants it faster, brother."

Dee squeezes my ass. "She'll have to wait," he pants, "I'm trying not to come. She's squeezing my cock so tight." I whimper, shoving my ass further back into him.

He takes a few deep breaths before pulling out and slamming back in. I groan and continue my original task. Squeezing Rook's cock, I begin pumping the base of him as I suck as much of him as I can into my mouth. I can feel my saliva sliding between my lips. I look up at Rook. He's panting hard and biting his lower lip to the point it's bleeding. His grip on my hair tightens, and he must see something in my gaze because he pants, "You look so fucking sexy wrapped around my cock."

I moan from the praise and squeeze around Dee as he thrusts harder into me. "Yes. Beautiful fucking female! All ours!" He reaches down and pinches my clit, tipping me over the edge. I scream around Rook's cock as I come.

"Fuck!" Rook yells as he tries to pull me off of him, but I clamp down and suck him as he comes. He pumps into my mouth a few more times as I suck and swallow him down.

Releasing my hold on Rook's cock, I reach underneath me and squeeze Dee's balls as I clamp down around him. He squeezes my ass and roars, slamming into me one last time before he comes. Not bad for having sex for the first time, let alone with two males.

I release Rook's cock, and his head falls back as he pants. I look over my shoulder to see Dee bracing himself with his hands on my hips.

He looks at me and smiles. "That was the most amazing fucking sex I have ever had." He slowly slides out of me, grunting.

Okay, that was a major ego boost!

He stands and walks over to the teacup then turns it on. He picks a scent and drops it into the water. Turning, he heads back over to me. I'm sitting on my heels slightly grossed out by the copious amounts of come dripping out of me. But will I complain? No. Why? Because the sex was totally worth it!

I watch as Rook slides into the bathtub as Dee bends down next to me. "In you go, darling." He grabs my arm and wraps it around his neck as he lifts me enough to get his arm behind my knees.

"I'll get come all over you," I squeak.

"Darling, you got come all over his dick. I don't think he's worried much about it," Rook says, laughing from his spot in the tub. He does have a point. Dee lets me slide into the tub, and Rook grabs my hips and places me right between his legs. "Lie back for me."

My head hits him mid-chest. I smell the aroma of the tub and smile. The smell has a tinge of cinnamon with a bit of sugar. Like a snickerdoodle. It's a combo of Dee's sweet scent and Rook's spicy cinnamon one. Sighing contently, I close my eyes and sag into Rook.

"Block her eyes for me, Dee."

I'm a little confused until I feel water cascade over my hair. I feel Rook's fingers work through my hair as he pours the water.

"Here's the shampoo, Rook."

I hear a snap, and then Rook chuckles. "Great choice, Dee."

Rook massages the suds into my hair, and I groan. Oh, fuck yeah! I love a good head massage, but a massage while washing my hair? Yep. I claimed the right males. Without prompting, Dee covers my face again as the suds are washed out.

"Lift your foot, darling." I lift my foot out of the tub as Dee requested, and he begins massaging my foot. I moan out my appreciation.

Rook chuckles behind me. "I think you hit our darling's melt button, Dee." I hear Dee's chuckle. I didn't even realize I fell asleep until I woke up an hour later, cuddled between the two males in bed.

CHAPTER TWENTY
Alyce

I stare at myself in the mirror as I study my abdomen. If I was being honest with myself, I couldn't see the scars from when I was thirteen. Laurel had made sure of that.

"Alyce!" Laurel screams as he enters the Principal's office. He's only had official custody of us for a year, but he had been taking care of us since the minute he turned eighteen after dad left us. It took two years of battling the courts for him to prove he could provide for us before he was finally granted custody. This wasn't going to look good on him.

"I'm sorry!" I cry as I hold the bandages to my bleeding abdomen.

He looks around the room. "Why the fuck is she still here?! She should be at the hospital! Where the fuck are the kids that did this to her?!"

The principal clears his throat. "We are trying to get to the bottom of this, Mr. Liddell. The girls she has accused of doing this have said they were nowhere near her. There is no one who can account for Ms. Liddell's whereabouts at the time of the incident. The girls have alibis."

"Fuck alibis!" He turns to me, eyes blazing. "Where the fuck was Alix?!"

I flinch at his tone. "He went to hang with some of his friends," I whisper.

He sighs and says, "I'm sorry I yelled." He turns at the sound of sneakers screeching down the hallway. Alix runs into the office, and Laurel sends him a death stare. "Nice of you to show up."

Edi runs in behind him wearing his football jersey. Huffing, he says, "I ran over here as fast as I could!"

Laurel turns his gaze to Edi. "You should be at your football practice. You have a big game this week, right?"

Edi shrugs, and his eyes meet mine. "There are more important things," he mutters.

Laurel kneels in front of me and asks gently, "What happened, Aly?"

"There were these girls who invited me over to hang out. I thought they were being nice, but they ambushed me and held me down and..." I choke on a sob.

He reaches up, wiping my tears away. He holds my cheek in his palm. "Breathe, kiddo. It's okay. I'm here now, and you're safe. Can I see?"

I nod, pulling away the bandages. I watch his eyes widen, then lift to mine. "Oh, kiddo," his voice breaks. He kisses my forehead as he stands. "Don't worry, I'll fix everything." He turns to Edi and murmurs, "Get her in the car. I'll be out there shortly."

Edi nods. He slips between Laurel and me and kneels as he asks softly, "Can I pick you up, Sis?"

I nod and he shifts me a little to get his arms under my knees. I wrap an arm around his neck as he lifts. I wince and my tears fall faster. He kisses my temple and says, "I'm sorry." As he turns to leave the room, my eyes catch Alix's, and I see him running his fingers roughly through his hair.

Releasing my hold around Edi's neck, I make a grabbing motion for him. "Come on, Alix. I need my cuddle buddy. Please."

His eyes fill with tears as he nods, making his way in my direction. "Yeah. I got you, baby Sis," he whispers hoarsely.

As Alix closes the door behind us, I can hear Laurel yell, "You will be hearing from my lawyers for allowing children to carve into my sister. This will END your career! I will be removing my brother and sister from this sad excuse of an educational system."

I'd never felt so proud to be his little sister as I did in that moment. After years of free laser treatments, the physical scars from that day were gone, but the emotional ones? Those were harder to erase.

I'm jerked out of my memories when there's a knock at the door. Realizing I'm still standing in front of the bathroom mirror in my new bra and underwear, I slip my new leather pants on as the door opens.

I look over my shoulder to find Rab smiling at me. I grin and ask, "Am I late meeting up with the others?"

Rab shrugs. "The others were getting worried not having you in sight, so I told them I would come check on you." He watches me as I slip my cloth undershirt on.

Grabbing the leather overlay, I raise a brow and tease, "Were they the only ones getting worried?"

He grins. "Who knows? Do you like your new clothes?"

Turning, I look at myself in the mirror and say, "It seems like a lot of leather to wear, but Rook said that these were the best fighting leathers Clubbz had to offer." Synching down the leather overlay, I turn to him. "They seem to fit well."

He nods as he narrows his eyes. "What's wrong?"

I smile and say, "Nothing."

He raises a brow in disbelief. "I have seen your true smile, Alyce. I can tell that's a forced one."

Smile dropping, I shrug. "Old monsters." Looking down, I flick the clasps on my bodice. "It seems you can heal physical wounds and scars, but the invisible ones seem to haunt the most."

"I've been told by a few that to get rid of our monsters we must run as fast as we can just to stay in place. And if we wish to go anywhere, we must run twice as fast as that." He sighs. I hear his steps, then his finger is under my chin, lifting my eyes to meet his. His eyes are filled with the fire of someone who runs from his own monsters. "Would you like to know what I say to that, Alyce?"

Watching that fire shift into ice, I whisper, "Yes."

"I say fight. Fight and fight until you can't fight anymore. Then fight some more. But do you know what the beauty of our group is? The amazing thing about having a Claimed?"

I shake my head, and he lowers his face to mine. When his lips are a breath away he says, "We can fight the monsters together. You have seven males ready to fight those monsters with you." He presses his lips softly against mine before backing away.

Then he smirks down at me. "So tell those monsters we are hunting them."

I'm in too much shock to say anything. He reaches up and threads his fingers into my hair before tugging. I squeak. He chuckles and asks, "Did you hear me, Alyce?"

"Yes."

He releases his hold on my hair, moving his hand down to caress my bottom lip with his thumb. "Good. My little Alyce. Such a good little Alyce." He shoves the tip of his thumb past my lips and pushes it deeper into my mouth. I swirl my tongue around it and he grunts. I suck on it hard before releasing it. He slowly removes it from my mouth, but not before I bite the end of his thumb.

I watch him adjust himself with his other hand, and I smile. He gives me a mischievous grin. "My little Alyce. You remind me of a blue rose. Smelling sweet and floral, looking delicate and fragile." He sucks the thumb I bit into his mouth, then turns to leave the bathroom before looking over his shoulder with a sensual smile. "But people often forget the thorns you must grasp to capture their beauty. Never lose your thorns, little Alyce. Your thorns are as beautiful as your delicate petals."

As we leave the woods and enter into Dymondz territory, I gasp. I didn't realize that the buildings would look like they were made of diamonds. They glitter in a range of colors as the sun sets. "Are the buildings made out of real diamonds?" I ask.

Chesh bumps my shoulder. "Dymondz territory is known for its advancement in technology and medicine. They believe in the advancement of the mind."

"So are they real diamonds?"

From the front, Rab calls out, "I'm assuming diamonds are something that comes from the Surface world?"

I nod. "Yeah. It's a mineral that if you heat hot enough and use enough pressure it turns into a sort of shiny crystal that people pay a lot of money for."

Rab nods in understanding. "You could call it diamonds. It's a stone that they find in the ground and also in the mountains close to the Spaydz territory."

I nod, continuing to look around as we walk through the territory. I wondered if we were going to stay in one of the sparkly buildings. Chesh bumps my shoulder again and asks, "Are you alright, Aly?"

"Yeah, why?"

He shrugs. "You seem a bit off today."

Sighing, I shrug. I should have known he would notice. I was still a bit distracted from this morning, and I was also a bit worried that Chesh would be upset because of what happened with the twins.

Chesh slides his hand into mine. "You know you can talk to me, right?"

I squeeze his hand. Chesh was the male every girl wanted. A male who listened to all of her problems. Who tried to help but didn't because he believed I was capable of helping myself too. He's my best friend, I realize. He's my best friend and a male I have feelings for, and I don't want to lose that friendship as we grow into something more with the Claiming.

"Can I ask you a question, Chesh?"

"Always."

Biting my lip, I ask, "Would you consider us friends?"

Chesh grins. "Of course!"

"And you also want to be something more than friends, right?"

"If I were to be so lucky then yes." He presses in closer, wrapping his tail around my abdomen.

I look down and smile. "But that wouldn't change us being friends, right?"

His tail tightens around my abdomen. "Of course not. Hatter and Arch have a relationship, and they are still best friends."

I nod, seeing his point. Clearing my throat, I say, "I also wanted to ask if you were upset with the fact that I slept with the twins instead of you first?"

Chesh gasps. "Why would I be upset? I am happy you have grown your relationship with the twins. They are very lucky males!"

I peek up at him through my lashes. "So you're not upset?"

His brows knit together. "Are you asking if I am upset that our relationship hasn't grown in that way?" I nod and he grins. "I appreciate that you are so worried about how I feel, but I am not upset. We are Claimed, and I am thrilled by that alone. If our relationship grows into more, I will be even more thrilled. A cat is very patient, and I do not mind waiting. If your relationships grow with the others before me that is okay, too. But may I ask for one thing?"

"Yes! Of course."

His ears flatten against his head. "Would you please not forget me? I have... I have been forgotten once. It was a horrid feeling. I only wish to not be forgotten. Also, if I may have your time and affection every so often," he says in a small voice.

Releasing his hand, I wrap my arms around his middle. "Of course, Chesh. I could never forget you. You are impossible to forget. You also don't have to ask for my time and affection. You can have it whenever you want."

He wraps his arms around me awkwardly as we walk. "What if you are with one of the others?"

"If you ever feel forgotten or left out, I want you to come to me, okay? I don't want you to ever feel like that. Do you understand, Chesh?"

He kisses the top of my head. "I understand, Kitten. Thank you."

"No, thank you for being such an amazing friend. Also an amazing Claimed." I feel him begin to purr as we continue walking down the path into a small town. I feel like I should be calling these males something other than a Claimed. It feels weird. Boyfriend feels wrong, and lover seems too sexual. Would Mate work? I'd have to ask the males once we settled down for the night.

CHAPTER TWENTY-ONE

Alyce

Chesh swings our arms as we walk into the building where we plan on staying the night. I look over and see him smiling widely. I suppose telling him that I could never possibly forget him has put him in a good mood. Looking around the building, I realize that I don't find it as fun as the place we stayed in Clubbz. This place seems a bit formal and stuffy, or maybe sterile is the right word.

The male at the front desk hands a key to Rab and gestures in the direction we should go to get to our room. We follow behind the others, winding through several hallways before getting to the door of our room. I know I will not be leaving the room without one of the guys because I would get lost.

As we enter, I realize the room is set up similarly to the one we had in Clubbz. There are several rooms attached to the main living area. Once we get in and have a quick look around, everyone goes their separate ways until later. Chesh tugs me toward one of the rooms. I look over my shoulder, watching to see which room Rab enters. I'll have to pay him a visit later; I feel like I haven't spent as much time with him as I have with the others. But he's also always leading the group which makes it harder to get to know him like I've been doing with the others.

As we enter the room, I run and jump up on the bed, squealing as I bounce. Sighing into the bed sheets, I lay there with my thoughts.

Chesh slides next to me and lies down beside me. "What's running through that mind of yours?" he asks.

Twisting my head, I look into his eyes. Am I allowed to talk to each of them about the others? Groaning, I say, "I have no idea how this relationship thing works in Wonderland."

He flips over so he's looking up at the ceiling. "Let me tell you a secret, neither do we," he assures me.

I laugh. "That's good to know. I don't know if I can talk to you guys about each other."

Chesh smirks. "Well, ask your question, and I'll tell you if I'm comfortable answering it or not."

He has a point. Flipping onto my back, matching Chesh, I look up at the ceiling. "Do you think Rab would mind if I stayed with him tonight? I feel like I've stayed with everyone except for him. He seems like he wants to be with me, but he's always busy leading us where we need to go. I was thinking that maybe he doesn't want a more romantic relationship with me."

Chesh hums and says, "Well I can tell you that Rab has feelings for you. I have learned a few things about him over the years. Having the ability to control time comes with some great benefits, but it also has its downfalls as well. He has the ability to control time for those he touches, but he cannot control what those people do with that time. Control can be both a blessing and a curse."

"That makes sense."

"After the war, I noticed his need for control got worse. His need to control his surroundings and how things play out during missions. I think the war reminded him that even if he can control time, he doesn't have control over everything."

Sitting up, I look down at Chesh and ask, "So what you're saying is that he has control issues?"

Chesh sighs. "What I'm saying is if you are wanting a more romantic and sexual relationship with him you need to know that his control goes deeper than simply leading us and keeping us safe."

Oh. OH! I feel my cheeks heat. Blushing, I nod. "Okay, so he's dominant in the bedroom. How do you know this?"

He winks at me. "When his control is slipping and he feels out of control, he often needs to boss someone around. Who better than a cat? He doesn't venture into sexual release often because he doesn't want to go too far. I'm a safe option."

If I think too much about that I may bust an ovary. Tugging on the tips of my hair, I say, "Alright, consider me warned."

"If you want to go visit him now you can. I won't stop you."

I look down at him as he smiles up at me. "Are you sure? I don't want to just leave you here."

He sits up, kisses me on the lips softly, and says, "We are all your Claimed. You aren't leaving me behind, just seeking out one of your other males who you haven't spent as much time with."

Taking a deep breath, I stand. "Okay." I rub him between his ears, causing him to purr before heading toward the door.

"Just make sure to share all the juicy details with me tomorrow," he says, laughing. Shaking my head, I leave the room and shut the door behind me. Heading toward Rab's door, I knock and call out, "Rab?" No answer. I slowly twist the knob. Opening the door, I slip through and close the door behind me. Looking around the room, I don't see him. "Rab?"

There's a moan coming from behind the door in the corner. Biting my lip, I debate between leaving or investigating. They are my Claimed, right? Steeling myself, I walk over to the door and knock. "Rab?" I hear another moan on the other side followed by a gasp. I slowly open the door.

Looking around the bathroom, I find Rab's naked form standing under the spray of water. He has one hand fisted on the tile in front of him, while his head is bowed and his ears hang limp in front of his face. My gaze lowers to his tight abdomen, and I see his other hand wrapped tightly around his cock as he pumps fast and hard.

My gaze races back up his body to find one red eye looking at me. He smiles darkly. "Such a naughty little Alyce." He continues to pump his cock, and I instantly grow hot, but I can't look away.

"Should I punish the peeping Alyce?" He pants as his knuckles grow white against the shower wall.

My mouth grows dry, and I lick my lips. "I don't know. Should you punish me?" I whisper.

His eyes close as he tightens his grip on his cock and pumps wildly. "Yes," he growls as his back arches and ribbons of come shoot across the tiled wall. He continues pumping himself as his eyes turn to meet mine. "Do you want to play, Alyce?"

I whine at his deep voice as heat pools between my legs. "Yes."

He grins. "Strip!"

His command instantly makes me rip off my clothes. I'm bare before him within seconds. "Good little Alyce. Now. Run."

I'm confused by the command until he steps out of the tub. He reaches over to the counter and picks up his leather gloves. I watch as he slowly slides each glove on. He smiles and says, "You didn't listen, Little Alyce." Then he races toward me. I squeal as I turn to run. I almost make it to the bed before hands are at my hips, and he's lifting me and throwing me on the bed. I screech as I bounce and flip, so I'm now facing the ceiling. I'm lying in the middle of the bed, and I look up at him. He's looking down at me like a predator, and I'm his prey. Let's be honest, I wouldn't mind him eating me.

He growls, looking down at me. "Such a beautiful Alyce." He crawls up the bed, and I feel his cock rub at my entrance. I moan. He grabs my wrists and pins them out at my sides. I see a flash of my past monsters before I shake them away. No. No! They are not ruining this moment. This is Rab!

"Where did you go?" he asks softly.

I didn't realize I had closed my eyes, but now I squeeze them tighter. "Nowhere."

His lips are suddenly next to my ear, and I feel his breath on my neck. "Where did you go, Alyce?"

I feel him pull away, and I can't hold back my words. "The monsters," I whisper.

It takes a moment before he growls and asks, "Someone held you down like this? Someone hurt you?"

I nod, trying to force the fear away. I feel his grip on my wrists loosen as he caresses his fingers down my arms. He moves my arms above my head before lightly gripping my wrists again. "Is this better, little Alyce?"

I can feel myself calming down, but the fear of being held down is still there. "Yes," I whisper.

"Open your eyes." His voice comes out as a command, but it's a soft command. Opening my eyes, they meet his red ones, and he smiles. "There you are, my beautiful female. Now, who is holding you?"

"You are," I say softly.

His smile turns sultry. "And who am I, Alyce?" He moves his hips so his cock rubs against my clit.

I moan. "Rab. You are Rab."

"Very good. Such a good Little Alyce. And what am I to you?"

"My Mate," I whisper. My eyes grow wide as they meet his. Fuck! I didn't mean to say that. I was going to ask everyone how they felt about that term before I used it.

His grip tightens around my wrist before loosening again as he growls appreciatively. "Yes. I'm your Mate. Do you know what that means, my sweet Alyce?"

I shake my head as he reaches down with one hand and places his cock at my entrance. His eyes meet mine as his ears flop in front of his face. He thrusts into me hard, and I scream. Moving his hand back up my body, he places it right above my shoulder. His other hand is still holding my wrists as he stays buried inside me.

I'm panting as he slams his lips against mine. He nips and bites at my lower lip. As he moves away, he looks down at me and says, "It means that you are mine. Mine to protect. Mine to pleasure."

I pant, "Yes! And you're mine."

He moans as he slides out and thrusts back in hard. He continues at a fast and hard pace until I'm whining. "Please."

"What do you want, little Alyce?"

"I want... I want to touch you," I whimper.

On his next thrust, he slams in deep. "How much do you want to touch me?" he teases. Bending down, he bites one of my nipples, then sucks it into his mouth.

My walls contract around him, and he growls around my breast before releasing it with a pop. "Don't you dare come before I tell you to."

I cry, "Please. I'm so close."

"What did I say, Alyce? Do you want to be punished?" he growls.

"Don't come," I pant.

"Until?"

"Until you say so." Wondering if I can press my luck, I add, "Sir." I've read enough books that I know what happens next. I feel his cock twitch.

He groans and demands, "Say it again." He moves to my other breast and bites down.

I scream, "Sir!"

He releases his hold on my wrist and moves his arm down to pin me in place as he pounds into me even faster. His other hand moves down my body, and he presses his thumb down on my clit. "You have permission to touch me."

I reach up and grasp his ears at the base. He circles my clit with his thumb and then presses down hard as he thrusts into me. "Come, Alyce!"

I scream as I tug hard on his ears. He comes with a shout and slams into me again as my cunt grips him tight. He continues to thrust slowly a few more times. I tug on his ears again and he growls as his cock jerks inside me. "Be careful, little Alyce. My ears are very sensitive."

I smile up at him. "Is that right, Sir?"

He groans, lowering his head until his lips are beside my ear. "You are going to be trouble. But I wouldn't change a thing. You are my little Alyce." He shifts so he can look me in the eyes and says, "You're my Little Rosebud."

I feel myself tearing up as I wrap my arms around his neck. I lift myself, placing my lips softly against his. Pulling away, I smile. "And you are my forever Mate."

He slowly pulls out of me and falls beside me. "Forever? Do you think we will last forever?" His eyes seem a bit haunted as they look into mine. Dark and haunted by the past.

Humming, I reply, "A certain cat told me that sometimes forever can only last a second. So I will hope for as many seconds as I can. As many seconds as I'm allowed. With all of you."

There's a tilt to his lips as he says, "Then I will enjoy forever for as long as it lasts."

CHAPTER TWENTY-TWO

Alyce

"We should reach the Dymondz castle soon," Rab announces from the front.

We continue walking through Dymondz territory, and the Wonderlanders stare at us as we pass. I'm not sure why they're staring at us, but maybe it has to do with the fact that seven males are escorting a lone female through town.

Chesh bumps my shoulder and asks, "So how did last night go?"

I laugh as I bump him back. "You're very curious to hear what I did with another male."

He shrugs. "I'm a cat. It's part of my charm."

I grin up at him. "Yes, it is, Chesh. Alright, but I'm not going to tell you everything."

"So no blow-by-blow?" He wiggles his brows with a wide grin.

I swat his shoulder. "No, I'm not giving you a blow-by-blow, Chesh," I choke out.

Chesh pouts, sticking out his very kissable lip. "Well, that's a shame. I would have loved to hear the details."

I roll my eyes. "Anyways. I walked in on him in the shower."

I watch as Chesh's tail flicks back and forth, and his ears perk up. "Oh! How did that go? Did he invite you in? Did you have shower sex? I'm not a fan of water myself, but that does sound sexy."

"Shh! Chesh, you don't need to talk so loud!" I hear a snort from behind me followed by a chuckle. I look over my shoulder to find Dee and Rook grinning. Whistling tea kettles! What am I going to do with these males? Why did I want to have a relationship with seven males? Oh, that's right, because they are all irresistible.

"It's not as if the others care. We are your Claimed."

Groaning, I say, "Just because they don't mind doesn't mean I want you yelling about it. I'm telling you, Chesh. Not the others. If the others want to know, they can come and ask me. You're my best friend, Chesh, and I want to talk to you about these things. On the Surface, having a best friend is a big deal." Kicking a rock, I sigh and say, "I didn't have friends."

Chesh slips his hand into mine and squeezes my fingers. He lowers his voice before saying, "We are your friends as well as your Claimed. I have not been a best friend before. Forgive me for my behavior, it seems to have upset you, and I do not wish to upset you, Kitten."

I lay my head on his shoulder. "It's a bit of a learning curve. I've gone from having no friends, to having you all as friends, to having seven Claimed males. I've never had a best friend before, but I feel like you are mine. I feel like I can confide in you about anything, and you will always be there for me no matter what. We have a connection."

"It does seem we have a connection," Chesh purrs.

"Like... like soul mates," I whisper.

Chesh's purring increases, but his voice seems hoarse as he whispers, "Soul mates."

I lift my head to peer up at him. His fang is biting into his lip. Brows knitting, I ask, "Chesh?"

His bright purple eyes seem to gleam with unshed tears as they meet mine. He lets out a choked laugh. "I don't know why my chest aches and feels so heavy." He swipes at his face as the tears start to spill over. "I'm sorry."

Capturing his hands in mine, I look around. The others are looking at us with varying levels of worry. "We need a moment. Where can we go?"

Hatter looks between Chesh and me, then nods. He looks around and sees a small building that will block us from view. "Follow me." He ushers us over to the side of the building until we are completely hidden from the others, then turns and walks to the edge of the building. Looking over his shoulder, he says, "I'll guard from here."

Nodding, I switch my focus to Chesh. His ears are flat against his head, his body is shaking, and his tail is wrapped tightly against his leg. My eyes finally meet his, and they are full of fear as he continues to sob, "I'm sorry. I'm sorry. I can stop crying. I can stop crying. I'm sorry. I'm sorry."

Pulling him down to the ground, my knees meet his. I release my grip on his wrists as I cup his face. He flinches as I caress his cheeks with my thumb. I feel my own eyes well up. "Cheshy. Chesh, it's okay."

"Crying makes them forget you. I have to be happy. Happy makes them stay. I'm sorry. I can be happy." He forces a smile.

Oh... oh, my poor Cheshire. "Cheshy, look at me."

"I can't. I can't until I stop. The ache in my chest won't go away. If I can make it go away, I'll be happy again."

"Cheshire, look at me." I make my voice as stern as I can. He needs this. He flinches at my tone but does as I say. "Chesh, you are allowed to cry. I want you to be happy, but I also want you to be who you are. If you feel sad or mad, I want you to feel those things."

His lip quivers. "But..."

"But nothing." I lean and press my forehead to his. "You are mine. My Cheshire. My Claimed. My soul mate. I will NEVER forget you. I will NEVER leave you for showing your emotions."

He sniffles. "Truly?"

I pull away to look into his eyes. "Truly," I repeat.

He mewls as fat tears roll down his face. I pull him closer, wrapping my arms around him tight, and rock him as he allows himself to feel. "My beautiful, Cheshy." I feel myself tear up as he wraps his arms around me tightly. The edge of his claws poke my skin, but I don't let go. I try to think of why the ache in his chest would make him cry. Then I realize it was because I called him my soul mate. He's never heard anyone call him Claimed let alone their Mate.

Biting my lip, I try to force my words not to sound broken as I say, "Chesh, the ache in your chest was because I called you my Mate wasn't it?" I feel his arms tighten around me even more, and he makes another mewling sound. "That ache happens to me too when I think about losing you guys. But also when I think about how happy I am with you. With all of you." I hold him until he calms down. His tail gradually unravels around his leg, and his ears slowly perk up.

He pulls away, wiping at his face. "I am sorry. I seem to have snotted all over you."

I chuckle. "It's alright. It's payback from when I snotted all over you. Remember?"

He gives me a soft smile. "Yes. Thank you."

"For what?"

"For allowing me to be your Claimed. For allowing me to be your Mate."

I lean forward, capturing his lips with mine. I slowly move my lips against his as he does the same. It's soft and sweet. I feel his fingers glide across my cheek as he tangles his fingers in my hair. I pull away to catch my breath. I smile, looking into his eyes, and say, "Thank you."

He arches a brow and asks, "For what?"

"For being my best friend."

"Is that better than being Claimed or being a Mate?"

Pulling further away, I stand and hold my hand out to him. "With you?"

He slides his hand into mine. "Does that make a difference?"

Pulling him up, I switch my grip to tangle my fingers through his. "With you, it does."

His lips tilt into a smile. "Then is it better?"

"With the others, we were friends, then Claimed. I don't like the word Claimed, so I'm switching it to Mate. But with you…" I grab his other hand and place it over my heart.

His eyes widen. "Your heart is beating so fast!"

I let out a nervous laugh and explain, "You were my first. The first person I met. The first friend I made in Wonderland. You were my first crush. You became my best friend. You may not have been the first one I verbally Claimed, but you were the first I Claimed in my heart. When I say you are my best friend, it's a combination of all my firsts."

He grins. "I wasn't your first sexual encounter in Wonderland."

I roll my eyes. "No, but you are the first one to know about them after."

He laughs. "True."

"I want you to know that it means everything to me that you're my best friend. Everything else is an extra bonus to our relationship."

He moves the hand resting over my heart to cup my face. "Then I shall cherish the title of being your best friend."

I grin up at him. "We should probably get back to the others; they are probably worried by now."

He nods. "You're probably right."

We jog up behind Hatter and he looks over his shoulder at us. "Ready?"

Chesh and I look at each other, then look back to Hatter with a smile. "Ready!" we say at the same time.

He nods as he escorts us back to our group. Everyone looks up at the sound of our footsteps. Hatter moves back into his position with Arch. Rab raises a brow and I smile. "Onward, Sir!"

I watch his ears twitch against the back of his head. His eyes darken as he grins and tells me, "Watch yourself, little Alyce." He turns and leads our group back to our original path. Hatter smirks as he pulls a laughing Arch along with him. I briefly look behind me as Chesh and I start to walk. Rook is smirking, and Dee is grinning while wiggling his brows.

Giggling, I face forward again. Chesh bumps my arm and asks, "So... what happened with Rab?"

Laughing, I share what happened with Rab. Blow. By. Blow. What? He asked for it.

CHAPTER TWENTY-THREE

Alyce

I stop on the gravel path and look up. And up. And up. Oh. My. Shattering tea cups. The castle is huge! It's... It's... "Glorious," I whisper. I didn't realize I said it loud enough for the others to hear.

Chesh chuckles beside me. "If you think this is glorious, you should see the Queen of Wonderland's castle."

My eyes snap to his. "Really?!"

He nods. "It's grander than this one."

I look back to the castle. How would the Queen's castle compare to a castle made out of crystal? "How so?"

Dee speaks up from behind me. "The Queen's castle is inspired by each Suit. So the outside has a bit of crystal from Dymondz and stone from the mountains in Spaydz. The inside is inspired by Clubbz, so there are dark wooden floors and doors. And the walls and decorations are inspired by Heartz, so there are some bright colors but also some pastels from the wildflowers."

Wow. It sounds beautiful. I couldn't wait to see it.

"It was hit hard in the war, and no one has been there since the White Queen sealed it shut, so it may not look as grand as it used to," Rook adds.

I shrug. "I'm sure it will look grand if it looks half as amazing in my mind as it does in person." I watch as Rab shakes hands with the guards, then opens the double doors.

As we pass one of the guards, I watch his eyes widen, and then he bows his head before saying, "It's an honor to see you again, Tweedles."

I look over my shoulder and arch a brow. "Tweedles?" I question.

Both males look stiff but nod toward the guard as we pass. Rook is still stiff as we enter the castle, but Dee sighs and says, "I hate when they call us that. I forgot that most of the guards here would remember us."

Bumping Chesh, I whisper, "Does being a Tweedle mean something?"

Chesh sighs, then he explains, "They were born in Spaydz. In Spaydz, your bloodline means a lot. Tweedle is their bloodline. They are the strongest and most sought-after warriors. Dee and Rook were the highest-ranking warriors to come out of Spaydz. They were the honorary Rooks of the White Queen and King until after the war." He briefly looks over his shoulder and then whispers, "They were released from duty when the King lost his life in the war. The Queen had no reason to keep them after his death when she fled to Dymondz. Rook blames himself for the King's death, but it wasn't his fault. Lives are lost in war."

Ah. The conversation I had with him the night I claimed everyone makes sense now. He felt like he failed not only the King, but also the Queen and he didn't want to fail me. Smiling up at Chesh, I pull him down for a kiss. Pulling away, he looks a bit surprised by the kiss. I squeeze his hand. "I better hold hands with the twins through this. They may need a little support." I look over my shoulder, noticing Rook is frowning and still stiff.

Chesh notices my gaze and says, "I believe you may be right, Kitten." He kisses my cheek before releasing my hand. "Go make sure our boys are good."

I nod. Letting Chesh walk ahead, I wait for Dee and Rook to catch up with me. I squeeze myself between them and we keep walking. Dee smiles down at me as I grab his hand and begin swinging our arms. "Did you need something, darling?" he asks.

I smile up at him. "Nope. I figured it may be a little weird coming back here and seeing some familiar faces, so I wanted to show my support."

Dee grins, pulling my hand up to his lips and kissing the back. "Thank you, darling."

Switching my gaze to Rook, I slip my other hand into his and give it a squeeze. He looks at me briefly, then looks back down at the ground. Squeezing his hand again, I ask worriedly, "Hey, you okay?"

Rook gives me a jerky nod. That would be a no, even if he's saying yes. Giving his hand a squeeze again, I wait until he looks at me before saying honestly, "I'm here. I'm not leaving. Whatever happens, won't change the fact that I care about you. You didn't fail anyone. And you won't fail me, okay?"

He looks at me for a moment. I think he's trying to see the truth in my eyes. He must have found what he was looking for after a few moments because I see him visibly relax. He still holds himself like the warrior he is, but the stiffness plaguing him since we got here is gone. He squeezes my hand back softly. "Thank you."

Grinning, I swing our combined arms as well while singing, "We're off to see the wizard! The wonderful Wizard of Oz!"

"We are about to meet with the White Queen, not a wizard of Oz," Dee states, completely confused by my words.

"I know, but I've always wanted to say that. Although, it's sorta like this. It's a completely different world meeting new people."

"What's Wizard of Oz?" Chesh yells from in front of me.

I laugh. "It's a story about this girl who is transported to another world by a tornado. She meets all these people, and they have a mission. They also have to avoid an evil witch."

Chesh hums. "Sounds interesting."

I nod. "You would be Toto, my trusty animal companion." I look between the twins and then at the others. "Hum. None of you really fit the other characters. I suppose the Red Queen could be the evil witch, but other than that..." I shrug.

"Interesting." Dee laughs.

"So I guess I should say we're off to see the White Queen, the wonderful White Queen of Wonderland." Wow, that doesn't have the same ring to it. It's also a mouthful.

"Yes. I suppose you could say that," Rook says as he smirks.

Rab clears his throat. "Now that we have come to that conclusion, are we good to continue? I believe the Queen is waiting on the other side of these doors."

I stand up straighter, ripping my hands out of the twin's hands and running them down my leathers. I'm about to meet a Queen! I look at the males around me. "Do I look okay? I should have worn a dress or something. I don't look fancy enough to meet a Queen," I ask as I ramble.

Rook and Dee tug my hands back into theirs. Dee smiles and answers, "You look beautiful, darling."

"Like a warrior," Rook says, squeezing my hand. "Which is better than looking like a Queen."

"Unless you're a Warrior Queen; I think that's even better," Chesh adds. He grins. "It's a good thing you're our Warrior Queen."

I roll my eyes, but I grin at him. "I'm not much of a warrior considering I can't use my magic or a sword or fight much."

Hatter shrugs. "Who says you have to be able to do all those things to be considered a warrior?"

"Everyone?"

"Are you asking us or telling us?" Rab asks, crossing his arms over his chest.

Feeling my cheeks heat, I change the subject. "Can we just go inside to meet the Queen now?"

Rab shakes his head. "Not until you admit you are a Warrior Queen."

"Fine! I'm a Warrior Queen."

Hatter snorts. "That didn't sound convincing at all."

"Say it with some confidence, Mouse." Arch says, smiling at me.

Rolling my eyes, I repeat, "I'm a Warrior Queen."

Chesh furrows his brows. "That was even less convincing, Kitten."

I square my shoulders and stand tall. "I'm a Warrior Queen."

Rook squeezes my hand. "Better."

"Now say it louder," Dee adds.

Taking a deep breath, I yell, "I AM A WARRIOR QUEEN!"

"Much better, little Alyce," Rab says, smirking as he turns and pushes open the double doors for us to enter.

Shattering Tea Cups. The Queen is several feet away in the center of the room hovering over a table, but her eyes are on us as we enter. And she's smiling. She pulls away from the table and says, "What a way of greeting." Her voice is ethereal, with a touch of command behind her words. I can see how she commands and leads people.

Rab bows his head before saying, "Thank you for meeting with us, White Queen."

She waves her hand in the air dismissing his words. "Every rebel is welcome in this territory." A male dressed in armor comes around and takes her hand as he guides her down from the elevated dais the table was on. He kisses her hand briefly before releasing her. I can see the love and adoration this male has for the female in front of him. His eyes shift from her back to us, and they harden.

She smiles. "I am also no longer the White Queen. A few years after the war, the ruler of this territory left the mantle to me when she passed." She looks to her side at the male and then back at us. "She passed after losing her male in the war. It can be heartbreaking to lose the love of your life."

The male beside her places his hand on her lower back and leans in close to kiss her cheek. She sighs and says, "Thankfully, I was blessed with two males. The passing of the White King was heartbreaking, but the White Knight has helped soften the blow. He has allowed me to continue my mission to stop the Red Queen's rule."

She glances at the two males by my side, smiling sadly at them. "I did not wish to release you from your duty. But I couldn't bear the thought of having the two of you continue to guard me when you could benefit the rebels so much more."

She glides over to stand in front of Dee and says, "You were an amazing guard, and I appreciated your company more than you know."

Dee bows his head. "It was an honor to serve, White Queen."

She laughs as she ruffles his hair affectionately. "You have grown so much since we last spoke. I am pleased to see you haven't lost the playful spark behind your eyes." She switches her attention to Rook and sighs as she moves to stand in front of him.

"I heard you have changed your name."

He nods, keeping his gaze fixed on the floor. "Yes, White Queen. I am now called Rook."

She smiles sadly. "Rook. I see." Sliding her forefinger under his chin, she raises his gaze to hers and says, "Rook, you were also an amazing guard for my husband. He cherished his time with you. He often spoke fondly of swordplay with you. I do not blame you for his death. The thought has never once crossed my mind to blame you."

Rook's hand tightens in mine as he clears his throat. "I was his guard. It was my fault he fell in the war," he says gruffly.

The White Knight moves to stand beside the Queen and replies, "My brother in arms was not a male who sat back while others fought. He might have been the King, but he fought alongside his people as well. He died a warrior's death. He died fighting for his people." He slaps a hand on Rook's shoulder. "He would not want you to blame yourself for his death."

Rook looks between the Knight and Queen and gives a jerky nod. I saw the gleam in his eyes as he tried to control his emotions. I knew he needed this. To be released of a burden that was no longer his to bear.

The Queen's eyes turn to me, and she smiles softly. "Is this the Warrior Queen that was yelling in my hall?" she teases.

My cheeks blaze as I reply, "Yes, White Queen."

"I feel I must address this since it seems to be continuing. I am no longer the White Queen. I am the Empress of Dymondz." She turns and heads toward the large throne in the corner. She spins and sits down before asking, "Now, what can the Dymondz do for you?"

I look toward Rab since he is the leader of our group. He raises a brow at me, and I gesture for him to take over. He smirks and explains, "Empress, we are needing to access the Looking Glass in the Queen of Wonderland's castle. Alyce passed through but wishes to make contact with her brothers before joining the fight in the war."

The Empress looks me over. "Are you sure she is who she says she is?"

The twins bristle beside me, but I speak up before they can say anything. "How would you like for me to prove to you who I am?"

She taps a finger to her lips, thinking. "Having the name is convincing, but I know for a fact that the Queen of Wonderland escaped through the Looking Glass with a weapon. The legend of the original Queen of Wonderland has been passed down to each Red and White Queen to assure our rule. The sword was called the Vorpal Sword. Do you have this weapon?"

My brows knit together as I think. I remember my necklace. I had taken it off the moment I got into Wonderland, putting it in my bag so it wouldn't get lost. This morning was the first time I had thought about it since coming to Wonderland. I had an overwhelming feeling that I needed to keep it on me today instead of in my bag.

Pulling the necklace out from under my shirt, I unclasp it and hold it out for her to see. "I've had it for as long as can remember. It hasn't changed size, though."

The Empress squints but then smiles. "The Vorpal Sword. It will change size once you inherit the Queen's powers."

"So I will have powers?"

She nods. "The Queen of Wonderland was one of the most powerful magic users in Wonderland. We will need to train you with a sword so you are familiar with the feel of one until the Vorpal Sword returns to size. We will also need to do some exercises to ensure that the magic does not control you once it is released."

"The magic can control me?" I ask, biting my lip in worry.

"Yes. Magic is very dangerous, and it takes years of training to learn control. Most Wonderlanders start at a young age before their powers ever manifest. As a Wonderlander the magic will grow as the male or female gets older. You have the unfortunate luck of having no experience and will have the power of an adult. It will be overwhelming and can cause you to go into magic overload."

"So when should we start training?" I ask.

She stands from her throne. "We will train as we travel to the Queen's castle. Rook and Dee will be the best warriors to show you swordplay. Between Rab, Mor, and I, we should be able to show you how to control the magic and give you exercises to make sure the power doesn't overwhelm you."

Wide-eyed, I ask, "So you are going to lead us to the castle?"

She says something to the White Knight and turns back to us. "I am the one who sealed the outside of the castle, so you will need me to access the Looking Glass." She grins. "I also have not been outside of this castle in some time. I am looking forward to the adventure. What better way to help the rebels than by helping the future Queen of Wonderland? "

Queen of Wonderland?! That escalated quickly. Though, the others have been saying that's what I am. I'm the future Queen of Wonderland. The blood of the original Alice runs through my veins. Whistling tea kettles! I did say I wanted to find where I belonged. But Queen? Queen was not on the list of possible possibilities. Though it wasn't on my impossibilities either.

She smiles as we make our way out of the throne room. "Also, I lied when I implied that I didn't know who you were," she admits.

I arch a brow. "How so?"

"Only a descendant from Alice can come and go through a Looking Glass. It's part of the magic. I locked up the castle so my sister could not destroy the mirror in her control of Wonderland."

I arch a brow. "So only a descendant of Alice can come and go through the Looking Glass?"

She shrugs. "That is what I have been told. Though, I have also heard that the magic of the mirror will allow others through so long as the Queen of Wonderland allows it."

Wow. This is a lot of information to digest. It makes sense though. The original Alice wouldn't want her enemies to follow her to the Surface. Taking a deep breath, I follow the others outside of the throne room. I may not be a Queen now, but I am a Warrior Queen, and Chesh did say that was better, right?!

CHAPTER TWENTY-FOUR

Alyce

I was severely exhausted after my mental exercises with the White Queen. I was going to continue calling her the White Queen in my head because calling her Empress felt weird. She had said it would be easier to work on mental exercises while walking, and once we got to a spot to settle for the night, I could work on sword fighting. I haven't gotten to the sword fighting yet due to being too exhausted the last two days.

My original thought was, how hard can mental exercise be? The answer... hard. Very hard. My first exercise was how to control my emotions during high-stress situations. The lesson consisted of breathing techniques and coming up with mental thoughts to calm myself. How could that be hard, you may ask? Well, Chesh would walk beside me as I was going through the exercises and swipe his tail lightly across my skin. It was VERY distracting.

The Queen didn't help. She just laughed and said that distractions are part of everyday life, and that I would have to find a way to fight past the distraction. She also taught me how to look for my magic within. She described how her magic felt and explained, "Yours will feel different, though. All magic is different. Magic often reflects who the person is. For example, Mor. His magic most likely feels fluttery and light, whereas Rab's magic would probably feel solid and have a constant beat like the ticking of a clock."

I nod, thinking. I remember the tug I used to get in my chest before I fell through the mirror, but since then, I haven't felt much. "I haven't felt anything since I got to Wonderland. But before, it always felt like a tugging in my chest."

She hums thoughtfully. "Then I would look inward, toward your center. Close to your chest. If that was where the tugging started, that's where your magic is located."

Tangling my hand through Chesh's, I close my eyes. I don't want to trip while walking in front of a Queen. How embarrassing would that be? But closing my eyes has helped me focus more. Trying to focus on anything that feels different, I try to remember how the tugging felt and where I felt it from. Suddenly, I feel a small warmth in the center of my chest. Like a small flame.

Opening my eyes, I say, "It feels like a small flame."

She smiles. "It may be small now, but that small flame is capable of becoming an inferno. It's slowly being fed the magic of Wonderland. But once it has fed, it will try to take over. Magic is like a living, breathing being. It experiences your thoughts and emotions. That's why strong and out-of-control emotions will cause your magic to spiral."

"So... I need to have a symbiotic relationship with my magic? Like venom?"

Her brows crinkle. "I am not sure what this term is or this being."

Shaking my head, I reply, "Sorry. Surface stuff. Um... So my magic and I have to live together in harmony. I depend on it for survival, and it depends on me to... I don't know... not die?"

She chuckles. "I suppose that's one way of looking at it. The magic doesn't exactly have a mind of its own, but it feeds off of the magic of Wonderland to make you stronger. It's reactionary if you have heightened emotions. If you are angry, you often want to cause damage to your magic and will respond by causing destruction. If you are scared, the magic may create a shield to protect you."

I nod. "That makes sense, I guess."

From the front, Rab announces, "We can settle here for the night. We should be able to reach the castle by the end of the day tomorrow." The males begin setting up the tents and starting a fire for the night.

"I will see you in the morning, Alyce." The Queen waves as she makes her way to the twin's tent.

Groaning, I turn toward the twins. I need to at least get the basics of sword-fighting down. I've seen stuff on the internet and in movies, but real-life fighting is different, I'm sure.

Rook runs into Rab's tent and returns with a shorter but still long sword. Ah, that's where they've been keeping their stuff. I was wondering where they've been sleeping since the Queen and the Knight have been staying in their tent.

He hands the sword over to me, hilt first. "The Vorpal blade is meant to be held by a female. Unfortunately, we do not have any blades for a female on us. This is the lightest blade we have."

I take the sword from him. It's lighter than I thought it would be. Backing away, so I don't accidentally cut anyone, I hold it up with two hands. "This is lighter than I thought it would be."

Dee smiles. "Good. Alright, we are going to teach you some basics."

Nodding, I lower the sword but make sure the tip doesn't touch the ground. "I'm ready!"

Rook unsheathes his own sword. "First, the point of the sword is the tip of the sword. Then you have the short and long edges of the sword. The short edge is on top. It's not sharp, so it's the false edge. The long edge is on the bottom and is sharp; that is the true edge. Those are the parts that make up the blade."

I nod, following along and looking at my own sword as a reference.

Dee speaks up, "Next is the hilt. The hilt is made up of the cross-guard, grip, and pommel. Your dominant hand needs to be under the cross-guard, and your non-dominant goes under that." When I don't change my grip, he nods. "Now, using your left hand, grip the sword tightly with your pinky, ring, and middle finger. Your other fingers should have a semi-tight grip on the sword."

Changing my grip a bit, I do as I'm told and nod for them to continue.

Rook steps up and demonstrates as he explains, "There are eight angles of attack: straight down, straight up, diagonally down to the right, diagonally down to the left, diagonally up to the right, diagonally up to the left, and left and right strikes horizontally."

Now, ladies, I'm not proud of what I'm about to admit. But... watching him demonstrate the sword moves? I didn't realize watching a male in a tight-cloth shirt doing sword moves was such a turn-on. Negate that statement. Of course, it's a turn-on! But imagining it and seeing it are two VERY different things. I drop my sword, and it clatters to the ground.

I scramble to pick it up. My eyes meet theirs, and I can feel myself blush. "Um... that was... that was a great demonstration. I think I learned so much."

Dee laughs. "Did you now, darling? What exactly did you learn?"

Straightening, I point my sword in his direction. "That I could totally fight you!" No. No, I could not fight him. I was just making this up to cover my blunder of dropping the sword. He knew that, and I knew that.

Suddenly, there's a whoosh of breath across my ear. "Could you fight both of us?" Rook's rough voice asks, sending shivers down my spine.

"Yes," I squeak. Well, that was convincing.

He chuckles as he kisses the side of my neck. "I don't think she will be able to handle this sword, brother."

I look up into Dee's eyes and smirk. "If I remember correctly. I was amazing at handling your swords."

His eyes sparkle with mischief. "Do you now? Are you sure you were handling the swords and not us?"

I lower my sword. With one hand, I reach behind me and caress Rook's thighs. His gasp against my neck makes me grin. "I remember handling one sword very well." Rook growls against my neck as I shift my hand away from his thigh and into his teal hair. I tug, and his hips pump forward against my back. I can feel how much he's enjoying this sword fight.

Dee's usual light and playful voice changes, and he mimics Rook's growl. "Maybe you should remind us of how well you handle our swords," he teases.

Tugging on Rook's hair again, he nips my neck, and I gasp, "Gladly."

I'm instantly thrown over Rook's shoulder before he stomps off toward Rab's empty tent with Dee following us. He throws me onto the bed, then they both strip.

I'm here to say that I proved my point when I made those males roar several times that night. I'm amazing at handing swords. No worries, though. They proved they could handle swords just as well.

"It's too early to walk," I whine. I really miss coffee. That is the first thing I am bringing back from the Surface. Tea doesn't cut it. Although Rab does make an AMAZING cup of tea. It isn't strong enough to wake a woman who was thoroughly plundered by two swords until the early hours of the morning, though. No regrets, though.

Chesh bumps my shoulder and teases, "Did you stay up too late, Kitten?"

Bumping him back, I laugh. "Yes. But it was totally worth it."

Chesh snickers. "I would have to agree, considering the satisfied grins those two have been wearing all morning." He points to the males behind us.

I look over my shoulder to find that both Dee and Rook have, as Chesh described, satisfied grins on their faces. I turn back to Chesh, rolling my eyes. "They said I didn't know how to handle a sword." Shrugging, I say, "I obviously proved them wrong."

"I think they proved they know how to handle swords as well." He points at my face. "You've got the equivalent satisfied grin on your face."

Laughing, I swat at his hand. "Fine! You're right."

The Queen hustles up beside me with a smile. "May I ask why the Tweedles are in such a good mood this morning? I have never seen them so happy before."

I blush instantly. "Um... well... you see..."

Chesh yowls in laughter before choking out, "She handled their swords."

I slap Chesh on the chest and turn back to the Queen. "Excuse him! He has no manners."

The Queen's brows furrow. "How would handling their swords make them happy?"

Chesh yowls even louder, and I don't think I can possibly get any redder.

Her eyes shift between Chesh and me, then they brighten. She covers her mouth as she giggles. "I see. Their swords."

I groan, covering my face. Just kill me now! I feel a gentle hand on my shoulder and look up to meet the Queen's soft gaze. "I am happy that they have found a female. You seem to be an honorable female, and I am happy you see their worth as males."

I furrow my brow. "They are amazing males. Why would I not see their worth?"

She sighs and explains, "Many females would judge their worth due to their rank. Tweedle males are extremely sought after due to their bloodline. If you include their ranking in the warrior cycle, many females would claim them simply because of that. You see them as males and only males. You do not see the bloodline or the rank." She looks over her shoulder, smiling as her eyes meet mine. "They are honorable males and deserve to be loved."

I study her for a moment and realize she's serious. She respects these males. I grin. "Thank you." A thought zips through my mind, and I bite my lip before asking, "May I say something? It may be a bold statement."

Her eyes brighten with intrigue. "I do love it when people are bold with me. Go ahead."

"I think we should be friends. I've never had a female friend before, and I think you would be a great friend to have. Also, I seem to be surrounding myself with several males. Don't get me wrong, Chesh is amazing to talk to, but having a female friend to talk to as well..." She interrupts me with a soft laugh.

Chesh snickers beside me. "She tends to ramble when she's nervous, Empress."

She smiles. "I see that. If I may also be so bold in saying that I would be honored to call you a friend. I also do not have many female companions."

I sigh. "Sweet."

"But if you are to call me friend, I would like you to call me Bianca instead of Empress. That way we are not calling each other by titles."

Nodding, I agree, "Deal."

The hours of walking go by quickly as Bianca and I talk and work on my mind exercises. Before I know it, I'm standing in front of a large stone and crystal castle. The males were right. This one is even grander than the Dymondz castle.

The Empress stands in front of the castle pressing her hand against the cold stone. "Give me a moment to undo the seal," she says.

We sit there for a few moments before there's an audible pop, then a whoosh of magic slides past us.

She smiles and turns to me. "All yours, Future Queen of Wonderland."

CHAPTER TWENTY-FIVE
Alyce

Walking up the stone steps of the castle, I'm trying to control my breathing. I'm caught between hyperventilating and holding my breath. I'm afraid. I don't know what it will mean if the Looking Glass is in the room at the top of the stairs. As we get to the top, I see the doors to the Queen's Quarter. They are ornate with golden filigree and the symbols of each Suit in the four corners. I'm at the door before my next blink, knob in hand. What if it's in there? Does that mean I have to leave and not come back? But what if it's not in there? Does that mean I won't be able to go home?

I feel a hand slip into my hand. "It'll be fine. No matter what," Chesh whispers beside me. I squeeze his hand in gratitude as I fling the door open. I look around the room to find a large bed. Wow. That's big enough for me and all the guys to fit on. Though, they did say that the original Alice had multiple lovers. I continue to sweep the room until my eyes meet the reflection of a mirror in the corner. It's a replica of the one I have in my room on the Surface.

Huffing out a breath, I release Chesh's hand and make my way toward it. Standing in front of it, I see my reflection shimmer, and then the blurry image of my apartment comes into view. I can't make out anything, but I know it's my room. I'm about to touch the surface but hesitate.

"What's wrong, Mouse?" Arch asks from behind me.

"I'm scared," I whisper.

Hatter comes up beside me. "What's to be afraid of?"

"What if this is all a dream?"

"A dream?" Rab asks.

Sighing, I tell them, "I've dreamed of Wonderland for so long. I've dreamed of you guys. What if I've gone mad, and this is all just a dream?"

"Didn't Chesh already tell you?" Dee asks, laughing.

The reflection shimmers again, so I can see all the males behind me. "Tell me what?" I see Chesh grinning as he bumps shoulders with Rook.

Rook rolls his eyes but gives me a smirk. "We're all mad here."

"Aren't the best people mad, though?" Arch asks, laughing.

I smile at all of them as I touch my fingertip to the mirror. The image wavers, showing me a blurry image of my apartment again.

Hatter slips his hand into mine. "Would it help the madness if I came along?"

My eyes widen. "You would go with me?"

He shrugs and replies, "We are planning on coming back with your brothers in tow, right?"

I nod, assuming the others are right and I can choose who gets through. Taking a deep breath, I push myself through the Looking Glass.

As I come through the other side, I have to hold in a gasp. All of my brothers are in my apartment. The mirror had been moved so that it was in the sight of the bed. Alix is asleep on my bed while Laurel and Edi are asleep on an air mattress on the floor.

Hatter follows through the Looking Glass behind me, his hand still in mine. "Who are these males on the floor?" he whispers.

"My brothers." My voice cuts out on a whimper.

"Ah, the ones on your mobile device."

Alix is the first to jolt awake. He looks around the room, rubbing his eyes. His eyes meet mine and widen. Rubbing his eyes again, he jumps up from the bed. "Alyce?" he asks as if he's not sure if he's really awake or not.

I nod, biting my lip to hold in the sob trying to escape.

He trips over the air mattress as he runs toward me. I let go of Hatter's hand as Alix pulls me into his arms and lifts me off the floor. My arms wrap around his shoulders as I hold him close. He doesn't put me down and my feet dangle above the floor. "You came back," he says, his voice breaking with each word.

"I promised, didn't I?" I can feel my eyes stinging with tears.

"I missed you so much, baby Sis," Alix sobs.

Alix had turned me enough so that I can see Laurel waking up from Alix tripping over their mattress. He looks around the room, confused until his eyes land on me. "Alyce!" he yells, jumping off the bed. That startles Edi awake, but I'm not able to see his reaction because Laurel tackles Alix and me to the ground.

Laurel's hand grasps the back of my head as we fall. We all let out a grunt, but Alix and Laurel refuse to let go. Laurel looks into my eyes and grasps the back of my head more firmly as he places a kiss on my forehead. Then looking into my eyes, I see the pain of my leaving reflected in his. "I was so scared when you went through that mirror," he tells me.

"I'm sorry," I whisper.

Shaking his head, he presses his forehead to mine as I see tears seep between his lids. "It's my job to protect you. It's my job to keep you safe." His voice breaks on the last word.

"You have, Laurel. You've been amazing. But I'm an adult now as much as you wish it otherwise," I say with a watery laugh.

He snorts. "I know. But it's still hard."

I feel another body land on top of us, and the air whooshes out of me. "Oh, whistling tea kettles! You guys are going to suffocate me!"

"Suffocate you with love! This is the consequence of leaving your brothers behind!" Edi shoves in between Laurel and me to place a sloppy kiss on my nose.

"Gross." I laugh.

"Need some help, Sugar?"

I roll my eyes at Hatter's question and the name. He knows I hate it, which was why he continued to use it. "I'm fine, Tar."

The guys must have been distracted by me because I notice all their heads shift to look at Hatter. Well, this is going to be fun.

"Who's the odd guy, Aly?" Edi questions from the top of the smash-Alyce-pile.

I groan. "Well, if all of you would get off of me, I could do introductions and explain why we are here," I sass. My brothers all shift so they can roll off of me. Hatter makes his way over to me, and I can see his smirk as he looks down at me.

"You should be glad it was I who joined you through the Looking Glass and not Chesh. I think he would have joined your brothers in smooshing you."

Rolling my eyes, I hold out my hand for him to help me up. "He would have called it a cat pile," I joke.

Reaching down, he pulls me up. "Or a cuddle pile. You know how he loves to cuddle."

Laughing, I smooth down my shirt. "You're probably right. Anyways, boys, this is Tarrant."

He grunts, "Sugar cube."

Ugh. "Fine! Apparently, I'm the only one who can call him that. This is Hatter. Hatter, these are my brothers Laurel, Edi, and Alix." I point to each brother as I say their names.

"Still doesn't answer the question of who this is." Laurel points at Hatter.

"Um... well. He's..." Before I can come up with something other than a lover, Hatter cuts in.

"I am one of the members of her harem," he states confidently.

Alix makes a choking sound as he laughs. Yep, I expected that. He did mention he's read all the same books I did. Which would include the reverse harem books. Unfortunately. I send him a glare. "Shut up."

He laughs. "Oh, come on! With all those books you read."

"What books? What's a harem?" Laurel looks lost as he tries to follow our conversation.

"I believe Alix is referring to the Alice books she reads. I'm assuming a few of them included reverse harem," Edi answers.

"That still doesn't answer the question of what a harem is and what that means for this bulky dude and our sister!" he yells out frustratedly.

Palming my face, I rub at my temples. Males. Why did I choose to start dating seven males? I send a glare over my shoulder at Hatter, and he holds his hands up, looking innocent. Innocent, my butt. The gleam of mischief in his eyes tells me otherwise. Sighing, I say, "The meaning of harem isn't important, but I'm in a relationship with multiple men."

"At the same time?" Laurel sounds horrified.

Raising a brow and crossing my arms over my chest, I stand taller. "Yes. At the same time."

"There's our Queen of Wonderland," Hatter whispers behind me. He sounds proud, which makes me stand even taller.

Laurel looks between Hatter and me. Standing taller himself, he spits out, "I won't have a bunch of guys passing my sister around like a whore!"

It's my turn to choke. Whore? Hatter comes up beside me. I can hear the anger in his voice as he says cooly, "Sir, I don't care who you are. I will not stand anyone speaking about our Queen in that manner." I shiver as he growls out the last part. What is it with these males and growling!?

"A Queen? So all these guys treat her like a Queen?" Laurel asks, sounding unconvinced.

I see Edi and Alix step back as Hatter moves in front of me, blocking Laurel from view. Damn it! Now I can't see anything! I tug on his shirt, but he refuses to move. Alpha male asshole. Tilting to the side enough so that I can see around Hatter, I see Edi and Alix with wide eyes. I give them a grin and a wave. They both shake their heads and laugh. I notice Hatter shifting into a fighting stance, so I put my hand on his shoulder. "You don't have to defend my honor, Tar."

Hatter peers over his shoulder, a glare on his handsome face. "He implied you were a whore!" he spits out the last word.

Rolling my eyes, I explain, "He's just being an overbearing brother." I raise onto the tips of my toes and kiss him on the cheek. "I wasn't offended."

He looks at me for a moment before sighing. "As you wish, my Queen." He shifts so I can stand beside him. Damn, you know Hatter is serious whenever he calls me Queen.

"Thank you." I brush my lips across his.

His eyes soften, "Can we go back home?"

I smile. "So you want me to stay in Wonderland?" I tease.

His brows furrow. "Of course!"

I rub the space between his brows and ask, "With you?"

Grabbing my wrist, he presses a kiss to my palm. "Yes," he whispers gruffly. I shift my hand enough to stroke his cheek, and he presses his hand against mine.

"How long would you like me to stay?" I ask quietly.

His gaze meets mine, and I can see the broken shards he's tried to hide. The fear of someone leaving him again. Of being left behind. Of being alone. He lowers his forehead to mine, whispering, "Forever, my Queen."

"How long is forever?" I whisper back.

He pulls away, looking into my eyes. Releasing his grip on my hand, he places his calloused hand against my cheek and strokes my cheek with his thumb. "Sometimes, just one second. If I am only allowed this moment." I watch his throat dip as he swallows down the emotion plaguing him. "If you choose to stay here and never return to Wonderland. If I'm only allowed this moment with you. This one second in time. I'll take it gladly."

Oh, my poor angry male. The one who fought the hardest not to get too close. Afraid of being alone. "You would have this moment with me. This one second, over never meeting me?" My eyes sting with emotion. He wouldn't, would he? Take the pain of losing someone compared to never knowing they existed? I've heard the saying. It's better to have loved and lost than to never have loved at all. But a male who has lost so much? Felt so much pain? Would he really wish for such a thing?

He presses his lips against mine, and I can't stop the tears from falling. It's soft and gentle but filled with so much emotion. He pulls back, wiping away my stray tears. "A second with you is worth a millennium without. I would choose you. Every. Time."

I move as quickly as I can, pressing my lips to his. It's a bit more forceful than I meant it to be, but I pour every bit of affection I've felt for this male since I first met him into it. Threading my fingers into his hair, I pull away. I make sure he is looking into my eyes and say, "I love you, Tar." I should have told the others how I felt before I left, but I was so afraid of this being a dream. I'll make sure to remedy that when we get back.

He grunts before sweeping me up into his arms. My legs dangle off the floor as he holds me in a tight hug. Why do I surround myself with so many tall males? His face is buried in the crook of my neck. "Truly?" he whispers.

I hold him close. "Truly."

"I love you too, Alyce," he whispers.

There's a throat clearing, and that's when I realize our entire heart-to-heart was in front of my brothers. Shattering tea cups! I pull away from Hatter, glancing at his face. It's slightly pink, making me grin. Embarrassed Hatter is an adorable look.

He grunts, "I'm still calling you Sugar."

I laugh as he places me gently on the ground. "I would expect nothing less." Turning to face my brothers, I say, "So I was going to ask you a question."

Edi bumps Laurel's shoulder. "I don't think you have to worry about these harem guys treating her like a whore."

Laurel grunts, "Yeah, we will see."

Rolling my eyes, I continue, "Anyways... My question. Would you guys like to travel to Wonderland and help defeat the Red Queen and put your sister on the throne instead?"

Alix throws his fist in the air. "Fuck yeah! I'm in. I don't care what's going on."

I grin and look at my other brothers, raising a brow.

Edi grins and says, "I'm in for an adventure." He elbows Laurel. "Don't act like you're not coming. You'll come just to interrogate these guys Aly's dating."

"It's not like I had anything important to do anyways," he mutters.

Clapping, I turn to Hatter. "You want to go through, and I'll meet you on the other side?" He looks panicked when I mention going after him. I grip both sides of his face and say softly, "I'll see you on the other side. I promise."

He taps the glass, and it shimmers. This time the image on the other side is much clearer. I can see the others pacing back and forth, and it makes me laugh. "You better get back there and let them know everything is okay." He nods, giving me one last look before passing through the Looking Glass. I watch him settle on the other side. The others rush him, and he points behind him at the mirror. All gazes look back at the mirror, and I give them a wave. They all visibly relax.

Edi saunters up next to the mirror, looking at the males and then back at Laurel shaking his head. "I can't believe you thought they would treat her like a whore." Then, without instruction, he pushes himself through the glass. I watch as he wobbles for a second and then turns with a laugh. He's looking right at me. He grins, pointing at our remaining brothers on this side. I can't hear what's going on on the other side, but I can read his lips, "It's your turn, bitches."

I roll my eyes. Leave it up to Edi to make it a competition. I look at my remaining brothers and ask, "Who's next?"

Alix sideglances Laurel then makes a mad dash to the mirror. "Last brother through is a rotten egg!" I watch as he runs right through the mirror and then tumbles to the ground on the other side. I see Edi bend over, laughing, and I see Alix on the ground throw his arms into the air in the universal, I'm okay gesture.

That makes me giggle. "Alright, Laurel, it's your turn." I look over to find him wide-eyed.

"This is real?"

Holding my hand out for him, I say, "Yes."

His hand shakes as he grasps mine, murmuring, "This is madness."

I grin a Cheshire worthy grin. "Didn't you hear? We're all mad in Wonderland."

CHAPTER TWENTY-SIX

Alyce

The moment I walk through the mirror, I release my brother's hand and run toward Chesh. He grins, catching me as I jump at him. "Hey, Little Kitten, we missed you," he says, purring into my neck.

"I wasn't gone that long."

His purr deepens. "A second without you here felt like an eternity in cat time."

I laugh, pulling away. "Is that so? It's a good thing I'm back then."

"It's purrfect."

Pressing my lips to his, I tug on his ears. He lets out a rumbling growl, and I grin against his lips. "I realized something while I was on the Surface for all eternity." I pull away enough to look into his eyes and watch as his pupils dilate, then contract back into slits.

"And what was this grand realization that took an eternity to find?"

I press my lips against his cat ears and say softly, "I love you, Chesh."

He mewls against my neck. Pulling away, he presses quick kisses all over my face, and I laugh. "Chesh!"

He places one last kiss on my lips and replies, "I love you too, Little Kitten."

I grin as I whisper, "I have other greetings, Chesh."

He growls, pressing a kiss to my nose before setting me on the ground. I turn to see the rest of my males already surrounding me. I laugh. I suppose I'll go around the circle they made.

I move to the next male. "Rook." I notice that he's removed his armor, then see that Dee has also removed his. I point to both of them and ask, "Why did you guys take off your armor?"

Dee laughs as he shifts so that he's now behind me, and Rook is in front. Is this going to be a twin sandwich?! Before I can ask what's going on, they smash me between the two of them. "So we can do this," Dee snickers.

"If you guys thought I would be against being smashed between two deliciously sexy males, you both thought wrong. Twin sandwich love!" They shift so that they are resting their foreheads on each other's shoulders. I'm short, but I feel extra cocooned in the hug with them like this.

I shift my head enough that my lips are pressed against Rook's ear, and I whisper, "I love you, Rook." I feel him try to pull me closer, but I can't get any closer, I'm already completely squished between the two of them.

He shifts his head enough that I can see his teal eye, his purple one still hidden in the shadow. "I don't feel worthy enough," he admits.

I press my lips against the corner of his and say sternly, "What happened in your past does not define your future. You can't go back to yesterday. You were a different person then."

He sighs, but I can see the tilt of his lips. "As the Queen decrees, so shall it be." He presses his lips against mine. "I love you as well, Aly."

Smiling, I twist to press my lips against Dee's ear. "I know you feel like I have to love you because I love your brother. That you feel like you're a package deal, and I won't love you for who you are." I nip his ear, and he growls, turning his head enough so I can see his purple eye, the teal one still hidden in the shadows. Capturing his gaze, I say, "I love you, Dee. Not because I love your brother, but for who you are as an individual. I see you and your brother as separate people. I may love you both, but you both show how you care in different ways. You contribute to this relationship in a different way that's all your own."

Closing his eyes, I'm cut off from seeing his reaction to my words. When he opens his eyes again, I see the gleam of emotion in them. His warm lips roughly meet mine, and I know he's trying to show me how much my words meant to him. I know the fears he hides. The females of Wonderland have treated these males horribly, and Dee's greatest fear was he would always be the "get one free." That he was the extra male attached to Rook because his brother would never leave him behind.

"I love you, Alyce. I am honored to be a male you count on. A male you have chosen to love." His normal light and playful voice sounds deeper at the moment.

I press a quick kiss to the corner of his lips. "I'm honored you've chosen me."

They both give me a quick squeeze before releasing me from my twin sandwich.

I shimmy my shirt back down; twin sandwich equals rumpled clothes. Not a complaint you will hear me making, though. I move toward Mor next as he smiles at me.

"Welcome back, Butterfly."

"It's great to be back." I say, sighing as I inhale his fresh rain scent. This male could serenade me to sleep with his smell alone.

He wraps his arms around me in a gentle hug. "I am glad you came back safely."

Pulling away slightly, I shift onto the tips of my toes so I can reach his lips. Pressing a soft kiss to his lips, I whisper, "I love you, Mor."

He smiles against my lips. "As I you, my beautiful Butterfly." He shifts, placing his lips against my ears. "You'll find that we all do."

He releases me as I walk to my next male. "Rab."

He gives me a wicked grin. "Yes, Alyce?" As I walk toward him, I notice he's removing his gloves.

I stop midstep. "You can't touch others without your gloves."

He shakes his head. "I can, but only with certain people."

"You've never touched me, though."

He notices that I'm not moving, so he begins walking toward me. "You are correct."

I stand motionless, but he's close enough to touch. I press my fingers against his chest to stop him from getting closer. "You will have a clock on your skin for me if you do this?"

He nods. "I will."

I shake my head and say, "No. I'm not worth the price of the clock on your skin. That clock will be there forever, Rab."

"You are worth any price," he whispers. He reaches out to touch my cheek, but I grip his wrist.

"Forever, Rab. With every broken clock, your life is shortened. You already have too many broken clocks. I won't be another broken clock to add to your shortened life."

He laughs. "You have seven males looking after you. We won't let you die in this war, Alyce." I look into his red eyes, and I can see his determination. This is his way of making sure I'm safe during the war. It's the only way he knows how to protect me.

I sigh, releasing his wrist. "Forever, Rab."

His soft, bare hand meets my cheek. He hisses, and I can see the pain etched on his face. Using his other hand, he unbuttons his shirt as he keeps eye contact with me. He opens his shirt enough for me to see the new tattoo etched into his skin.

I gasp. Reaching out a tentative hand, I caress the new tattoo over his heart. It's a blue rose with a clock face. I watch as the hands tick away.

Rab's thumb softly caresses my cheek, "Forever and always, you will be with me."

I look back into his soft red eyes and say, "I love you."

He smiles as he bends down, pressing his lips firmly against mine. Pulling away, he replies, "I love you, too."

I press my lips roughly against his once more, then reluctantly pull away, remembering his bare hands. "Put your gloves back on. I don't want you accidentally touching anyone else."

He laughs. "Yes, my Queen."

Turning, I head toward Arch but remember. "Also, no more touching people without me knowing."

"So I shouldn't touch Mor?" he teases, but I can hear the laughter in his voice.

Turning, I glare at him. "Gloves on unless you already have their clock, understood?" He gives me a half-assed salute, and I can't help but laugh. Back on my original path, I find Arch standing next to Hatter.

I watch his ears twitch as he winks at me. "Glad to see that Hatter didn't break you. Did you two enjoy venturing to the Surface, Mouse?"

Looking up at him, I stand on my tiptoes to reach for one of his ears and tug on it. He groans. Laughing, I caress his ears. "I had a blast, Arch. Were you good while I was away?"

His half-lidded gaze meets mine. "I was the best Hare you ever saw, my Queen." His voice sounds breathy as he lowers down to the ground on his knees. I can hear the others in the background ushering my brothers out of the room. Smart idea. I already completely forgot they were here. Arch runs his hands from the back of my calves up my thighs and settles them on my ass.

Now that his head is level with my upper abdomen, I reach for his other ear, tugging it lightly, and he groans. "What do you think, Tar? Do you think he was a good Hare?"

Hatter laughs as he pulls a chair over from the corner and settles onto it to watch the show. "I'm sure he'll say he was a good Hare, but how are we to know?"

Humming in agreement, I tease, "He does have a point, Arch." I bite the tip of his ear between my teeth as I tug. His grip on my ass tightens as he shoves his face into my skin to dampen the sound of his whine. "I think you were a good Hare. A very good Hare. I think I should reward you."

"Yes, my Queen," he whimpers.

Keeping my grip on his ears light, I order, "Remove your slacks, Arch." I have never seen a male rip off his clothes so fast in my life. I grin as I see that he went commando. His cock is currently standing tall and proud, seeping with pre-cum. "What a good Hare."

His hands find their way back to my ass and squeeze. He's panting now. "Always for you, my Queen."

Looking over at Hatter, I say, "Come over here and join the fun."

He raises a brow and then shrugs. Pulling off his shirt in one of those manly one-armed moves they do so effortlessly, he makes his way over to us and asks, "Where would you like me, Sugar?"

"Behind Arch. Grip his cock for me." Hatter nods. Lowering himself to his knees, he shimmies up behind Arch. He nips Arch's neck before reaching down and gripping his cock roughly. Arch whines, pulling my shirt into his mouth as he bites down. Hatter begins a slow pace as he milks Arch's cock. He moans around my shirt, and I tug on his ears so he's looking at me.

"Now, Arch, I want you to remove my underwear." I order, grinning as he moans at the thought. He moves his hands under my skirt and pulls my underwear down. I step out of them, and the cool brush of air instantly makes my hot cunt pulse with moisture. I moan, "Now eat me like I'm the last dessert you will ever get!"

Without further instruction, he shoves my skirt up and impales my wet cunt with his tongue. I scream, gripping his ears tight as my legs suddenly turn to jello. I hear a scraping sound and open my eyes to find Hatter moving the chair he was sitting in. Placing the chair behind me, he orders, "Sit."

Arch pauses as I sit. Once I'm seated, he grabs my hips again and positions me so that my ass is barely on the seat. Before I can say how that isn't going to help, he throws my legs over his shoulders with a devilish smirk. "Trust me?" he asks.

Hatter has moved back behind Arch and continues pumping Arch's cock. Arch moans as he settles his face back between my legs. He raises a brow at me, and I realize I didn't answer him. "Yes."

"Good." He slowly lowers his head and sucks on my clit. I reach back up and grasp one of his ears as my other hand tangles in the hair between his ears. I pull him deeper into me, wanting to find the climax I was so close to reaching before he stopped. Fuck, this is so much better than a vibrator! Not realizing I closed my eyes, I open them and look down to find Arch's heated eyes on me. I feel his fingers between my thighs before he thrusts a finger into my wet cunt.

"Yes!" I yell, trying to push myself deeper onto his fingers. He gives a few slow thrusts before adding another finger. He curves them just right, and I explode with a scream. Breathing heavily, I look down to find Arch grinning. I shift to sit further back onto the chair before he grips my hips, stopping me.

"You thought we were done?"

I arch a brow. Well I came, wasn't that normal? A woman orgasms, and it's over. "Well, I came. Isn't it your turn?"

Both Hatter and Arch laugh darkly. Arch pulls me back to my original position and says, "The fun isn't over till you are thoroughly pleasured out of your mind."

"But what about you?"

He looks confused. "What do you mean?"

"You're pleasuring me, but what about your pleasure?"

"Me? Pleasuring you is my pleasure," he replies. I tug on his ear before he can lower himself.

"I want you to get satisfaction out of this too," I tell him.

He looks over his shoulder at Hatter who has stopped pumping him, then back to me. "What we are doing is fine."

I realize he's afraid to ask for what he wants. I look up at Hatter and realize he is, too. It occurs to me that they've never added a female into this dynamic before, and I realize that the offer they gave me was a front to make sure I didn't still judge them. Reaching for Hatter, he stands and hovers over Arch's shoulder. I can see the bulge in his slacks. I beckon him closer with a grin. When he's close enough, I grip the back of his head and thread my fingers through his hair. Tugging roughly, I drag him toward me, so my lips smash against his.

He's motionless for a moment, and then he threads his fingers into my hair. I bite his lip, tugging as I look up at him. His eyes are dark and filled with lust. Pulling away, I look down to see Arch watching us. His breathing is quick. The tip of his tongue peeks out and wets his lips. "You want to kiss him, don't you?" I can see him ready to say no out of habit, but I give him a smile and say, "He is a great kisser." I move back to Hatter, slamming my lips to his. I press the tip of my tongue against the slit of his lips begging for him to open. There's a slight hesitation on his part, but then he opens up for me, and I plunge my tongue into his mouth, tangling my tongue with his. The grip he has in my hair tightens as he moans.

The fingers of my other hand find Arch's ear, and I tug. He groans as he moves a hand between my legs, finding my folds. I tug hard as he plunges two fingers into my needy cunt. I pull away from Hatter, nipping at his bottom lip in the process. Releasing the grip I had on Arch's ear, I encourage the two males to kiss. I press Hatter's face toward Arch's. They both look at me and then at each other. Arch hits a spot that makes me moan. I look at the two males, still hesitating as they look at each other. "Kiss. Please."

Hatter makes the first move as he lowers himself and presses his lips softly against Arch's. I groan as I tighten around Arch's fingers. As if the moan was encouragement enough, Hatter's hand snaps out and grips the back of Arch's head. I watch as Hatter's tongue pierces the space between Arch's lips. Watching these two males kiss, fuck! I feel myself tighten around Arch's fingers again, and he stops, pulling his fingers out. I whine in disappointment. He pulls away from kissing Hatter and shoves the fingers that were inside me into Hatter's mouth.

"Taste her. Doesn't she taste better than any dessert in Wonderland?" Arch's gruff voice makes me tighten around air, making me whimper.

Hatter sucks Arch's fingers clean and says, "She is delectable. You should enjoy her while I fuck you, Arch." I watch Arch's eyes widen, then grow hooded.

"Do it!" I whine in frustration. I am so close!

Hatter grins. "Very well. I'll need lube." Without hesitation, he reaches over Arch and shoves two large fingers into my aching cunt. He gives two hard thrusts before I'm coming all over his hand. "Seems Arch worked you up without following through." I'm not sure what came out of my mouth, but I think it was a bunch of garbled words that didn't make sense through my pleasure-hazed brain.

Trying to catch my breath, I watch as Arch positions himself in front of me and bends as Hatter comes up behind him. "Better get in position, Arch because I'm worked up something maddening. This will be hard and fast."

Arch moves so his face is in between my legs again. Throwing my legs over his shoulder once more, he wraps his arms around the top of my thighs. "Ready."

Hatter's cock glistens with my come that was all over his hand. He positions his hand on the top of Arch's ass and circles his hole with his thumb. He presses his thumb in, massaging the hole.

Arch is panting as he looks up at me. His eyes are glassy with pleasure as he says, "You can hold onto my ears."

I meet Hatter's eyes, and he smirks. "Tug his ears right as I shove my cock in. He'll love it."

"Don't! I'll come too quick," he whines.

I thread my fingers through his hair, stopping at the base of his ears. "We will build you back up. Be a good Hare and let the pleasure consume you. Embrace the madness."

I look back up to Hatter, and he nods. I adjust my grip on Arch's ears and watch as Hatter positions himself with his cock at Arch's entrance. I tug roughly on Arch's ears as Hatter slams all the way into him with one thrust. Arch yells as ribbons of come explode from his cock.

Hatter grunts, "Such a good Hare, Archy."

"Such a good Archy." I praise as I stroke his ears. His glassy eyes meet mine, and he shivers as the last bit of come rolls down his erect cock.

"Better get into position to pleasure our Queen before I start fucking this ass," Hatter pants, and I watch as sweat rolls down his face. His grip on Arch's hips tightens as he forces himself not to move.

A glassy-eyed Arch shoves his face in between my splayed legs. He nips and sucks on my clit. Groaning, I wrap my legs around his head, forcing him closer. His gruff laughter tickles my hot and achy cunt. "Please," I whimper. Arch plunges his tongue inside me as Hatter pulls back and thrusts deeply into Arch. Arch moans and the vibration heightens my pleasure.

"More," I pant, "I need more!"

Arch shifts his hold on my thighs enough that his thumb pushes on my clit. I cry out in pleasure, but it's still not enough. My head rolls back onto the chair, and I tug harder on his ears, needing more.

Hearing Hatter's grunt, I open my eyes to find him. I can tell he's close, too, but he wants me to find my pleasure first. He pounds harder into Arch, his knuckles turning white from the tight grip he has on Arch's hips. "If you're not going to fuck her, I will," he grunts, emphasizing his statement by pulling out of him, and then thrusting back in hard.

Arch grunts against my cunt. He looks up at me, and I whimper, "More! I need more." He shifts his arms from around my hips and places them on the ground. "Hatter, stop," he pants. Hatter pauses his thrusting with a growl.

"Get off the chair," Arch orders me. I let go of his ears as he reaches for his discarded slacks and wipes his come off of the floor below him. Throwing the slacks away, he looks back at me and demands, "Under me now."

I lie on the ground and shimmy myself underneath him. I can feel the tip of his cock at my entrance. He glides his cock into my pussy, and I almost come from the feeling. Yes! I groan, and reach up for his ears again.

Panting, I say, "You have control of the fucking, Hatter."

Hatter shifts a little closer. With his hands on Arch's hips, he pulls Arch's cock out of me as he glides into Arch's ass. His laugh is gruff. "Be careful when you ask for more, Alyce. I'm going to fuck you with his cock." That's the only warning I get as Hatter forces Arch's hip down, making his cock thrust into me.

I moan. "I want it fast and hard, Hatter. Can you handle that?" I ask as I tighten around Arch's cock, and he swears.

"Fuck, the way she clamps down on my cock. I'm not going to last long in this position."

Hatter laughs. "Challenge accepted, my Queen." He begins to fuck Arch's ass hard, and I can feel every thrust.

Our moans and grunts meld together until Arch's cock hits just the right spot, and I explode. Arch follows with a yell, panting into my neck. With one last thrust, Hatter follows with a roar.

Hatter pulls out of Arch slowly and falls to the ground on my right. He's panting, and I look to see come still seeping out of his cock. Damn, this male had a lot of come. I watch as his softening cock hardens again. Damn, and a short recovery time.

Looking back up at the male hovering over me, I tug on his ears to bring his lips down to mine. I feel him pulse inside me once again as he moans around my lips.

"If you haven't noticed, my ears are very sensitive."

I grin. "I did notice."

He smiles down at me, and I press my lips to his again. Pulling away, I look into his eyes. "I love you, Arch."

Pressing his lips to mine again, he pulls away, beaming as he says, "I love you, Mouse."

CHAPTER TWENTY-SEVEN
Alyce

To say that I'm not embarrassed as we walk out of the Queen's chamber would be a lie. And to say I'm embarrassed would be an understatement. The moment we open the doors, all eyes swing to us. Covering my face, I mumble, "Seriously?! None of you could find anywhere else to be other than right outside the door?"

"I enjoyed hearing what was going on," Chesh says as he grins.

"This is new territory, and this castle is unsecured. It's best we stay together," Rab reasons.

I peek between my fingers and look around. The Empress is missing along with the Knight. But, unfortunately, my brothers are here with the males. Huffing, I pull my hands away when I see Rab smirking. "You couldn't send my brothers with the Empress and the Knight?!"

Rab shrugs. "They refused to leave without you."

Groaning, I look over at my brothers. Alix has a shit-eating grin on his face, while Edi looks torn between awe and disgust. Laurel... Oh, Shattering Tea Cups. He looks like he wants to murder the two males beside me for touching me. I can only imagine what they heard in this hallway.

I raise a brow. "Seriously? You chose to stay and listen to your sister have sex instead of joining the Empress?"

His mouth opens for a second, then closes it as his face turns red. He's about to say something, but Alix interrupts him, "Impressive. Who knew our little sister was so dominant."

Laurel chokes on what I assume is spit, and Edi slaps a hand to his face before yelling, "Fuck, Alix! I had to listen to her have sex for the last few minutes. I do not want a recap of everything! Fuck, there isn't enough bleach in the world to scrub away the mental images nor the noises coming out of that room."

"You didn't have to stick around," I screech, embarrassed.

Edi points a finger at me. "Well, I can assure you I will not be making that mistake again!"

Alix just laughs and says, "I think Laurel is about to self-destruct."

I look over to find that my brother does indeed look as if he is about to explode. The vein in his temple is pulsing. Huffing, I march over to him and stab him in the chest with my finger. "I am twenty-one years old. I am allowed to have sex! You are not my dad. You are my brother, so start acting like it."

He sputters, "I am not acting like Dad!"

"I didn't say like Dad. I said you are acting like A dad. Two different things. You old man."

"I am not old!"

I smirk and tease, "You're like what? Twenty-nine. You're almost thirty. You're old." Edi and Alix cackle with laughter beside me.

He looks between the three of us and rolls his eyes. "Whatever. You three act like children."

I push past him, walking down the stairs that lead out of the Queen's chamber. "This child will kick your butt in a sword fight."

He yells after me, "Yeah! Well... well..."

"That's what I thought, old man." I laugh. I can't help but smile as I make my way down the stairs. Fucking with my brothers is a little sister's full time job. Damn, I missed them. I can hear Alix and Edi yelling old man jokes as they follow behind me. My smile widens even more. Yep. I missed the fuck out of them. And that's saying something considering I try not to cuss.

We make our way outside to where the tents are already set up for the night. I look around, thinking this land has to be somewhat secure. The Red Queen would have to know that her sister has wards up around this castle. As soon as that thought crosses my mind though, I am proved wrong. I hear a loud screech and jump at the sound then a loud roar shakes me to the core. I look up into the air and find a large swarm of black dots. Jabberwocky. Wonderful. A roar sounds again and looking toward the noise I see Bandersnatch running toward us from the Heartz border.

I am not prepared for this. Yeah, I've been practicing my sword fighting, but it's been with the sword Dee gave me. I don't have that sword on me. I only have the Vorpal sword, and it's still small. I haven't been able to get my magic to change its shape. Even if I could get the sword to change shape, I'm severely lacking when it comes to the actual use of a sword during a fight.

How did they get here so fast?! Then I realize that the wave of power released when the Empress removed her seal on the castle must have alerted the Red Queen that this territory was no longer protected.

I look around to find all of my males preparing to fight. Rab is already running toward the advancing Bandersnatch holding a sword in each hand. Mor shifts into his cursed form, taking to the skies to fight the swarm of Jabberwocky converging on us. Chesh shifts into his cursed form as well, following Rab to join the fight. Hatter and Arch rush in the opposite direction. Hatter starts throwing hat pins as Arch guards his back, shooting several rounds from his pistol. Rook and Dee form a tight circle with Bianca and the Knight to guard my brothers.

I feel my magic crackle behind my chest, but I smother it. In my lessons, I've been taught not to let my magic control me, instead that I need to control it. Taking a deep breath, I let just enough magic flow through me, hoping it finally cooperates with me. As if my magic knows this is a life or death situation, the small sword necklace suddenly transforms into a big, long sword. I let myself feel the brief elation that it finally worked before shaking off my emotions and focusing. I take the stance Rook taught me and ready myself to fight for my life.

I wait for a Bandersnatch to run toward me. I haven't mastered running while using a sword yet, so I'll have to fight the only way I know how. It opens its large maw to attack, and I slash upwards cutting across its thick neck. Warm blood sprays my face, and I'm surprised by the color as I look down at the dark yellow blood covering my chest. I wonder if Mor and Chesh would bleed a normal color or if they have the same colored blood as these beasts due to their cursed forms. Shaking that thought away, I try to focus once more. I'm panting as I carve through another beast. Gulping down a breath, I take a second to look around.

All of my males are covered in yellow and red blood, including Mor and Chesh. I guess that answers that question. Hissing, I stab the head of the Banderstanch that took advantage of my distracted state. I shake out my arm not holding the sword, and look down to see a large gash running down my forearm. That will teach me not to get distracted in battle.

I look up quickly when I hear a shriek. My eyes widen as a Jabberwok dives down at me. I crouch down, lifting my sword over my head as I scream. But before the Jabberwock touches me, a blue-scaled Jabberwock snatches the other Jabberwock about to attack me. Mor! I watch as he shakes the Jabberwock as if it's a toy. He shakes it until the neck of the beast is severed, and its body falls to the ground. Mor throws the head away and looks down at me as he beats his wings. He makes a chirping sound as he tilts his head to the side. I grin up at him and say, "I'm fine. Thank you for the save."

He makes a louder chirping noise, and I laugh. "I'm fine, I promise. Go help the others." I make a shooing motion at him. He grunts at me, then flaps his wings, spinning to fight off the dwindling number of Jabberwocky in the sky.

I quickly glance around me to take note of everyone and how many more beasts we have left to fight. Noticing that Rab and Chesh are now heading to help with the few beasts attacking the circle around my brothers, I shift my gaze to find Hatter and Arch still fighting off a few beasts, but they seem to be handling it fine. My attention snaps back as a growl sounds beside me. I quickly crouch as a Bandersnatch jumps at me. I lift my sword upward as he jumps over me, and yellow blood rains down over me as the Bandersnatch falls beside me.

My gaze returns to my brothers as the others kill the last beast. I hear a guttural bellow in the direction I last noticed Hatter and Arch and my stomach drops. I quickly turn to find Arch screaming as he shoots several rounds into a Bandersnatch that is now lying beside Hatter on the ground. I hear the thump of each round as Arch shoots until his gun clicks empty. He screams again, the guttural sound making my heart drop as he falls beside Hatter on the ground.

My breath quickens as I run. As if knowing that I no longer need it, my sword returns to necklace size, and I shove it into my breast pocket. I hear the others yelling behind me, but I ignore their voices as I run. I ignore my body's protests as my thighs and lungs scream in pain. Nothing matters except getting to Hatter.

I slide as my knees hit the now-wet ground. It's soaked in blood. Hatter's messy black hair is on full display as his hat lays in a puddle of yellow blood beside him. His head is laying in Arch's lap, and Arch is softly brushing the messy hair off his sweaty brow.

Looking down at Hatter, I see a bloody gash running from his chest to his abdomen. I want to scream and cry. It's pouring blood. I look up to meet Arch's eyes, and I can tell from the tears tracking down his dirty face that this isn't good.

"It's okay, Hatter. We got you," he whispers.

Hatter coughs and bright red blood sprays across my face. Fuck. FUCK! What do I do? What do I do? How did this day go from being amazing to nightmarish so quickly?!

The Empress slides up on his other side. "Okay. Okay. We don't have any equipment here to heal him properly," she says as her eyes meet mine. "This is going to be all on you."

My eyes widen in shock and fear. "Me?"

She nods and explains, "You can feed him some of your magic to help him heal. It won't be pleasant for him, though."

I shake my head. "I've only now started learning how to use my magic. I can't do this, Bianca!" A hand rests on my shoulder offering me strength.

I look over to find Mor smiling gently down at me. "You've got this Butterfly."

Biting my lip, I look back at Arch. He gives me a weak smile and nods. Eyes lowering, they meet Hatter's. The light in his eyes is slowly dimming as he gurgles in his attempt to breathe. He's looking at me, and I can see that he's trying to talk. "Don't talk, Hatter."

He gives me a bloody smirk and starts to mouth, "I... I love..."

"Don't you dare say you love me right now like you are saying goodbye!" I scream. "Our forever isn't done yet! I will fight time itself for more seconds with you, Tar! Do you understand!?" I can feel tears streaming down my face, but I don't care. I will not allow this male who has finally allowed himself to have a relationship with Arch and me, to die.

His nod is shaky. He moves his hand from the ground to grip my thigh, giving it a weak squeeze.

Huffing out a breath, I look to the Empress and beg, "What do I do?"

She smiles as she looks between Hatter and me. "Alright. We need to place something between his teeth so he doesn't cause himself any more damage. This is going to hurt."

Alix rushes over, unbuckling his belt. It slides through his belt loops and he quickly hands it to Arch. "From personal experience, I find a leather belt is the best when you need something to not bite through."

Arch raises a brow but takes the belt. Folding it in half, he places it between Hatter's lips. When Alix doesn't elaborate, Arch's gaze moves to me. He quirks a brow and I groan, "We had a complicated childhood." Arch just nods, his gaze moving back to Hatter.

"Alright, Alyce, you are going to place your hands on his sternum." Bianca adjusts my hands the way she wants and says, "Good. Now the hard part will be trying to control the magic. Heightened emotions will make the magic want to take over, so strong emotions like fear, anger, and even love will make it harder to control. You will need to try and stay as calm as possible."

I nod, taking a deep breath. Calm. Calm. I can totally handle that. Closing my eyes, I take another deep breath focusing only on Bianca's voice.

Her voice sounds like a whisper as she continues to instruct me. "Now I need you to focus on that flutter of power inside of you. I know you can feel it."

Latching onto that whisper of power in my chest it lashes out. I grip it tightly, taking a deep breath in and letting it out slowly. Controlled and calm. I can feel that it still wants to fight me, but I have a solid grip on it as I whisper, "Got it. Now what?"

"Slowly let the warmth of that power seep into your arms, then into your hands as it flows out of your fingers."

Nodding, I pull the power from my chest, letting it fill me with warmth. It still wants to fight though, and I can feel it thrashing, wanting to be let out. Then, suddenly, there's a hand threading into my hair, tugging. "Focus, Little Alyce."

Rab's bark and tight grip help ground me as I take control of the power again, letting it flow through my arms and into my hands. My hands feel like they are suddenly on fire as the power seeps out of my fingers. Hatter's body jerks suddenly and his grip on my thigh tightens to the point where I'm biting my lip not to match his screams. I refuse to open my eyes because I know I'll stop the moment I see the pain in his.

I hear Arch's crying increase as he whispers words I can't hear over Hatter's roars of pain.

I can feel the stickiness of his blood coating my hands as he thrashes and a copper tang fills my nose. I fight not to gag, pouring as much power as I can into Hatter. His death grip on my thigh suddenly loosens and he quiets. I feel the power wanting to take over at my sudden panic that he's dead. That I couldn't save him. The grip in my hair tightens and I hear, "Focus. He's just passed out."

I'm feeling slightly light-headed when Bianca finally says, "Stop. He can heal the rest on his own. You will pass out from magic overload!"

I fight with my magic for what feels like hours when finally the magic is sucked back into a tiny flame inside my chest, and I gasp for air. The pressure on my head is gone and my eyes shoot open. Looking down, I instantly regret it. My hands are covered in red and my vision blurs as it mixes with the past. My hands are covered in blood as I pull them away from my carved abdomen. No. No! Shaking my head, I'm looking back down at Hatter's marred skin.

Panting, my vision blurs again, and I scream when a hand lands on my shoulder. I scramble to the side trying to get away from the hands as I huddle into myself and start rocking. I can hear murmuring and some raised voices, but I can't understand what they are saying over the thumping heartbeat in my head.

I flinch when I hear Laurel's voice. "Alyce?" he calls gently. I tighten my grip around my legs, trying to get the dark visions to go back where they belong. I hear his soft voice in front of me. "Hey, Aly. Can you look at me?"

I shake my head, no. I need the memories to go away.

"Hey, Sis. We need you to look at us okay?" Edi softly whispers at my side.

I finally look up to see Laurel crouching in front of me. He has a sad smile on his face as he says, "Hey, kiddo. I'm going to touch your face okay?"

I nod as I whimper. Please make it stop. Make the memories stop.

He slowly reaches out, cupping my face. "We are going to help okay? Edi and Alix are going to help, and you aren't going to take your eyes off of me okay, kiddo?" I feel them each pulling at my arms. I turn to look, but Laurel turns my face back to his. "You keep your eyes on me, remember?"

I feel Edi and Alix wipe my arms with something soft. It makes me wonder what they have. How? Then I watch Laurel grab something from over his shoulder. A brightly colored towel. Where did they get the towel? Laurel wipes my face as the others scrub my hands.

My heart rate starts to slow, and I can feel the haze and panic ebb away. Then I remember the blood. The blood was from Hatter. Hatter! My eyes jerk to Laurel's, "HATTER!" I scream.

Laurel grips my face tighter. "He's fine, Aly. Arch took him to their tent. We are more worried about you right now."

My eyes wander, and I realize the others are all watching me. Bianca nods to me and turns, walking away with the White Knight. Aside from Arch and Hatter missing, the others are all staring. Dee and Rook are standing behind me as if guarding to make sure no other threats attack. Mor looks worried as his wings seem to flutter in rapid succession. Rab looks as if he wants to murder someone. Although, he was the one who noticed my fear of being held down. I'm sure my instant panic over the blood AFTER I healed Hatter and my scream at being touched clued him in as to why. And Chesh, my poor Chesh is tugging at his ears as tears stream down his face.

My voice wobbles as I whisper, "Cheshy." He instantly shifts into the size of a house cat and runs into my lap. Realizing I'm still covered in blood, I yell, "Chesh, the blood!" I pull my arms out of my brother's hands to try and stop Chesh.

Mewling, Chesh continues running at me. "I don't care!"

Sighing, I pull him into my arms. I hold him close to my chest as he shoves his face into my neck. "I'm sorry," I whisper.

I must have said that loud enough for the others to hear because I see my brother's eyes harden. He opens his mouth to say something, but Rab interrupts him.

"What do you have to be sorry about? You saved Hatter's life. You shouldn't be apologizing for anything."

"I'm sorry I freaked out because of the blood." I look into his bright red eyes. "The monsters were too much."

"And what did I tell you about those monsters, little Alyce?" he asks.

"That... that we would fight them together."

"Correct, little Alyce." He looks at the males surrounding us. "So let us fight them with you."

I watch as Laurel looks around at the others as well. I see the small smile he's trying to hide. His gaze meets mine as he says, "I like them." He leans forward and kisses my forehead. Pulling away just enough to look me in the eye, he adds, "But I'll still kick their asses if they break your heart."

I let out a watery laugh. "I would expect nothing less."

"I suppose I need to pass the torch of your care to them now," he grunts.

I look between him and my other brothers. "I'll always need my big brothers, that won't ever change," I tell Laurel.

I can see his eyes glistening, but he gives me a smile. "Good because you can't get rid of us that easily." He looks at Edi and Alix. "I suppose we should get to the tent and settle down." His eyes meet mine as he whispers, "I'll give you the privacy you need to tell them what you need."

My eyes widen in surprise. "Really? Thank you."

He shrugs. "You were right. I need to start acting like your brother and not your dad, as you put it." Standing he says, "The twins said we could use Mor's tent for the night. They said we couldn't use the Castle till it was secured."

Alix kisses me on one cheek as Edi kisses the other, and it makes me laugh. "Love you, Sis," Edi whispers as he follows Laurel.

Walking backward in their direction, Alix grins. "Love you, Sis."

I watch them until the flaps close behind them. Sighing, I ask, "Do you guys mind if we talk in the tent with Hatter? I want to make sure he's okay."

The twins come up beside me and each grip an arm, gently pulling me up from the ground as I hold onto a still-weeping Chesh.

Rab nods. "Let's get you cleaned up first, Rosebud."

Giving the males a half smile, we head to Hatter's tent. I try to sort out my thoughts and how I'm going to tell them the story of my greatest nightmare. This wasn't going to be fun. For anyone. But they deserve to know.

CHAPTER TWENTY-EIGHT

Alyce

Chesh refuses to leave my side as I bathe. He's lying next to the bath as the others wait behind the makeshift curtain. Hatter was sleeping when I entered, and Arch was wiping him down with a cloth.

"Are you okay, Kitten?" Chesh whispers. He's now in male form, head lying against the edge of the tub as he looks at me. His face is still dirty, and I can see the path his tears took as they rolled down his face. His eyes are red-rimmed and shadowed.

Sitting up, I reach out and wipe the dirt from his face. His breath hitches as he closes his eyes. The tips of his canines bite into his lip as more tears escape. "Cheshy. Are you okay?"

His hand comes up and grips my wrist holding my hand against his cheek. He rubs his cheek against my palm. "I was so scared when Hatter got hurt. I thought we were going to lose him."

"I know, Chesh. He'll be okay now."

He nods and opens his eyes, focusing on me. His normally bright purple eyes seem so dark. "You screamed. You screamed when I touched you. I thought I hurt you." His voice breaks at the end.

It was he who touched me? Oh. Oh, my poor Chesh! "Chesh, you would never hurt me! I know that. My head was stuck in the past."

He presses harder into my palm. "You backed away, and my chest hurt so bad. I don't know what I would do if I hurt you, Kitten."

I jump out of the tub and pull him into my arms. I know I'm completely naked and he's covered in dirt and blood, but I don't care. "Chesh, you would never hurt me!"

He pulls away, looking into my eyes. "But what if I hurt you the way the person who hurt you did?!"

I grip both sides of his face so he's really looking at me. "You would NEVER hurt me the way they did. NEVER Chesh! Do you hear me?"

He must see something in my eyes because slowly he nods. He looks down and gives me a small smile. "I may have made you dirty again."

I look down to find myself covered in dirt and blood again. Laughing, I jump back into the bath, rinsing off before grabbing a towel. Holding out a hand, I decide to get this over with. "Let's go sit down, and I can tell everyone what happened."

He nods, taking my hand. The others follow behind as I tuck the towel in at the top and sit on Arch's empty bed. Looking around at the others, I watch as they take spots around the tent. Mor and Chesh sit beside me on the bed while the twins continue standing guard at the tent's opening. Rab stands at the end of Arch's bed looking down at me. He nods for me to start.

Looking over to find Arch sitting next to Hatter as he lies in his bed, I'm surprised to find him squinting at me.

I gasp, "Hatter you're awake!"

He groans, "Keep your voice down, Sugar. I'm awake enough to listen, not function. My head hurts."

"Sorry," I whisper.

He smirks. "Out with it, Sugar. I know you're trying to stall."

I huff out a sigh. "Fine. When I was younger it was hard for me to make friends. My family had the reputation of going mad. My mother was in the mental institute, and my dad had already left. So that left my older brothers to watch over me. Laurel had finally received custody of us and was working all the time to provide for us. Edi was on the football team and was trying to get a scholarship to college. Alix and I had just turned thirteen, and Alix was trying to make friends. Since he was my twin, and we were usually always together, he often got teased because of me."

Shifting on the bed, I slide my hands into Mor's and Chesh's. Sighing, I continue, "Alix had finally made some friends and was meeting with them after school. This left me to walk home by myself. I had stayed around school a bit, and a few girls from my class asked me to play with them. I didn't know at the time that it was a trap. They had asked me about my mom, and then suddenly, I had several people holding me down."

Fighting off the memories that want to surface, I shake my head and continue, "One of the girls lifted up my shirt and carved psycho into my abdomen." The males around me growl, and I jump, startled.

Chesh scoots closer to me and rests his head on my shoulder. He begins purring. "It's okay. You're safe," he murmurs.

Feeling the vibrations of his purring throughout my body, I relax. I close my eyes and continue my story. "I passed out from the pain and then woke up outside by myself. I ran as fast as I could to the Principal's office and told him everything. He questioned the girls I remembered being there and said that he couldn't do anything about it. I knew that. They were rich and would find a way out of it no matter what. He called my brother, and within minutes, he was there slamming the door open. I'm pretty sure he broke every traffic law to get to my school that fast."

I grin, remembering. "I was so proud to be his sister that day. He sued the school for everything it was worth. I had laser treatments done once the wounds healed." Pulling my hands out of Mor's and Chesh's, I open my towel to reveal my smooth skin. "It took several treatments, but the scars are no longer there."

"The mental ones are still there, though," Rook grunts from the front of the tent.

I nod. "Yes." Looking toward Rab, I say, "Being held down triggers my memories."

His ears droop as he rasps, "Which is why you freaked out when the plants held you down, and when..."

I nod, looking over to Hatter, I say, "The blood is a new thing. I didn't know being covered in blood would trigger the memories."

Hatter growls, "Don't you dare apologize!"

Suddenly feeling overwhelmed, I bite my lip and say, "So now everyone knows. Would you guys mind if I went to sleep now?"

Chesh and Mor kiss my cheeks and say goodnight as they head toward the entrance. Rab walks over to me and kisses the top of my head. "Get some sleep, Rosebud."

I nod. Rook and Dee hustle over quickly, each kissing a cheek at the same time. They pull away. "Sleep well, darling."

Realizing I was in the same tent with Hatter and Arch, I flip over in the bed to face away from them. The weight of today slams into me hard. Tears spring to my eyes as I slip under the blankets and cover myself completely. Hiding, I bite my lip to stop the sobs wanting to escape.

"Sugar, come over here."

I suck in a silent breath and mumble, "I'm fine."

Hatter grunts. "Either you come over here with Arch and me, or we are coming over there."

I stay silent, hoping he'll think I'm asleep. I hear a grunt followed by Arch cursing. I rip the covers off and look over to find Hatter sitting up. Arch is giving me a pleading look. Sighing, I jump out of bed and slide into the bed next to Hatter. I press a hand to his chest. "I'm here. Now lie down."

He nods his approval as Arch snuggles back down into his other side. I lay down facing Arch, and I can see the worry in his eyes. I close my eyes and fight the emotions and tears. I open my eyes when I feel soft fingers caressing my cheeks. Arch gives me a sad smile and says, "It's okay. Let it out."

I bite my lip as I feel fingers tangle in my hair and massage my scalp. Hatter's chest vibrates as he growls and says, "I'm okay. I'm alive. I'm here."

"Tar…" I whisper.

"Let it out, Sugar."

A sob escapes me as I watch silent tears roll down Arch's face while he continues caressing my cheek with his thumb. I feel Hatter move above me as he kisses the top of my head. His other arm comes around Arch and holds him close. Arch lets out a keening sound as Hatter whispers, "I love you. Both of you."

And with those words, I sob even harder. Heaving sobs escape me as my hand comes up, and I grasp Arch's wrist. I press my cheek harder against his palm. I can no longer see Arch in front of me, but I can hear his muffled cries as he sobs into Hatter's chest.

Hatter holds us close through it all, whispering, "I love you. It's okay. I'm here."

I'm not sure when Arch and I finally quiet, but both of us are held tightly against Hatter. We both fall asleep surrounded by Hatter's muddled but masculine scent. Black licorice and mint. I think that will be my favorite scent for a while.

CHAPTER TWENTY-NINE

Alyce

I groan as I wake. Cuddling is nice. I love cuddling. Cuddling and sleeping all night in a full-size bed with two LARGE males while trying not to fall off the bed is almost impossible, though. Note to self, when I finally move into the castle, I need a LARGE bed. Maybe a bed that's so big it takes up most of the far wall in the corner of the Queen's bed chambers. I wasn't about to use the bed that was already there. I stretch until my back makes a loud crack.

"Shit, Sugar! Did you break your back?"

Lifting my head off Hatter's chest, I shift to look up at him. His gaze is a bit sleepy, but his eyes are narrowed on me. "Why would you think I broke my back?"

He lifts a brow. "That crack sounded as if a Bandersnatch sat on you and shattered every bone."

I shrug. "It's normal to me. I didn't even realize it was that loud."

Arch yawns and asks sleepily, "How does your back sounding as if it's breaking in half sound normal to you?"

I laugh and say, "I don't know. My back gets stiff when I'm lying in odd positions, so I have to stretch to relieve some of the pressure."

Arch frowns. "If you were uncomfortable, you could have moved to the other bed."

Rolling my eyes, I move to a sitting position. Now, I would love to say due to forgetting to put clothes on before I fell asleep that I managed to slide out of the bed in a very sexy way. But what I really managed to do was get my foot caught in the bed sheets and proceed to fall out of the bed, landing on the floor.

Groaning, I cover my face. How is it possible that I am this clumsy? I hear a roar of laughter above me and uncover my face to see Hatter peering over the side of the bed, laughing. I can't say I'm mad at his laughter, though. The way his eyes glisten with tears from laughing so hard, and his black hair is disheveled from sleep, I can't help but smile up at him. Arch is peering down at me over Hatter's shoulder with a wide grin. He looks between Hatter and me, chuckling.

Hatter wipes at his eyes. "I've got to say there's no greater sight than seeing you sprawled across my floor naked. The added show was a bonus."

My smile dims a bit when I see the bandage covering his chest and abdomen. My eyes meet his but he's still smiling. "I'm alright. I promise. I feel great this morning."

Arch kisses his cheek. "We should probably change the bandages and get you cleaned up. I could only wipe you down last night, but I'm sure a nice shower will help with your muddled scent."

Hatter twists, kissing Arch back. "Muddled scent?"

Sighing, I pull myself up off the floor and wrap myself with a sheet. "You normally smell like black licorice and mint," I tell him.

Arch nods. "It's still there, but it's covered up with the iron tang of blood and decay."

Hatter looks between both of us and sighs, giving in. "Fine." He points toward a drawer in the corner and says, "Take a shirt, Sugar. Chesh has been peeking through the tent flaps for the last few hours, waiting for you to wake up. You may want to go check on him."

He looks over his shoulder and smiles up at Arch. He quickly flips in the bed pinning Arch down and pecks small kisses all over his face until Arch is laughing. I smile as well. Hatter pulls away from Arch and smiles down at him. "Thank you for taking care of me. I would like to return the favor."

Arch looks over at me raising a brow. Pulling a shirt over my head, I shake my head and say, "Enjoy each other. I'm going to go check on Chesh. I'll meet you guys outside for breakfast."

Hatter turns his gaze to me. He crooks a finger at me and I walk over. I'm an arm's length away when his hand shoots out and threads through my hair. He tugs me closer until his lips meet mine. His lips softly dance across mine in a slow caress. He slides his hand out of my hair until he's cupping my cheek. He pulls away, caressing my cheek with his thumb, and says quietly, "Thank you for saving my life."

"You saved me first, remember?" I whisper.

He smiles. "I suppose I did." He kisses my lips again softly before saying, "I love you."

I hum against his lips. "I love you too." I will NEVER tire of hearing this male say he loves me.

Hatter pulls away. "You better be off to check on Chesh."

I nod, leaning down and kissing Arch. I smile as I pull away. "Love you! Oh, and have fun you two."

I hear Hatter growl, "Oh we will." Then I hear Arch moan as I leave the tent. Smiling, I head toward Chesh's tent. I open the flap enough to announce myself first. I didn't think Chesh would be doing something in here that would require me to announce myself, but I did learn my lesson. "Chesh? You in here?" I call out.

I hear some rustling and then he yells, "Just a minute, Kitten!"

Hum. Curious. He sounds... frazzled. He's never frazzled. "Are you alright?"

His voice is muffled. "Yes! Just a minute."

Alrighty then. Guess I'm waiting. I look down at myself. Well... shattering tea cups. I look around the camp. Thankfully Bianca and the White Knight are still in their tent. Unfortunately, I have four males staring at me intently. Each one with a smirk, their eyes dancing with laughter.

I forgot to put on more clothing. I'm standing outside the tent dressed only in one of Hatter's shirts. Bare thighs showing and a slight breeze whispering under the shirt, hitting bare skin. Fidgeting under their stares, I call, "Chesh? I'm sorta out here in nothing but a shirt. Can I come in now?"

He's huffing like he's been running around his tent all morning. Curious. He has a shy grin as he greets me, "Morning, Kitten."

I arch a brow. "Good morning. What are you up to?"

He smiles as he sweeps open the tent flaps and gestures me inside. I gasp as I enter. The room is decorated with blue rose petals. I see that he captured some fireflies and they flutter around in little glass jars lighting up the room. I continue looking around the room and find the bathtub is filled with water and has bubbles and rosebuds floating on the surface. "Chesh..." I whisper in awe.

"I... I wanted to do something for you."

I look over to find his ears flat against his head and tail swishing rapidly. He's rubbing the back of his neck as his eyes meet mine. His cheeks are bright pink. "This is the sweetest thing anyone has ever done for me!" Looking back at the room, I sputter, "How... this is... what made you do this?"

His eyes brighten. "I was talking to your brothers, and they explained dating to me. It sounded wonderful, and I wanted to do it with you." He gestures at the room. "They said I needed to woo you. I do not understand that term, but they said that if I did this you would be properly wooed." He looks at me. One ear popping up to attention, he asks, "Are you wooed? Did I do it correctly?"

I feel tears stinging my eyes as I look around the room. He did all of this... for me. To show he cared.

"Oh no! You're crying. Crying is bad! I did something wrong!"

I shake my head with a giggle. "No. This is amazing. You wooed me very much. I love it!"

His other ear pops up, and he smiles "Truly!?"

I nod as I slide my hand into his and pull him toward his bed, which is completely covered in rose petals. I turn, walking backward as I tug him along. The back of my knees hit the edge of the bed, and I fall backward, tugging him with me. We land with a whoosh and petals fly up around us.

I grin, looking into his purple eyes. I slide my fingers through his hair and say, "Thank you, Chesh."

I can see him visibly swallow. "Um... of course, Kitten. Anything for you."

He hovers over me. My fingers move to the edge of his ears. I massage the edge and his eyes seem to glow as he begins to purr. His purr vibrates my entire body, and I gasp. No underwear.

He leans to put his weight on one arm as he lifts his other hand, and his fingers caress up and down my arm. His purr deepens, and it sends electricity straight to my clit. My fingers instantly latch into his hair, and I tug.

He growls. "Are you sure, Aly?"

Not realizing I closed my eyes, I open them to meet his dark purple gaze. I lift my head and press my lips softly to his. I pull away and grind myself against him. "Yes."

He pulls away, jumping to his feet. He rips his pants off and is instantly on top of me again. His fingers graze the tops of my thighs as he slowly lifts Hatter's shirt. Fingers slowly explore my body as he lifts the shirt high enough until his palms hover over my breasts.

Now I'm not a large breasted woman, but I'm a good handful. Although, maybe a handful is generous when compared to his hands. He bends down and licks my peaked nipples, and I hiss out a breath. He grins and says, "Like small strawberries. I do love strawberries, Aly."

He slides the shirt off and throws it to the side. He shimmies back down, kissing a trail down over my stomach, stopping where I had told them my scars used to be. His gaze meets mine as he presses several kisses over the spot and tells me, "No one will ever hurt you again. My sweet Kitten."

He moves further down until his face is directly above my, now soaked, cunt. He spreads my legs further apart, so I'm now completely on display for him. His eyes seem to glow as he looks back up at me. "I do love pussy." He lowers himself keeping eye contact as he makes one long stroke over my cunt with his tongue. He purrs deeply as he licks his lips, adding, "And I love cream."

He lowers himself again and throws my thighs over his shoulders. He nips at my clit and I squeal. He immediately thrusts his tongue into my cunt. The pain turns into immediate pleasure. My fingers tangle in his hair, and I tug him closer. He purrs and the vibration sends me into an immediate orgasm.

That was the fastest orgasm I have ever had! But he isn't done. Continuing to suck and tongue me, he doesn't allow my orgasm to ebb off but continues feeding it as he purrs louder. I dig my fingers into his head not knowing if I want to push him away or pull him closer. The pleasure is too much! Too much.

I scream through my next orgasm as he sucks hard on my clit. I have no idea how he's doing the things he's doing, but right now my pleasure-hazed brain doesn't care. He pulls away, licking his lips, his face wet with my pleasure.

His dark gaze meets mine, and he has a satisfied grin on his face. I pant out the first thing that comes to mind, "Now you better fuck me, Chesh."

I grin when I see the surprise that lights his gaze before he growls and says, "As my kitten wishes."

I look down to find his cock seeping with precum. Seems he was enjoying eating me as much as I enjoyed being eaten. He lines himself up and slowly slides inside of me. It's so agonizingly slow that I'm whimpering. I immediately grab onto his ears and tug. "Fuck me!" I beg.

His gaze meets mine, and I watch as the soft Chesh vanishes, and a new Chesh takes his place. A darker Chesh. The beast. He growls as he slowly slides out and then slams back into me.

I gasp at how full I feel in that moment. He continues his pace of slowly sliding out, then slamming back into me, hard. My eyes meet his, and I can see something warring behind his. I can see he needs something. I tug on his ears again and he growls, crushing his lips to mine. It's not soft and loving. This. This is filled with desperation and a frenzied need.

He pulls away and snarls, "Mine. You are my Kitten. My Mate! You aren't allowed to leave. You can't leave me. Never. Mine."

And that's when it clicks. His sweet exterior hides the beast within. The beast that has been rejected by every female he has ever met in Wonderland. Every female until me. He slams his lips back onto mine, and I meet his frenzied and desperate kisses. I try to put every emotion I have ever felt for this male into this kiss. I pull away, gasping as I come again. His hips seem to stutter for a moment as my cunt squeezes his cock.

He thrusts into me faster now. Desperate. He's growling. "Say it!"

I pant. "Say what?" I ask, my brain lost in a pleasure-filled haze.

His gaze meets mine, and it's filled with so much need. The need to be accepted and not left behind. The need to be loved. So I softly smile up at him and promise, "I won't leave you, Cheshy. Ever."

He slams into me with another growl. I continue, "I'm your kitten." He's biting his lip and I can see his canines digging in deep. "I'm your Mate."

I can see that he's so close. So close to ecstasy. "I love you, Chesh."

"Please," he pants. His eyes glow a dark purple as he continues to thrust hard into me. His bends so our foreheads touch and he demands, "Say it."

"You are mine. My Mate!" I cry out. He slams into me as he keens, and I feel the gush as he comes. He's panting, his forehead still against my own. His eyes are on mine, and I watch as the glow slowly dissipates. "I love you so much, Kitten."

I kiss his lips softly. "I know." Then I remember that the bathtub was filled when I came in. I give him a sheepish smile and ask, "Do you think the water is still warm?"

He laughs. "It's still warm."

I wiggle under him and he groans. I laugh. "You want to join me?"

He smiles down at me softly and answers, "Always and anywhere."

CHAPTER THIRTY
Alyce

Chesh and I finished our bath, and I think I've convinced Chesh to love baths. Although, it may only be when I'm in the bathtub with him. After we get out, we dress and make our way out to the center of the camp to eat and have our morning meeting.

Rab quirks a brow as Chesh and I make our way over. Noticing my wet hair, he asks, "Did you have a good bath, Aly?"

Sitting on a large mushroom, I pull Chesh down to sit next to me. "I had a great bath, Rab."

He smirks a bit. "Was Hatter and Arch's bathtub not good enough?"

I look over to see Hatter and Arch sitting next to each other. Arch is snuggled in close, and Hatter has a soft smirk on his lips as he looks down at him. Hatter's eyes meet mine, and his smirk widens. Looks like someone enjoyed himself. My eyes turn back to Rab, and I shrug. "It was a little crowded. Plus it doesn't look like they are complaining." Hatter snorts and Arch laughs.

Rab's eyes darken. "I see. Was it crowded in Chesh's bathtub as well?"

I smirk. "I don't know. Was it crowded, Chesh?"

Chesh purrs beside me, "I'm a cat. We are VERY flexible, Kitten."

I shiver, and I see Rab's eyes flash with hunger. I lick my lips, "Hum. Well, I suppose it wasn't crowded." Then I purr, "Sir."

Rab's ears, no longer hidden by his hat, twitch on the top of his head, and I watch as he shifts a bit on the tree stump where he's sitting. Suddenly, my brother asks, "What are the plans for the war?" Causing both of us to jerk to attention as if a whip had snapped.

I pull my gaze from Rab's, finding Laurel looking at all of us expectantly. I look over his shoulder and find Edi and Alix. Bianca and the Knight are close behind. I huff out a sigh, damn I forgot about them. Again. My eyes meet Alix's as he looks between Rab and me. He waggles his brows at me, and I can't help but laugh. Leave it up to Alix to make me feel less awkward that they saw me flirting with Rab.

Alix sits on my other side and whispers, "So... have you done the dirty with him yet?"

I choke on my spit. "What!?"

Alix smirks. "You know rumpy pumpy."

I feel my cheeks heat as I hiss, "Alix!"

Chesh bumps my arm and says, "I think he's asking if you have had sex with Rab yet, Kitten."

"I know what he's asking. It seems to be an inappropriate thing to ask your sister, though."

Alix shrugs with a grin. "I'm curious how your relationship with all of these guys works."

Chesh smiles. "She is our Mate." He seems to preen as he says it, and I can't help but smile. He's so proud to say I'm his Mate.

Alix quirks a brow. "What does Mate mean?"

Sighing, I explain, "In Wonderland the women choose the men. Although, they call each other female and male here. Anyways, when a female chooses a male they are considered Claimed. I didn't like the way they described what a Claiming meant, so I changed it."

Alix considers that for a moment and shrugs. "So all of these guys are your Mates?"

I nod. "Yes, all of these males are my Mates." I point to the White Knight and clarify, "Except him. He is Claimed by the Empress."

The Knight stiffens for a moment before the Empress presses a soft kiss to his cheek. I watch the tilt of his lips as he looks down at her. I can see the love he has for her as he smiles, placing a soft kiss on her forehead.

I'm surprised by the quick kiss against my cheek. Turning, I see Chesh smiling at me, the same loving look in his eyes. Slipping my hand into his, I turn back to my brother and find him looking around the camp. Brows knitting, I follow his gaze to find all my males watching me with soft smiles. Laurel and Edi are watching my males as well. I feel my cheeks heat as I whisper, "Why are you guys all staring at me?"

"We love hearing you say we are your Mates," Mor says softly, and I watch his wings flutter before disappearing in a puff of blue glitter.

I giggle as his cheeks pinken. His wings are the secret to his emotions, so he hid them. I hear a throat clear and turn to find Laurel looking between Edi and Alix. His eyes aren't on me but on the males around me.

"So all of you care about my sister," he grunts. I'm not sure if that's a statement or a question.

"Laurel," I hiss in protest.

Dee laughs. "I don't think care is the right word for what we feel for Alyce."

Rook growls, "She's our darling."

Arch smirks. "Our little mouse."

"Our Sugar." Hatter winks.

Mor smiles. "Our beautiful butterfly."

"My Little Alyce. Our delicate Rosebud," Rab rasps.

Chesh grins. "Our purrfect Kitten."

My cheeks heat, but I smile. I didn't realize I had so many nicknames. "And they are... well... my males." I don't have nicknames for them, but I feel like claiming them as my males is an accurate term. I look at my brothers, but they aren't looking at me. They are still looking at the males around me.

"What exactly does that mean?" Edi asks.

As if rehearsed, the males say at once, "She's our Mate."

Hatter's deep voice adds, "She's the heart of our broken and battered group."

I feel my eyes burn with tears as Chesh squeezes my hand. "A group of males who don't deserve her love and compassion."

No! They are wrong, they deserve everything. I'm the one who doesn't deserve all of their love. I begin to protest, but Rook interrupts, "But we are eternally grateful that she has chosen to Claim us anyways."

I look at each of my males as tears begin to slide down my face. Rab stands and makes his way over, kneeling in front of me. He reaches up slowly. Gently, he cups my face in his large callused hands as he wipes away my tears with his thumbs.

Smiling softly, he says, "So to answer your question. We care very deeply for this female. Our family was broken. But this female... a female who has healed seven broken males." He leans forward and presses a soft kiss to my lips before pulling away. His voice breaks with his next words. "I will be forever grateful for this female. I will cherish every second I have with her."

Chesh presses in close and kisses my cheek, adding, "We love her."

"How do you know you love her? How do you know it isn't just lust? She hasn't been here that long," Alix asks from beside me. I want to look over at him. To see his face. I know he's asking because of my past. He doesn't want me to get hurt by a bunch of guys.

Rab holds my face, refusing to let my gaze shift to Alix. So I whisper, "All you need to know is that I love them. That's all that matters." These males have done amazing things to boost my non-existent confidence. I've had doubts about how this relationship would work. If it was even going to last. Because, how could these seven males love me? I'm just a broken and scared woman.

Alix grunts, "No it's not, Aly."

Hatter speaks up, "Because love is terrifying. It's scary to let a person see all your faults and broken parts. I'm afraid."

I peer over Rab's shoulder to find Hatter watching me. He looks to Arch beside him and then back at me. "I'm afraid she will still reject the male I truly am. The male who I have let her see. The male who is still broken, but slowly healing."

Arch slides his hand into Hatter's, smiling at me as his eyes glisten with emotion. "Lust is easy. There is no emotion required with lust. Love is difficult. It requires letting the other person see the broken, battered parts of your soul."

My eyes roam to Rook as he adds, "Love is wanting to protect that person with your whole being and fearing it won't be enough."

"Fearing that the female only wishes to be with you because she is also with your brother. But finding she cares for you as well. That she will stand next to me proudly and claim that I am hers," Dee says, his voice deep with emotion.

"Love is finding a female who looks beyond the beautiful exterior," Mor whispers, "and see's the fractured soul of a male who wishes to be more than a discarded toy for someone else's pleasure."

I bite my lip, trying to fight the well of emotions inside of me. All I want to do is hold my males and show them how much I love them. How much they have come to mean to me in such a short amount of time.

Chesh lays his head on my shoulder as he purrs softly. "Love is utterly terrifying. But it's an exhilarating rush when the female you love, loves you back."

"A radiant rose," Rab murmurs softly. "Where others see thorns and sneer of false beauty. Who have tried to belittle and stomp her into the ground. To destroy her," he says, growling, "We see delicate petals, broken and scarred, but no less beautiful. We will not be deterred by her thorns. They are there to protect and speak of her strength and power."

Rab's gaze shifts to Alix beside me. "She is our Warrior Queen, and we will protect her at any cost."

Edi speaks up, "So you're like her knights in shining armor?"

Chesh snickers as Hatter's deep voice rumbles, "Knights are honorable and noble males."

Rab releases my face as he stands. His eyes darken as he looks between my brothers. "We are no such creatures."

I see Laurel stiffen. "Then what are you?" he asks.

Rab smirks. It's not the dark smirks he gives me when we play, but a dangerous one that holds a promise of death. He looks at the males around him before looking my brother in the eye and announcing, "We are her dark legion to command."

Chesh growls in agreement beside me before saying, "And we will eradicate anyone who wishes to harm our female again."

I shiver. These males would annihilate everyone in Wonderland for me. I watch Laurel's reaction to their words. That's when I see it. The glimmer of emotion that he's trying to hide. He's afraid. His eyes meet mine and I gasp. I broke something in him when I left that day. When he watched me pass through the mirror, I broke something. The little sister he has protected since birth was suddenly out of his reach.

"Laurel?" I whisper. I don't really know what I'm asking when I say his name.

His hard eyes soften as he gives me a weak smile. He must see something in my eyes because he whispers back, "I needed to know, kiddo."

I knit my brows in confusion until I see the look in his eyes when his gaze shifts back to my males. He seems to gauge all the males for a moment before nodding. Trust. He wanted to make sure he could trust them. He was asking invasive questions to see what they would do. I watch as he turns to the Empress and asks the same question as earlier, "So what are our plans for the war?"

I'm stunned. He's acting as if this whole conversation didn't happen. The others, realizing the interrogation is over, move back to their seats as well. Did I hallucinate the whole conversation? I hear Alix chuckle beside me.

He leans in and whispers, "It seems guys in Wonderland aren't that much different than back home."

I raise an eyebrow in question.

He smirks. "It's a guy thing. Say how you feel and move on."

I roll my eyes. "So everything is good now?"

He shrugs. "We know they care. We know we can trust them. That's all that really matters. They said what they said, we said what we needed to say. All good."

I huff out a sigh, shaking my head. Guys are weird. But I understand why my brothers needed the reassurance. They only trusted each other when I was growing up. I tune out the battle plans as Dee hands me a plate of food with a smile. I grin at him and begin shoveling food into my mouth. I'm going to need fuel and energy to prepare for the battle ahead.

CHAPTER THIRTY-ONE

Alyce

"Spread your legs apart, Alyce!" Rook yells across from me. If it wasn't for the fact that what he said sounded so dirty, I would have yelled back. Instead I smirk.

"Are you sure you want me to do that in front of everyone?" I tease. As I watch, his eyes darken.

He grunts, "Focus!"

Sighing, I spread my legs further apart and continue my sword exercises. Right. Must focus. I need to make sure I'm ready for the fight when it comes. I got lucky in the last fight, but the fight to come will be worse. Sweat slides down my face as I concentrate on my arm movements and how I place my feet.

I startle mid-strike when suddenly, Dee appears in front of me with a grin. "Hey, darling. You want to spar with me?"

Huffing out a breath, I sheath my practice blade. The males wanted me to practice with the Vorpal blade, but Bianca said that she didn't want me to strain my magic. She thought that I was getting a better grasp on it and didn't want me to cause an issue by using it to keep the Vorpal blade in its larger sword form.

Shrugging, I ask, "Are we doing hand-to-hand, or do you want me to keep practicing with swords?" Hand-to-hand combat has also been added to my practices. Rab had said he wanted me to be prepared in case my sword gets knocked out of my hands during battle.

He grins, wiggling his brows. "Hand to hand."

Laughing, I get into my fighting stance and tease, "You just want a reason to get your hands all over me."

He shrugs. "It's an added bonus." He mirrors my stance. "Ready?"

I nod. I'm startled when he runs at me, but I lower myself in preparation, remembering that he may have the muscle and strength, but I'm small and fast. He reaches out for me, and I duck, racing around him and slapping his thick ass. I return to my fighting stance as he turns.

He raises a brow. "So we're fighting like that are we?"

I grin and taunt, "What? Can't handle a slap on the butt?"

His eyes darken as he smirks. "You have no idea what you've started, darling."

"Are we going to fight or not?" I tease.

He straightens from his fighting stance and smiles darkly before calling out, "Mor!"

My brows knit in confusion as I look over to find Mor looking up from the war table we set up to make battle plans. He lifts a brow in question. "Yes?"

"Why don't you come over here and practice some hand-to-hand combat? Our little Alyce needs some practice with a faster opponent."

Mor straightens and walks over to Dee. "Wouldn't Chesh be better suited for this? My wings tend to get in the way of hand-to-hand combat."

Dee bends and whispers something in Mor's ear. I strain to hear what they are saying, but I can't make out anything. Mor's eyes widen and then darken as his eyes meet mine. I watch as his wings disappear in a burst of blue glitter.

Dee gives me a dark chuckle as he backs away and says, "Good luck, darling." What in the name of shattering tea cups did I get myself into? My eyes meet Mor's and he smiles as he lowers into a fighting stance. I mimic his stance.

"Ready, Little Butterfly?"

I arch a brow. "Umm... yes?"

I jump when I hear Dee yell, "Begin!"

Mor doesn't move from his spot, and neither do I. We both gauge each other. Someone has to break the standoff, but he just continues smirking at me. Huffing out a sigh, I run at him. However, I miss him completely as my fist glides past him only meeting air. I feel a soft finger caress down my spine, and I gasp.

I turn to find Mor's blue eyes, which are filled with amusement, on me. I growl, realizing what's happening. I would have won against Dee because I'm short and fast. But with Mor, Mor is still tall, but he has sleek, athletic muscle instead of bulk like Dee.

Eyes narrowing, I lower back into my fighting stance. He's grinning at me, and that only infuriates me more. These males think they can win? I'm going to show them just how dirty I can play. "Are you only going to stand there, or are you going to fight me?"

He smirks, and I squeak when he's suddenly in front of me. Dang, he's faster than I thought he was. He places a chaste kiss against my lips and then jerks away. He spins behind me, and I turn quickly, only to find him several feet away.

Dee is laughing, and Mor chuckles softly. "Are you sure you want to play this game, Butterfly?"

Realizing that my mouth is hanging open, I snap it shut. Grunting, I slide the hair tie off my wrist and put my hair up in a high pony. I'm thankful I remembered to pack a few ties in my bag. Although, I didn't find them until I was unpacking my bag yesterday. It's a pity. It would have been nice to have had my hair up when we were hiking through the forest instead of being hot and sweaty with my hair down.

Lowering back into my fighting stance, I smile and taunt, "I'm ready if you are."

His eyes seem to darken as he smirks. "Then let's play."

He runs at me. I swerve in time, and my fingers caress lightly across his back. Right where his wings would be. He groans as he spins, and I can see the heat in his gaze. This time when he comes at me I'm not able to dodge him, and he lightly caresses the tips of my breast.

Before I know it he's a few feet away again. I can see the bulge in his pants, and it makes me smirk. But when my eyes meet his, I notice he is smirking too, except his eyes are on my chest. I look down and realize that his brief touch has caused my nipples to pebble through my cloth shirt.

After what feels like hours, I'm panting, and we are at a standoff. Mor's eyes are hooded as he watches my chest rise and fall rapidly. My pussy is pulsing with need, and I know my panties are soaked. With every slight caress against my thigh or breast, my need grew.

Lost in my desire, I jump when I hear Dee's voice. "Both of you need a bath. Go!" he orders.

I stand tall, trying to make myself look completely unaffected by our game. I pass Mor as I make my way toward Chesh's tent, which is where I usually take baths. A hot breath caresses the back of my neck, and I freeze when a deep voice says, "Wrong tent, Little Butterfly. I'm not done with our game."

I try not to whimper at the promise in his voice. A shiver races down my spine, but I nod. Leading the way, I turn and head in the direction of Mor's tent. I slip into his tent, and he slips past me, quickly making his way over to the bath area. I didn't notice the last time I was in here, but he doesn't have a bath like the others. Instead, the area has pebbles on the ground, and a shower head and faucet handles are on the wall of the tent. How does he get the water to flow out of the shower head? When I take baths the guys have to bring in water from a local body of water.

I point to the shower and ask, "How do you have a shower?"

He looks over his shoulder at me. "With the combination of Arch's inventions and my magic, the water pumps from a basin of water. The water is then filtered and recycled in a continuous cycle until I'm done showering." He turns the knobs and water begins flowing out of the shower head. Cool. Magic here is amazing.

He looks me up and down and smirks. "Are you planning on showering with clothes on?"

I roll my eyes. Keeping my eyes locked on him, I slowly shimmy out of my pants and underwear. I smirk when I see his breathing increase. Kicking my pants off to the side, I grip the edge of my shirt and slip it over my head. I hear him hiss, and I grin. I didn't put a bra on this morning because it's uncomfortable when I have my full leathers on.

I slowly walk toward him and slip under the waterfall of warm water. He continues to stare at me, so I smile and tease, "Are you planning on showering with clothes on?"

He rips off his clothes and throws them over his shoulder before slipping into the water with me. His chest is heaving against mine as he looks down at me. I caress my fingertips up his chest until my fingers slip into his blue hair. As I tug softly, I feel the bulge of his dick jump against my abdomen. I pull him down until my lips meet his. He groans against my lips, and I nip at his bottom lip.

I'm suddenly up against the wall as his hands grip my ass and squeeze. I deepen the kiss and he hungrily accepts. I slip my other hand down his back until I feel a line of raised skin. It's then that I realize that's where his wings usually are. My fingertips press against the raised skin, and he growls, jerking his hips against my abdomen.

He's panting when he pulls away. He looks into my eyes and asks, "Are you sure you want to do this?"

My brows knit. Why would I not want to do this? "Why wouldn't I?" I ask as I press my fingers against the raised skin again. His eyes seem to glow an even brighter blue. Is that a powerful shifter thing? Or is it a magic thing? Maybe both?

He groans, biting his lip. "Aly." He's panting as he whispers, "Are you sure you want to be with a male like me?"

"A male like you?" I'm severely confused. What does he mean? A shifter? I've been with three other shifters. A cursed male? I've been with Chesh.

He presses his forehead against mine. "A used male," he whispers. Almost too softly for me to hear.

That's when it clicks. Other females have used him as their personal sex toy. My fingers tangle in his hair, and I grip it tight. Using his hair, I pull his head away from mine and force him to look into my eyes as I say, "You are mine. My Mate. My male. Mine."

He growls, and his wings burst into view in a cloud of glitter. His grip on my ass tightens. "Then I'll make you mine," he says, his voice rough. He slips backward only far enough to position his cock at my entrance.

I groan, "Yes."

"You're so wet for me, Little Butterfly. You enjoyed our game, didn't you?"

My hand, which was originally resting against the skin of his back, shifts to the base of his wing. My eyes meet his and I smile. "Yes. But it's not over yet." I tug hard on his sensitive wing and he slams his cock into me, filling me in one thrust.

I scream at the sudden fullness. He groans, resting his head on my shoulder as he pants, "You're so tight, Butterfly." Shifting his grip, he holds me so that he's holding my ass with one hand, and the other is resting against my head. His glowing blue eyes meet mine, and he asks, "Ready?"

I whimper, wiggling my butt. "Yes."

He slowly slides out and then slams back in. My fingers tighten in his hair, and I pull his face to mine, crushing my lips to his. This kiss isn't soft or loving. It's hot and needy. I caress my fingertips across his wings, loving how he growls against my lips and slams into me hard and deep. I can feel myself tightening around him. I pull away panting, "So close... so close, Mor."

He shifts his grip on my ass again so his other hand can slip in between us. He softly caresses a thumb across my swollen clit, and I whine. Slamming into me roughly once more, he presses his thumb hard against my clit, and that's all it takes, I explode. I scream his name as he continues slamming into me.

"Again," he grunts.

I shake my head. How can I possibly come again?

He nips the side of my neck and yells, "Again!" He circles my clit softly, simultaneously hitting my G-spot then presses hard on my clit once more and bites down on my neck. Fuck! I come again with a shout, milking his cock. But he's still refusing to come.

He kisses the spot he bit and says, "You're so beautiful when you come, Little Butterfly." He continues fucking me, and I can feel tears pricking the corners of my eyes. How is it possible to feel so much pleasure?!

My eyes open to meet his. The glow in his eyes seems brighter. He's biting his lip, trying to make this last for as long as he can, but fuck that! I release my hold on his hair and slide my hand down to hold the base of his other wing. "Come for me," I moan as I pull on his wings. He slams into me with a yell, and I can feel his release. He pants as he rests his head on my shoulder. His hold on my ass tightens as his come seeps out of me, dripping onto the shower floor. Who knew shifters had so much?

My hands slip up his back and into his hair again. I run my fingers through his hair, massaging his scalp. He shivers, placing a soft kiss against my neck. We don't move, and I'm okay with that. Savoring this moment of connection.

I feel his lips move against my neck as he whispers, "I love you, Little Butterfly."

"I love you, Mor," I whisper back.

CHAPTER THIRTY-TWO

Alyce

There is something different in the air today. It feels thick, seeming to seep into every open space, clogging it with dark intentions. It feels as if Wonderland knows something bad is going to happen today. Maybe it's the magic of Wonderland wisping around me. I think it's warning me that Wonderland will be changed after today.

I strap on the additional knife holsters Hatter and Rook demanded I wear. They want me to use my non-magical knives before wielding the Vorpal sword if possible. Bianca had shrugged and agreed that me using every other source before relying on magic would help save my magic for when it was needed.

I walk out of the tent, and everyone turns to look at me. I look around, and I can tell that my males can sense the change in the air as well. Bianca nods to me then turns back to talk to her male. My brothers give me questioning glances, not understanding what will become of today.

Alix points at me and asks, "What's with the full warrior outfit?"

I look at my males before turning my gaze to him. "I'm preparing for war."

"War?" Laurel questions. He looks between all of us, brows knitting together. "What do you mean war? I thought we had more time."

Rab speaks up, "It seems Wonderland thinks otherwise."

"Wonderland?" Edi looks down at the ground and then back up at Rab. "You make it sound like Wonderland is alive."

Chesh grins and explains, "It is in a way. The magic of Wonderland feeds those who have power. Those who are magic-wielding are more sensitive to the changes in Wonderland due to the shift in magic."

My brothers still seem confused, but I shrug because I don't know how to explain it any better than that. I don't fully understand Wonderland yet.

Arch breaks into the conversation. "So I stayed up last night making these." He pulls out three small pistols. He spins one around, handing the butt end to Laurel first. "I'm not sure how weapons on the Surface work, but these guns are an aim-and-shoot weapon. It doesn't take much skill." He hands the other two pistols to Edi and Alix.

I smile at how thoughtful my Hare is. "You made pistols for my brothers."

He shrugs. "They didn't take to swordplay very well. They can use a knife well enough, but I would only recommend a sword in an emergency."

I walk up to Arch, wrap my arms around his middle, and squeeze him gently. "Thank you," I say, trying to convey how much I appreciate him.

He hugs me back. "I wouldn't let your brothers enter a battle without something, Mouse." I turn in his arms, so I can look at my brothers.

"So, how do these work?" Laurel asks.

Arch releases me and walks over to him. He points at different parts of the gun, "This is your safety lever. These guns have unlimited ammo, so you will not have to worry about reloading. With a little help from Mor, I was able to link the clip to Wonderland's magic. As long as we are in an area where it can feed off of the magic around us, you will have ammo."

"What's the ammo?" Edi questions curiously.

"The ammo is a ball of energy due to it feeding from the magic around us." Arch pulls out his own gun and removes the clip. "Mine has typical bullets with a little magic embedded in them. Your guns will cause damage, but depending on where you hit the target depends on if it's a kill shot or not."

Hatter walks up beside Arch. He has leather straps in his hands, and that's when I realize he has holsters for the guns. He holds out one of the holsters. "I managed to find some leftover leather. These should work for you guys to hold the guns in place."

My brothers each take a holster and strap it on then place the pistol inside. Alix grins. "Look at me now. I'm such a badass."

I snort. "You're only a badass if you can shoot."

He smirks at me and replies, "Oh, I can shoot."

My easy banter with my brother ends when I notice movement coming from the mountains surrounding Spaydz. There's also movement coming from the Dymondz territory. I'm about to pull one of my knives when I notice Bianca waving a hand in the air. I look at her and she smiles.

"It's our backup."

My brows knit together. "Our backup?" I didn't realize we would have backup. I suppose with the numbers the Red Queen has, surely we wouldn't be able to defeat her alone, but I didn't know someone had reached out to the other Suits.

Bianca must see the confusion on my face. "I informed my third-in-command before we left Dymondz that they needed to reach out to Spaydz to join the rebellion. I told them to arrive here as soon as possible." She looks off into the distance. "I wasn't sure if they would make it in time," she explains.

Dee and Rook come up beside me, hands on the hilts of their swords. Their eyes don't deviate from where the Spaydz are converging. We wait silently until Bianca's third-in-command greets her with a smile. "It is wonderful to see you are well, Empress." I'm surprised that her third-in-command is a female. She's short and slim but radiates power.

Bianca nods as she smiles. "I see you were able to convince the Spaydz to join."

The third-in-command's face sours. "It took some bargaining, but as you can see, we finally agreed on something. "I didn't doubt you for a moment." She pats the small female's shoulder and then points to the camp. "Why don't you and the others sit for a while and rest."

The female smiles as she nods. Looking over her shoulder she commands, "Let's go. Sit and rest before the battle begins."

The ruler of Spaydz marches toward us. She glances at me briefly before turning toward Bianca and bowing her head. "Greetings, Empress." Her voice is deep and sultry.

Bianca does the same. "Greetings, Commander."

The Commander's eyes roam over the group until they freeze on Dee and Rook. I can feel them both stiffen at her gaze. She smiles seductively as she makes her way to us. She ignores me completely as she greets the males. "The Tweedle brothers. You have filled out nicely since the last time I saw you." She reaches up to touch them, but I slap her hand away.

I feel myself growl as I say, "Do not touch them."

She raises a brow. "Ah, is this your new keeper?"

I stand on my tiptoes to get at least some height on this amazon of a female. I glare at her and inform her, "I am their Mate." I feel as Dee and Rook slide their free hands onto my back in silent support. I feel their strength as I feel my power try to take over, but I smother it. I'm not sure if I succeed because the Commander's eyes widen, so I smile darkly and add, "They are MY males." Then I growl to emphasize. "MINE. So back the FUCK off."

Alix laughs. "Oh shit! Aly said an adult word." I turn my glare on him, and he holds his hands up in surrender, smiling.

The Commander looks me over before yelling over her shoulder, "Rest!" She smirks at me as she bows her head then turns to join the others in the camp.

I huff out a breath. "What just happened?! Did I seriously just slap the ruler of Spaydz's hand?!" I mutter.

Dee and Rook chuckle, and Dee bumps my shoulder. "That was amazing, darling."

Rook bumps my other side. "That was sexy."

I slap both of them on the chest. "I'm serious!"

Rook takes one of my hands and kisses my palm. "You did nothing wrong."

Dee does the same to my other hand. "She will respect you now."

I arch a brow skeptically. "Really?"

They both nod. I sigh and state, "Females are weird here."

They tug on my hands as we make our way over to the camp to join everyone. We will rest and feast until the battle. Until we fight to free Wonderland.

CHAPTER THIRTY-THREE

Alyce

Something in the air shifts, and we all stand immediately. The sun is starting to set, and the sky is painted in beautiful reds and oranges. Like the sky is on fire. Like Wonderland knows the land will soon be covered in blood. Bianca starts yelling orders to her people as they spread out to cover as much land as possible. The Commander of Spaydz is rallying her troops as they do the same.

I look to Rab, our leader. He looks at us. Meeting each of us in the eyes, he gives us a nod. "Stay alive," he orders. His eyes meet mine, and he smiles. "We have a female to make happy."

I smirk. "Like you males could do anything else."

Chesh wraps me in a hug and squeezes tight. "Stay safe, Kitten." He presses a kiss to the top of my head before pulling away. He gives me a wink then takes off running toward the front lines, shifting into his cursed form as he runs.

Mor's wings catch my eye, and I turn to look at him. I give him a smirk, and he returns it. "I'll keep an eye on you from the skies," he says before shattering into a puff of blue glitter as thousands of Blue Morpho butterflies take to the sky. I'm sure I'll see him in his cursed form as well once the battle begins.

Dee and Rook come up beside me, each taking a side as they smash a kiss to my cheeks, squishing my face from the force. I giggle as they pull away. Dee looks down at me, concern etching his face. "Remember the techniques we taught you. Protect vital parts."

I nod as I rise on tiptoes and kiss his lips softly. "Never stop. Never stop fighting,"

He smirks and says, "Be safe, darling." I nod as he pulls away to join the Spaydz troops.

I look at Rook who has a smile on his face, but I can tell it's forced. I rise and kiss his lips gently as I whisper, "I remember everything you guys taught me."

He caresses my cheek as his smile falls, worry replacing his features. "Be safe, alright? If you need help, just yell. One of us will be at your side in seconds."

"Be safe yourself," I demand. He smirks as he presses his lips to mine quickly before pulling away and following after his brother.

I hear the screech of Jabberwocky in the distance and stiffen at the sound. This is it. Hatter and Arch are next to me within moments.

Hatter's rough voice grunts, "We'll stay next to you."

Arch nods, adding, "We won't leave your side."

I shake my head and say, "I'll be fine. Help protect my brothers. They haven't had as much training as I've had."

"Not happening, Sugar." Hatter growls.

I place my hand on his forearm. "Please, Hatter. You two are the best protection they have. I don't trust the other Suits to protect them."

Hatter's eyes meet mine. I can see the struggle in his eyes. The battle between protecting me or my brothers. Arch puts a hand on his shoulder, and Hatter switches his gaze to look at him.

"She's right, Hatter."

Hatter looks back at me, growls and says, "Fine! But you better not have a scratch on you when the battle ends."

I smirk. "No promises."

He smashes his lips to mine. Pulling away, he whispers, "I love you, Sugar. Please be safe." He runs off in the direction of my brothers before I can say anything back.

Arch huffs out a laugh. "He still doesn't do well with emotions in high-pressure situations."

I laugh. "He's come so far, though." I shift my eyes to Arch and see him smiling at Hatter's as he walks away.

His eyes shift down to me as he agrees, "He has." His ears droop as he bends down to kiss my nose, and his eyes shimmer as he pulls away. "He's right, though. Be safe. We all love you too much to see you hurt, Mouse."

I tug on one of his ears and laugh when he grunts. "You both need to be safe for me too. Protect each other." He nods as he pulls away, running off to catch up with Hatter.

I sigh when Rab comes up next to me. His sensual voice wraps around me as he asks, "You ready for battle?"

"Is anyone ever ready for battle?" I counter.

His fingers twine in mine as the distant roars of Bandersnatch greet us. He squeezes my hand and asks worriedly, "Do you regret coming to Wonderland?"

I squeeze his hand back in reassurance. "Nope."

He snorts out a laugh. "How?"

"How do I not regret coming to Wonderland?"

"Yes."

"Because," I pause for a moment when I hear the clashing of swords in the distance. Roars and screams now greet us. I look up at the male beside me and say truthfully, "Because I met all of you."

"How are we worth all of this?" He gestures to the fighting now moving closer to us.

I release his hand as I pull out duel knives. "Because I meddled with madness."

"That doesn't answer my question, Alyce."

I smirk and start walking but turn to walk backward, facing Rab so I can explain, "I meddled with the madness of Wonderland and found it made more sense than the world I belonged to. I found people who make my heart smile. I found my Wonderland. And if I have to fight to keep it, then I will."

He raises a brow as he smirks. "So are you saying you're mad now?"

I laugh as I spin to face the oncoming army. "I'm afraid so. But all the best people are, don't you know?" I feel my magic singing inside me, but I don't allow it free. Not yet. I need to keep in control.

Rab is suddenly beside me, and he laughs. "Well I suppose I'll join the madness then."

The clattering of swords begins around us, and I ready my knives. "Then let's fight for our Wonderland," I yell before running into the battle with Rab right behind me. A Bandersnatch jumps toward us to attack, but the creature freezes in front of me. I slash through its throat then spin to glare at Rab. "Do. Not. Control my time unless you have to. I will not be the reason your magic is depleted."

His eyes widen at my tone, and he must see something in my face because he nods. "Yes, my Queen."

I nod, turning to continue fighting off the enemies. I'm slashing through Bandersnatch after Bandersnatch when I look around and realize that Rab and I have become separated. Looking around quickly, I try to take measure of my males. They are all stilll fighting, covered in yellow and red blood. That's when I realize that the Red Queen has males fighting on her side wearing fighting leathers resembling playing cards.

I scream when I feel a hot slash down my back. My magic tries to flare inside me, but I force it down as I turn to find one of those playing card males. His face is empty of emotion, seeming more like a puppet being controlled by its master. He tries to slash out at me again, and I block it, but he has so much force behind the slash that it knocks my knife out of my hand. I rip at the necklace around my neck and release a small amount of my magic to allow the sword to grow.

Slashing across the male's abdomen, he falls as red blood bubbles out of the wound. I want to vomit with the realization that these males may be acting like dolls, but they bleed just like the rest of us. Trying to breathe through the nausea, another playing card male makes his way toward me. I fight him off as well but realize that these males are built for battle. I catch something red out of the corner of my eye and look in the direction of the castle to find the Red Queen racing across the battlefield, completely untouched by the battle, not even bothering to fight. I turn to go after her, but before I can, another playing card male slashes his sword in my direction.

How are we supposed to win this battle? I look across the battlefield to find Dymondz medics carrying fallen soldiers as quickly as they can to tend to their wounds. I need to end this. I need to end this battle so no more Wonderlanders die.

CHAPTER THIRTY-FOUR

Alyce

I look around the battlefield and watch as both comrades and enemies fall. Blood soaks the ground. I can feel the heat in my chest growing. The Vorpal sword grows hot in my hands. Searching the battlefield, I find Rab's hands out in front of him as he stops time for our comrades that he has clocks for. The enemies around them freeze and are killed in an instant. He's breathing hard, swiping at his face to keep the sweat from rolling into his eyes. As I watch, Mor guards him, taking out soldiers in his Jabberwock form.

Looking for the others, I find Hatter and Arch back-to-back. As I watch, Hatter throws hat pin after hat pin while Arch uses his handmade pistol. Hatter reaches down to get another hat pin and finds he has run out. He reaches behind him and pulls a knife from Arch's back holster. He steps forward as if to run through the battlefield when Arch stops him with a hand on his hip.

Hatter looks back at him with an arched brow. Arch's ears flatten as he turns toward Hatter and hands him his gun. He pulls several cartridges out of his pocket and places them into the now-empty pocket of Hatter's leg holster. Arch steps away from Hatter to enter the battlefield himself, but he's stopped by a hand wrapping around the back of his neck. Hatter pulls Arch to him, so their foreheads meet. I watch the intimate look that passes between them.

Hatter says something to Arch, and I watch as Arch responds. Hatter continues talking, and Arch nods with a smile. Hatter smashes his lips to Arch's briefly before turning away. He begins using Arch's gun to take down enemies. Hatter covers Arch as he takes off, weaving through the bodies, and picking up hat pins as he goes. I didn't realize how fast Arch was, even in male form. My brothers join Hatter in covering Arch as he runs through the fallen bodies.

Glancing away, I look for the last of my males. I find the twins in a similar position, facing back-to-back. They look every bit like the warriors they were born to be. But they each have blood covering their armor and exposed skin. I can see rips and tears in their cloth undershirts.

I can't let anyone else die because the Red Queen wants control over all of Wonderland. This needs to stop. The warmth behind my chest grows into a wildfire. If I let the magic control me, would it be worth it? Bianca said that if the magic consumes me, I could die. Would my death be worth saving everyone in Wonderland? Yes. I nod to myself as I release the control I have over my magic. I scream as I'm consumed by its flame. I hear my name being yelled, but I can't hear anything else beyond the thumping of my blood in my ears.

I look around the battlefield and find that the Red Queen has made it into the castle and is on one of the terraces overlooking the ground. My eyes meet the Red Queen's and her eyes are wide with fear. I walk across the battlefield as warriors, both friend and foe, move out of my way instantly. I'm close enough to hear the Queen gasp as she says, "This isn't possible. The power of the Queen of Wonderland was lost with Alice."

I feel a spike of pain and look down to find that one of the playing card males has stabbed me with one of my forgotten knives. As I look, I find that blood is only slowly seeping out of the wound. The Vorpal sword slips out of my hand, my grip around the hilt seeming foreign.

I catch a flash of color in the reflection of the soldier's sword as he pulls it out of me. The soldier is not frozen, yet he stands there, mouth agape as he stares at me. "My... My... My Queen?"

Despite being smeared with my blood, the sword is still clear enough for me to see my reflection. If I were of sound mind, I may have recoiled in fear myself. My eyes are glowing a bright white as swirls of red and white wisp around me. There's a smoky crown of white and red atop my head. I'm also holding twin red globes of power in my hands. I look badass but seriously scary at the same time. I watch from the backseat of my own mind as the woman in the reflection smiles a sinister smile.

My gaze finds the Red Queen's again. "Did you not know that I am her descendant? The descendants of the Queen your ancestor tried to kill in order to take over a throne that was not hers to take." My voice sounds ethereal as I walk toward her. I hold one of the red orbs of power up, bouncing it in my hand. "Should I kill you without mercy? Shall I end your life the way you have so many other Wonderlanders?"

She steps back and says nervously, "You wouldn't."

I arch a brow. "Wouldn't I?" I raise my arm, about to throw the energy ball when Bianca steps in front of her sister.

"Alyce, if I may. This isn't how you should start your rule. Have a trial amongst the people. Have them make the decision. Allow the formation of true rulers amongst the Suits again. Be the Queen they deserve." Her eyes plead for me to accept her offer. I would, if I could, but the power inside of me is consuming my every thought.

I try to force the words past my lips, but all I can manage is, "Run!" I watch Bianca's eyes widen as she grabs her sister and ducks right as my power is let loose. I try to aim the ball of power toward the farthest point away I can.

Time stops and Rab is suddenly in front of me. "Hey, Aly."

"Don't touch me! I'll hurt you," I screech.

His hands cup my face and he says, "It will be okay. Let everything out. You need to control the magic."

Shaking my head, I argue, "I can't. You need to kill me now." He looks down, seeing the blood now seeping faster from my stab wound. It seems my magic can control the flow of blood, but now that I am trying to fight for control, my magic can't fight for control and control the bleeding at the same time. His eyes shift to the forgotten soldier behind me, then back to me. "Seems I may be doing the job myself," I grunt.

He grips my cheeks tighter. "I am not letting you die on this battlefield. Now fight! I know you can do it." His voice softens. "I know new magic can be overwhelming. Take a deep breath, and let the excess magic flow from you slowly."

Biting my lip, I try to do as he says. Searching for the magic, I try to suffocate it enough to control the release, but it rams against my mind forcefully, fighting my hold. I grit my teeth. "It's too strong."

His eyes glisten with unshed tears as he looks around the battlefield, then back at me, helplessly. "This is all I can do. There isn't anyone who can help. I don't know what else to do," he yells in frustration, "I don't have a useful power to help!"

I grasp onto his wrist and smile. "You are doing what you do best. Stopping me from hurting anyone else."

"But I can't help you!" he bellows. "You're hurting yourself, and I don't know how to help!"

The blood loss is slowly making my mind hazy, but I have to hold on so my magic doesn't consume me and hurt Rab. Can't hurt Rab. I can't hurt Rab. Think Alyce. What would a badass main character do in this situation? I think of all the books I have ever read. Then an idea hits me, but it's going to hurt, and I'm not sure Rab will be okay with this plan. I caress his arm, knowing he's going to hate this idea, but it's the only way I can think of to stop my magic and get the medical attention I need. "Knock me out," I whisper.

His eyes widen. "What?"

"Hit me hard enough to knock me out. That will allow the magic to seep out slowly, and you can rush me to medical for the Dymondz to treat."

He jerks as if I've slapped him. "I could never! I would never harm you!"

I grip his arm tightly. "This is the only way you won't lose me, Rab. This is how you can help."

He leans his forehead to mine, breathing rapidly. "Okay. Okay." He pulls away, looking around us, and finds the Vorpal sword a few steps away. He rushes over and picks it up. Making sure that the bottom of the hilt is facing down, he looks back up at me and I can see the pain swirling behind his eyes. "Are you sure?"

I nod and say, "Yes. I trust you."

Stray tears fall from his eyes. "I love you, my Little Rosebud."

I grin at the nickname. It reminds me of the tattoo over his heart. "I love you, Rab." He hesitates for only a second before bringing the hilt down on the side of my head. Before the darkness consumes me, I hear someone scream my name.

CHAPTER THIRTY-FIVE

Rab

I throw the sword down as I catch her and release time.

"Alyce!" I hear the fear in Chesh's voice as he screams her name. I keep a hold of her as we fall to the ground. Fuck! My magic is low. I pause time for only her. If I can hold onto time long enough, we can get her to the Dymondz healers.

"Rab!" Mor yells as he slides up next to me. "Rab you won't be able to carry her to the medics in your condition. Hand her to me."

Chesh slides in next. "Why isn't she breathing?!" he cries.

My vision blurs as I huff, "I'm holding on to time. She was bleeding, and I didn't want her to bleed out before we reach the healers." I can hear the voices of her brothers in the background, but I can't focus on them. I need to focus on her. On my Little Rosebud.

"Rab, you are going to burn out if you use any more of your magic," Chesh whines worriedly.

I grunt, "I'll hold on as long as I can."

Mor places a hand on my shoulder and asks, "Can you still hold on to time in your shifted form?"

I understand what he's asking. Whether in male or shifted form, I can manipulate time, but if my magic is too low, I won't be able to do it in my shifted form. I nod. "I think so."

He nods looking at Chesh. "I need you to shift. I'll hold onto Alyce and Rab as you race us to the medics," he tells him.

Chesh immediately shifts into his Bandersnatch form, then lies on the ground.

Mor looks at me. He shifts closer as we switch our hold on Alyce. Before my grip on her falls away, I shift. Moving so that I'm snuggled up under her neck, I close my eyes to concentrate on my hold of her clock.

Mor races over to Chesh, jumping onto his back. Chesh takes off, racing to the medics and leaving everyone else behind. They know where to go to meet us. I take a deep breath of her fresh floral scent now tainted with the coppery scent of blood.

"Don't worry, Rab, we will save her," he says, but I'm not sure who he's trying to reassure, himself or me.

Chesh growls in confirmation. It feels like it's been hours, but I'm sure it's only been minutes before Chesh slides to a stop. Mor slides off of Chesh, carrying me and Alyce into the makeshift hospital for the fallen. I can feel myself creeping into magic overload.

"Release the clock on Alyce, Rab," Mor commands.

I do as he says, and I'm instantly consumed by darkness. I fall into a deep sleep where the only images I see are Alyce consumed by blood.

CHAPTER THIRTY-SIX
Alyce

I come to, feeling a light weight on my chest. Curious. Both of my sides feel warm too. Squinting, I look to see what's on my chest. Lying there is a kitten size Chesh, purring as he sleeps. My eyes shift to my left and find a small white rabbit, his nose twitching as he rests his head on my arm. Switching my gaze to the right, I see a brown Hare with his face tucked into the crook of my arm.

Feeling more awake, I look around the room to find thousands of Blue Morpho butterflies. I notice one glide down before it lands on my nose. "Hello Mor," I rasp. At the sound of my voice, three males suddenly appear in front of me. The sudden movement causes the butterfly sitting on my nose to fly away. Hatter, Dee, and Rook all peer down at me, looking distressed.

"Hey, Sugar. Do you need anything?"

I glance up at Hatter and try to smile. "I could use some water," I say, my voice rough. Dee runs out of the room. Hatter and Rook sit at the end of the bed, placing a hand on each of my feet. "How is everyone?" I ask.

Rook shakes his head. "Don't worry about us." I wiggle my fingers at him. He sounds exhausted as he sighs and takes my hand.

"Rook, how are you doing?" I know what happened to me is bringing up old memories of his charge the White King dying in the War.

"I'm fine, Aly." His words don't match his eyes as I see them glisten with unshed tears.

Dee runs back into the room but pauses, looking between his brother and me. He looks back at me, and I try to plead with my eyes. Rook needs us, but he won't listen if it comes from me right now. Dee nods, setting the glass of water on the side table. "I think we all need a cuddle," he says quietly.

I grin up at Dee. "Yes."

"We shouldn't, what if we hurt…" Before Rook can protest anymore, I tug on his hand as Dee grasps the back of his neck. His face lands on my abdomen. "She's hurt," he protests.

It did hurt a little bit, but my stab wound is on the other side of where he landed. It actually doesn't hurt too badly, there's only a sting of pain compared to what it was. I shush him, letting go of his hand as I caress the side of his face. I hear his breathing hitch as he shifts to slide his arms under my lower back. His hold is tight but not uncomfortable. I can feel his silent tears seeping through to my skin. I shift my hand to slip my fingers through the teal hair at the top of his head.

Turning my head to my right, I find Dee kneeling on the ground. His face is right next to mine, and he's biting his lower lip as tears track down his face. "I'm sorry," I rasp.

He shifts forward, kissing me softly. Pulling away, he smiles sadly. "No need to be sorry. You had us worried, though."

"I love you, Dee."

His smile turns genuine. "I love you too," he says softly. He lays his head down next to mine and closes his eyes.

I turn to the other side, finding Hatter kneeling similarly. He reaches up, threading his fingers through my hair. I close my eyes, briefly enjoying the sensations. I feel a kiss on my forehead, and my eyes slowly open and lift to his. My strong male refuses to cry, but I can see the glassy sheen to them now.

"I missed you, Sugar," he whispers.

I know what he's trying to say, but he's attempting to control his emotions. He's trying to stay strong while his friends break. "I love you, Tar."

He shifts forward, kissing me softly, then pulls away and says, "I love you forever."

I smile. "Forever seems like a long time."

"Forever doesn't seem long enough, if I'm honest," he replies.

"Agreed." I shift my gaze back over to my other males, noticing they are all asleep. I look back at Hatter, noticing his lids drooping. "I'm okay. You can sleep now."

He shakes his head and argues, "Someone should stay awake."

I smirk. "I think Mor has that covered."

He looks around the room and watches as a butterfly glides down and lands on my forehead. I can see the smirk working on his lips. "I suppose you're right." He lays his head next to mine, keeping his fingers threaded through my hair. His breathing soon evens out, and I'm surrounded by warmth and feeling more loved than I ever thought possible. With the sound of their steady breathing and their warmth surrounding me, I fall into a peaceful sleep.

My peaceful sleep is disturbed by whispered voices. I hear mumbled words but can't make them out. Then I recognize one of the voices as Laurel. I grumble, "Five more minutes." The voices stop suddenly, and I feel a hand brush gently through my hair. I open my eyes enough to squint up and find Laurel smiling softly down at me.

"It's good to see you awake, kiddo."

I look to see who else is in the room. Edi and Alix are at the end of my bed, along with Mor. Hum... where is everyone? I look back to Laurel and ask, "Where is everyone?"

Edi slides up on my other side and sits on the edge of the bed. "The others are getting something to eat and drink."

I nod and close my eyes, still feeling exhausted. Alix tugs on my toes, and I open my eyes again to glare. He grins. "What? You've been sleeping for days. We were worried."

Sighing, I say, "You could have woken me up."

Laurel shakes his head. "You needed your rest to heal. We checked on you each day, but your guys stayed with you the whole time."

I arch a brow. "Where were you guys?"

Edi rubs the back of his head. "We were helping the Empress with the fallen and with cleaning up the castle."

"We were also helping guard the Red Queen so some of the soldiers could rest or eat," Alix adds.

I smile. "You guys don't have to help out. I'm sure we can get you back through the Looking Glass if you want."

Alix snorts. "Like we would leave without making sure you were okay."

"Plus, as your older brothers, helping make sure our little sister's kingdom is at least somewhat organized is the polite thing to do," Edi says, laughing.

I roll my eyes. "I'm sure that's the only reason."

Edi smirks and jokes, "The ladies here are interesting. You can't fault me for being curious."

"It's females. And yes, I can."

Laurel pushes Edi off the bed with a snort of laughter as Edi dramatically falls off. Laurel looks back down at me before saying, "We wanted to come by and check on you since Mor said you had finally woken up yesterday."

"ALY!"

I hear my name screeched from the door and look up to find Chesh, Rab, and Arch standing in the doorway. Chesh is leading the way, but upon seeing me awake, he drops the cup in his hand and runs toward me. I can already see tears streaming down his face. Alix jumps out of the way when Chesh launches himself over the edge of the bed. Laurel jumps out of the way as well as Chesh lands on me.

I let out a huff as he lands on me. Shattering Tea Cups! I wasn't expecting a mass of a male to land on me. At least my wound has healed enough with magic that there's only a slight twinge of pain.

"Chesh!" Mor chastises.

Chesh slides his arms under my armpits and nuzzles his face into my neck. I wave off Mor's worry as I wrap my arms around a shaking Chesh. "It's okay," I soothe as I run my fingers through his hair and he mewls into my neck. I look at Rab and Arch, and I can see they are fighting not to run to me as well. I smile and use my free hand to wave them over. "You two come here."

As if that was all they were waiting on, they rush to either side of me. Rab slides onto the left side of the bed. Due to my hand currently running through Chesh's hair on that side, Rab slides his hand into my hair and begins tugging it softly. He lays his head next to mine on his bicep.

I close my eyes at his gentle touch. He whispers, "You scared the shit out of me."

"I'm sorry," I whisper back.

"You need to stay with us alright, Rosebud?"

"Forever," I vow.

Arch had slid onto the bed on my right side. He lifts my arm and slides under it, so his head now rests on my bicep. My arm is just long enough that I can caress the tips of his ears. He shivers in my arms and snuggles closer. "I missed your voice."

"My voice?"

"It was so quiet without you," he whispers.

I open my eyes to look to my left first and shift enough until I'm able to kiss Rab on his nose. He smirks and leans in, pressing his lips to mine softly. He pulls away, and I smile. "I love you, Rab."

His eyes shimmer. "I love you too, Little Rosebud." His eyes close as he continues playing with my hair.

I shift a bit to press a kiss to the top of Chesh's head right between his flattened ears. "I love you, Chesh."

I hear his rough reply, "I love you, Kitten."

I look to my right to find Arch looking up at me. I smile down at him as I caress the tips of his ears. "I love you, Arch."

He bites his lip, trying to keep the tears I see glistening in his eyes from falling as he says, "I love you, Mouse." He squeezes his eyes shut as he snuggles in closer to me.

I feel warm and loved by these males. My gaze shifts, and it falls upon Mor standing next to the bed. He's looking down at me with love and affection. I smile up at him. "Thank you," I say.

He raises a brow. "For what?"

"For watching over us while we slept. For looking after me and keeping me safe."

His eyes widen for a moment, and then they soften. "You're welcome," he says gruffly.

I'm going to need to snuggle him next. Maybe later, when everyone is gone again, I will snuggle him all alone. I'm so comfortable, I feel my eyes getting heavy again.

"Go back to sleep, Aly."

I sigh, giving in to the temptation of sleep. But first I whisper, "I love you, Mor."

I hear his soft reply as the brush of his wings caresses my cheeks. "I love you, my beautiful Butterfly."

CHAPTER THIRTY-SEVEN
Alyce

It's been a week, and I've been officially cleared by the Dymondz medics. I had to admit Dymondz has amazing health personnel. I may have to ask Bianca if I can hire a few of her staff to have here. Here being a relative term considering I have no idea what condition the castle is in. Actually, I have no idea what the area around the castle looks like either. Pushing through the flaps of the medical tent, I'm blinded by the sun.

Shattering tea cups! I blink my eyes several times to clear away the spots. Has it always been that bright, or has being restricted to the darkened tent caused my aversion to the bright sun? I blink a few more times and gasp at the sight in front of me. The surrounding area is bright green with mushrooms and flowers growing everywhere. Wasn't there a bloodbath here a week or so ago?

I'm immersed in the color combinations of tiger lilies, irises, pansies, tulips, lilacs, and even roses. The flowers aren't talking like the books say, though. Which I'm slightly disappointed about but also glad about. The thought of talking flowers creeps me out a bit. But the roses catch my eye. They are blue. I thought the roses in Wonderland were supposed to be red? I squeal when I see a cactus move in the distance. What in the world? Then it races past me, and I realize it's a cat. What would that be called?! A cat-tus? I let out a soft squeak when my name is called behind me. Turning, I find Mor smiling softly at me.

I grin. "Mor!" I wrap my arms around him tightly.

He wraps his arms around me, laughing. "Good morning to you too, Aly."

I give him one last squeeze before pulling away. He releases me, and I slide my hand into his. "I haven't had a chance to cuddle with you yet! Cuddles are required tonight."

He smiles and says, "I'm sorry, Little Butterfly. I've been a bit busy helping the others with the castle."

I quirk a brow. "The castle?" I ask, slightly confused.

He nods.

"Okay, you are going to have to explain that to me, but first..." I wave to the surrounding area. "How do the grounds look this amazing after everything that happened here?"

He looks around and shrugs. "It seems Wonderland is thriving now that the Red Queen is no longer in power."

"How does Wonderland understand who is in charge?"

"Magic, I suppose. It doesn't feel like the malicious and controlling power of the Red Queen, though. Instead, it feels like a much gentler power radiating from the center of Wonderland." He points to the blue roses. "It's why the roses are blue."

"Blue?"

He nods and pulls a necklace out of his pocket. He holds it out to me, and I realize it's the blue rose necklace they bought me in Clubbz. I'd forgotten that I had placed it in one of the small, buckled pockets of my leathers. I wanted to wear it all the time but figured I could keep it close instead. I pull my hair up, signaling him to put it on me. He unclasps it, placing it around my neck before pulling away with a smile.

He points to the rose and says, "It has recognized you as the true ruler of Wonderland."

My eyes widen, looking down at the small rose. I knew this was what the outcome would be, but now that it's here... Whistling tea kettles! This is real! I'm the ruler of Wonderland! I look back up at Mor, and he must see the panic on my face.

He cups my face with both hands. "Breathe, Little Butterfly. You're not alone. The coronation won't be for a while. Wonderland is still healing, and we need to deal with the Red Queen as well. You will have time to grasp this new idea."

"What if I never grasp the idea?" I rasp.

He smiles. "You will be an amazing Queen. I'm sure the idea of being Queen may never feel real, but, you have us. We will be by your side the whole time. Every step of the way."

"Forever?"

He kisses my nose. "Forever."

Shaking away the fear, I huff out a sigh. "So you said something about the castle?"

He smirks as he slips his hand into mine. He tugs, and we begin walking in the direction of the castle. "It will be easier if I show you."

"Can you at least give me a hint?"

"We worked together to make the castle a livable space again," he tells me.

"Who is we?"

Mor laughs. "The males and I. And your brothers helped with a few tasks as well."

I snort. "If my brothers were involved, I'm a little scared."

Mor sets his hand on the newly clean wooden doors to the castle. "Are you ready?"

I shrug. "I guess so."

He pushes the doors open, and I gasp. The once shabby and dusty inside is no more. In its place is the most beautiful place I have ever seen, and that includes the Dymondz castle. The crumbling stone archways have been fixed, and the stone floors are clean and shiny. Where the once dark entryway sat, there are now beautiful, large crystal chandeliers lighting the space. My hand slips out of Mor's as I walk further into the space. There are sweeping staircases leading up to rooms and fire-lit hallways. I twirl around the wide-open area taking in all of the colors.

"So... do you like it?" he asks nervously.

"Like it? I love it!"

He smiles. "Good." Taking my hand, he leads me up the stairs. Once we reach the top he veers off in the direction of the Queen's Chambers.

"You cleaned the Queen's Chambers too?"

He smirks. "We did the whole castle."

I choke on my spit in shock. "In a week?!" I blurt.

He nods. "The other Suits wanted to help as well, but it was mainly the seven of us and your brothers." He pushes the doors open immediately.

I'm floored. This room isn't the same room I entered when I went back through the Looking Glass. The room is now painted a light blue and has a crystal chandelier that reflects the light coming through the windows. It's bathed in rainbows from the light reflecting off the crystal. I spot the Looking Glass placed in the corner of the room. Safely away from the main entrance into the room.

The others filter into the room with us, and I'm suddenly surrounded by my males. Chesh squeezes himself up next to me and grins. "Welcome home, Kitten."

I feel tears stinging my eyes as I look at each of my males. Home. I've wanted to feel like I belonged somewhere for so long. It's true that home is where your heart is, and my heart is with these males. But it's wonderful to have a place to call my own. Where each of us can rest and relax. "Home?" I ask.

Hatter's deep voice comes from behind me. "A place where we can be ourselves."

I feel Hatter's arms wrap around my waist, and I lean back into him. Chesh squeezes my hand, and I look over at him.

"A place where you can be happy."

"Where WE can be happy," I amend.

He smiles. "Where we can be happy."

"Home..." I grin at the words. "I like the sound of that."

CHAPTER THIRTY-EIGHT
Alyce

Three months later...

"So the decision has been made," Bianca commands from the dias of the Grand Hall. We decided to have the meeting at my castle since it's a centralized location. My castle. That is still weird to say. I'm standing behind her as she announces the decision that the people made regarding what to do with the Red Queen. I entrusted her with the communication between Suits and the people for the Red Queen's conviction. She insisted that I be in charge due to being the, soon to be, Queen of Wonderland, but I had argued that I wasn't experienced in the politics of Wonderland yet, and it would be better for someone who knew Wonderland better than me.

That unfortunately meant she was in charge of her sister's conviction. "...The people are tied in their decision. She is to be either beheaded, as she has done to many Wonderlanders, or be sentenced to life imprisonment. This leaves the final decision to the leaders of the four Suits and the Queen of Wonderland to break any ties."

Well, shattering tea cups. Bianca points to the Commander of Spaydz to start the vote. The Commander nods and says, "Death."

The Lady of Clubbz votes next. "Imprisonment."

The Countess of Heartz seems to struggle with her decision. She sighs. "My people suffered under her hand, and I was unable to do anything. For my people, I will vote for death."

Bianca looks at me, and I can see the indecision warring in her eyes. This is her sister. She looks at her Knight, and he slips his hand into hers. She grunts, "Imprisonment."

My eyes meet Rab's. My leader in all things, except for this. This will be my first decision as the Queen of Wonderland. It doesn't matter that we haven't had the coronation yet. These rulers are looking to me as if I'm already the Queen. Rab smiles. He nods as he mouths. "You know what to do."

I did. It was my role as the Queen to rule with all aspects of the Suits. I need to rule with love and compassion for all my subjects, no matter if they are innocent or guilty. But I also need to lead with my logic and mind. To not let my personal feelings get in the way. To be honest and loyal to my people. And lastly, to rule with honor and bring justice to Wonderland.

I shift my shoulders back to stand taller as I announce my decision. "Life imprisonment will be the outcome of this trial. The people deserve to find closure, but the life of one will not bring back all the lives lost. The blood of lives lost must end here. She will be contained within a cell in Spaydz. They have the highest level of security. She will not be pampered and will pay for her sins each day of her confinement until her life and her magic are returned to Wonderland from where they once began. Today marks the day Wonderland will heal and begin anew." My voice sounded as if it were coming from another woman. I didn't even recognize the power emanating from me as I spoke. My eyes meet each of the rulers.

The Lady of Clubbz gives me a smile as she stands from her seat and says, "Thank you for your honesty. I will return to my people and give them the verdict." She bows before leaving the chamber.

The Heartz Countess is next. She smiles as she bows. "Thank you for your compassion. I will leave to tell my people. We will take this time to heal and grow. If you need anything from Heartz, please let me know."

The Commander stands, and I'm not going to lie; I'm still intimidated by her. She's an amazon woman, and I'm sure she could kill me in seconds if she wanted to. She holds out her hand to me. I look down at it, and then over to Dee and Rook. What is the custom here?! Dee and Rook grasp each other's forearms and then nod to the Commander. Right! I grasp her forearm, and she grasps mine. I have to hold back a wince at how tight her grip is. Dang, this woman is strong!

She bows her head. "Thank you for your justice. I will take the prisoner away immediately. She will be secure on our journey back." She releases my arm, and I do the same. She stomps away with several males following behind her.

That leaves Bianca, the last ruler. My eyes find hers, and I can see the tears swimming in her eyes. She whispers, "Thank you."

I shrug. "I only did what was right."

She stands, walking over to me. Wrapping me in a hug, she says, "I know. That's why I'm saying thank you. You could have easily sent her to death. I wouldn't have stopped you."

I hug her back. "I'm not sure how, but I knew what I needed to do. It wouldn't have been right to sentence her to death."

Bianca pulls away, wiping at her face. She smiles. "I suppose I should get back to Dymondz and let everyone know the decision."

I nod but then remember something. "But first, you need to teach me how to magically spell the mirror so my brothers can come and go from the Surface." I made my brothers go back through the mirror after I was fully healed. Which was about three months ago. They were not happy, but I told them they had been away for too long and needed to get back to their lives. The only way they could come back to Wonderland was if

I went through the mirror first. Which was bothersome considering how crazy my life has become.

"Right! Let's go then." She leads the way up to the now secure room for the mirror. I thought it would be better in there than in the bedroom in case my brothers were able to look into the mirror and see what was going on in Wonderland. Talk about awkward if my brothers saw what I did with my males.

Remembering the question that has been burning in my brain since I first came to Wonderland, I finally ask, "Why did I drop out of the sky when I first came to Wonderland?"

Bianca laughs, "Because the mirror on the Surface did not have a connection to the one in the castle yet. The moment you walked through the Looking Glass on this side, it created the connection."

Hmm. I suppose that makes sense. I'm glad I won't fall through the air when I enter Wonderland now. Rook slides the key into the lock and opens the mirror room. The males thought it was stupid that I called it that, but what else was I supposed to call it? Rook or Dee always had the key since they were now in charge of security. They also trained a small group of males the Spaydz Commander sent us in thanks for saving Wonderland. I didn't understand the gesture, but Rook told me that I had gained her respect, and this was how she showed it.

Bianca pulls me over to the mirror. "Now due to you being the descendant of the original Alice you will need blood for this spell," she instructs.

I groan, "Blood?"

She nods and repeats, "Blood."

Then I smirk, holding my hand out to Hatter. "Prick me, Tar."

Rolling his eyes, he pulls out one of his hat pins, but I can see his smirk. "I can prick you with something much larger later, Sugar." He winks as he quickly stabs my finger.

Bianca rolls her eyes but smiles. She grabs onto my hand and starts making designs on the glass. She nods before releasing my hand. "Alright, that should do it."

My hand is suddenly in a warm mouth. I look over to find Chesh grinning around my finger. "No worries, Kitten. I'll make it better."

I moan and Bianca claps her hands in front of my face. "Pay attention," she admonishes.

I rip my finger out of Chesh's mouth as he chuckles. I wipe my finger on my slacks and look up to Bianca. "Sorry. What do you need me to do?"

"I need you to say this spell."

"What spell?" I ask. Bianca touches my forehead, and my mind is suddenly filled with several spells in a language that's foreign but also familiar. Also, a neat trick.

"The spell is in the native tongue of Wonderland. Not many people speak it anymore. You will find that only the scholars in Spaydz are able to speak it."

The spell I need seems to glow gold within my mind, and my own magic seems to pulse in recognition of the old language. I may not be able to read it, but my magic seems to know what to do. I have become better with my magic over the last few months, and I'm now able to have a steady flow of magic within myself without it fighting me. I take a breath and let my magic do the rest.

Those who wish to enter
Must be judged and pass.
Heart and Mind must be pure,
Honesty and Justice are true,
With the blessing of the Queen,
You may enter till the next.

The mirror seems to whine for a moment, and then it starts to glow. The blood smeared across the mirror appears to soak into the glass, and then my old room on the Surface comes into view.

"Anyone you feel is worthy of walking through the mirror will now be able to do so."

I turn back to Bianca and ask, "Anyone?"

She nods, pointing to the males beside me. "If they want to pass to the Surface they will be able to without you now. Your brothers should also be able to pass freely."

"Thank you!"

She bows her head. "I'll be taking my leave now. Until I see you at the coronation."

Ugh... The coronation is in three months. I'm not sure I'm ready for it. I look back into the mirror and laugh when I notice my brothers have moved it, so I can see the clock on my old nightstand. They should be getting off work soon. I look at my males and tell them, "I'm going to pop through really quick and write them a note. Do you guys mind getting a few of the guest rooms ready for them? I'm sure they will immediately come through the mirror once they read the note."

They all nod and everyone leaves except Dee. I raise a brow, and he smirks. "Someone has to make sure you come back."

I roll my eyes. "Of course, I will come back."

He shrugs. "I was planning on staying until your brothers read the note. A familiar face instead of one of the guards would be better. We've also moved the mirror since they were last here, so they won't know how to navigate the castle to find us."

I stand on my tiptoes and he bends down, so I can kiss him quickly. I smile as I walk through the mirror. "I love you, Dee."

"I love you too, darling."

CHAPTER THIRTY-NINE

Alyce

One week until the coronation...

The guys are up to something. They have been sneaking around the last few weeks, and I know they are planning something. I know it doesn't have anything to do with the coronation because everything for that event has been finalized for a month. They have been sneaking off to the Surface without me. My brothers have assured me that they are with my males the entire time. That would make me feel better if I didn't know how crazy my brothers could get.

Currently, I'm pacing the floor in the mirror chamber. Yes, I changed it from the mirror room to the mirror chamber. It sounds more official. The others still thought it was weird, but they conceded. They said I was the Queen, so I could call the rooms whatever I wanted. My eyes jerk up when I see the glow of the mirror. Rab and Mor walk through, laughing. I halt my pacing when I see Rab's smile. He still doesn't do it enough, and he's so handsome when he does.

They both halt when they see me, causing the others to bump into them as they enter the room. Hatter and Arch end up on the floor on top of each other as Dee and Rook trip over their fallen bodies. They manage to catch themselves as Chesh transforms quickly into his cat form, floating in the air to avoid the pile of bodies.

I tap my foot on the ground in irritation. "What is going on? You guys have been secretive the last few weeks and are slipping through the mirror more often than ever."

I hear Hatter groan from the floor. "Watch the knee, Archy."

"I wasn't going to knee you in the dick, Tar. I like that part of you too much to damage it."

Hatter chuckles. "I'm sure you do."

I clap my hands to get everyone's attention. "Something is going on. You guys are horrible at trying to be sneaky with whatever this plan is. What is going on?!" I'm trying not to yell, but I'm feeling the months of frustration from planning the coronation blow into me. The stress of not feeling adequate enough for this position. And on top of everything, my males are keeping secrets from me.

Rab clears his throat and says, "We have a date night planned for tonight. We were getting the last few things we needed."

"Really?" I sound way more skeptical than I meant to.

Mor holds up a bag that I didn't notice when they walked through. "Really, Little Butterfly."

I sigh. "A date night?"

Chesh explodes in a puff of purple glitter, changing back into his male form. "Yes, a date night, Little Kitten. You have seemed stressed lately, and we want to help relax you with a date."

Arch comes up behind me and begins massaging my shoulders. I groan as my body seems to melt under his strong hands. "We want you to go upstairs, take a warm bath, and try to relax. Chesh is going to set out some clothes for you to change into for the date afterward. Once you're dressed, come down to the courtyard."

I'm skeptical, but I play along. Why not? Arch hits a tight spot in my shoulders, and I groan. I didn't realize how much stress I held in my shoulders and back. "Okay," I mumble.

Arch laughs. "Alright, Little Mouse." He gives my shoulders one last squeeze and then pulls away. He kisses my cheek and says, "Go relax in the bath for however long you want. We will be waiting."

I whine, "But... the massage."

He smirks. "I'll massage you later, Little Mouse."

"Alright," I murmur, feeling my cheeks heat when he winks. Clearing my throat, I turn away from my males and head up to our bed chamber. Opening the large doors to our room, I make my way over to the large bathroom. Hatter and Arch have been making changes to the bathroom over the last few months. We were able to get a tub from Clubbz, and I absolutely love the large teacup. It's big enough to hold all eight of us. Over in the corner of the bathroom is a large shower as well. With some help from Mor, we were able to set the whole castle up with running water. We no longer had to go to the stream to get water to fill up the tub or do other chores around the castle.

I turn on the water, letting it rise from the bottom of the teacup. I shift through the tiny drawers above the tub and pick out a scent to throw in the bath. Smiling when I find the blue rose scent is overflowing, I pull out a few tea bags and throw them into the tub. Turning off the water, I undress and slip into the warm water. I groan as my muscles instantly relax.

I've been in here for what feels like hours before the water runs cold, and I finally get out. Slipping out of the bathroom, I find clothes lying on the bed. I smile. Chesh is a sneaky one alright. Moving closer to the bed, I gasp when I realize that the outfit is reminiscent of the one I wore when we went to the festival in Clubbz. The dress is a light blue, but instead of it being short like the one in Clubbz, this one is floor length. The dress looks to be satin with a sheer overlay that's covered in dark blue roses. It has the same corset top with the sleeves being sheer and off the shoulder. The sleeves are long and flowy instead of the short simple sleeves the other dress had.

Next to the dress sits a silver circlet headdress that has vines and small blue roses with a blue sapphire in the middle. There's a diamond in the center that will dip down into the center of my forehead.

Next to the dress are a pair of white lace flats that when I look closer, I can see the lace pattern makes roses. And lastly is the blue rose necklace I got the night of the festival. Running back to the bathroom, I curl my hair into soft rivulets.

Once I'm dressed, I look in the mirror. I don't look like the same girl who first fell through the Looking Glass. I look... like a Queen. Nodding to myself, I make my way down the winding stairs and out to the courtyard. Once I get outside I look around and freeze. The courtyard is surrounded by fairy lights. How did they get the fairy lights to work? There are jars filled with fireflies creating a path, which leads further into the courtyard. I follow the path. Rounding the corner, I gasp when I find all of my males. They are all dressed in suits from the Surface, but that's not what catches my eye first. They are all kneeling on one knee.

I cover my mouth as each of them pulls out a box from behind their backs. Each box varies in size.

Rab smiles and explains, "We didn't think it appropriate to get you seven rings, so we got you something from each of us as well as a ring we all agreed upon."

"What... what..." I can't find the words; they've rendered me speechless.

Rab stands, making his way over to me. He kneels in front of me again and opens the box he's holding. "Your brothers explained the customs of the Surface when a man wants to marry a woman, but since we are males of Wonderland we wanted to make a few changes. This is my gift to you. With this, I pledge my life and loyalty to you. Forever and always. Will you accept this gift and become my wife?"

I stare at him, my jaw on the floor. Is he asking only for himself or for all of them? He must see the question burning in my eyes because he smiles and says, "This is only on my behalf. The others will ask on their own."

I finally look at the gift he's holding, and I feel tears gather in my eyes. It's a delicate-looking choker with two blue roses framing a dangling circular golden plate. The plate reads, 'Precious Rosebud.' I look into Rab's eyes and smile. "I would be honored to become your wife," I say, my voice raspy with emotion.

He grins as he stands, clasping the choker around my neck. He places a soft kiss against my lips and says, "You look beautiful Little Rosebud." He steps away, allowing the next male to come forward. Mor kneels in front of me next.

Mor opens his box, and I gasp. Inside is a pair of dangling earrings that look like the wings of a Blue Morpho butterfly. I look into his eyes, and he smiles. "This was one of the butterflies that fell in battle. I wanted to do something special with this small piece of me. It took the artist on the Surface a long time to make these and to make sure the wings didn't rip in the process. I would be honored if you accepted this gift and became my wife."

He now had a broken butterfly tattooed on his body due to the loss of this small piece of himself. Instead of allowing Wonderland to take back this small piece of magic, he preserved it. It may seem dark to some people, but I see this gift for what it is. He's giving me a part of himself. He's trusting me with one of his precious butterflies. "Yes," I rasp as silent tears stream down my face. He stands, placing the earrings where they belong. I can feel the warmth of his magic that still resides in the fallen wings as they caress the sides of my neck when they swing. He wipes away my tears as he presses a soft kiss to my nose and steps away.

Hatter steps up next and kneels. He takes a deep breath, seemingly nervous, which makes me smile. He opens the box and grimaces. "I wasn't sure what gift to give you. I've never given a gift before. The only thing I could think of was giving you something that was both beautiful and could protect you." He pulls out a small and delicate hat pin. Looking up at me he says, "It looks small and delicate. Like you."

I snort, but he continues with a smile, "But I have found that even the things we think are delicate and small can be dangerous too."

He hands me the small hat pin. Its shaft is black, and the end is extremely sharp. But on the other end is a dark blue rose. It has small chains dangling from it that have silver roses attached to the end.

"We have a leather holster for you that you can strap to your leg to use in battle." I watch as he stands and shifts a bit as he looks into my eyes. I can see the vulnerability he is trying to hide as he says, "With this gift, I hope you will accept me as your husband. I would be honored if you would be my wife."

I stand on my tiptoes and kiss him, wrapping my free hand around the back of his head to deepen the kiss. I feel him moan against my lips. I pull away smiling and look into his dark gaze as I reply, "I would be honored to call you my husband, Tar."

Something in his gaze shifts as he slams his lips to mine. He pulls away, panting. Pressing his forehead against mine, he whispers, "Thank you."

Smiling, I pull away to look into his eyes. "For what?" I ask quietly.

He caresses my cheek, looking at me as if I was the only female in the world. "For being the female I always wished for but never thought I would meet. For being the female I thought I never deserved but forced her way into my heart anyways." He kisses me again softly, walking away before I have the chance to say anything else, allowing Arch to take his spot. I look around, trying to find a place to put my sharp hat pin. Rab comes up behind me, smirking as he places a velvet box beside me on the ground.

He winks. "I have a feeling you will need this, Little Alyce."

I'm about to ask why when Arch kneeling in front of me grabs my attention. Turning back to give Arch my full attention, I find him smirking as he opens his box. Inside is one of his handmade pistols, but this one is different. It's small enough to fit into my hand perfectly. "I made some modifications to the pistol I made for your brothers. This one will be fed by your magic and your magic alone, so no one will be able to use this pistol except for you."

I lift the small pistol out of the box. It looks delicate. It's beautiful, decorated with filigree and small roses. I notice etching on the bottom of the butt of the pistol. Holding it closer, I smile when I read, 'For the Queen of Wonderland, My Little Mouse.' I lower myself, placing the pistol in the velvet box beside me before standing again.

"I would be honored if you would be my wife, Little Mouse," Arch says sweetly.

I smile, nodding. "Yes."

He grins, standing and kissing my lips quickly before making his way over to Hatter. He slips his hand into Hatter's and presses a kiss to Hatter's cheek. I watch Hatter's eyes widen before they soften on Arch. He smiles before placing a kiss on the top of his head. I love how Hatter is now opening up more in his relationship with Arch.

I turn back when I hear a throat clear. In true twin fashion, both Dee and Rook are kneeling in front of me together. I smile down at both of them. They each reveal a box and open them at the same time. I laugh when I see what's inside. My males seem to think I need an abundance of weapons. Inside each box is a knife, but the knives are twins of each other, just like Dee and Rook. They pull out the knives revealing their beauty. My males have all continued the rose theme.

The hilt of each knife is covered in intricate roses. They hold the knives out to me, bowing their heads. In unison, they say, "We would be honored if you would accept these gifts and become our wife."

I take each knife and place them in the velvet box. Staying at their level, I place a finger under each of their chins and raise them so their eyes meet mine. I look at Rook first and reply, "I would be honored to be your wife, Rook." I lean forward and kiss his lips gently. Pulling away, I look at Dee next. "I would be honored to be your wife, Dee." I tell him as I kiss his lips gently as well. Standing now, they rise with me and smash their lips against each of my cheeks. My laugh is a bit weird with my face squished.

They pull away smiling. They make their way over to the others leaving only Chesh. He saunters over to me with his feline grace and grins as he kneels. His box is small. Before he opens it, he looks me up and down. "You are currently wearing my gift, and you look absolutely purrfect in it."

My brows knit together as I look at the small box. His grin widens. "So... since you are wearing my gift, I was in charge of this." He opens the box revealing a ring. The ring is absolutely breathtaking. It looks as if it belongs in a fairytale. What catches my eye are the seven small stones embedded in the band, surrounded by smaller diamonds. I look back up at Chesh. "It took us forever to find the right ring. Your brothers explained that the stones are called birthstones, and we each picked a stone we liked the most."

He pulls the ring out of the box and holds it out to me. "I would be honored to call you my wife. Will you marry us?" he asks.

I can't stop the torrent of tears that seem to explode out of me. I cover my mouth as I nod. Holding out my left hand, he slides the ring into place, and it fits perfectly. He wraps me in his arms as I continue to cry. I'm not sure why I'm crying so much.

Chesh holds me tighter and coos, "It's okay, Little Kitten. I've got you. You're stuck with us forever now."

That's it! I've been so afraid that they would still leave me. Leave me like everyone else has. Except for my brothers. But that's brotherly love. This is different. They could leave. They were under no obligation to stay. Yeah, we called each other Mates, but that's just a word. I feel the others circle around me and add their warmth to Chesh's as they all hold me close.

I've been so afraid they were going to leave these last few months. They were constantly sneaking around and leaving Wonderland to go to the Surface. But this was what they had been planning. They had talked to my brothers and wanted to do something that was done on the Surface. They wanted to commit to me, not only in the way Wonderlanders did but also where I was from.

I let out all of the doubt and fear I've felt for the last few months as I hold Chesh tighter. These were my Males. They were mine. Forever.

CHAPTER FORTY

Alyce

Day of the Coronation & Wedding...

Today is the day. Today is the day!!! Oh, whistling tea kettles! I have been working overtime this past week to get everything I needed done for the wedding done. No, I didn't need a place or decorations. That was covered with the Coronation. But I needed a dress and items to represent each of the guys. They gave me such fantastic gifts, and I wanted to do the same for them. So where better to get everything than on the Surface? I had to get my brothers involved because, of course, they were my bridesmen. Yes, I looked it up. It's a thing. But in true female fashion, I made Bianca my Maid of Honor. I also made Alix my Male of Honor because he has always been there for me. Laurel and Edi were in charge of distracting my males, so they didn't see the gifts or my dress.

They were truly the best too. Alix helped me find the best place to get my dress, and Bianca helped me pick out dresses to try on. The dress that I picked? It has a stunning lace corset top with a lace overlay skirt. It flows beautifully, but what made me say yes to the dress? It's dark blue at the bottom and has an ombre effect as it goes up, so it fades to the lightest of blues before fading into white midway up the dress. I thought it would look wonderful with Mor's butterfly wing earrings. I also found a small white top hat will be wonderful to put Hatter's hat pin in. I also got white leather holsters for Arch and the twin's gifts.

Next on the list were gifts for the guys. Dee and Rook were first. After several hours of research and Alix's help, I found a blacksmith. He had several premade swords for sale, and I immediately found two that spoke to me. The blacksmith was nice enough to discount the leather belts and scabbards.

For Hatter, I was able to find a store that sold hat pins, and I'm not going to lie, I bought too many. But they all looked so awesome, and I couldn't not buy them! I hoped that Hatter would love them!

I found a leather gun holster that would be amazing for Arch's new pistol. When I had asked him why he didn't carry it, he'd said, "I can't find enough leather to make a holster. It's fine, Little Mouse." It was an astonishing pistol that he had worked hard on for the last few months, and I hated that he wasn't able to carry it around with his other pistol.

Chesh was my easiest to find a gift for. I bought him the softest and cuddliest blanket I could find. I also bought a crap ton of Rom-Com movies I knew he would love. His gift was a date night full of cuddles and movies.

Rab and Mor were my hardest males to shop for. It took me two days of research to find a suitable tattoo artist who could fit me in. For Rab, I wanted a tattoo of a rabbit and a clock. He had my clock forever etched into his skin, and I wanted to get a clock for him. It wouldn't tick the way mine does against his skin, but I hoped he would like it. I knew it would hurt, but I chose to put the tattoo in the same place mine was on Rab, right over my heart. Thankfully my magic helped with the pain. My tattoo artist insisted I come back the next day for the second tattoo. I didn't argue because it might look weird if I was able to sit for two tattoos in one day.

The next morning, I greeted my tattoo artist with a smile as she sat me down and etched out my second design. Now, I know wing tattoos are a bit cliche, but I knew I had to have Mor's beautiful Blue Morpho wings on my back. They took up more than half my back. I have never been more thankful for my magic.

I'm now staring at myself in the mirror. My makeup and hair are done, but I'm still in my robe because I had asked Alix to get the guys. I didn't want them to see me in my wedding dress yet, but I wanted to give them their gifts before the wedding. Bianca, on the other hand, said they weren't allowed to come into the bedroom, so I would have to do the gift exchange from the other side of the door. I wasn't sure how showing Rab and Mor my gifts would happen, but I'm sure Bianca would have an idea.

I hear a knock on the bedroom door and smile as I hear my brother on the other side say, "Bianca said you weren't allowed in. Do you want to anger her right now? She is a woman on a mission, and I am not getting in her way. She scares the shit out of me."

I laugh on the other side of the door. "You should listen to Alix. She's taking the position of Maid of Honor very seriously," I warn.

"Hey, Sis. I got your males for you. How exactly are we doing this gift exchange?"

Bianca is next to the door in an instant. "Alyce is going to stay on this side, and I will open the door and hand over the gifts." She looks at me next and says, "You may be the Queen, but I am in charge right now."

I hold my hands up in a placating gesture and say, "Sure thing, Empress."

She rolls her eyes but smiles before opening the door just wide enough so that the males can only see her. She looks at me and asks, "Who's first?"

I look down at the gifts I placed next to the door. I had decided to give the gifts in the order they had given me mine but backward. "Chesh." I pick up his box and hand it over to Bianca.

She smiles taking it. "Chesh. You're up first."

"Really?" I smile hearing Chesh's voice. I hear him rip open the paper on the box. I had put a note on top of everything, so I hope he reads it. "For date night, love your Kitten."

I hear his purr begin as he asks excitedly, "Are these Surface movies?"

"They are."

I know when he pulls out the blanket because his purr gets louder. "This is so soft, Kitten. Thank you."

"I figured we could do a date night and watch movies in my room on the Surface." I say through the door.

"I can't wait, Kitten."

Bianca looks at me with a grin. "He wants to hug you so bad."

I smile and slide my hand around the corner of the door. His hand is instantly in mine. He squeezes it and says, "I love you, Kitten."

"I love you too, Cheshy." He gives my hand another squeeze before releasing it.

"Who's next, Aly?" the Empress asks.

I bend down, grabbing only one box first. "Dee and Rook." I hand the first box to her. "This is Dee's." I grab the other box and hand it over as well. "This is Rook's."

I know when they open the boxes because they both gasp in unison. I bite my lip in anticipation. Do they like them?

I hear Dee's awed voice first. "You got us swords?"

"Yes," I whisper.

"These are handcrafted," Rook states, his voice deep and breathless.

"Yes."

I see both of their hands creep around the corner of the door, so I slide both my hands in there and feel them squeeze my hands.

Rook's deep voice seems choked. "In Spaydz, when a female gifts a male with a sword..."

Dee picks up speaking where Rook left off. "It means that the female finds the male loyal and protective. She has deemed that male her protector for as long as she finds him worthy."

Well, shattering teacups. I didn't realize the gift of a sword meant so much. I squeeze their hands and say, "Of course, I find you worthy. You are both loyal and protective. I would be honored to have you as protectors, forever."

"For as long as you find us worthy," Rook chokes out.

"Which will be for as long as my heart beats," I whisper.

They both squeeze my hand and say in unison, "Thank you."

"I love you both."

"We love you too," Dee says as they release my hands.

"Next?" Bianca whispers.

"Arch," I state and hand her the next box.

I hear Arch's chuckle when he opens his gift. "How did you even remember that conversation? We only talked about my new pistol once."

I smile. "Well, I could hear in your voice how much you wanted to wear your new pistol, and I knew it would be a while before you found enough leather to make your own holster, so I thought it would be the perfect gift."

"It is the perfect gift, Little Mouse. Thank you." He slides his hand around the corner of the door, and I grip his hand. He gives my hand a squeeze and says, "Love you, Mouse."

"Love you too, Arch." He slips his hand out of mine and steps away. I pick up the next gift. "Next is Hatter."

Bianca nods, taking the gift. She hands the box to the male on the other side of the door, and I hear him growl my name when he opens it. "Alyce."

"I couldn't pick. They were all amazing. I figured having extra hat pins wouldn't hurt either."

"These are too beautiful to use in battle, Sugar Cube."

I rub the back of my neck, a bit embarrassed. "I mean a few maybe."

"I'll put them in my hats. This is too precious a gift to use for blood-shed."

I slide my hand to the other side of the door. "I love you Tar."

I hear his sigh, and he grips my hand. "I love you, Aly." He squeezes my hand before moving away from the door.

I look to Bianca and say, "My gifts for Mor and Rab are on my body. How do you want to do this?"

Her eyes widen before she nods. "Who is first?"

"Mor."

"Where is the gift?" she asks.

I turn, untying my robe, and lower it so she can see my back. I don't have a bra on, so my back is completely bare except for the large Blue Morpho butterfly wings.

I hear her gasp. "Oh, Alyce. They are beautiful," she whispers.

I look over my shoulder at her. "Really? You think he will like them?"

She shakes her head. "Like them? He will love them." She claps her hands. "Okay, he's not allowed to see your face because of your makeup, so keep your face down. Your robe is low enough, so hold it tightly against you. I'll stand in front of you so he can't take a quick peek of you." She gives me a wink and moves to stand in front of me. "Mor, you are allowed to come into the room to view your gift."

I hear the shuffle of feet before I hear him gasp and murmur, "Little Butterfly."

I feel the soft touch of his fingers as they run over the bright blue wings on my back. "Do you like them?"

He presses a soft kiss to the center of my back before resting his forehead against the top of my back. "Like is too weak a word for what I feel. You have marked your body with my wings. Not even my wings because these are more beautiful than I could ever imagine my own to be."

"I didn't know if this would be a gift you would like," I admit.

I feel him pull away as he places a hand against the center of my back. I feel his hand warm as he whispers under his breath. Suddenly, I feel the soft flutter of wings against my back and gasp.

"It's only an illusion, and it will only last for a few seconds, but I had to see what you would look like with my wings."

I know Bianca didn't want Mor to see my face, but I can't help looking over my shoulder. My eyes widen when I see that my tattooed wings have come to life. They seem to flutter in my amazement, and I can feel the ghost of the flutter against my skin. I look further to find Mor staring at the wings with silent tears rolling down his face. "Mor?"

His eyes flick up to mine, and a breathtaking smile takes over his face. "This is my greatest wish. To find a female with wings like mine. And, here you stand."

"You said it was only an illusion." As soon as I finish the words the spell breaks, and my wings shatter into blue fractals before disappearing.

His smile widens. "The magic was an illusion. But your wings are real." He closes his eyes. "I should have closed them the moment you turned, but I couldn't look away."

I shift the robe back over my shoulders and tie it. I make my way over to him and wipe away the tears still rolling down his face. He grips my wrist, turning his face to press a kiss to my palm. "Thank you for this gift, Little Butterfly."

I stand on my tiptoes and press a soft kiss to his lips. Pulling away, I whisper, "I love you, Mor."

He releases my wrist before wrapping me tightly in his arms. His tears have stopped falling, but his voice is rough as he says, "I love you too, my Little Butterfly." He squeezes me tighter before releasing me. He turns before opening his eyes to leave the room.

I huff out a sigh and look over my shoulder to apologize, "Sorry I broke the rules, Bianca."

She waves a hand in the air. "I suppose it couldn't be helped. I'm sure Rab is going to see your face too."

I untie my robe once more and lower it over my shoulders to reveal my upper chest.

She smiles. "You know what, I'll stay over by the door. Rab, it's your turn."

She shuffles over to the door as Rab looks behind the door and sees me. He smiles before lowering his gaze to my exposed upper chest. His eyes widen, and he gently rubs the clock that is in the same spot on his chest. My clock. I wanted to mirror my clock with his.

He walks over until he is standing in front of me, then lifts a hand to finger the tattoo before stopping himself. He looks me in the eye for a moment then back down at the clock. His brows furrow as if he's trying to process what I've done. His eyes meet mine and I can see the utter awe in them before he asks, "You have a clock?"

I nod. "I wanted a clock for you."

His fingers caress the still clock. "It doesn't tick."

I shake my head. "The Surface doesn't have that kind of magic. My magic is also unable to make it tick."

He presses his hand against the tattoo and mutters a soft spell. Suddenly there's a soft click, and he pulls his hand away smiling. I look down to find the clock ticking quietly. He caresses it again and explains, "Now, it will tick as long as it can feel my magic. When the clock stops ticking you know that my magic is gone."

I press my hand against the clock on his chest and whisper, "To match mine."

He nods. "We are forever connected now."

I smile up at him. "Forever is a long time."

He presses a soft kiss against my lips before pulling away and saying, "Sometimes forever is just one second. But I will cherish every second I have with you."

Bianca interrupts our moment by clapping her hands. I look over to find her smiling. "Alright males! Everyone to your designated areas. I need to get the bride and future Queen ready."

Rab laughs as she pushes him out the door.

Bianca points at me and says excitedly, "Let's go!"

I laugh as I make my way back to the bathroom to finish getting ready. I slip my white leather holsters in place instead of a garter. The pistol from Arch fits perfectly. My twin knives from Dee and Rook settle into their holster perfectly as well. I slide into my dress and let Bianca tie the corset bodice. I place the hat pin Hatter got me into the small white top hat, and Bianca twists my hair into a low bun, pulling out a few blonde rivulets to frame my face.

She pins the hat in my hair before pulling the white veil connected to the hat over the top half of my face. She smiles as she helps clip Rab's necklace around my neck. Next, she grabs Mor's butterfly earrings and helps slip them into my ears.

She grins. "Last item." She walks over to the counter and pulls out a box with the white lace shoes Chesh bought me. Kneeling in front of me, she helps me slip the shoes onto my feet. Then she stands, taking a few steps away from me. She covers her mouth, and I see tears glistening in her eyes.

"Don't you dare start crying!" I reprimand. If she starts, I'll start, and she worked too hard on my makeup to waste it.

She fans her face as she looks up at the ceiling. "You're right! I couldn't help it!"

"Well figure it out! I can't mess up this makeup!" I turn and grab the closest thing to me and throw it at her.

She squeals when a makeup brush hits her. "What was that for?!"

"To make you stop crying. Did it work?"

She starts giggling and says, "Yes, I suppose it did."

I stand up straight. "Alright! Let's get on with my happily ever after!" I exclaim.

She holds out a hand and I grasp it. She walks me to the door before pausing. I lift a brow in question. Grinning, she tells me, "This isn't your happily ever after, Alyce."

"What's that supposed to mean?"

"Happily ever after, implies that the story ends."

"So what would this be then?"

She opens the door. "You are only closing the book on the story that brought you to this point."

"Wouldn't that mean my story is ending?"

She pulls me out of the door, ushering me down the stairs to the Grand Hall. "Of the female you were, yes. But the amazing thing about your story is that you're just opening the book to your new life."

"So, what's this new book?" I joke.

She laughs. "The story of the Queen of Wonderland and her seven husbands, of course." Bianca releases me and takes her spot to enter the Grand Hall. She looks over her shoulder and adds, "Happily ever after implies no more adventures. But you have so many more adventures to encounter. Your story will end only when you do. So keep turning the page. Start another book. Enjoy every moment. Have a happily ever... forever."

I smile as she turns around and the doors open. I feel the tick of Rab's clock against my chest. I can feel the magic of my wings fluttering on my back, left behind by Mor's magic. I feel the weight of the holsters on my thighs holding Arch's and the twin's weapons and the pressure of the top hat on my head holding Hatter's gift. Last but not least, I wiggle my toes in the lace shoes from Chesh.

Bianca is right. My story is only changing, not ending. The music starts, signaling me to walk down the aisle, and I begin walking. Smiling as I make my way down the aisle to my forever. My happily ever... forever.

About the Author

Ivy Cole is a longtime lover of writing and has wanted to publish her books for years. She loves Reverse Harem of many kinds. She's an indie author and can't wait to share future books with you.

Want to follow Ivy Cole and see future books? Follow her at:

https://www.facebook.com/groups/508646927449550/

Want all things, Ivy Cole? Click her Linktree to access all her social media accounts.

https://linktr.ee/ivycoleauthor

ALSO BY

<u>Books Also by Ivy Cole</u>

Underground Syndicate Series:

Underworld

Tartarus

Why Choose Fables:

Meddling with Madness (Wonderland Retelling)

The Washington Wraiths

Ice Me Baby (Liz, Mac, Dean)